Praise for Arundhati Roy's

THE MINISTRY OF UTMOST HAPPINESS

"Magisterial. . . . *The Ministry of Utmost Happiness* works its empathetic magic upon a breathtakingly broad slate."
—*O, The Oprah Magazine*

"To read Roy is to build a sense of wonder, incrementally. To ask questions not of what we're seeing of late, but what we've been staring at the whole time." —*The Globe and Mail*

"A fiercely unforgettable novel about gender, terrorism, India's caste system, corruption and politics. . . . A love story with characters so heartbreaking and compelling they sear themselves into the reader's brain." —*USA Today*

"Thrilling. . . . [Roy's] luminous passages span eras and regions of the Indian subcontinent and artfully weave the stories of several characters into a triumphant symphony."
—*Minneapolis Star Tribune*

"A lustrously braided and populated tale." —*Vanity Fair*

"Roy's second novel proves as remarkable as her first. . . . Through [the characters'] archetypal interactions, juxtaposed with Roy's glorious social details, you will have been granted a powerful sense of their world, of the complexity, energy and diversity of contemporary India." —*Financial Times*

"Through rich storytelling and gorgeous prose, Roy doesn't just reject jingoistic slogans and nationalistic narratives celebrating the making of modern India—she unmasks them."
—*Toronto Star*

"Full of bright moments and good beginnings. . . . There are moments in the book of real humour and grace. . . . Moments that are brief but nevertheless unforgettable." —*National Post*

"Epic in scale, but intimately human in its concerns, the long-awaited story dazzles with its kaleidoscopic narrative approach and unforgettable characters."
—*Elle*

"The novel weaves the personal and the political with powerful results. . . . Roy turns her lens outward to examine India's rich but violent history and the catastrophic lingering effects of Partition."
—*Esquire*

"A riotous carnival, as wryly funny and irreverent as its author."
—*The Guardian*

"A deeply rewarding work. . . . Images in *The Ministry of Utmost Happiness* . . . wedge themselves in the mind like memories of lived experience."
—*Slate*

"A rich, romantic, and sprawling tale. . . . You're guaranteed to fall in love with the characters and be swept up by the writing."
—*Glamour*

"One of the best protest novels ever written. . . . Roy elucidates the conversation around power and diversity in a way that no other author does."
—*Los Angeles Review of Books*

ARUNDHATI ROY

THE MINISTRY OF UTMOST HAPPINESS

Arundhati Roy is the author of *The God of Small Things*, which won the Booker Prize and has been translated into more than forty languages. She also has published several books of nonfiction including *The End of Imagination, Capitalism: A Ghost Story*, and *The Doctor and the Saint*. She lives in New Delhi.

THE
MINISTRY
OF
UTMOST
HAPPINESS

A NOVEL

ARUNDHATI ROY

PENGUIN

an imprint of Penguin Canada, a division of
Penguin Random House Canada Limited

Penguin Canada

320 Front Street West, Suite 1400, Toronto, Ontario M5V 3B6, Canada

First published in Hamish Hamilton hardcover by Penguin Canada, 2017.
Simultaneously published in the United States by Alfred A. Knopf, a
division of Penguin Random House LLC, New York, in Great Britain by
Hamish Hamilton, an imprint of Penguin Books Ltd., a division of Penguin
Random House Ltd., London, and in India by Penguin Books Pvt Ltd, a
division of Penguin Random House India, New Delhi.

Published in this edition, 2018

3 4 5 6 7 8 9 10

Cover design by Two Associates
Author photograph and cover photographs © Mayank Austen Soofi

Printed and bound in the United States of America.

Library and Archives Canada Cataloguing in Publication data
available upon request.

ISBN 978-0-7352-3436-9
eBook ISBN 978-0-7352-3435-2

www.penguinrandomhouse.ca

Penguin
Random House
PENGUIN CANADA

To,

The Unconsoled

CONTENTS

CONTENTS

THE MINISTRY OF UTMOST HAPPINESS

I mean, it's all a matter of your heart . . .

—NÂZIM HIKMET

At magic hour, when the sun has gone but the light has not, armies of flying foxes unhinge themselves from the Banyan trees in the old graveyard and drift across the city like smoke. When the bats leave, the crows come home. Not all the din of their homecoming fills the silence left by the sparrows that have gone missing, and the old white-backed vultures, custodians of the dead for more than a hundred million years, that have been wiped out. The vultures died of diclofenac poisoning. Diclofenac, cow aspirin, given to cattle as a muscle relaxant, to ease pain and increase the production of milk, works—worked—like nerve gas on white-backed vultures. Each chemically relaxed, milk-producing cow or buffalo that died became poisoned vulture bait. As cattle turned into better dairy machines, as the city ate more ice cream, butterscotch-crunch, nutty-buddy and chocolate-chip, as it drank more mango milkshake, vultures' necks began to droop as though they were tired and simply couldn't stay awake. Silver beards of saliva dripped from their beaks, and one by one they tumbled off their branches, dead.

Not many noticed the passing of the friendly old birds. There was so much else to look forward to.

I

WHERE DO OLD BIRDS GO TO DIE?

She lived in the graveyard like a tree. At dawn she saw the crows off and welcomed the bats home. At dusk she did the opposite. Between shifts she conferred with the ghosts of vultures that loomed in her high branches. She felt the gentle grip of their talons like an ache in an amputated limb. She gathered they weren't altogether unhappy at having excused themselves and exited from the story.

When she first moved in, she endured months of casual cruelty like a tree would—without flinching. She didn't turn to see which small boy had thrown a stone at her, didn't crane her neck to read the insults scratched into her bark. When people called her names—clown without a circus, queen without a palace—she let the hurt blow through her branches like a breeze and used the music of her rustling leaves as balm to ease the pain.

It was only after Ziauddin, the blind imam who had once led the prayers in the Fatehpuri Masjid, befriended her and began to visit her that the neighborhood decided it was time to leave her in peace.

Long ago a man who knew English told her that her name written backwards (in English) spelled Majnu. In the English version of the story of Laila and Majnu, he said, Majnu was called Romeo and Laila was Juliet. She found that hilarious. "You mean I've made a *khichdi* of their story?" she asked. "What will they do when they find that Laila may actually be Majnu and Romi was really Juli?" The next time he saw her, the Man Who Knew English said he'd made a mistake. Her name spelled backwards would be Mujna, which wasn't a name and meant nothing at all. To this she said, "It doesn't matter. I'm all of them, I'm Romi and Juli, I'm Laila and Majnu. *And* Mujna, why not? Who says my name is Anjum? I'm not Anjum, I'm Anjuman. I'm a *mehfil*, I'm a gathering. Of everybody and nobody, of everything and nothing. Is there anyone else you would like to invite? Everyone's invited."

The Man Who Knew English said it was clever of her to come up with that one. He said he'd never have thought of it himself. She said, "How could you have, with your standard of Urdu? What d'you think? English makes you clever automatically?"

He laughed. She laughed at his laugh. They shared a filter cigarette. He complained that Wills Navy Cut cigarettes were short and stumpy and simply not worth the price. She said she preferred them any day to Four Square or the very manly Red & White.

She didn't remember his name now. Perhaps she never knew it. He was long gone, the Man Who Knew English, to wherever he had to go. And she was living in the graveyard behind the government hospital. For company she had her steel Godrej almirah in which she kept her music—scratched records and tapes—an old harmonium, her clothes, jewelry, her father's poetry books, her photo albums and a few press clippings that had survived the fire at the Khwabgah. She hung the key around her neck on a black thread along with her bent silver toothpick. She slept on a threadbare Persian carpet that she locked up in the day and unrolled between two graves at night (as a private joke, never the same two on consecutive nights). She still smoked. Still Navy Cut.

One morning, while she read the newspaper aloud to him, the old imam, who clearly hadn't been listening, asked—affecting a casual air—"Is it true that even the Hindus among you are buried, not cremated?"

Sensing trouble, she prevaricated. "True? Is what true? What is Truth?"

Unwilling to be deflected from his line of inquiry, the imam muttered a mechanical response. "Sach Khuda hai. Khuda hi Sach hai." Truth is God. God is Truth. The sort of wisdom that was available on the backs of the painted trucks that roared down the highways. Then he narrowed his blindgreen eyes and asked in a slygreen whisper: "Tell me, you people, when you die, where do they bury you? Who bathes the bodies? Who says the prayers?"

Anjum said nothing for a long time. Then she leaned across and whispered back, untree-like, "Imam Sahib, when people speak of color—red, blue, orange, when they describe the sky at sunset, or moonrise during Ramzaan—what goes through your mind?"

Having wounded each other thus, deeply, almost mortally, the two sat quietly side by side on someone's sunny grave, hemorrhaging. Eventually it was Anjum who broke the silence.

"You tell me," she said. "You're the Imam Sahib, not me. Where do old birds go to die? Do they fall on us like stones from the sky? Do we stumble on their bodies in the streets? Do you not think that the All-Seeing, Almighty One who put us on this Earth has made proper arrangements to take us away?"

That day the imam's visit ended earlier than usual. Anjum watched him leave, tap-tap-tapping his way through the graves, his seeing-eye cane making music as it encountered the empty booze bottles and discarded syringes that littered his path. She didn't stop him. She knew he'd be back. No matter how elaborate its charade, she recognized loneliness when she saw it. She sensed that in some strange tangential way, he needed her shade as much as she needed his. And she had learned from experience that Need was a warehouse that could accommodate a considerable amount of cruelty.

Even though Anjum's departure from the Khwabgah had been far from cordial, she knew that its dreams and its secrets were not hers alone to betray.

2

KHWABGAH

She was the fourth of five children, born on a cold January night, by lamplight (power cut), in Shahjahanabad, the walled city of Delhi. Ahlam Baji, the midwife who delivered her and put her in her mother's arms wrapped in two shawls, said, "It's a boy." Given the circumstances, her error was understandable.

A month into her first pregnancy Jahanara Begum and her husband decided that if their baby was a boy they would name him Aftab. Their first three children were girls. They had been waiting for their Aftab for six years. The night he was born was the happiest of Jahanara Begum's life.

The next morning, when the sun was up and the room nice and warm, she unswaddled little Aftab. She explored his tiny body— eyes nose head neck armpits fingers toes—with sated, unhurried delight. That was when she discovered, nestling underneath his boy-parts, a small, unformed, but undoubtedly girl-part.

Is it possible for a mother to be terrified of her own baby? Jahanara Begum was. Her first reaction was to feel her heart constrict and her bones turn to ash. Her second reaction was to take another look to make sure she was not mistaken. Her third reaction was to recoil from what she had created while her bowels convulsed and a thin stream of shit ran down her legs. Her fourth reaction was to contemplate killing herself and her child. Her fifth reaction was to pick her baby up and hold him close while she fell through a crack between the world she knew and worlds she did not know existed. There, in the abyss, spinning through the darkness, everything she had been sure of until then, every single thing, from the smallest to the biggest, ceased to make sense to her. In Urdu, the only language she knew, all things, not just living things but *all* things—carpets, clothes, books, pens, musical instruments—had a gender. Everything was either masculine or feminine, man or woman. Everything except her baby. Yes of course she knew there was a word for those like him— *Hijra*. Two words actually, *Hijra* and *Kinnar*. But two words do not make a language.

Was it possible to live outside language? Naturally this question did not address itself to her in words, or as a single lucid sentence. It addressed itself to her as a soundless, embryonic howl.

Her sixth reaction was to clean herself up and resolve to tell nobody for the moment. Not even her husband. Her seventh reaction was to lie down next to Aftab and rest. Like the God of the Christians did, after he had made Heaven and Earth. Except that in his case he rested after making sense of the world he had created, whereas Jahanara Begum rested after what she created had scrambled her sense of the world.

It wasn't a real vagina after all, she told herself. Its passages were not open (she checked). It was just an appendage, a baby-thing. Perhaps it would close, or heal, or go away somehow. She would pray at every shrine she knew and ask the Almighty to show her mercy. He would. She knew He would. And maybe He did, in ways she did not fully comprehend.

The first day she felt able to leave the house, Jahanara Begum took baby Aftab with her to the dargah of Hazrat Sarmad Shaheed, an easy, ten-minute walk from her home. She didn't know the story of Hazrat Sarmad Shaheed then, and had no idea what turned her footsteps so surely in the direction of his shrine. Perhaps he had called her to him. Or perhaps she was drawn to the strange people she had seen camped there when she used to walk past on her way to Meena Bazaar, the kind of people who in her earlier life she would not have deigned to even glance at unless they'd crossed her path. Suddenly they seemed to be the most important people in the world.

Not all the visitors to Hazrat Sarmad Shaheed's dargah knew his story. Some knew parts of it, some none of it and some made up their own versions. Most knew he was a Jewish Armenian merchant who had traveled to Delhi from Persia in pursuit of the love of his life. Few knew the love of his life was Abhay Chand, a young Hindu boy he had met in Sindh. Most knew he had renounced Judaism and embraced Islam. Few knew his spiritual search eventually led him to renounce orthodox Islam too. Most knew he had lived on the streets of Shahjahanabad as a naked fakir before being publicly executed. Few knew the reason for his execution was not the offense caused by his public nakedness but the offense caused by his apostasy. Aurangzeb, emperor at the time, summoned Sarmad to his court and asked him to prove he was a true Muslim by reciting the Kalima: *la ilaha illallah, Mohammed-ur rasul Allah*—There is no God but Allah, and Mohammed is His Messenger. Sarmad stood naked in the royal court in the Red Fort before a jury of Qazis and Maulanas. Clouds stopped drifting in the sky, birds froze in mid-flight and the air in the fort grew thick and impenetrable as he began to recite the Kalima. But no sooner had he started than he stopped. All he said was the first phrase: *la ilaha*. There is no God. He could not go any further, he insisted, until he had completed his spiritual search and could embrace Allah with all his heart.

Until then, he said, reciting the Kalima would only be a mockery of prayer. Aurangzeb, backed by his Qazis, ordered Sarmad's execution.

To suppose from this that those who went to pay their respects to Hazrat Sarmad Shaheed without knowing his story did so in ignorance, with little regard for facts and history, would be a mistake. Because inside the dargah, Sarmad's insubordinate spirit, intense, palpable and truer than any accumulation of historical facts could be, appeared to those who sought his blessings. It celebrated (but never preached) the virtue of spirituality over sacrament, simplicity over opulence and stubborn, ecstatic love even when faced with the prospect of annihilation. Sarmad's spirit permitted those who came to him to take his story and turn it into whatever they needed it to be.

When Jahanara Begum became a familiar figure at the dargah she heard (and then retailed) the story of how Sarmad was beheaded on the steps of the Jama Masjid before a veritable ocean of people who loved him and had gathered to bid him farewell. Of how his head continued to recite his poems of love even after it had been severed from his body, and how he picked up his speaking head, as casually as a modern-day motorcyclist might pick up his helmet, and walked up the steps into the Jama Masjid, and then, equally casually, went straight to heaven. That is why, Jahanara Begum said (to anyone who was willing to listen), in Hazrat Sarmad's tiny dargah (clamped like a limpet to the base of the eastern steps of the Jama Masjid, the very spot where his blood spilled down and collected in a pool), the floor is red, the walls are red and the ceiling is red. More than three hundred years have gone by, she said, but Hazrat Sarmad's blood cannot be washed away. Whatever color they paint his dargah, she insisted, in time it turns red on its own.

The first time she made her way past the crowd—the sellers of ittars and amulets, the custodians of pilgrims' shoes, the cripples, the beggars, the homeless, the goats being fattened for slaughter on Eid and the knot of quiet, elderly eunuchs who had taken up residence under a tarpaulin outside the shrine—and entered the tiny red chamber, Jahanara Begum became calm. The street sounds grew faint and seemed to come from far away. She sat in a corner with her baby asleep on her lap, watching people, Muslim as well as Hindu, come in ones and twos, and tie red threads, red bangles and chits of paper to the grille around the tomb, beseeching Sarmad to bless them. It was only after she noticed a translucent old man with dry, papery skin and a wispy beard of spun light sitting in a corner, rocking back and forth, weeping silently as though his heart was broken, that Jahanara Begum allowed her own tears to fall. *This is my son, Aftab*, she whispered to Hazrat Sarmad. *I've brought him here to you. Look after him. And teach me how to love him.*

Hazrat Sarmad did.

FOR THE FIRST FEW YEARS of Aftab's life, Jahanara Begum's secret remained safe. While she waited for his girl-part to heal, she kept him close and was fiercely protective of him. Even after her younger son, Saqib, was born she would not allow Aftab to stray very far from her on his own. It was not seen as unusual behavior for a woman who had waited so long and so anxiously for a son.

When Aftab was five he began to attend the Urdu–Hindi madrassa for boys in Chooriwali Gali (the bangle-seller's lane). Within a year he could recite a good part of the Quran in Arabic, although it wasn't clear how much of it he understood—that was true of all the other children too. Aftab was a better than average student, but even from the time he was very young it became clear that his real gift was music. He had a sweet, true singing voice and could pick up a tune after hearing it just once. His parents decided to send him to Ustad Hameed Khan, an outstanding young musician who taught Hindustani classical music to groups of children in his cramped quarters in Chandni Mahal. Little Aftab never missed a single class. By the time he was nine he could sing a good twenty minutes of *bada khayal* in Raag Yaman, Durga and Bhairav and make his voice skim shyly off the flat rekhab in Raag Pooriya Dhanashree like a stone skipping over the surface of a lake. He could sing Chaiti and Thumri with the accomplishment and poise of a Lucknow courtesan. At first people were amused and even encouraging, but soon the snickering and teasing from other children began: *He's a She. He's not a He or a She. He's a He and a She. She-He, He-She Hee! Hee! Hee!*

When the teasing became unbearable Aftab stopped going to his music classes. But Ustad Hameed, who doted on him, offered to teach him separately, on his own. So the music classes continued, but Aftab refused to go to school any more. By then Jahanara Begum's hopes had more or less faded. There was no sign of healing anywhere on the horizon. She had managed to put off his circumcision for some years with a series of inventive excuses. But young Saqib was waiting in line for his, and she knew she had run out of time. Eventually she did what she had to. She mustered her courage and told her husband, breaking down and weeping with grief as well as relief that she finally had someone else to share her nightmare with.

Her husband, Mulaqat Ali, was a hakim, a doctor of herbal medicine, and a lover of Urdu and Persian poetry. All his life he had worked for the family of another hakim—Hakim Abdul Majid, who founded a popular brand of sherbet called Rooh Afza (Persian for "Elixir of the Soul"). Rooh Afza, made of khurfa seeds (purslane), grapes, oranges, watermelon, mint, carrots, a touch of spinach, khus khus, lotus, two kinds of lilies and a distillate of damask roses, was meant to be a tonic. But people found that two tablespoons of the sparkling ruby-colored syrup in a glass of cold milk or even just plain water not only tasted delicious, but was also an effective defense against Delhi's scorching summers and the strange fevers that blew in on desert winds. Soon what had started out as medicine became the most popular summer drink in the region. Rooh Afza became a prosperous enterprise and a household name. For forty years it ruled the market, sending its produce from its headquarters in the old city as far south as Hyderabad and as far west as Afghanistan. Then came Partition. God's carotid burst open on the new border between India and Pakistan and a million people died of hatred. Neighbors turned on each other as though they'd never known each other, never been to each other's weddings, never sung each other's songs. The walled city broke open. Old families fled (Muslim). New ones arrived (Hindu) and settled around the city walls. Rooh Afza had a serious setback, but soon recovered and opened a branch in Pakistan. A quarter of a century later, after the holocaust in East Pakistan, it opened another branch in the brand-new country of Bangladesh. But eventually, the Elixir of the Soul that had survived wars and the bloody birth of three new countries, was, like most things in the world, trumped by Coca-Cola.

Although Mulaqat Ali was a trusted and valued employee of Hakim Abdul Majid, the salary he earned was not enough to make ends meet. So outside his working hours he saw patients at his home. Jahanara Begum supplemented the family income with what she earned from the white cotton Gandhi caps she made and supplied in bulk to Hindu shopkeepers in Chandni Chowk.

Mulaqat Ali traced his family's lineage directly back to the Mongol Emperor Changez Khan through the emperor's second-born son, Chagatai. He had an elaborate family tree on a piece of cracked parchment and a small tin trunk full of brittle, yellowed papers that he believed verified his claim and explained how descendants of shamans from the Gobi Desert, worshippers of the Eternal Blue Sky, once considered the enemies of Islam, became the forefathers of the Mughal dynasty that ruled India for centuries, and how Mulaqat Ali's own family, descendants of the Mughals, who were Sunni, came to be Shia. Occasionally, perhaps once every few years, he would open his trunk and show his papers to a visiting journalist who, more often than not, neither listened carefully nor took him seriously. At most the long interview would merit an arch, amusing mention in a weekend special about Old Delhi. If it was a double spread, a small portrait of Mulaqat Ali might even be published along with some close-ups of Mughal cuisine, long shots of Muslim women in burqas on cycle rickshaws that plied the narrow filthy lanes, and of course the mandatory bird's-eye view of thousands of Muslim men in white skullcaps, arranged in perfect formation, bowed down in prayer in the Jama Masjid. Some readers viewed pictures like these as proof of the success of India's commitment to secularism and inter-faith tolerance. Others with a tinge of relief that Delhi's Muslim population seemed content enough in its vibrant ghetto. Still others viewed them as proof that Muslims did not wish to "integrate" and were busy breeding and organizing themselves, and would soon become a threat to Hindu India. Those who subscribed to this view were gaining influence at an alarming pace.

Regardless of what appeared or did not appear in the newspapers, right into his dotage Mulaqat Ali always welcomed visitors into his tiny rooms with the faded grace of a nobleman. He spoke of the past with dignity but never nostalgia. He described how, in the thirteenth century, his ancestors had ruled an empire that stretched from the countries that now called themselves Vietnam and Korea all the way to Hungary and the Balkans, from Northern Siberia to the Deccan plateau in India, the largest empire the world had ever known. He often ended the interview with a recitation of an Urdu couplet by one of his favorite poets, Mir Taqi Mir:

Jis sar ko ghurur aaj hai yaan taj-vari ka
Kal uss pe yahin shor hai phir nauhagari ka

The head which today proudly flaunts a crown
Will tomorrow, right here, in lamentation drown

Most of his visitors, brash emissaries of a new ruling class, barely aware of their own youthful hubris, did not completely grasp the layered meaning of the couplet they had been offered, like a snack to be washed down by a thimble-sized cup of thick, sweet tea. They understood of course that it was a dirge for a fallen empire whose international borders had shrunk to a grimy ghetto circumscribed by the ruined walls of an old city. And yes, they realized that it was also a rueful comment on Mulaqat Ali's own straitened circumstances. What escaped them was that the couplet was a sly snack, a perfidious samosa, a warning wrapped in mourning, being offered with faux humility by an erudite man who had absolute faith in his listeners' ignorance of Urdu, a language which, like most of those who spoke it, was gradually being ghettoized.

Mulaqat Ali's passion for poetry was not just a hobby separate from his work as a hakim. He believed that poetry could cure, or at least go a long way towards curing, almost every ailment. He would prescribe poems to his patients the way other hakims prescribed medicine. He could produce a couplet from his formidable repertoire that was eerily apt for every illness, every occasion, every mood and every delicate alteration in the political climate. This habit of his made life around him seem more profound and at the same time less distinctive than it really was.

It infused everything with a subtle sense of stagnancy, a sense that everything that happened had happened before. That it had already been written, sung, commented upon and entered into history's inventory. That nothing new was possible. This could be why young people around him often fled, giggling, when they sensed that a couplet was on its way.

When Jahanara Begum told him about Aftab, perhaps for the first time in his life Mulaqat Ali had no suitable couplet for the occasion. It took him a while to get over the initial shock. When he did, he scolded his wife for not having told him earlier. Times had changed, he said. This was the Modern Era. He was sure that there was a simple medical solution to their son's problem. They would find a doctor in New Delhi, far away from the whisper and gossip that went on in the mohallas of the old city. The Almighty helps those who help themselves, he told his wife a little sternly.

A week later, dressed in their best clothes, with an unhappy Aftab fitted out in a manly steel-gray Pathan suit with a black embroidered waistcoat, a skullcap and jootis with toes curled like gondolas, they set off for Nizamuddin basti in a horse-drawn tanga. The ostensible purpose of their day out was that they were going to inspect a prospective bride for their nephew Aijaz—the youngest son of Mulaqat Ali's older brother, Qasim, who had moved to Pakistan after Partition and worked for the Karachi branch of Rooh Afza. The real reason was that they had an appointment with a Dr. Ghulam Nabi, who called himself a "sexologist."

Dr. Nabi prided himself on being a straight-talking man of precise and scientific temper. After examining Aftab he said he was not, medically speaking, a Hijra—a female trapped in a male body—although for practical purposes that word could be used. Aftab, he said, was a rare example of a Hermaphrodite, with both male and female characteristics, though outwardly, the male characteristics appeared to be more dominant. He said he could recommend a surgeon who would seal the girl-part, sew it up. He could prescribe some pills too. But, he said, the problem was not merely superficial. While treatment would surely help, there would be "Hijra tendencies" that were unlikely to ever go away. (*Fitrat* was the word he used for "tendencies.") He could not guarantee complete success. Mulaqat Ali, prepared to grasp at straws, was elated. "Tendencies?" he said. "Tendencies are no problem. Everybody has some tendency or the other . . . tendencies can always be managed."

Even though the visit to Dr. Nabi did not provide an immediate solution to what Mulaqat Ali saw as Aftab's affliction, it benefited Mulaqat Ali a great deal. It gave him coordinates to position himself, to steady his ship that was pitching perilously on an ocean of couplet-less incomprehension. He was now able to convert his anguish into a practical problem and to turn his attention and his energies to something he understood well: How to raise enough money for the surgery?

He cut down on household expenses and drew up lists of people and relatives from whom he could borrow money. Simultaneously, he embarked on the cultural project of inculcating manliness in Aftab. He passed on to him his love of poetry and discouraged the singing of Thumri and Chaiti. He stayed up late into the night, telling Aftab stories about their warrior ancestors and their valor on the battlefield. They left Aftab unmoved. But when he heard the story of how Temujin—Changez Khan—won the hand of his beautiful wife, Borte Khatun, how she was kidnapped by a rival tribe and how Temujin fought a whole army virtually single-handedly to get her back because he loved her so much, Aftab found himself wanting to be her.

While his sisters and brother went to school, Aftab spent hours on the tiny balcony of his home looking down at Chitli Qabar—the tiny shrine of the spotted goat who was said to have had supernatural powers—and the busy street that ran past it and joined the Matia Mahal Chowk. He quickly learned the cadence and rhythm of the neighborhood, which was essentially a stream of Urdu invective—*I'll fuck your mother, go fuck your sister, I swear by your mother's cock*—that was interrupted five times a day by the call to prayer from the Jama Masjid as well as the several other smaller mosques in the old city. As Aftab kept strict vigil, day after day, over nothing in particular, Guddu Bhai, the acrimonious early-morning fishmonger who parked his cart of gleaming fresh fish in the center of the chowk, would, as surely as the sun rose in the east and set in the west, elongate into Wasim, the tall, affable afternoon naan khatai–seller who would then shrink into Yunus, the small, lean, evening fruit-seller, who, late at night, would broaden and balloon into Hassan Mian, the stout vendor of the best mutton biryani in Matia Mahal, which he dished out of a huge copper pot. One spring morning Aftab saw a tall, slim-hipped woman wearing bright lipstick, gold high heels and a shiny, green satin salwar kameez buying bangles from Mir the bangle-seller who doubled up as caretaker of the Chitli Qabar. He stored his stock of bangles inside the tomb every night when he shut shrine and shop. (He had managed to ensure that the working hours coincided.) Aftab had never seen anybody like the tall woman with lipstick. He rushed down the steep stairs into the street and followed her discreetly while she bought goats' trotters, hairclips, guavas, and had the strap of her sandals fixed.

He wanted to be her.

He followed her down the street all the way to Turkman Gate and stood for a long time outside the blue doorway she disappeared into. No ordinary woman would have been permitted to sashay down the streets of Shahjahanabad dressed like that. Ordinary women in Shahjahanabad wore burqas or at least covered their heads and every part of their body except their hands and feet. The woman Aftab followed could dress as she was dressed and walk the way she did only because she wasn't a woman.

Whatever she was, Aftab wanted to be her. He wanted to be her even more than he wanted to be Borte Khatun. Like her he wanted to shimmer past the meat shops where skinned carcasses of whole goats hung down like great walls of meat; he wanted to simper past the New Life-Style Men's Hairdressing Salon where Iliyaas the barber cut Liaqat the lean young butcher's hair and shined it up with Brylcreem. He wanted to put out a hand with painted nails and a wrist full of bangles and delicately lift the gill of a fish to see how fresh it was before bargaining down the price. He wanted to lift his salwar just a little as he stepped over a puddle—just enough to show off his silver anklets.

It was not Aftab's girl-part that was just an appendage.

He began to divide his time between his music classes and hanging around outside the blue doorway of the house in Gali Dakotan where the tall woman lived. He learned that her name was Bombay Silk and that there were seven others like her, Bulbul, Razia, Heera, Baby, Nimmo, Mary and Gudiya, who lived together in the haveli with the blue doorway, and that they had an Ustad, a guru, called Kulsoom Bi, older than the rest of them, who was the head of the household. Aftab learned their haveli was called the Khwabgah—the House of Dreams.

At first he was shooed away because everybody, including the residents of the Khwabgah, knew Mulaqat Ali and did not want to get on the wrong side of him. But regardless of what admonition and punishment awaited him, Aftab would return to his post stubbornly, day after day. It was the only place in his world where he felt the air made way for him. When he arrived, it seemed to shift, to slide over, like a school friend making room for him on a classroom bench. Over a period of a few months, by running errands, carrying their bags and musical instruments when the residents went on their city rounds, by massaging their tired feet at the end of a working day, Aftab eventually managed to insinuate himself into the Khwabgah. Finally the day dawned when he was allowed in. He entered that ordinary, broken-down home as though he were walking through the gates of Paradise.

The blue door opened on to a paved, high-walled courtyard with a handpump in one corner and a Pomegranate tree in the other. There were two rooms set behind a deep verandah with fluted columns. The roof of one of the rooms had caved in and its walls had crumbled into a heap of rubble in which a family of cats had made its home. The room that hadn't crumbled was a large one, and in fairly good condition. Its peeling, pale green walls were lined with four wooden and two Godrej almirahs covered with pictures of film stars—Madhubala, Waheeda Rehman, Nargis, Dilip Kumar (whose name was really Muhammad Yusuf Khan), Guru Dutt and the local boy Johnny Walker (Badruddin Jamaluddin Kazi), the comedian who could make the saddest person in the world smile. One of the cupboards had a dim, full-length mirror mounted on the door. In another corner there was a beaten-up old dressing table. A chipped and broken chandelier with only one working bulb and a long-stemmed, dark brown fan hung from the high ceiling. The fan had human qualities—she was coy, moody and unpredictable. She had a name too, Usha. Usha wasn't young any more and often needed to be cajoled and prodded with a long-handled broom and then she would go to work, gyrating like a slow pole dancer. Ustad Kulsoom Bi slept on the only bed in the haveli with her parakeet, Birbal, in his cage above her bed. Birbal would screech as though he was being slaughtered if Kulsoom Bi was not near him at night. During Birbal's waking hours he was capable of some weapons-grade invective that was always preceded by the half-snide, half-flirtatious *Ai Hai!* that he had picked up from his housemates. Birbal's choicest insult was the one most commonly heard in the Khwabgah: *Saali Randi Hijra* (Sister-fucking Whore Hijra). Birbal knew all the variations. He could mutter it, say it coquettishly, in jest, with affection and with genuine, bitter anger.

Everyone else slept in the verandah, their bedding rolled up in the day like giant bolsters. In winter, when the courtyard grew cold and misty, they all crowded into Kulsoom Bi's room. The entrance to the toilet was through the ruins of the collapsed room. Everybody took turns to bathe at the handpump. An absurdly steep, narrow staircase led to the kitchen on the first floor. The kitchen window looked out on to the dome of the Holy Trinity Church.

Mary was the only Christian among the residents of the Khwabgah. She did not go to church, but she wore a little crucifix around her neck. Gudiya and Bulbul were both Hindus and did occasionally visit temples that would allow them in. The rest were Muslim. They visited the Jama Masjid and those dargahs that allowed them into the inner chambers (because unlike biological women Hijras were not considered unclean since they did not menstruate). The most masculine person in the Khwabgah, however, did menstruate. Bismillah slept upstairs on the kitchen terrace. She was a small, wiry, dark woman with a voice like a bus horn. She had converted to Islam and moved into the Khwabgah a few years ago (the two were not connected) after her husband, a bus driver for Delhi Transport Corporation, had thrown her out of their home for not bearing him a child. Of course it never occurred to him that he might have been responsible for their childlessness. Bismillah (formerly Bimla) managed the kitchen and guarded the Khwabgah against unwanted intruders with the ferocity and ruthlessness of a professional Chicago mobster. Young men were strictly forbidden to enter the Khwabgah without her express permission. Even regular customers, like Anjum's future client—the Man Who Knew English—were kept out and had to make their own arrangements for their assignations. Bismillah's companion on the terrace was Razia, who had lost her mind as well as her memory and no longer knew who she was or where she came from. Razia was not a Hijra. She was a man who liked to dress in women's clothes. However, she did not want to be thought of as a woman, but as a man who wanted to be a woman. She had stopped trying to explain the difference to people (including to Hijras) long ago. Razia spent her days feeding pigeons on the roof and steering all conversations towards a secret, unutilized government scheme (*dao-pech*, she called it) she had discovered for Hijras and people like herself. As per the scheme, they would all live together in a housing colony and be given government pensions and would no longer need to earn their living doing what she described as *badtameezi*—bad behavior—any more. Razia's other theme was government pensions for street cats. For some reason her unmemoried, unanchored mind veered unerringly towards government schemes.

Aftab's first real friend in the Khwabgah was Nimmo Gorakhpuri, the youngest of them all and the only one who had completed high school. Nimmo had run away from her home in Gorakhpur where her father worked as a senior-division clerk in the Main Post Office. Though she affected the airs of being a great deal older, Nimmo was really only six or seven years older than Aftab. She was short and chubby with thick, curly hair, stunning eyebrows curved like a pair of scimitars, and exceptionally thick eyelashes. She would have been beautiful but for her fast-growing facial hair that made the skin on her cheeks look blue under her make-up, even when she had shaved. Nimmo was obsessed with Western women's fashion and was fiercely possessive of her collection of fashion magazines sourced from the second-hand Sunday book bazaar on the pavement in Daryaganj, a five-minute walk from the Khwabgah. One of the booksellers, Naushad, who bought his supply of magazines from the garbage collectors who serviced the foreign embassies in Shantipath, kept them aside, and sold them to Nimmo at a hefty discount.

"D'you know why God made Hijras?" she asked Aftab one afternoon while she flipped through a dog-eared 1967 issue of

Vogue, lingering over the blonde ladies with bare legs who so enthralled her.

"No, why?"

"It was an experiment. He decided to create something, a living creature that is incapable of happiness. So he made us."

Her words hit Aftab with the force of a physical blow. "How can you say that? You are all happy here! This is the Khwabgah!" he said, with rising panic.

"Who's happy here? It's all sham and fakery," Nimmo said laconically, not bothering to look up from the magazine. "No one's happy here. It's not possible. *Arre yaar*, think about it, what are the things you normal people get unhappy about? I don't mean *you*, but grown-ups like you—what makes them unhappy? Price-rise, children's school-admissions, husbands' beatings, wives' cheatings, Hindu-Muslim riots, Indo-Pak war—*outside* things that settle down eventually. But for us the price-rise and school-admissions and beating-husbands and cheating-wives are all *inside* us. The riot is *inside* us. The war is *inside* us. Indo-Pak is *inside* us. It will never settle down. It *can't*."

Aftab desperately wanted to contradict her, to tell her she was dead wrong, because *he* was happy, happier than he had ever been before. He was living proof that Nimmo Gorakhpuri was wrong, was he not? But he said nothing, because it would have involved revealing himself as not being a "normal people," which he was not yet prepared to do.

It was only when he turned fourteen, by which time Nimmo had run away from the Khwabgah with a State Transport bus driver (who soon abandoned her and returned to his family), that Aftab fully understood what she meant. His body had suddenly begun to wage war on him. He grew tall and muscular. And hairy. In a panic he tried to remove the hair on his face and body with Burnol—burn ointment that made dark patches on his skin. He then tried Anne French crème hair remover that he purloined from his sisters (he was soon found out because it smelled like an open sewer). He plucked his bushy eyebrows into thin, asymmetrical crescents with a pair of home-made tweezers that looked more like tongs. He developed an Adam's apple that bobbed up and down. He longed to tear it out of his throat. Next came the unkindest betrayal of all—the thing that he could do nothing about. His voice broke. A deep, powerful man's voice appeared in place of his sweet, high voice. He was repelled by it and scared himself each time he spoke. He grew quiet, and would speak only as a last resort, after he had run out of other options. He stopped singing. When he listened to music, anyone who paid attention would hear a high, barely audible, insect-like hum that seemed to emerge through a pinhole at the top of his head. No amount of persuasion, not even from Ustad Hameed himself, could coax a song out of Aftab. He never sang again, except to mockingly caricature Hindi film songs at ribald Hijra gatherings or when (in their professional capacity) they descended on ordinary people's celebrations—weddings, births, house-warming ceremonies—dancing, singing in their wild, grating voices, offering their blessings and threatening to embarrass the hosts (by exposing their mutilated privates) and ruin the occasion with curses and a display of unthinkable obscenity unless they were paid a fee. (This is what Razia meant when she said *badtameezi*, and what Nimmo Gorakhpuri referred to when she said, "We're jackals who feed off other people's happiness, we're Happiness Hunters." *Khushi-khor* was the phrase she used.)

Once music forsook Aftab he was left with no reason to continue living in what most ordinary people thought of as the real world—and Hijras called *Duniya*, the World. One night he stole some money and his sisters' nicer clothes and moved into the Khwabgah. Jahanara Begum, never known for her shyness, waded in to retrieve him. He refused to leave. She finally left after making Ustad Kulsoom Bi promise that on weekends, at least, Aftab would be made to wear normal boys' clothes and be sent home. Ustad Kulsoom Bi tried to honor her promise, but the arrangement lasted only for a few months.

And so, at the age of fifteen, only a few hundred yards from where his family had lived for centuries, Aftab stepped through an ordinary doorway into another universe. On his first night as a permanent resident of the Khwabgah, he danced in the courtyard to everybody's favorite song from everybody's favorite film— "Pyar Kiya To Darna Kya" from *Mughal-e-Azam*. The next night at a small ceremony he was presented with a green Khwabgah dupatta and initiated into the rules and rituals that formally made him a member of the Hijra community. Aftab became Anjum, disciple of Ustad Kulsoom Bi of the Delhi Gharana, one of the seven regional Hijra Gharanas in the country, each headed by a Nayak, a Chief, all of them headed by a Supreme Chief.

Though she never visited him there again, for years Jahanara Begum continued to send a hot meal to the Khwabgah every day. The only place where she and Anjum met was at the dargah of Hazrat Sarmad Shaheed. There they would sit together for a while, Anjum nearly six feet tall, her head demurely covered in a spangled dupatta, and tiny Jahanara Begum, whose hair had begun to gray under her black burqa. Sometimes, they held hands surreptitiously. Mulaqat Ali for his part was less able to accept the situation. His broken heart never mended. While he continued to give his interviews, he never spoke either privately or publicly of the misfortune that had befallen the dynasty of Changez Khan. He chose to sever all ties with his son. He never met Anjum or spoke to her again. Occasionally they would pass each other on the street and would exchange glances, but never greetings. Never.

Over the years Anjum became Delhi's most famous Hijra. Film-makers fought over her, NGOs hoarded her, foreign correspondents gifted her phone number to one another as a professional favor, along with numbers of the Bird Hospital, Phoolan Devi, the surrendered dacoit known as "Bandit Queen," and a contact for the Begum of Oudh who lived in an old ruin in the Ridge Forest with her servants and her chandeliers while she staked her claim to a nonexistent kingdom. In interviews Anjum would be encouraged to talk about the abuse and cruelty that her interlocutors assumed she had been subjected to by her conventional Muslim parents, siblings and neighbors before she left home. They were invariably disappointed when she told them how much her mother and father had loved her and how *she* had been the cruel one. "Others have horrible stories, the kind you people like to write about," she would say. "Why not talk to *them*?" But of course newspapers didn't work that way. She was the chosen one. It had to be her, even if her story was slightly altered to suit readers' appetites and expectations.

Once she became a permanent resident of the Khwabgah, Anjum was finally able to dress in the clothes she longed to wear—the sequined, gossamer kurtas and pleated Patiala salwars, shararas, ghararas, silver anklets, glass bangles and dangling earrings. She had her nose pierced and wore an elaborate, stone-studded nose-pin, outlined her eyes with kohl and blue eye shadow and gave herself a luscious, bow-shaped Madhubala mouth of glossy-red lipstick. Her hair would not grow very long, but it was long enough to pull back and weave into a plait of false hair. She had a strong, chiseled face and an impressive, hooked nose like her father's. She wasn't beautiful in the way Bombay Silk was, but she was sexier, more intriguing, handsome in the way some women can be. Those looks combined with her steadfast commitment to an exaggerated, outrageous kind of femininity made the real, biological women in the neighborhood—even those who did not wear full burqas—look cloudy and dispersed. She learned to exaggerate the swing in her hips when she walked and to communicate with the signature spread-fingered Hijra clap that went off like a gunshot and could mean anything—Yes, No, Maybe, *Wah! Behen ka Lauda* (Your sister's cock), *Bhonsadi ke* (You arsehole born). Only another Hijra could decode what was specifically meant by the specific clap at that specific moment.

On Anjum's eighteenth birthday Kulsoom Bi threw a party for her in the Khwabgah. Hijras gathered from all over the city, some came from out of town. For the first time in her life Anjum wore a sari, a red "disco" sari, with a backless choli. That night she dreamed she was a new bride on her wedding night. She awoke distressed to find that her sexual pleasure had expressed itself into her beautiful new garment like a man's. It wasn't the first time this had happened, but for some reason, perhaps because of the sari, the humiliation she felt had never been so intense. She sat in the courtyard and howled like a wolf, hitting herself on her head and between her legs, screaming with self-inflicted pain. Ustad Kulsoom Bi, no stranger to these histrionics, gave her a tranquilizer and took her to her room.

When Anjum calmed down Ustad Kulsoom Bi talked to her quietly in a way she had never done before. There was no reason to be ashamed of anything, Ustad Kulsoom Bi told her, because Hijras were chosen people, beloved of the Almighty. The word *Hijra*, she said, meant a Body in which a Holy Soul lives. In the next hour Anjum learned that the Holy Souls were a diverse lot and that the world of the Khwabgah was just as complicated, if not more so, than the Duniya. The Hindus, Bulbul and Gudiya, had both been through the formal (extremely painful) religious castration ceremony in Bombay before they came to the Khwabgah. Bombay Silk and Heera would have liked to do the same, but they were Muslim and believed that Islam forbade them from altering their God-given gender, so they managed, somehow, within those confines. Baby, like Razia, was a man who wanted to remain a man but be a woman in every other way. As for Ustad Kulsoom Bi, she said she disagreed with Bombay Silk and

Heera's interpretation of Islam. She and Nimmo Gorakhpuri—who belonged to different generations—had had surgery. She knew a Dr. Mukhtar, she said, who was reliable and close-lipped and did not spread gossip about his patients in every gali and *koocha* of Old Delhi. She told Anjum she should think it over and decide what she wanted to do. Anjum took three whole minutes to make up her mind.

Dr. Mukhtar was more reassuring than Dr. Nabi had been. He said he could remove her male parts and try to enhance her existing vagina. He also suggested pills that would undeepen her voice and help her develop breasts. At a discount, Kulsoom Bi insisted. At a discount, Dr. Mukhtar agreed. Kulsoom Bi paid for the surgery and the hormones; Anjum paid her back over the years, several times over.

The surgery was difficult, the recovery even more so, but in the end it came as a relief. Anjum felt as though a fog had lifted from her blood and she could finally think clearly. Dr. Mukhtar's vagina, however, turned out to be a scam. It worked, but not in the way he said it would, not even after two corrective surgeries. He did not offer to refund the money though, neither in whole nor in part. On the contrary, he went on to make a comfortable living, selling spurious, substandard body parts to desperate people. He died a prosperous man, with two houses in Laxmi Nagar, one for each of his sons, and his daughter married to a wealthy building contractor in Rampur.

Although Anjum became a sought-after lover, a skilled giver of pleasure, the orgasm she had when she wore her red disco sari was the last one of her life. And though the "tendencies" that Dr. Nabi had cautioned her father about remained, Dr. Mukhtar's pills did undeepen her voice. But it restricted its resonance, coarsened its timbre and gave it a peculiar, rasping quality, which sometimes sounded like two voices quarreling with each other instead of one. It frightened other people, but it did not frighten its owner in the way her God-given one had. Nor did it please her.

Anjum lived in the Khwabgah with her patched-together body and her partially realized dreams for more than thirty years.

She was forty-six years old when she announced that she wanted to leave. Mulaqat Ali was dead. Jahanara Begum was more or less bedridden and lived with Saqib and his family in one section of the old house at Chitli Qabar (the other half was rented to a strange, diffident young man who lived amidst towers of second-hand English books piled on the floor, on his bed and on every available horizontal surface). Anjum was welcome to visit occasionally, but not to stay. The Khwabgah was home to a new generation of residents; of the old ones only Ustad Kulsoom Bi, Bombay Silk, Razia, Bismillah and Mary remained.

Anjum had nowhere to go.

PERHAPS FOR THIS REASON, nobody took her seriously.

Theatrical announcements of departure and impending suicide were fairly routine responses to the wild jealousies, endless intrigue and continuously shifting loyalties that were a part of daily life in the Khwabgah. Once again, everybody suggested doctors and pills. Dr. Bhagat's pills cure everything, they said. Everyone's on them. "I'm not Everyone," Anjum said, and that set off another round of whispers (For and Against) about the pitfalls of pride and what did she think of herself?

What *did* she think of herself? Not much, or quite a lot, depending on how you looked at it. She had ambitions, yes. And they had come full circle. Now she wanted to return to the Duniya and live like an ordinary person. She wanted to be a mother, to wake up in her own home, dress Zainab in a school uniform and send her off to school with her books and tiffin box. The question was, were ambitions such as these, on the part of someone like herself, reasonable or unreasonable?

Zainab was Anjum's only love. Anjum had found her three years ago on one of those windy afternoons when the prayer caps of the Faithful blew off their heads and the balloon-sellers' balloons all slanted to one side. She was alone and bawling on the steps of the Jama Masjid, a painfully thin mouse of a thing, with big, frightened eyes. Anjum guessed that she was about three years old. She wore a dull green salwar kameez and a dirty white hijab. When Anjum loomed over her and offered her a finger to hold, she glanced up briefly, grasped it and continued to cry loudly without pause. The Mouse-in-a-hijab had no idea what a storm that casual gesture of trust set off inside the owner of the finger that she held on to. Being ignored instead of dreaded by the tiny creature subdued (for a moment at least) what Nimmo Gorakhpuri had so astutely and so long ago called Indo-Pak. The warring factions inside Anjum fell silent. Her body felt like a generous host instead of a battlefield. Was it like dying, or being born? Anjum couldn't decide. In her imagination it had the fullness, the sense of entirety, of one of the two. She bent down and picked the Mouse up and cradled her in her arms, murmuring all the while to her in both her quarreling voices. Even that did not scare or distract the child from her bawling project. For a while Anjum just stood there, smiling joyfully, while the creature in her arms cried. Then she set her down on the steps, bought her some bright pink cotton candy and tried to distract her by chatting nonchalantly about adult matters, hoping to pass the time until whoever owned the child came to get her. It turned out to be a one-way conversation, the Mouse did not seem to know much about herself, not even her name, and did not seem to want to talk. By the time she had finished with the cotton candy (or it had finished with her) she had a bright pink beard and sticky fingers. The bawling subsided into sobs and eventually into silence. Anjum stayed with her on the steps for hours, waiting for someone to come for her, asking passersby if they knew of anybody who was missing a child. As evening fell and the great wooden doors of the Jama Masjid were pulled shut, Anjum hoisted the Mouse on to her shoulders and carried her to the Khwabgah. There she was scolded and told that the right thing to do under the circumstances was to inform the Masjid Management that a lost child had been found. She did that the next morning. (Reluctantly, it has to be said, dragging her feet, hoping against hope, because by now Anjum was hopelessly in love.)

Over the next week announcements were made from several mosques several times a day. No one came forward to claim the Mouse. Weeks went by, still no one came looking. And so, by default, Zainab—the name Anjum chose for her—stayed on in the Khwabgah where she was lavished with more love by more mothers (and, in a manner of speaking, fathers) than any child could hope for. She did not take very long to settle into her new life, which suggested that she had not been unduly attached to her old one. Anjum came to believe that she had been abandoned and not lost.

In a few weeks she began to call Anjum "Mummy" (because that's what Anjum had begun to call herself). The other residents (under Anjum's tutelage) were all called "Apa" (Auntie, in Urdu), and Mary, because she was Christian, was Mary Auntie. Ustad Kulsoom Bi and Bismillah became "Badi Nani" and "Chhoti Nani." Senior and Junior Granny. The Mouse absorbed love like sand absorbs the sea. Very quickly she metamorphosed into a cheeky young lady with rowdy, distinctly bandicoot-like tendencies (that could only barely be managed).

Mummy, in the meanwhile, grew more addle-headed by the day. She was caught unawares by the fact that it was *possible* for one human being to love another so much and so completely.

At first, being new to the discipline, she was only able to express her feelings in a busy, bustling way, like a child with its first pet. She bought Zainab an unnecessary amount of toys and clothes (frothy, puff-sleeved frocks and Made-in-China squeaking shoes with flashing heel-lights), she bathed, dressed and undressed her an unnecessary number of times, oiled, braided and unbraided her hair, tied and untied it with matching and unmatching ribbons that she kept rolled up in an old tin. She overfed her, took her for walks in the neighborhood and, when she saw that Zainab was naturally drawn to animals, got her a rabbit—who was killed by a cat on his very first night at the Khwabgah—and a he-goat with a Maulana-style beard who lived in the courtyard and every now and then, with an impassive expression on his face, sent his shiny goat pills skittering in all directions.

The Khwabgah was in better condition than it had been for years. The broken room had been renovated and a new room built on top of it on the first floor, which Anjum and Mary now shared. Anjum slept with Zainab on a mattress on the floor, her long body curled protectively around the little girl like a city wall. At night she sang her to sleep softly, in a way that was more whisper than song. When Zainab was old enough to understand, Anjum began to tell her bedtime stories. At first the stories were entirely inappropriate for a young child. They were Anjum's somewhat maladroit attempt to make up for lost time, to transfuse herself into Zainab's memory and consciousness, to reveal herself without artifice, so that they could belong to each other completely. As a result she used Zainab as a sort of dock where she unloaded her cargo—her joys and tragedies, her life's cathartic turning points. Far from putting Zainab to sleep, many of the stories either gave her nightmares or made her stay awake for hours, fearful and cranky. Sometimes Anjum herself wept as she told them. Zainab began to dread her bedtime and would shut her eyes tightly, simulating sleep in order not to have to listen to another tale. Over time, however, Anjum (with inputs from some of the junior Apas) worked out an editorial line. The stories were successfully childproofed, and eventually Zainab even began to look forward to the night-time ritual.

Her top favorite was the Flyover Story—Anjum's account of how she and her friends walked home late one night from Defense Colony in South Delhi all the way back to Turkman Gate. There were five or six of them, dressed up, looking stunning after a night of revelry at a wealthy Seth's house in D-Block. After the party they decided to walk for a while and take in some fresh air. In those days there was such a thing as fresh air in the city, Anjum told Zainab. When they were halfway across the Defense Colony flyover—the city's only flyover at the time—it began to rain. And what can anyone possibly do when it rains on a flyover?

"They have to keep walking," Zainab would say, in a reasonable, adult tone.

"Exactly right. So we kept walking," Anjum would say. "And then what happened?"

"Then you wanted to soo!"

"Then I wanted to soo!"

"But you couldn't stop!"

"I couldn't stop."

"You had to keep walking!"

"I had to keep walking."

"So we soo-ed in our ghagra!" Zainab would shout, because she was at the age when anything to do with shitting, pissing and farting was the high point, or perhaps the *whole* point, of all stories.

"That's right, and it was the best feeling in the world," Anjum would say, "being drenched in the rain on that big, empty flyover, walking under a huge advertisement of a wet woman drying herself with a Bombay Dyeing towel."

"And the towel was as big as a carpet!"

"As big as a carpet, yes."

"And then you asked that woman if you could borrow her towel to dry yourself."

"And what did the woman say?"

"She said, *Nahin! Nahin! Nahin!*"

"She said, *Nahin! Nahin! Nahin!* So we got drenched, and we kept walking . . ."

"With *garam-garam* (warm) soo running down your *thanda-thanda* (cold) legs!"

Inevitably at this point Zainab would fall asleep, smiling. Every hint of adversity and unhappiness was required to be excised from Anjum's stories. She loved it when Anjum transformed herself into a young sex-siren who had led a shimmering life of music and dance, dressed in gorgeous clothes with varnished nails and a throng of admirers.

And so, in these ways, in order to please Zainab, Anjum began to rewrite a simpler, happier life for herself. The rewriting in turn began to make Anjum a simpler, happier person.

Edited out of the Flyover Story, for example, was the fact that the incident had happened in 1976, at the height of the Emergency declared by Indira Gandhi that lasted twenty-one months. Her spoiled younger son, Sanjay Gandhi, was the head of the Youth Congress (the youth wing of the ruling party), and was more or less running the country, treating it as though it was his personal plaything. Civil Rights had been suspended, newspapers were censored and, in the name of population control, thousands of men (mostly Muslim) were herded into camps and forcibly sterilized. A new law—the Maintenance of Internal Security Act—allowed the government to arrest anybody on a whim. The prisons were full, and a small coterie of Sanjay Gandhi's acolytes had been unleashed on the general population to carry out his fiat.

On the night of the Flyover Story, the gathering—a wedding party—that Anjum and her colleagues had descended on was broken up by the police. The host and three of his guests were arrested and driven away in police vans. Nobody knew why. Arif, the driver of the van that brought Anjum & Co. to the venue, tried to bundle his passengers into his van and make a getaway. For this impertinence he had the knuckles of his left hand and his right kneecap smashed. His passengers were dragged out of the Matador, kicked on their backsides as though they were circus clowns and instructed to scram, to run all the way home if they did not want to be arrested for prostitution and obscenity. They ran in blind terror, like ghouls, through the darkness and the driving rain, their make-up running a lot faster than their legs could, their drenched diaphanous clothes limiting their strides and impeding their speed. True, it was only a routine bit of humiliation for Hijras, nothing out of the ordinary, and nothing at all compared to the tribulations others endured during those horrible months.

It was nothing, but still, it was something.

Notwithstanding Anjum's editing, the Flyover Story retained some elements of truth. For instance, it really did rain that night. And Anjum really did piss while she ran. There really was an advertisement for Bombay Dyeing towels on the Defense Colony flyover. And the woman in the advertisement really did flat out refuse to share her towel.

A YEAR BEFORE ZAINAB was old enough to go to school, Mummy began to prepare for the event. She visited her old home and, with her brother Saqib's permission, brought Mulaqat Ali's collection of books to the Khwabgah. She was often seen sitting cross-legged in front of an open book (not the Holy Quran), moving her mouth as her finger traced a line across the page, or rocking back and forth with her eyes closed, thinking about what she had just read, or perhaps dredging the swamp of her memory to retrieve something that she once knew.

When Zainab turned five, Anjum took her to Ustad Hameed to begin singing lessons. It was clear from the start that music was not her calling. She fidgeted unhappily through her classes, hitting false notes so unerringly that it was almost a skill in itself. Patient, kind-hearted Ustad Hameed would shake his head as though a fly was bothering him and fill his cheeks with lukewarm tea while he held down the keys of the harmonium, which meant that he wanted his pupil to try once more. On that rare occasion when Zainab managed to arrive somewhere in the vicinity of the note, he would nod happily and say, "That's my boy!"—a phrase he had picked up from *The Tom and Jerry Show* on Cartoon Network, which he loved and watched with his grandchildren (who were studying in an English Medium school). It was his highest form of praise, regardless of the gender of his student. He bestowed it on Zainab not because she deserved it, but out of regard for Anjum and his memory of how beautifully she (or he—when she was Aftab) used to sing. Anjum sat through all the classes. Her high, hole-in-the-head insect hum reappeared, this time as a discreet usher endeavoring to discipline Zainab's wayward voice and keep it true. It was useless. The Bandicoot couldn't sing.

Zainab's real passion, it turned out, was animals. She was a terror on the streets of the old city. She wanted to free all the half-bald, half-dead white chickens that were pressed into filthy cages and stacked on top of each other outside the butcher shops, to converse with every cat that flashed across her path and to take home every litter of stray puppies she found wallowing in the blood and offal flowing through the open drains. She would not listen when she was told that dogs were unclean—*najis*—for Muslims and should not be touched. She did not shrink from the large, bristly rats that hurried along the street she had to walk down every day; she could not seem to get used to the sight of the bundles of yellow chicken claws, sawed-off goats' trotters, the pyramids of goats' heads with their staring, blind, blue eyes and the pearly white goats' brains that shivered like jelly in big steel bowls.

In addition to her pet goat, who, thanks to Zainab, had survived a record three Bakr-Eids unslaughtered, Anjum got her a handsome rooster who responded to his new mistress's welcoming embrace with a vicious peck. Zainab wept loudly, more from heartbreak than pain. The peck chastened her, but her affection for the bird remained undiminished. Whenever Rooster Love came upon her she would wrap her arms around Anjum's legs and deliver a few smacking kisses to Mummy's knees, turning her head to look longingly and lovingly at the rooster between kisses so that the object of her affection and the party receiving the kisses were not in any doubt about what was going on and who the kisses were really meant for. In some ways, Anjum's addle-headedness towards Zainab was proportionately reflected in Zainab's addle-headedness towards animals. None of her tenderness towards living creatures, however, got in the way of her voracious meat eating. At least twice a year Anjum took her to the zoo inside Purana Qila, the Old Fort, to visit the rhinoceros, the hippopotamus and her favorite character, the baby gibbon from Borneo.

A few months after she was admitted into KGB (Kindergarten—Section B) in Tender Buds Nursery School in Daryaganj—Saqib and his wife were registered as her official parents—the usually robust Bandicoot went through a patch of ill health. It wasn't serious, but it was persistent, and it wore her out, each illness making her more vulnerable to the next. Malaria followed flu followed two separate bouts of viral fever, one mild, the second worrying. Anjum fretted over her in unhelpful ways and, disregarding grumbles about her dereliction of Khwabgah duties (which were mostly administrative and managerial now), nursed the Bandicoot night and day with furtive, mounting paranoia. She became convinced that someone who envied her (Anjum's) good fortune had put a hex on Zainab. The needle of her suspicion pointed steadfastly in the direction of Saeeda, a relatively new member of the Khwabgah. Saeeda was much younger than Anjum and was second in line for Zainab's affections. She was a graduate and knew English. More importantly, she could speak the new language of the times—she could use the terms *cis-Man* and *FtoM* and *MtoF* and in interviews she referred to herself as a "transperson." Anjum, on the other hand, mocked what she called the "trans-france" business, and stubbornly insisted on referring to herself as a Hijra.

Like many of the younger generation, Saeeda switched easily between traditional salwar kameez and Western clothes—jeans, skirts, halter-necks that showed off her long, beautifully muscled back. What she lacked in local flavor and old-world charm she more than made up for with her modern understanding, her knowledge of the law and her involvement with Gender Rights Groups (she had even spoken at two conferences). All this placed her in a different league from Anjum. Also, Saeeda had edged Anjum out of the Number One spot in the media. The foreign newspapers had dumped the old exotics in favor of the younger generation. The exotics didn't suit the image of the New India—a nuclear power and an emerging destination for international finance. Ustad Kulsoom Bi, wily old she-wolf, was alert to these winds of change, and saw benefit accrue to the Khwabgah. So Saeeda, though she lacked seniority, was in close competition with Anjum to take over as Ustad of the Khwabgah when Ustad Kulsoom Bi decided to relinquish charge, which, like the Queen of England, she seemed in no hurry to do.

Ustad Kulsoom Bi was still the major decision-maker in the

Khwabgah, but she was not actively involved in its day-to-day affairs. On the mornings her arthritis troubled her she was laid out on her charpai in the courtyard, to be sunned along with the jars of lime and mango pickle, and wheat flour spread out on newspaper to rid it of weevils. When the sun got too hot she would be returned indoors to have her feet pressed and her wrinkles mustard-oiled. She dressed like a man now, in a long yellow kurta—yellow because she was a disciple of Hazrat Nizamuddin Auliya—and a checked sarong. She wound her thin white hair that barely covered her scalp into a tiny bun pinned to the back of her head. On some days her old friend Haji Mian, who sold cigarettes and paan down the street, would arrive with the audio cassette of their all-time favorite film, *Mughal-e-Azam*. They both knew every song and every line of dialogue by heart. So they sang and spoke along with the tape. They believed nobody would ever write Urdu like that again and that no actor would ever be able to match the diction and delivery of Dilip Kumar. Sometimes Ustad Kulsoom Bi would play Emperor Akbar as well as his son Prince Salim, the hero of the film, and Haji Mian would be Anarkali (Madhubala), the slave-girl Prince Salim had loved. Sometimes they would exchange roles. Their joint performance was really, more than anything else, a wake for lost glory and a dying language.

One evening Anjum was upstairs in her room putting a cold compress on the Bandicoot's hot forehead when she heard a commotion in the courtyard—raised voices, running feet, people shouting. Her first instinct was to assume that a fire had broken out. This happened often—the huge, tangled mess of exposed electric cables that hung over the streets had a habit of spontaneously bursting into flames. She picked Zainab up and ran down the stairs. Everybody was gathered in front of the TV in Ustad Kulsoom Bi's room, their faces lit by flickering TV light. A commercial airliner had crashed into a tall building. Half of it still protruded out, hanging in mid-air like a precarious, broken toy. In moments a second plane crashed into a second building and turned into a ball of fire. The usually garrulous residents of the Khwabgah watched in dead silence as the tall buildings buckled like pillars of sand. There was smoke and white dust everywhere. Even the dust looked different—clean and foreign. Tiny people jumped out of the tall buildings and floated down like flecks of ash.

It wasn't a film, the Television People said. It was really happening. In America. In a city called New York.

The longest silence in the history of the Khwabgah was finally broken by a profound inquiry.

"Do they speak Urdu there?" Bismillah wanted to know.

Nobody replied.

The shock in the room seeped into Zainab and she stirred out of her fever dream only to tumble straight into another. She wasn't familiar with television replays, so she counted ten planes crashing into ten buildings.

"Altogether ten," she announced soberly, in her new, Tender Buds English, and then refitted her fat, fevered cheek back into its parking slot in Anjum's neck.

The hex that had been put on Zainab had made the whole world sick. This was powerful *sifli jaadu*. Anjum stole a sly, sidelong glance at Saeeda to see whether she was brazenly celebrating her success or affecting innocence. The crafty bitch was pretending to be as shocked as everybody else.

By December Old Delhi was flooded with Afghan families fleeing warplanes that sang in their skies like unseasonal mosquitoes, and bombs that fell like steel rain. Of course the great politicos (which, in the old city, included every shopkeeper and Maulana) had their theories. For the rest, nobody really understood

exactly what those poor people had to do with the tall build-
ings in America. But how could they? Who but Anjum knew
that the Master Planner of this holocaust was neither Osama bin
Laden, Terrorist, nor George W. Bush, President of the United
States of America, but a far more powerful, far stealthier, force:
Saeeda (née Gul Mohammed), r/o Khwabgah, Gali Dakotan,
Delhi—110006, India.

In order to better understand the politics of the Duniya that
the Bandicoot was growing up in, as well as to neutralize or at
least pre-empt the educated Saeeda's *sifli jaadu*, Mummy began
to read the papers carefully and to follow the news on TV (whenever the others would let her switch away from the soaps).

The planes that flew into the tall buildings in America came as
a boon to many in India too. The Poet–Prime Minister of the
country and several of his senior ministers were members of
an old organization that believed India was essentially a Hindu
nation and that, just as Pakistan had declared itself an Islamic
Republic, India should declare itself a Hindu one. Some of its
supporters and ideologues openly admired Hitler and compared
the Muslims of India to the Jews of Germany. Now, suddenly, as
hostility towards Muslims grew, it began to seem to the Organization that the whole world was on its side. The Poet–Prime
Minister made a lisping speech, eloquent, except for long, exas-
perating pauses when he lost the thread of his argument, which
was quite often. He was an old man, but had a young man's way
of tossing his head when he spoke, like the Bombay film stars
of the 1960s. "The Mussalman, he doesn't like the Other," he
said poetically in Hindi, and paused for a long time, even by his
own standards. "His Faith he wants to spread through Terror."
He had made this couplet up on the spot, and was exceedingly
pleased with himself. Each time he said *Muslim* or *Mussalman* his

lisp sounded as endearing as a young child's. In the new dispensation he was considered to be a moderate. He warned that what
had happened in America could easily happen in India and that
it was time for the government to pass a new anti-terrorism law
as a safety precaution.

Every day Anjum, new to the news, watched TV reports about
bomb blasts and terrorist attacks that suddenly proliferated like
malaria. The Urdu papers carried stories of young Muslim boys
being killed in what the police called "encounters," or being
caught red-handed in the act of planning terrorist strikes and
arrested. A new law was passed which allowed suspects to be
detained without trial for months. In no time at all the prisons
were full of young Muslim men. Anjum thanked the Almighty
that Zainab was a girl. It was so much safer.

As winter set in, the Bandicoot developed a deep, chesty cough.
Anjum gave her teaspoons of warm milk with turmeric and kept
awake at night listening to her asthmatic wheeze, feeling utterly
helpless. She visited the dargah of Hazrat Nizamuddin Auliya
and spoke to one of the less mercenary Khadims whom she knew
well about Zainab's illness and asked him how she could neutralize Saeeda's *sifli jaadu*. Matters had got out of control, she
explained, and now that it concerned much more than the fate of
one little girl, she, Anjum, who was the only one who knew what
the problem was, had a responsibility. She was prepared to go
to any lengths to do what needed to be done. She was prepared
to pay any price, she said, even if it meant going to the gallows.
Saeeda had to be stopped. She needed the Khadim's blessings.
She became theatrical and emotional, people began to stare and
the Khadim had to calm her down. He asked her whether she
had visited the dargah of Hazrat Gharib Nawaz in Ajmer since
Zainab had come into her life. When she said that for one reason
or another she hadn't been able to, he told her that *that* was the

problem, not anybody's *sifli jaadu*. He was a little stern with her about allowing herself to believe in witchcraft and voodoo when Hazrat Gharib Nawaz was there to protect her. Anjum was not wholly convinced, but agreed that not visiting Ajmer Sharif for three years had been a serious lapse on her part.

It was late February by the time Zainab recovered enough for Anjum to feel that she could leave her for a few days. Zakir Mian, the Proprietor and Managing Director of A-1 Flower, agreed to travel with Anjum. Zakir Mian was a friend of Mulaqat Ali's and had known Anjum since she was born. He was in his mid-seventies now, too old to be embarrassed about being seen traveling with a Hijra. His shop, A-1 Flower, was basically a hip-high cement platform, a meter square, located under the balcony of Anjum's old home, at the corner where Chitli Qabar opened into the Matia Mahal Chowk. Zakir Mian had rented it from Mulaqat Ali—and now from Saqib—and had run A-1 Flower from there for more than fifty years. He sat on a piece of burlap all day, making garlands out of red roses and (separately) out of brand-new currency notes that he folded into tiny fans or little birds, for bridegrooms to wear on the day of their nikah. His main challenge was and had always been to keep the roses fresh and damp and the currency notes crisp and dry within the small space of his shop. Zakir Mian said he needed to go to Ajmer and then on to Ahmedabad in Gujarat where he had some business with his wife's family. Anjum was prepared to travel with him to Ahmedabad rather than risk the harassment and humiliation (of being seen as well as of being *un*seen) that she would have to endure if she traveled back on her own from Ajmer. Zakir Mian, for his part, was frail now, and happy to have someone to help him with his luggage. He suggested that while they were in Ahmedabad they could visit the shrine of Wali Dakhani, the seventeenth-century Urdu poet, known as the Poet of Love, whom Mulaqat Ali had been immensely fond of, and seek his blessings too. They sealed their travel plans by laughingly reciting a couplet by him—one of Mulaqat Ali's favorites:

Jisey ishq ka tiir kaari lage
Usey zindagi kyuun na bhari lage

For one struck down by Cupid's bow
Life becomes burdensome, isn't that so?

A few days later they set off by train. They spent two days in Ajmer Sharif. Anjum pushed her way through the press of devotees and bought a green-and-gold chadar for one thousand rupees as an offering to Hazrat Gharib Nawaz in Zainab's name. She called the Khwabgah from public payphones on both days. On the third day, anxious about Zainab, she called again from the Ajmer railway station platform just before she boarded the Gharib Nawaz Express to Ahmedabad. After that there was no news either from her or from Zakir Mian. His son called his mother's family home in Ahmedabad. The phone was dead.

THOUGH THEY HAD NO NEWS from Anjum, the news from Gujarat was horrible. A railway coach had been set on fire by what the newspapers first called "miscreants." Sixty Hindu pilgrims were burned alive. They were on their way home from a trip to Ayodhya where they had carried ceremonial bricks to lay in the foundations of a grand Hindu temple they wanted to construct at the site where an old mosque once stood. The mosque, the Babri Masjid, had been brought down ten years earlier by a screaming mob. A senior cabinet member (who was in the Opposition then, and had watched as the screaming mob tore down the mosque) said the burning of the train definitely looked like the work of Pakistani terrorists. The police arrested hundreds of Muslims—all auxiliary Pakistanis from their point of view—from the area around the railway station under the new terrorism law and threw them into prison. The Chief Minister of Gujarat, a loyal member of the Organization (as were the Home Minister and the Prime Minister), was, at the time, up for re-election. He appeared on TV in a saffron kurta with a slash of vermilion on his forehead, and with cold, dead eyes ordered that the burnt bodies of the Hindu pilgrims be brought to Ahmedabad, the capital of the state, where they were to be put on display for the general public to pay their respects. A weaselly "unofficial spokesperson" announced unofficially that every action would be met with an equal and opposite reaction. He didn't acknowledge Newton of course, because, in the prevailing climate, the officially sanctioned position was that ancient Hindus had invented all science.

The "reaction," if indeed that is what it was, was neither equal nor opposite. The killing went on for weeks and was not confined to cities alone. The mobs were armed with swords and tridents and wore saffron headbands. They had cadastral lists of Muslim homes, businesses and shops. They had stockpiles of gas cylinders (which seemed to explain the gas shortage of the previous few weeks). When people who had been injured were taken to hospital, mobs attacked the hospitals. The police would not register murder cases. They said, quite reasonably, that they needed to see the corpses. The catch was that the police were often part of the mobs, and once the mobs had finished their business, the corpses no longer resembled corpses.

Nobody disagreed when Saeeda (who loved Anjum and was entirely unaware of Anjum's suspicions about her) suggested that the soap operas on TV be switched off and the news be switched on and left on in case, by some small chance, they could pick up a clue about what might have happened to Anjum and Zakir Mian. When flushed, animated TV news reporters shouted out their Pieces-to-Camera from the refugee camps where tens of thousands of Gujarat's Muslims now lived, in the Khwabgah they switched off the sound and scanned the background hoping to catch a glimpse of Anjum and Zakir Mian lining up for food or blankets, or huddled in a tent. They learned in passing that Wali Dakhani's shrine had been razed to the ground and a tarred road built over it, erasing every sign that it had ever existed. (Neither the police nor the mobs nor the Chief Minister could do anything about the people who continued to leave flowers in the middle of the new tarred road where the shrine used to be. When the flowers were crushed to paste under the wheels of fast cars, new flowers would appear. And what can anybody do about the connection between flower-paste and poetry?) Saeeda called every journalist and NGO worker she knew and begged him or her to help. Nobody came up with anything. Weeks went by with no news. Zainab recovered from her bout of illnesses and went back to school, but outside school hours she was querulous and clung to Saeeda night and day.

TWO MONTHS LATER, when the murdering had grown sporadic and was more or less tailing off, Zakir Mian's eldest son, Mansoor, went on his third trip to Ahmedabad to look for his father. As a precaution he shaved off his beard and wore red puja threads on his wrist, hoping to pass off as Hindu. He never found his father, although he did learn what had happened to him. His inquiries led him to a small refugee camp inside a mosque on the outskirts of Ahmedabad, where he found Anjum in the men's section, and brought her back to the Khwabgah.

She had had a haircut. What was left of her hair now sat on her head like a helmet with ear muffs. She was dressed like a junior bureaucrat in a pair of dark brown men's terry cotton trousers and a checked, short-sleeved safari shirt. She had lost a good deal of weight.

Zainab, though momentarily a little frightened by Anjum's new, manly appearance, got over her fear and propelled herself into her arms shrieking her delight. Anjum held her close, but responded to the tears and questions and welcoming embraces of the others impassively, as though their greetings were an ordeal that she had no choice but to put up with. They were hurt and a little frightened by her coldness, but uncharacteristically gracious in their empathy and concern.

As soon as she could, Anjum went up to her room. She emerged hours later, in her normal clothes, with lipstick and make-up and a few pretty clips in her hair. It soon became obvious that she did not want to talk about what had happened. She would not answer questions about Zakir Mian. "It was God's will," was all she would say.

During Anjum's absence Zainab had begun to sleep downstairs with Saeeda. She returned to sleeping with Anjum, but Anjum noticed that she had started calling Saeeda "Mummy" too.

"If she's Mummy, then who am I?" Anjum asked Zainab a few days later. "Nobody has two Mummies."

"*Badi* Mummy," Zainab said. Big Mummy.

Ustad Kulsoom Bi gave instructions that Anjum was to be left in peace to do whatever she wanted, for as long as she wanted.

What Anjum wanted was to be left alone.

She was quiet, disconcertingly so, and spent most of her time with her books. Over the course of a week she taught Zainab to chant something that nobody in the Khwabgah could understand. Anjum said it was a Sanskrit chant, the Gayatri Mantra. She had learned it while she was in the camp in Gujarat. People there said it was good to know so that in mob situations they could recite it to try to pass off as Hindu. Though neither she nor Anjum had any idea what it meant, Zainab picked it up quickly and chanted it happily at least twenty times a day, while she dressed for school, while she packed her books, while she fed her goat:

Om bhur bhuvah svaha
Tat savitur varenyam
Bhargo devasya dhimahi
Dhiyo yo nah pracodayat

One morning Anjum left the house, taking Zainab with her. She returned with a completely transformed Bandicoot. Her hair was cropped short and she was dressed in boy's clothes; a baby Pathan suit, an embroidered jacket, jootis with toes curled upward like gondolas.

"It's safer like this," Anjum said by way of explanation. "Gujarat could come to Delhi any day. We'll call him Mahdi."

Zainab's wailing could be heard all the way down the street—by the chickens in their cages and the puppies in their drains.

An emergency meeting was called. It was scheduled during the two hours of regular power cut so that there would be no complaints from anybody about having to miss the serials on TV. Zainab was sent to spend the evening with Hassan Mian's grandchildren. Her rooster was in his customary snoozing place on a shelf beside the TV. Ustad Kulsoom Bi addressed the meeting propped up on her bed, her back supported by a rolled-up razai. Everyone else sat on the ground. Anjum skulked sullenly in the doorway. In the hissing blue light of the Petromax lantern Kulsoom Bi's face looked like a dried riverbed, her thinning white hair the receding glacier from which the river once rose. She had put in her uncomfortable set of new dentures for the occasion.

She spoke with authority and a great sense of theater. Her words appeared to be directed at the new initiates who had just joined the Khwabgah, but her tone was directed at Anjum.

"This house, this household, has an unbroken history that is as old as this broken city," she said. "These peeling walls, this leaking roof, this sunny courtyard—all this was once beautiful. These floors were covered with carpets that came straight from Isfahan, the ceilings were decorated with mirrors. When Shahenshah Shah Jahan built the Red Fort and the Jama Masjid, when he built this walled city, he built our little haveli too. For us. Always remember—we are not just *any* Hijras from *any* place. We are the Hijras of Shahjahanabad. Our Rulers trusted us enough to put their wives and mothers in our care. Once we roamed freely in their private quarters, the zenana, of the Red Fort. They're all gone now, those mighty emperors and their queens. But *we* are still here. Think about that and ask yourselves why that should be."

The Red Fort had always played a major part in Ustad Kulsoom Bi's recounting of the history of the Khwabgah. In the old days, when she was able-bodied, a trip to the fort to watch the Sound and Light show was a mandatory part of the initiation rites for new arrivals. They would go in a group, dressed in their best clothes, with flowers in their hair, holding hands, risking life and limb as they plunged through the Chandni Chowk traffic—a confusion of cars, buses, rickshaws and tangas driven by people who somehow managed to be reckless even at an excruciatingly slow speed.

The fort loomed over the old city, a massive sandstone plateau, so vast a part of the skyline that local people had ceased to notice it. Had Ustad Kulsoom Bi not insisted, perhaps nobody from the Khwabgah would ever have worked up the nerve to go in, not even Anjum, who had been born and raised in its shadow. Once they crossed the moat—full of garbage and mosquitoes—

and walked through the great gateway, the city ceased to exist. Monkeys with small, mad eyes paraded up and down the towering sandstone ramparts that were built on a scale and with a grace the modern mind could not conceive of. Inside the fort it was a different world, a different time, a different air (that smelled distinctly of marijuana) and a different sky—not a narrow, street-wide strip that was barely visible through a tangle of electric wires, but a boundless one in which kites wheeled, high and quiet, up in the thermals.

The Sound and Light show was an old-government-approved version (the new government had not got its hands on it yet) of the history of the Red Fort and the emperors who had ruled from it for more than two hundred years—from Shah Jahan, who built it, to Bahadur Shah Zafar, the last Mughal, who was sent into exile by the British after the failed uprising of 1857. It was the only formal history Ustad Kulsoom Bi knew, though her reading of it may have been more unorthodox than its authors intended. During their visits, she and her little crew would take their place with the rest of the audience, mostly tourists and schoolchildren, on the rows of wooden benches under which dense clouds of mosquitoes lived. To avoid being bitten the audience had to assume a posture of enforced nonchalance and swing their legs through every coronation, war, massacre, victory and defeat.

Ustad Kulsoom Bi's special area of interest was the mid-eighteenth century, the reign of Emperor Mohammed Shah Rangeela, legendary lover of pleasure, of music and painting—the merriest Mughal of them all. She primed her acolytes to pay particular attention to the year 1739. It began with the thunder of horses' hooves that came from behind the audience and moved through the fort, faint at first and then louderLouderLOUDER. That was Nadir Shah's cavalry riding all the way from Persia, galloping through Ghazni, Kabul, Kandahar, Peshawar, Lahore and Sirhind, plundering city after city as it galloped towards

Delhi. Emperor Mohammad Shah's generals warn him of the approaching cataclysm. Unperturbed, he orders the music to play on. At this point in the show the lights in the Diwan-e-Khas, the Hall of Special Audience, would turn lurid. Purple, red, green. The zenana would light up in pink (of course) and echo with the sound of women's laughter, the rustling of silk, the *chhann-chhann-chhann* of anklets. Then, suddenly, amidst those soft, happy, lady-sounds would come the clearly audible, deep, distinct, rasping, coquettish giggle of a court eunuch.

"There!" Ustad Kulsoom Bi would say, like a triumphant lepidopterist who has just netted a rare moth. "Did you hear that? That is *us*. That is our ancestry, our history, our story. We were never commoners, you see, we were members of the staff of the Royal Palace."

The moment passed in a heartbeat. But it did not matter. What mattered was that it *existed*. To be present in history, even as nothing more than a chuckle, was a universe away from being absent from it, from being written out of it altogether. A chuckle, after all, could become a foothold in the sheer wall of the future.

Ustad Kulsoom Bi would be furious with anyone who missed the chuckle after all the effort she had put into pointing it out. So furious, in fact, that in order to avoid what could turn into a public spectacle, the newbies were advised by the older ones to pretend they had heard it even if they hadn't.

Once Gudiya tried to tell her that Hijras had a special place of love and respect in Hindu mythology. She told Kulsoom Bi the story of how, when Lord Ram and his wife, Sita, and his younger brother Laxman were banished for fourteen years from their kingdom, the citizenry, who loved their king, had followed them, vowing to go wherever their king went. When they reached the outskirts of Ayodhya where the forest began, Ram turned to his people and said, "I want all you men and women to go home and wait for me until I return." Unable to disobey their king, the men and women returned home. Only the Hijras waited faithfully for him at the edge of the forest for the whole fourteen years, because he had forgotten to mention them.

"So we are remembered as the forgotten ones?" Ustad Kulsoom Bi said. "Wah! Wah!"

Anjum remembered her first visit to the Red Fort vividly for reasons of her own. It was her first outing after she had recovered from Dr. Mukhtar's surgery. While they queued for tickets most people gawked at the foreign tourists, who had a separate queue and more expensive tickets. The foreign tourists in turn gawked at the Hijras—at Anjum in particular. A young man, a hippy with a piercing gaze and a wispy Jesus beard, looked at her admiringly. She looked back at him. In her imagination he became Hazrat Sarmad Shaheed. She pictured him standing proud and naked, a slim, slight figure, before the jury of malevolent bearded Qazis, not flinching even when they sentenced him to death. She was a little taken aback when the tourist walked up to her.

"You are fery beautiful," he said. "A photo? May I?"

It was the first time anybody had ever wanted to photograph her. Flattered, she threw her red-ribboned braid over her shoulder coyly and looked at Ustad Kulsoom Bi for permission. It was granted. So she posed for the photograph, leaning awkwardly against the sandstone ramparts, her shoulders thrown back and her chin tilted up, brazen and timorous all at once.

"Sankyou," the young man said. "Sankyou very much."

She never saw it, but it was the beginning of something, that photograph.

Where was it now? God only knew.

Anjum's drifting mind returned to the meeting in Ustad Kulsoom Bi's room.

It was the decadence and indiscipline of our Rulers that brought ruin on the Mughal Empire, Ustad Kulsoom Bi was saying. Princes frolicking with slave women, emperors running around naked, living lives of opulence while their people starved—how could an empire like that have hoped to survive? Why *should* it have survived? (Nobody who had heard her playing Prince Salim in *Mughal-e-Azam* would have guessed that she disapproved of him so thoroughly. Nor would anybody have suspected that, notwithstanding her pride about the Khwabgah's vintage and its proximity to royalty, she harbored a socialist's anger about the Mughal Rulers' profligacy and their people's penury.) She then went on to make a case for principled living and iron discipline, the two things that according to her were the hallmark of the Khwabgah—its strength and the reason it had survived through the ages, while stronger, grander things had perished.

Ordinary people in the Duniya—what did they know about what it takes to live the life of a Hijra? What did they know about the rules, the discipline and the sacrifices? Who today knew that there had been times when all of them, including she, Ustad Kulsoom Bi herself, had been driven to begging for alms at traffic lights? That they had built themselves up, bit by bit, humiliation by humiliation, from there? The Khwabgah was called Khwabgah, Ustad Kulsoom Bi said, because it was where special people, *blessed* people, came with their dreams that could not be realized in the Duniya. In the Khwabgah, Holy Souls trapped in the wrong bodies were liberated. (The question of what would happen if the Holy Soul were a man trapped in a woman's body was not addressed.)

However, Ustad Kulsoom Bi said, *however*—and the pause that followed was one that was worthy of the lisping Poet–Prime Minister—the central edict of the Khwabgah was *manzoori*. Consent. People in the Duniya spread wicked rumors about Hijras kidnapping little boys and castrating them. She did not know and could not say whether these things happened elsewhere, but in the Khwabgah, as the Almighty was witness, nothing happened without *manzoori*.

She then turned to the specific subject at hand. The Almighty has sent our Anjum back to us, she said. She won't tell us what happened to her and Zakir Mian in Gujarat and we cannot force her to. All we can do is surmise. And sympathize. But in our sympathy we cannot allow our principles to be compromised. Forcing a little girl to live as a boy against her wishes, even for the sake of her own safety, is to incarcerate her, not liberate her. There is no question of that happening in our Khwabgah. No question at all.

"She's *my* child," Anjum said. "*I* will decide. I can leave this place and go away with her if I want to."

Far from being perturbed by this declaration, everybody was actually relieved to see a sign that the old drama queen in Anjum was alive and well. They had no reason to worry because she had absolutely nowhere to go.

"You can do as you like, but the child will stay here," Ustad Kulsoom Bi said.

"All this time you spoke about *manzoori*, now *you* want to decide on her behalf?" Anjum said. "We'll ask her. Zainab will want to come with me."

Talking back to Ustad Kulsoom Bi in this way was considered unacceptable. Even for someone who had survived a massacre. Everybody waited for the reaction.

Ustad Kulsoom Bi closed her eyes and asked for the rolled-up razai to be removed from behind her. Suddenly tired, she turned to the wall and curled up, using the crook of her arm as a pillow. With her eyes still shut and her voice sounding as though it was coming from far away, she instructed Anjum to see Dr. Bhagat and to make sure that she took the medicines he prescribed.

The meeting ended. The members dispersed. The Petromax lantern was carried out of the room hissing like an annoyed cat.

ANJUM HADN'T MEANT what she said, but having said it, the idea of leaving took hold and coiled around her like a python.

She refused to go to Dr. Bhagat, so a little delegation headed by Saeeda went on her behalf. Dr. Bhagat was a small man with a clipped military mustache who smelled overwhelmingly of Pond's Dreamflower talcum powder. He had a quick, birdy manner and a way of interrupting his patients as well as himself every few minutes with a dry, nervous sniff accompanied by three staccato taps of his pen on the tabletop. His forearms were covered with thick black hair but his head was more or less hairless. He had shaved a broad strip of hair off his left wrist, over which he wore a tennis player's toweling sweatband, over which he wore his heavy gold watch so that he had a clear, unobscured view of the time. That morning he was dressed the way he dressed every day—in a spotless white terry cotton safari suit and shiny white sandals. A clean white towel hung over the back of his chair. His clinic was in a shithole locality, but he was a very clean man. And a good one too.

The delegation trooped in and sat down on what chairs were available, some perched on the arms of the others' chairs. Dr. Bhagat was used to seeing his patients from the Khwabgah in twos and threes (they never came alone). He was a little taken aback at the multitude that descended on him that morning.

"Which one of you is the patient?"

"None of us, Doctor Sahib."

Saeeda, the spokesperson, with occasional clarifications and elucidations from the others, described Anjum's altered behavior as carefully as she could—the brooding, the rudeness, the *reading* and, most seriously, the insubordination. She told the doctor about Zainab's illnesses and Anjum's anxiety. (Of course she had no means of knowing about Anjum's *sifli jaadu* theory and her own part in it.) The delegation had, after detailed consultations with each other, decided to leave Gujarat out of it because:

(a) They didn't know what, if anything, had happened to Anjum there.

And,

(b) Because Dr. Bhagat had a biggish silver (or perhaps it was only silver-plated) statue of Lord Ganesh on his table and there was always smoke from a fresh incense stick curling up his trunk.

Certainly there were no concrete conclusions to be drawn from this latter fact, but it made them unsure of his views on what had happened in Gujarat. So they decided to err on the side of abundant caution.

Dr. Bhagat (who, like millions of other believing Hindus, was in fact appalled by the turn of events in Gujarat) listened attentively, sniffing and tapping the table with his pen, his bright, beady eyes magnified by thick lenses set in gold-framed spectacles. He furrowed his brow and thought for a minute about what he had been told and then asked whether Anjum's wanting to leave the Khwabgah had led to the Reading or the Reading had led to her wanting to leave. The delegation was divided on the issue. One of the younger delegates, Meher, said that Anjum had told her that she wanted to move back to the Duniya and help the poor. This set off a flurry of merriment. Dr. Bhagat, not smiling, asked them why they thought it so funny.

"*Arre*, Doctor Sahib, which Poor would want to be helped by *us*?" Meher said, and they all giggled at the idea of intimidating poor people with offers of help.

On his prescription pad Dr. Bhagat wrote in tiny, neat handwriting: *Patient formerly of outgoing, obedient, jolly-type nature now exhibits disobedient, revolting-type of personality.*

He told them not to worry. He wrote them a prescription. The pills (the ones that he always prescribed to everybody) would calm her down, he said, and give her a few good nights' sleep, after which he would need to see her personally.

Anjum flatly refused to take the pills.

As the days passed, her quietness gave way to something else, something restless and edgy. It coursed through her veins like an insidious uprising, a mad insurrection against a lifetime of spurious happiness she felt she had been sentenced to.

She added Dr. Bhagat's prescription to the things she had piled up in the courtyard, things she had once treasured, and lit a match. Among the incinerated items were:

Three documentary films (about her)

Two glossy coffee-table books of photographs (of her)

Seven photo features in foreign magazines (about her)

An album of press clippings from foreign newspapers in more than thirteen languages including the *New York Times*, the London *Times*, the *Guardian*, the *Boston Globe*, the *Globe and Mail*, *Le Monde*, *Corriere della Sera*, *La Stampa* and *Die Zeit* (about her).

The smoke from the fire rose and made everybody, including the goat, cough. When the ash cooled, she rubbed it into her face and hair. That night Zainab moved her clothes, shoes, school bag and rocket-shaped pencil box into Saeeda's cupboard. She refused to sleep with Anjum any more.

"Mummy's never happy," was the precise, merciless reason she gave.

Heartbroken, Anjum emptied her Godrej almirah and packed her finery—her satin ghararas and sequined saris, her jhumkas, anklets and glass bangles—into tin trunks. She made herself two Pathan suits, one pigeon gray and one mud brown; she bought a second-hand plastic anorak and a pair of men's shoes that she wore without socks. A battered Tempo arrived and the almirah and tin trunks were loaded on to it. She left without saying where she was going.

Even then, nobody took her seriously. They were sure she'd be back.

ONLY A TEN-MINUTE TEMPO RIDE from the Khwabgah, once again Anjum entered another world.

It was an unprepossessing graveyard, run-down, not very big and used only occasionally. Its northern boundary abutted a government hospital and mortuary where the bodies of the city's vagrants and unclaimed dead were warehoused until the police decided how to dispose of them. Most were taken to the city crematorium. If they were recognizably Muslim they were buried in unmarked graves that disappeared over time and contributed to the richness of the soil and the unusual lushness of the old trees.

The formally constructed graves numbered less than two hundred. The older graves were more elaborate, with carved marble tombstones, the more recent ones, more rudimentary. Several generations of Anjum's family were buried there—Mulaqat Ali, his father and mother, his grandfather and grandmother. Mulaqat Ali's older sister Begum Zeenat Kauser (Anjum's aunt) was buried next to him. She had moved to Lahore after Partition. After living there for ten years she left her husband and children and returned to Delhi, saying she was unable to live anywhere except in the immediate vicinity of Delhi's Jama Masjid. (For some reason Lahore's Badshahi Mosque did not work out as a substitute.) Having survived three attempts by the police to deport her as a Pakistani spy, Begum Zeenat Kauser settled down in Shahjahanabad in a tiny room with a kitchen and a view of her beloved mosque. She shared it with a widow roughly her own age. She earned her living by supplying mutton korma to a restaurant in the old city where foreign tour groups came to savor local food. She stirred the same pot every day for thirty years and smelled of korma the way other women smelled of ittar and perfume. Even when life left her, she was interred in her grave smelling like a delicious Old Delhi meal. Next to Begum Zeenat Kauser were the remains of Bibi Ayesha, Anjum's oldest sister, who had died of tuberculosis. A little distance away was the grave of Ahlam Baji, the midwife who'd delivered Anjum. In the years before her death, Ahlam Baji had grown disoriented and obese. She would float regally down the streets of the old city, like a filthy queen, her matted hair twisted into a grimy towel as though she had just emerged fresh from a bath in ass's milk. She always carried a tattered Kisan Urea fertilizer sack that she crammed with empty mineral-water bottles, torn kites, carefully folded posters and streamers left behind by the big political rallies that were held in the Ramlila grounds nearby. On her grimmer days Ahlam Baji would accost the beings she had helped bring into the world, most of whom were grown men and women with children of their own, and abuse them in the foulest language, cursing the day they were born. Her insults never caused offense; people usually reacted with the wide, embarrassed grins of those who are called on stage to be guinea pigs in magic shows. Ahlam Baji was always fed, always offered shelter. She accepted food— rancorously—as though she was doing the person who offered it a great favor, but she turned down the offer of shelter. She insisted on remaining outdoors through the hottest of summers and the bitterest of winters. She was found dead one morning, sitting bolt upright outside Alif Zed Stationers & Photocopiers, with her arms around her Kisan Urea sack. Jahanara Begum insisted she be buried in the family graveyard. She organized for the body to be bathed and dressed and for an imam to say the final prayers. Ahlam Baji had, after all, midwifed all her five children.

Next to Ahlam Baji's grave was the grave of a woman on whose

tombstone it said (in English) "Begum Renata Mumtaz Madam."
Begum Renata was a belly dancer from Romania who grew up in
Bucharest dreaming of India and its classical dance forms. When
she was only nineteen she hitchhiked across the continent and
arrived in Delhi where she found a mediocre Kathak guru who
exploited her sexually and taught her very little dance. To make
ends meet she began to perform cabarets in the Rosebud Rest-
O-Bar located in the rose garden—known to locals as No-Rose
Garden—in the ruins of Feroz Shah Kotla, the fifth of the seven
ancient cities of Delhi. Renata's *nom de cabaret* was Mumtaz. She
died young after being thwarted in love by a professional cheat
who disappeared with all her savings. Renata continued to long
for him even though she knew he had deceived her. She grew
distraught, tried to cast spells and call up spirits. She began to go
into long trances during which her skin broke out in boils and
her voice grew deep and gravelly like a man's. The circumstances
of her death were unclear, though everybody assumed it was suicide. It was Roshan Lal, the taciturn headwaiter of the Rosebud
Rest-O-Bar, gruff moralizer, scourge of all the dancing girls (and
the butt of all their jokes), who surprised himself by organizing her funeral and visiting her grave with flowers, once, twice
and then, before he knew it, every Tuesday (his day off). It was
he who organized the tombstone with her name on it and who
maintained its "keep-up," as he called it. It was he who added
"Begum" and "Madam," the posthumous prefix and suffix to her
name(s) on the tombstone. Seventeen years had gone by since
Renata Mumtaz died. Roshan Lal had fat varicose veins running
up his thin shins and had lost the hearing in one ear, but still he
came, clanking into the graveyard on his old black bicycle, bringing fresh flowers—gazanias, discounted roses and, when he was
pressed for money, a few strings of jasmine that he bought from
children at traffic lights.

Other than the main graves, there were a few whose provenance was contested. For example the one that simply said "Badshah." Some people insisted Badshah was a lesser Mughal prince who had been hanged by the British after the rebellion of 1857, while others believed he was a Sufi poet from Afghanistan. Another grave bore only the name "Islahi." Some said he was a general in Emperor Shah Alam II's army, others insisted he was a local pimp who had been knifed to death in the 1960s by a prostitute whom he had cheated. As always, everybody believed what they wanted to believe.

On her first night in the graveyard, after a quick reconnaissance, Anjum placed her Godrej cupboard and her few belongings near Mulaqat Ali's grave and unrolled her carpet and bedding between Ahlam Baji's and Begum Renata Mumtaz Madam's graves. Not surprisingly, she didn't sleep. Not that anyone in the graveyard troubled her—no djinns arrived to make her acquaintance, no ghosts threatened a haunting. The smack addicts at the northern end of the graveyard—shadows just a deeper shade of night—huddled on knolls of hospital waste in a sea of old bandages and used syringes, didn't seem to notice her at all. On the southern side, clots of homeless people sat around fires cooking their meager, smoky meals. Stray dogs, in better health than the humans, sat at a polite distance, waiting politely for scraps.

In that setting, Anjum would ordinarily have been in some danger. But her desolation protected her. Unleashed at last from social protocol, it rose up around her in all its majesty—a fort, with ramparts, turrets, hidden dungeons and walls that hummed like an approaching mob. She rattled through its gilded chambers like a fugitive absconding from herself. She tried to dismiss the cortège of saffron men with saffron smiles who pursued her with infants impaled on their saffron tridents, but they would not be dismissed. She tried to shut the door on Zakir Mian, lying neatly folded in the middle of the street, like one of his crisp cash-birds. But he followed her, folded, through closed doors on his flying carpet. She tried to forget the way he had looked at her just before the light went out of his eyes. But he wouldn't let her.

She tried to tell him that she had fought back bravely as they hauled her off his lifeless body.

But she knew very well that she hadn't.

She tried to un-know what they had done to all the others—how they had folded the men and unfolded the women. And how eventually they had pulled them apart limb from limb and set them on fire.

But she knew very well that she knew.

They.

They, who?

Newton's Army, deployed to deliver an Equal and Opposite Reaction. Thirty thousand saffron parakeets with steel talons and bloodied beaks, all squawking together:

Mussalman ka ek hi sthan! Qabristan ya Pakistan!

Only one place for the Mussalman! The Graveyard or Pakistan!

Anjum, feigning death, had lain sprawled over Zakir Mian. Counterfeit corpse of a counterfeit woman. But the parakeets, even though they were—or pretended to be—pure vegetarian (this was the minimum qualification for conscription), tested the breeze with the fastidiousness and proficiency of bloodhounds. And of course they found her. Thirty thousand voices chimed together, mimicking Ustad Kulsoom Bi's Birbal:

Ai Hai! Saali Randi Hijra! Sister-fucking Whore Hijra. Sister-fucking Muslim Whore Hijra.

Another voice rose, high and anxious, another bird:

Nahi yaar, mat maro, Hijron ka maarna apshagun hota hai.

Don't kill her, brother, killing Hijras brings bad luck.

Bad luck!

Nothing scared those murderers more than the prospect of bad luck. After all, it was to ward off bad luck that the fingers that gripped the slashing swords and flashing daggers were studded with lucky stones embedded in thick gold rings. It was to ward off bad luck that the wrists wielding iron rods that bludgeoned people to death were festooned with red puja threads lovingly tied by adoring mothers. Having taken all these precautions, what would be the point of willfully courting bad luck?

So they stood over her and made her chant their slogans.

Bharat Mata Ki Jai! Vande Mataram!

She did. Weeping, shaking, humiliated beyond her worst nightmare.

Victory to Mother India! Salute the Mother!

They left her alive. Unkilled. Unhurt. Neither folded nor unfolded. She alone. So that *they* might be blessed with good fortune.

Butchers' Luck.

That's all she was. And the longer she lived, the more good luck she brought them.

She tried to un-know that little detail as she rattled through her private fort. But she failed. She knew very well that she knew very well that she knew very well.

The Chief Minister with cold eyes and a vermilion forehead would go on to win the next elections. Even after the Poet–Prime Minister's government fell at the Center, he won election after election in Gujarat. Some people believed he ought to be held responsible for mass murder, but his voters called him Gujarat ka Lalla. Gujarat's Beloved.

FOR MONTHS ANJUM LIVED in the graveyard, a ravaged, feral specter, out-haunting every resident djinn and spirit, ambushing bereaved families who came to bury their dead with a grief so wild, so untethered, that it clean outstripped theirs. She stopped grooming herself, stopped dyeing her hair. It grew dead white from the roots, and suddenly, halfway down her head, turned jet black, making her look, well . . . *striped*. Facial hair, which she had once dreaded more than almost anything else, appeared on her chin and cheeks like a glimmer of frost (mercifully a lifetime of cheap hormone injections stopped it from growing into an all-out beard). One of her front teeth, stained dark red from chewing paan, grew loose in her gums. When she spoke or smiled, which she did rarely, it moved up and down terrifyingly, like a harmonium key playing a tune of its own. The terrifyingness had its advantages though—it scared people and kept nasty, insult-hurling, stone-throwing little boys at bay.

Mr. D. D. Gupta, an old client of Anjum's, whose affection for her had transcended worldly desire long ago, tracked her down and visited her in the graveyard. He was a building contractor from Karol Bagh who bought and supplied construction material—steel, cement, stone, bricks. He diverted a small consignment of bricks and a few asbestos sheets from the building site of a wealthy client and helped Anjum construct a small, temporary shack—nothing elaborate, just a storeroom in which she could lock her things if she needed to. Mr. Gupta visited her from time to time to make sure she was provided for and did not harm herself. When he moved to Baghdad after the American invasion of Iraq (to capitalize on the escalating demand for concrete blast walls), he asked his wife to send their driver with a hot meal for Anjum at least three times a week. Mrs. Gupta, who thought of herself as a Gopi, a female adorer of Lord Krishna, was, according to her palmist, living through her seventh and last cycle of rebirth. This gave her license to behave as she wished without worrying that she would have to pay for her sins in her next life. She had her own amorous involvements, although she maintained that when she attained sexual climax, the ecstasy she felt was for a divine being and not for her human lover. She was extremely fond of her husband but was relieved to have his physical appetites taken off her plate, and therefore more than happy to do him this small favor.

Before he left, Mr. Gupta bought Anjum a cheap mobile phone and taught her how to answer it (incoming calls were free) and how to give him what he described as a "missed call" if she needed to speak to him. Anjum lost it within a week, and when Mr. Gupta called from Baghdad the phone was answered by a drunk who wept and demanded to speak to his mother.

In addition to this kind-heartedness, Anjum also received other visitors. Saeeda brought the apparently heartless, but in truth traumatized, Zainab a few times. (When it became apparent to Saeeda that the visits caused both Anjum and Zainab too much pain, she stopped bringing her.) Anjum's brother, Saqib, came once a week. Ustad Kulsoom Bi herself, accompanied by her friend Haji Mian and sometimes Bismillah, would come by in a rickshaw. She saw to it that Anjum received a small pension from the Khwabgah, delivered to her in cash in an envelope on the first of every month.

The most regular visitor of all was Ustad Hameed. He would arrive every day except on Wednesdays and Sundays, either at dawn or at twilight, settle down on someone's grave with Anjum's harmonium and begin his haunting *riaz*, Raag Lalit in the morning, Raag Shuddh Kalyan in the evenings—*Tum bin kaun khabar mori lait* . . . Who other than you will ask for news of me? He studiously ignored the insulting audience-requests for the latest Bollywood hit or popular qawwali (nine out of ten times it was *Dum-a-Dum Mast Qalandar*) shouted out by the vagabonds and drifters who gathered outside the invisible boundary of what had, by consensus, been marked off as Anjum's territory. Sometimes the tragic shadows on the edge of the graveyard rose to their feet in a dreamy, booze- or smack-induced haze and danced in slow motion to a beat of their own. While the light died (or was born) and Ustad Hameed's gentle voice ranged over the ruined landscape and its ruined inhabitants, Anjum would sit cross-legged with her back to Ustad Hameed on Begum Renata Mumtaz Madam's grave. She would not speak to him or look at him. He didn't mind. He could tell from the stillness of her shoulders that she was listening. He had seen her through so much; he believed that if not he, then certainly music, would see her through this too.

But neither kindness nor cruelty could coax Anjum to return to her old life at the Khwabgah. It took years for the tide of grief and fear to subside. Imam Ziauddin's daily visits, their petty (and sometimes profound) quarrels, and his request that Anjum read the papers to him every morning, helped draw her back into the Duniya. Gradually the Fort of Desolation scaled down into a dwelling of manageable proportions. It became home; a place of predictable, reassuring sorrow—awful, but reliable. The saffron men sheathed their swords, laid down their tridents and returned meekly to their working lives, answering bells, obeying orders, beating their wives and biding their time until their next bloody outing. The saffron parakeets retracted their talons and returned to green, and camouflaged themselves in the branches of the Banyan trees from which the white-backed vultures and sparrows had disappeared. The folded men and unfolded women visited less frequently. Only Zakir Mian, neatly folded, would not go away. But in time, instead of following her around, he moved in with her and became a constant but undemanding companion.

Anjum began to groom herself again. She hennaed her hair, turning it a flaming orange. She had her facial hair removed, her loose tooth extracted and replaced with an implant. A perfect white tooth now shone like a tusk between the dark red stumps that passed for teeth. On the whole it was only slightly less alarming than the previous arrangement. She stayed with the Pathan suits but she had new ones tailored in softer colors, pale blue and powder pink, which she matched with her old sequined and printed dupattas. She gained a little weight and filled out her new clothes in an attractive, comfortable way.

But Anjum never forgot that she was only Butchers' Luck. For the rest of her life, even when it appeared otherwise, her relationship with the Rest-of-Her-Life remained precarious and reckless.

As the Fort of Desolation scaled down, Anjum's tin shack scaled up. It grew first into a hut that could accommodate a bed, and then into a small house with a little kitchen. So as not to attract undue attention, she left the exterior walls rough and unfinished. The inside she plastered and painted an unusual shade of fuchsia. She put in a sandstone roof supported on iron girders, which gave her a terrace on which, in the winter, she would put out a plastic chair and dry her hair and sun her chapped, scaly shins while she surveyed the dominion of the dead. For her doors and windows she chose a pale pistachio green. The Bandicoot, now well on her way to becoming a young lady, began to visit her again. She always came with Saeeda, and she never spent the night. Anjum never asked or insisted, or even made her feelings manifest. But the pain from this one wound never deadened, never diminished. On this count her heart simply would not agree to mend.

Every few months the municipal authorities stuck a notice on Anjum's front door that said squatters were strictly prohibited from living in the graveyard and that any unauthorized construction would be demolished within a week. She told them that she wasn't living in the graveyard, she was dying in it—and for this she didn't need permission from the municipality because she had authorization from the Almighty Himself.

None of the municipal officers who visited her was man enough to take the matter further and run the risk of being embarrassed by her legendary abilities. Also, like everyone else, they feared being cursed by a Hijra. So they chose the path of appeasement and petty extortion. They settled on a not-inconsiderable sum of money to be paid to them, along with a non-vegetarian meal, on Diwali as well as Eid. And they agreed that if the house expanded the sum would expand proportionately.

Over time Anjum began to enclose the graves of her relatives and build rooms around them. Each room had a grave (or two) and a bed. Or two. She built a separate bathhouse and a toilet with its own septic tank. For water she used the public hand-pump. Imam Ziauddin, who was being unkindly treated by his son and daughter-in-law, soon became a permanent guest. He rarely went home any more. Anjum began to rent a couple of rooms to down-and-out travelers (the publicity was strictly by word of mouth). There weren't all that many takers because obviously the setting and landscape, to say nothing of the innkeeper herself, were not to everybody's taste. Also, it must be said, not all the takers were to the innkeeper's taste. Anjum was whimsical and irrational about whom she admitted and whom she turned away—often with unwarranted and entirely unreasonable rudeness that bordered on abuse (*Who sent you here? Go fuck yourself in the arse*), and sometimes with an unearthly, savage roar.

The advantage of the guest house in the graveyard was that unlike every other neighborhood in the city, including the most exclusive ones, it suffered no power cuts. Not even in the summer. This was because Anjum stole her electricity from the mortuary, where the corpses required round-the-clock refrigeration. (The city's paupers who lay there in air-conditioned splendor had never experienced anything of the kind while they were alive.) Anjum called her guest house Jannat. Paradise. She kept her TV on night and day. She said she needed the noise to steady her mind. She watched the news diligently and became an astute political analyst. She also watched Hindi soap operas and English film channels. She particularly enjoyed B-grade Hollywood vampire movies and watched the same ones over and over again. She couldn't understand the dialogue of course, but she understood the vampires reasonably well.

Gradually Jannat Guest House became a hub for Hijras who, for one reason or another, had fallen out of, or been expelled from, the tightly administered grid of Hijra Gharanas. As word spread about the new guest house in the graveyard, friends from the past reappeared, most incredibly, Nimmo Gorakhpuri. When they first met, Anjum and she held each other and wept like star-crossed sweethearts reunited after a long separation. Nimmo became a regular visitor, often spending two or three days at a stretch with Anjum. She had grown into a resplendent figure, large, jeweled, perfumed and immaculately groomed. She came in her own little white Maruti 800 from Mewat, a two-hour drive from Delhi, where she owned two flats and a small farm. She had become a goat-magnate who traded in exotic goats that she sold for serious money to wealthy Muslims in Delhi and Bombay for slaughter on Bakr-Eid. She chuckled as she told her old friend the tricks of the trade and described the spurious techniques of overnight goat-fattening and the politics of goat-pricing in the pre-Eid goat-market. She said that from next year her business would go online. Anjum and she agreed that for old times' sake they would celebrate the next Bakr-Eid together in the graveyard with the best specimen in Nimmo's stock. She showed Anjum goat portraits on her swanky new mobile phone. She was as obsessed with goats as she had once been with Western women's fashion. She showed Anjum how to tell a Jamnapari from a Barbari, an Etawa from a Sojat. Then she showed her an MMS of a rooster who seemed to say "Ya Allah!" each time he flapped his wings. Anjum was floored. *Even a simple rooster knew!* From that day onwards her faith deepened.

True to her word, Nimmo Gorakhpuri presented Anjum with a young black ram with biblical, curled horns—the same model,

Nimmo said, as the one Hazrat Ibrahim had sacrificed on the mountain in place of his beloved son Ismail, except that theirs was white. Anjum put the ram in a room of his own (with a grave of his own) and reared him lovingly. She tried to love him just as much as Ibrahim had loved Ismail. Love, after all, is the ingredient that separates a sacrifice from ordinary, everyday butchery. She wove him a tinsel collar and put bells on his ankles. He loved her too, and followed her wherever she went. (She took care to take the bells off his ankles and conceal him from Zainab when she visited, because she knew what that would lead to.) By the time Eid came around that year, the old city was teeming with retired camels with faded tattoos, buffaloes and goats as big as small horses, waiting to be slaughtered. Anjum's ram was full-grown, almost four feet tall, all lean meat and muscle and slanting yellow eyes. People came to the graveyard just to have a look at him.

Anjum booked Imran Qureishi, the rising star among the new crop of young butchers in Shahjahanabad, to perform the sacrifice. He had several prior bookings and said he would not be able to come until late afternoon. When the day of Bakr-Eid dawned, Anjum knew that unless she went to the old city and brought him herself, interlopers would snatch him away out of turn. Dressed as a man, in a clean, ironed Pathan suit, she spent the whole morning trailing Imran from house to house, street corner to street corner while he went about his business. His last appointment was with a politician, a former member of the Legislative Assembly, who had lost the previous election by an embarrassing margin of votes. To minimize his defeat and show his constituency that he was already preparing for the next election, he had decided to put on an opulent display of piety. A sleek, fat water buffalo, her skin oiled and shining, was dragged through the narrow streets that were only as wide as she was, to a crossing where there was some room for maneuver. Positioned diagonally, teth-

ered to a lamp post with her front legs hobbled, she just about
fitted into what passed off as a street crossing. Excited people,
dressed in new clothes, crowded doorways, windows, little balconies and terraces to watch Imran perform the sacrifice. He
arrived, making his way through the crowd, slim, quiet, unas-
suming. As the murmur of the crowd grew louder the buffalo's
skin twitched and her eyes began to roll. Her huge head with
its horns that swept backwards in an oblong arc began to sway
back and forth, as though she was in a trance at a classical music
concert. With a deft judo move Imran and his helper rolled her
over on to her side. In a moment he had cut open her jugular
and ducked out of the way of the fountain of blood that pumped
up into the air, its rhythm matching the beating of her failing
heart. Blood sprayed across the downed shutters of shops, on to
the faces of smiling politicians on the tattered old posters pasted
on the walls. It flowed down the street past parked motorcycles,
scooters, rickshaws and cycles. Little girls in jeweled slippers
squealed and stepped out of its way. Little boys pretended not to
mind and the more naughty ones stamped their feet softly in the
red puddles and admired their bloody shoe-prints. It took a while
for the buffalo to bleed to death. When she did, Imran opened
her up and laid her organs out on the street—heart, spleen,
stomach, liver, entrails. Since the street sloped downwards, they
began to slip away like odd-shaped boats on a river of blood.
Imran's helper rescued them and put them on more even ground.
The skinning and cutting-up would be done by the supporting
cast. The superstar wiped his cleaver on a piece of cloth, scanned
the crowd, caught Anjum's eye and nodded imperceptibly. He
slipped through the crowd and walked away. Anjum caught up
with him at the next chowk. The streets were busy. Goatskins,
goat horns, goat skulls, goat brains and goat offal were being
collected, separated and stacked. Shit was being extruded from
intestines that would then be properly cleaned and boiled down

into soap and glue. Cats were making off with delectable booty. Nothing went to waste.

Imran and Anjum walked up to Turkman Gate from where they took an autorickshaw to the graveyard.

Anjum, Man of the House for the moment, held a knife over her beautiful ram and said a prayer. Imran slit his jugular, and held him down while he shuddered and the blood flowed out of him. Within twenty minutes the ram was skinned, cut up into manageable pieces, and Imran was gone. Anjum made little parcels of mutton to distribute the sacrifice in the way it is Written: a third for the family, a third for nears and dears, a third for the poor. She gave Roshan Lal, who had arrived that morning to greet her on Eid, a plastic packet containing the tongue and part of a thigh. She kept the best pieces for Zainab, who had just turned twelve, and for Ustad Hameed.

The addicts ate well that night. Anjum, Nimmo Gorakhpuri and Imam Ziauddin sat out on the terrace and feasted on three kinds of mutton dishes and a mountain of biryani. Nimmo gifted Anjum a mobile phone with the rooster MMS already installed on it. Anjum hugged her and said she now felt she had a direct line to God. They watched the MMS a few more times. They described the video in detail to Imam Ziauddin, who listened with his eyes but was not as enthusiastic as they were about its evidentiary value. Then Anjum tucked her new phone safely into her bosom. This one she did not lose. In a few weeks, through the good offices of his driver, who still brought messages from his boss to Anjum, D. D. Gupta got her new number and was back in touch with her from Iraq where he seemed to have decided to live.

The morning after Bakr-Eid, Jannat Guest House received its second permanent guest—a young man who called himself Saddam Hussain. Anjum knew him a little and liked him a lot, so she offered him a room at a rock-bottom price—less than it would have cost him to rent one in the old city.

When Anjum first met Saddam he worked in the mortuary. He was one of about ten young men whose job it was to handle the cadavers. The Hindu doctors who were required to conduct post-mortems thought of themselves as upper caste and would not touch dead bodies for fear of being polluted. The men who actually handled the cadavers and performed the post-mortems were employed as cleaners and belonged to a caste of sweepers and leatherworkers who used to be called Chamars. The doctors, like most Hindus, looked down on them and considered them to be Untouchable. The doctors would stand at a distance with handkerchiefs masking their noses and shout instructions to the staff about where incisions were to be made and what was to be done with the viscera and the organs. Saddam was the only Muslim among the cleaners who worked in the mortuary. Like them, he too had become something of an amateur surgeon.

Saddam had a quick smile and eyelashes that looked as though they had worked out in a gym. He always greeted Anjum with affection and often ran little errands for her—buying her eggs and cigarettes (she trusted nobody with her vegetable shopping) or fetching a bucket of water from the pump on the days she had a backache. Occasionally, when the workload at the mortuary was less hectic (usually September to November, when people on the streets were not dying like flies of the heat, the cold, or dengue), Saddam would drop in, Anjum would make him tea and they'd share a cigarette. One day he disappeared without leaving word. When she asked, his colleagues told her he had had a run-in with one of the doctors and been fired. When he reappeared that morning after Eid, a whole year later, he looked a little gaunt, a little battered, and was accompanied by an equally gaunt and battered white mare whose name he said was Payal. He was dressed stylishly, in jeans and a red T-shirt that said *Your*

Place or Mine? He wore his sunglasses even when he was indoors. He smiled when Anjum teased him but he said it didn't have anything to do with style. He told her the strange story of how his eyes had been burned by a tree.

After he was fired from the mortuary, Saddam said, he drifted from job to job—he worked as a helper in a shop, a bus conductor, selling newspapers at the New Delhi railway station and finally, in desperation, as a bricklayer on a construction site. One of the security guards at the site became a friend and took Saddam to meet his boss, Sangeeta Madam, in the hope that she might give him a job. Sangeeta Madam was a plump, cheerful widow who, notwithstanding her jolly-type personality, and her love for Bollywood songs, was a tough-hearted labor contractor whose security company, Safe n' Sound Guard Service (SSGS), controlled a pool of five hundred security guards. Her office, in the basement of a bottle factory, was in the new industrial belt that had sprung up on the outskirts of Delhi. The men on her roster had a twelve-hour working day and a six-day week. Sangeeta Madam's commission was 60 percent of their salary, which left them with barely enough for food and a roof over their heads. Still they flocked to her in their thousands—retired soldiers, laid-off workers, trainloads of desperate villagers freshly arrived in the city, educated men, illiterate men, well-fed men, starving men. "There were many security companies whose offices were all next to each other," Saddam told Anjum. "What a sight we made on the first of every month when we went to collect our pay . . . thousands of us . . . You got the feeling that there were only three kinds of people in this city—security guards, people who need security guards, and thieves."

Sangeeta Madam was among the better paymasters. So she had her pick of the men. She recruited the ones who looked relatively less malnourished and gave them half a day's training—basically, she taught them how to stand straight, how to salute, how to say "Yes, sir," "No, sir," "Good morning, sir" and "Good-night, sir." She equipped them with a cap, a pre-knotted tie that came on an elastic loop, and two sets of uniforms with SSGS embroidered on the epaulettes. (They had to pay a deposit worth more than the price of the uniforms in case they ran off without returning them.) She spread her little private army across the city. They guarded homes, schools, farmhouses, banks, ATMs, stores, malls, cinema halls, gated housing communities, hotels, restaurants and the embassies and high commissions of poorer countries. Saddam told Sangeeta Madam that his name was Daya-chand (because every idiot knew that in the prevailing climate a security guard with a Muslim name would have been considered a contradiction in terms). Being a literate, pleasant-looking man in good health, he got the job easily. "I'll be watching you," Sangeeta Madam told him on his very first day, looking him up and down appreciatively. "If you can prove you are a good worker, I'll make you a supervisor in three months." She sent him out as one of a team of twelve men to the National Gallery of Modern Art where one of India's most famous contemporary artists, a man from a small town who had risen to international stardom, was holding a solo show. The security for the show had been subcontracted to Safe n' Sound.

The exhibits, everyday artifacts made of stainless steel—steel cisterns, steel motorcycles, steel weighing scales with steel fruit on one side and steel weights on the other, steel cupboards full of steel clothes, a steel dining table with steel plates and steel food, a steel taxi with steel luggage on its steel luggage rack—extraordinary for their verisimilitude, were beautifully lit and displayed in the many rooms of the gallery, each room guarded by two Safe n' Sound guards. Even the cheapest exhibit, Saddam said, was the price of a two-bedroom LIG (Lower Income Group) flat. So, all put together, according to his calculations, they cost as much as a whole housing colony. *Art First*, a cutting-edge contemporary art magazine owned by a leading steel magnate, was the main sponsor of the show.

Saddam (Dayachand) was given sole charge of the signature exhibit in the show—an exquisitely made half-scale, but absolutely life-like, stainless-steel Banyan tree, with stainless-steel aerial roots that hung all the way down to the ground, forming a stainless-steel grove. The tree came in a gigantic wooden crate, shipped in from a gallery in New York. He watched it being uncrated and placed on the lawns of the National Gallery, secured with underground bolts. It had stainless-steel buckets, stainless-steel tiffin carriers and stainless-steel pots and pans hanging from its branches. (Almost as though stainless-steel laborers had hung up their stainless-steel lunches while they plowed stainless-steel fields and sowed stainless-steel seeds.)

"That part I just didn't understand," Saddam told Anjum.

"And the rest you did?" Anjum asked, laughing.

The artist, who lived in Berlin, had sent strict instructions that he did not want any kind of protective fence or cordon to be built around the tree. He was keen for viewers to commune with his work directly, without any barriers. They were to be allowed to touch it and to wander through the grove of roots if they wanted to. Most of them did, Saddam said, except when the sun was high and the steel was burning hot to the touch. Saddam's job was to make sure nobody scratched their names into the steel tree or damaged it in any way. It was also his responsibility to keep the tree clean and to make sure the imprints from the hundreds of hands that touched it were wiped away. For this task he was given a specially designed ladder, a supply of Johnson's Baby Oil and fragments of old, soft saris. It seemed an improbable method, but it actually worked. Cleaning the tree was not a problem, he said. The problem was keeping an eye on it when the sun reflected off it. It was like being asked to keep an eye on the sun. After the first two days Saddam asked Sangeeta Madam for permission to wear sunglasses. She turned down his request, saying it would look inappropriate and the museum management was bound to take offense. So Saddam developed a technique of looking at the tree for a couple of minutes and then looking away. Still, by the time seven weeks had passed and the tree was re-crated and shipped to Amsterdam for the artist's next show, Saddam's eyes were singed. They smarted and watered continuously. He found it impossible to keep them open in daylight unless he used sunglasses. He was dismissed from Safe n' Sound Guard Service because nobody had any use for an ordinary security guard who dressed as though he was a film star's bodyguard. Sangeeta Madam told him he was a great disappointment to her and had completely belied her expectations. His response was to call her some terrible names. He was physically ejected from her office.

Anjum cackled her appreciation when Saddam told her what those names were. She gave him the room she had built around her sister Bibi Ayesha's grave.

Saddam built a temporary stable abutting the bathhouse for Payal. She stood there all night, snuffling and harrumphing, a pale night mare in the graveyard. In the daytime she was Saddam's business partner. Saddam and she did the rounds of the city's larger hospitals. He stationed himself outside the hospital gates and busied himself with one of her hooves, tapping it worriedly with a small hammer, pretending he was re-shoeing it. Payal went along with the charade. When the anxious relatives of seriously ill patients approached him Saddam would reluctantly agree to part with the old horseshoe to bring them good luck. For a price. He also had a supply of medicines—some commonly prescribed antibiotics, Crocin, cough syrup and a range of herbal remedies—that he sold to the people who flocked to the big government hospitals from the villages around Delhi. Most of them camped in the hospital grounds or on the streets because they were too poor to rent any kind of accommodation in the city. At night Saddam rode Payal home through the empty streets like a prince. In his room he had a sack of horseshoes. He gave Anjum one that she hung on her wall next to her old catapult. Saddam had other business interests too. He sold pigeon-feed at certain spots in the city where motorists stopped to seek quick benediction by feeding God's creatures. On his non-hospital days Saddam would be there with small packets of grain and ready change. After the motorist sped away, he would, quite often, much to the chagrin of the pigeons, sweep up the grain and put it back into a packet, ready for his next customer. All of it—short-changing pigeons and exploiting sick people's relatives—was tiring work, especially in summer, and the income was uncertain. But none of it involved having a boss and that was the main thing.

Soon after Saddam moved in, Anjum and he, partnered by Imam Ziauddin, began another initiative. It started by accident and then evolved on its own. One afternoon Anwar Bhai, who ran a brothel nearby on GB Road, arrived in the graveyard with the body of Rubina, one of his girls, who had died suddenly of a burst appendix. He came with eight young women in burqas, trailed by a three-year-old boy, Anwar Bhai's son by one of them. They were all distressed and agitated, not just by Rubina's passing, but also because the hospital returned her body with the eyes missing. The hospital said that rats had got to them in the mortuary. But Anwar Bhai and Rubina's colleagues believed that Rubina's eyes had been stolen by someone who knew that a bunch of whores and their pimp were unlikely to complain to the police. If that wasn't bad enough, because of the address given on the death certificate (GB Road), Anwar Bhai could not find a bathhouse to bathe Rubina's body, a graveyard to bury her in, or an imam to say the prayers.

Saddam told them they had come to the right place. He asked them to sit down and got them something cold to drink while he created an enclosure behind the guest house with some of Anjum's old dupattas wrapped around four bamboo poles. Inside the enclosure he put out a piece of plywood raised off the ground on a few bricks, covered it with a plastic sheet and asked the women to lay Rubina's corpse on it. He and Anwar Bhai collected water from the handpump in buckets and a couple of old paint cans and ferried them to the improvised bathhouse. The corpse was already stiff, so Rubina's clothes had to be cut open. (Saddam produced a razor blade.) Lovingly, flapping over her body like a drove of ravens, the women bathed her, soaping her neck, her ears, her toes. Equally lovingly they kept a sharp eye out for anyone among them who might be tempted to slip off and pocket a bangle, a toe-ring or her pretty pendant. (All jewelry— fake as well as real—was to be handed over to Anwar Bhai.) Mehrunissa worried that the water might be too cold. Sulekha insisted Rubina had opened her eyes and closed them again (and that shafts of divine light shone out from where her eyes had been). Zeenat went off to buy a shroud. While Rubina was being prepared for her final journey, Anwar Bhai's little son, dressed in denim dungarees and a prayer cap, paraded up and down, goose-stepping like a Kremlin guard, in order to show off his new (fake) mauve Crocs with flowers on them. He made a great production of noisily crunching Kurkure from the packet Anjum had given him. Occasionally he tried to peep into the shed to see what his mother and his aunties (whom he had never seen in burqas in all his short life) were up to.

By the time the body had been bathed, dried, perfumed and wrapped in a shroud, Saddam, with the help of two of the addicts, had dug a respectably deep grave. Imam Ziauddin said the prayers and Rubina's body was interred. Anwar Bhai, relieved and grateful, pressed five hundred rupees on Anjum. She refused to take it. Saddam refused too. But he was not one to pass up a business opportunity.

Within a week Jannat Guest House began to function as a funeral parlor. It had a proper bathhouse with an asbestos roof and a cement platform for bodies to be laid out on. There was a steady supply of gravestones, shrouds, perfumed Multani clay (which most people preferred to soap) and bucket-water. There was a resident imam on call night and day. The rules for the dead (same as for the living in the guest house) were esoteric—warm, welcoming smiles or irrational roars of rejection, depending on nobody-really-knew-what. The one clear criterion was that Jannat Funeral Services would only bury those whom the grave-yards and imams of the Duniya had rejected. Sometimes days went by with no funerals and sometimes there was a glut. Their record was five in one day. Sometimes the police themselves—whose rules were as irrational as Anjum's—brought bodies to them.

When Ustad Kulsoom Bi passed away in her sleep she was buried in grand fashion in the Hijron Ka Khanqah in Mehrauli. But Bombay Silk was buried in Anjum's graveyard. And so were many other Hijras from all over Delhi.

(In this way, Imam Ziauddin finally received the answer to his long-ago question: "Tell me, you people, when you die, where do they bury you? Who bathes the bodies? Who says the prayers?")

Gradually Jannat Guest House and Funeral Services became so much a part of the landscape that nobody questioned its prov-enance or its right to exist. It existed. And that was that. When Jahanara Begum died at the age of eighty-seven, Imam Ziaud-din said the prayers. She was buried next to Mulaqat Ali. Bismil-lah, when she died, was buried in Anjum's graveyard too. And so was Zainab's goat, who could have made it into the *Guinness Book of World Records* for accomplishing an unheard-of feat (for a goat): dying of natural causes (colic) after surviving a record sixteen Bakr-Eids in Shahjahanabad. The credit for that of course belonged not to him, but to his fierce little mistress. Of course the *Guinness Book* had no such category.

Though Anjum and Saddam shared the same home (and graveyard), they rarely spent time together. Anjum enjoyed lazing around, but Saddam, stretched between his many enterprises (he had sold his pigeon-feed business, it being the least remunerative), had no time to spare and hated TV. On one unusual morning of enforced leisure Anjum and he sat on an old red taxi seat that they used as a sofa, drinking tea and watching TV. It was the 15th of August, Independence Day. The timid little Prime Minister who had replaced the lisping Poet–Prime Minister (the party he belonged to did not officially believe India was a Hindu Nation) was addressing the nation from the ramparts of the Red Fort. It was one of those days when the insularity of the walled city had been invaded by the rest of Delhi. Massive crowds organized by the Ruling Party filled the Ramlila grounds. Five thousand schoolchildren dressed in the colors of the national flag did a flower drill. Petty influence-peddlers and smallwigs who wanted to be seen on TV seated themselves in the front rows so they could convert their visible proximity to power into business deals. A few years ago, when the lisping Poet–Prime Minister and his party of bigots were voted out of office, Anjum had rejoiced and lavished something close to adoration on the timid, blue-turbaned Sikh economist who replaced him. The fact that he had all the political charisma of a trapped rabbit only enhanced her adulation. But of late she had decided that it was true what people said—that he really was a puppet and someone else was pulling the strings. His ineffectualness was strengthening the forces of darkness that had begun to mass on the horizon and slouch through the streets once again. Gujarat ka Lalla was still the Chief Minister of Gujarat. He had developed a swagger and begun to talk a lot about avenging centuries of Muslim Rule. In every public speech, he always found a way to bring in the measurement of his chest (fifty-six inches). For some odd reason it *did* seem to impress people. There were rumors that he was getting ready for his "March to Delhi." On the subject of Gujarat ka Lalla, Saddam and Anjum were in perfect sync.

Anjum watched the Trapped Rabbit—who barely had a chest at all—standing in his bulletproof enclosure with the Red Fort looming behind him, reeling off dense statistics about imports and exports to a restive crowd that had no idea what he was talking about. He spoke like a marionette. Only his lower jaw moved. Nothing else did. His bushy white eyebrows looked as though they were attached to his spectacles and not his face. His expression never changed. At the end of his speech he raised his hand in a limp salute and signed off with a high, reedy *Jai Hind!* (Victory to India!) A soldier, who was almost seven feet tall and had a bristling mustache as broad as the wingspan of a baby albatross, unsheathed his sword from its scabbard and shouted a salute at the little Prime Minister, who seemed to shudder in fright. When he walked away, only his legs moved, nothing else did. Anjum switched off the TV in disgust.

"Let's go up to the roof," Saddam said hastily, sensing the approach of one of her moods, which usually spelled trouble for everybody within a half-kilometer range.

He went on ahead and put out an old rug and a few hard pillows with flowered pillowcases that smelled of rancid hair oil. There was a hint of a breeze and the Independence Day kite-flyers were already out. There were some kite-flyers in the graveyard too, not doing too badly. Anjum arrived with a saucepan of fresh, hot tea and a transistor. Saddam and she lay down, staring up (Saddam in his sunglasses) at the dirty sky dotted with bright paper kites. Lolling next to them, as though he too had decided to take a day off after a hard, working week, was Biroo (sometimes called Roobi), a dog Saddam had found wandering down the pavement of a busy road, wild-eyed and disoriented, with a mess of transparent tubes dangling out of him. Biroo was a beagle who had either escaped from or outlived his purpose in a pharmaceuticals testing lab. He looked worn and rubbed out, like a drawing someone had tried to erase. The usually rich black, white and tan beagle colors were dimmed by a smoky, greyish patina that may of course have had nothing to do with the drugs that were tested on him. When Biroo first came to live in Jannat Guest House he was troubled by frequent epileptic fits and snorting, debilitating reverse sneezes. Each time he recovered from the exhaustion of a seizure, he emerged as a different character—sometimes friendly, sometimes horny, sometimes sleepy, sometimes snarly or lazy—as unreasonable and unpredictable as his adopted mistress. Over time his fits had grown less frequent and he had stabilized into what became his more or less permanent Lazy Dog avatar. The reverse sneezes lived on.

Anjum poured a little tea into a saucer and blew into it to cool it down for him. He slurped it up noisily. He drank everything Anjum drank, ate everything that she ate—biryani, korma, samosas, halwa, falooda, phirni, zamzam, mangoes in summer, oranges in winter. It was terrible for his body, but excellent for his soul.

In a while the breeze picked up and the kites soared, but then the mandatory Independence Day drizzle began. Anjum roared at it as though it was an uninvited guest—*Ai Hai!* Motherfucking whore rain! Saddam laughed but neither of them moved, waiting to see if it was a major or a minor. It was a minor, and soon stopped. Absent-mindedly, Anjum began to rub down Biroo's coat, wiping off the delicate frost of raindrops on it. Getting wet in the rain reminded her of Zainab and she smiled to herself. Uncharacteristically, she began to tell Saddam about the Fly-over Story (the edited version) and how much the Bandicoot had loved it when she was a little girl. She went on sunnily, describing Zainab's pranks, her love of animals, and how quickly she had picked up English at school. All of a sudden, when her reminiscence was at its most cheerful, Anjum's voice(s) broke and her eyes filled with tears.

"I was born to be a mother," she sobbed. "Just watch. One day Allah Mian will give me my own child. That much I know."

"How is that possible?" Saddam said, reasonably, entirely unaware that he was entering treacherous territory. "Haqeeqat bhi koi cheez hoti hai." There is, after all, such a thing as Reality.

"Why not? Why the hell not?" Anjum sat up and looked him in the eye.

"I'm just saying . . . I meant realistically . . ."

"If you can be Saddam Hussain, I can be a mother." Anjum didn't say it nastily, she said it smilingly, coquettishly, sucking on her white tusk and her dark red teeth. But there was something steely about the coquetry.

Alert, but not worried, Saddam looked back at her, wondering what she knew.

"Once you have fallen off the edge like all of us have, including our Biroo," Anjum said, "you will never stop falling. And as you fall you will hold on to other falling people. The sooner you understand that the better. This place where we live, where we have made our home, is the place of falling people. Here there *is* no *haqeeqat*. *Arre*, even *we* aren't real. We don't really exist."

Saddam said nothing. He had grown to love Anjum more than he loved anyone else in the world. He loved the way she spoke, the words she chose, the way she moved her mouth, the way her red, paan-stained lips moved over her rotten teeth. He loved her ridiculous front tooth and the way she could recite whole verses of Urdu poetry, most—or all—of which he didn't understand. Saddam knew no poetry and very little Urdu. But then, he knew other things. He knew the quickest way to skin a cow or buffalo without damaging the hide. He knew how to wet-salt the skin and marinate it with lime and tannin until it began to stretch and stiffen into leather. He knew how to calibrate the sourness of the marinade by tasting it, how to scud the leather and strip it of hair and fat, how to soap it, bleach it, buff, grease and wax it till it shone. He also knew that the average human body contains between four and five liters of blood. He had watched it spill and spread slowly across the road outside the Dulina police post, just off the Delhi-Gurgaon highway. Strangely, the thing he remembered most clearly about all that was the long line-up of expensive cars and the insects that flitted in the beams of their headlights. And the fact that nobody got out to help.

He knew it was neither plan nor coincidence that had brought him to the Place of Falling People. It was the tide.

"Who are you trying to fool?" Anjum asked him.

"Only God." Saddam smiled. "Not you."

"Recite the Kalima . . ." Anjum said imperiously, as though she were Emperor Aurangzeb himself.

"La ilaha . . ." Saddam said. And then, like Hazrat Sarmad, he stopped. "I don't know the rest. I'm still learning it."

"You're a Chamar like all those other boys you worked with in the mortuary. You weren't lying to that Sangeeta Madam *Haramzaadi* Bitch about your name, you were lying to *me* and I don't know why, because I don't care what you are . . . Muslim, Hindu, man, woman, this caste, that caste, or a camel's arsehole. But why call yourself Saddam Hussain? He was a bastard, you know."

Anjum used the word *Chamar* and not *Dalit*, the more modern and accepted term for those that Hindus considered to be "untouchable," in the same spirit in which she refused to refer to herself as anything other than Hijra. She didn't see the problem with either Hijras or Chamars.

For a while they lay side by side, in silence. And then Saddam decided to trust Anjum with the story he had not told anybody before—a story about saffron parakeets and a dead cow. His too was a story about luck, not butchers' luck perhaps, but some similar strain.

She was right, he told Anjum. He *had* lied to her and told the truth to Sangeeta Madam *Haramzaadi* Bitch. Saddam Hussain was his chosen name, not his real name. His real name was Dayachand. He was born into a family of Chamars—skinners—in a village called Badshahpur in the state of Haryana, only a couple of hours away by bus from Delhi.

One day, in answer to a phone call, he and his father, along with three other men, hired a Tempo to drive out to a nearby village to collect the carcass of a cow that had died on someone's farm.

"This was what our people did," Saddam said. "When cows died, upper-caste farmers would call us to collect the carcasses—because they couldn't pollute themselves by touching them."

"Yes, yes, I know," Anjum said, in a tone that sounded suspiciously like admiration. "Some of them are very neat and clean. They don't eat onions, garlic, meat . . ."

Saddam ignored that intervention.

"So we would go and collect the carcasses, skin them, and turn the hides into leather . . . I'm talking about the year 2002. I was still in school. You know better than me what was going on then . . . what it was like . . . Yours happened in February, mine in November. It was the day of Dussehra. On our way to pick up the cow we passed a Ramlila maidan where they had built huge effigies of the demons . . . Ravan, Meghnad and Kumbhakaran, as high as three-storeyed buildings—all ready to be blown up in the evening."

No Old Delhi Muslim needed a lesson about the Hindu festival of Dussehra. It was celebrated every year in the Ramlila grounds, just outside Turkman Gate. Every year the effigies of Ravan, the ten-headed "demon" King of Lanka, his brother Kumbhakaran and his son Meghnad grew taller and were packed with more and more explosives. Every year the Ramlila, the story of how Lord Ram, King of Ayodhya, vanquished Ravan in the battle of Lanka, which Hindus believed was the story of the triumph of Good over Evil, was enacted with greater aggression and ever-more generous sponsorship. A few audacious scholars had begun to suggest that the Ramlila was really history turned into mythology, and that the evil demons were really dark-skinned Dravidians—indigenous rulers—and the Hindu gods who vanquished them (and turned them into Untouchables and other oppressed castes who would spend their lives in service of the new rulers) were the Aryan invaders. They pointed to village rituals in which people worshipped deities, including Ravan, that in Hinduism were considered to be demons. In the new dispensation however, ordinary people did not need to be scholars to know, even if they could not openly say so, that in the rise and rise of the Parakeet Reich, regardless of what may or may not have been meant in the scriptures, in saffron parakeetspeak, the evil demons had come to mean not just indigenous people, but everybody who was not Hindu. Which included of course the citizenry of Shahjahanabad.

When the giant effigies were blown up, the sound of the explosions would boom through the narrow lanes of the old city. And few were in doubt about what that was meant to mean.

Every year, the morning after Good had vanquished Evil, Ahlam Baji, the midwife-turned-wandering-queen with filthy hair, would go to the Ramlila grounds, sift through the debris, and return with bows and arrows, sometimes a whole handlebar mustache, or a staring eye, an arm, or a sword that stuck out of her fertilizer bag.

So when Saddam spoke of Dussehra, Anjum understood it in all its vast and varied meanings.

"We found the dead cow easily," Saddam said. "It's always easy, you just have to know the art of walking straight into the stink. We loaded the carcass on to the Tempo and started driving home. On the way we stopped at the Dulina police station to pay the Station House Officer—his name was Sehrawat—his cut. It was a previously-agreed-upon sum, a per-cow rate. But that day he asked for more. Not just for more, for *triple* the amount. Which meant we would have actually been losing money to skin that cow. We knew him well, that Sehrawat. I don't know what came over him that day—maybe he wanted the money to buy alcohol that night, to celebrate Dussehra, or maybe he had a debt to pay off, I don't know. Maybe he was just trying to take advantage of the political climate of the time. My father and his friends tried to plead with him, but he wouldn't listen. He got angry when they said they didn't even have that much money on them. He arrested them on the charge of 'cow-slaughter' and put them in the police lock-up. I was left outside. My father didn't seem worried when he went in, so I wasn't either. I waited, assuming they were just doing some hard bargaining and would soon come to an agreement. Two hours went by. Crowds of people passed by on their way to the evening fireworks. Some were dressed as gods, Ram, Laxman and Hanuman—little kids with bows and arrows, some with monkey's tails and their faces painted red, some were demons with black faces, all going to take part in the Ramlila. When they walked past our truck, they all held their noses because of the stink. At sunset, I heard the explosions of the effigies being blown up and the cheers of the people watching. I was upset that I had missed all the fun. In a while people began to return home. There was still no sign of my father and his friends. And then, I don't know how it happened—maybe the police spread the rumor, or made a few phone calls—but a crowd started to collect outside the police station demanding the 'cow-killers' be turned over to them. The dead cow in the Tempo, stinking up the whole area, was proof enough for them. People began to block traffic. I didn't know what to do, where to hide, so I mingled with the crowd. Some people started shouting *Jai Shri Ram!* and *Vande Mataram!* More and more joined in and it turned into a frenzy. A few men went into the police station and brought my father and his three friends out. They began to beat them, at first just with their fists, and with shoes. But then someone brought a crowbar, someone else a carjack. I couldn't see much, but when the first blows fell I heard their cries . . ."

Saddam turned to Anjum.

"I have never heard a sound like that . . . it was a strange, high sound, it wasn't human. But then the howling of the crowd drowned them. I don't need to tell you. You know . . ." Saddam's voice dropped to a whisper. "Everybody watched. Nobody stopped them."

He described how once the mob had finished its business the cars switched their headlights on, all together, like an army convoy. How they splashed through puddles of his father's blood as if it were rainwater, how the road looked like a street in the old city on the day of Bakr-Eid.

"I was part of the mob that killed my father," Saddam said.

Anjum's desolate fort with its humming walls and secret dungeons threatened to rise around her again. Saddam and she could almost hear each other's heartbeats. She couldn't bring herself to say anything, not even to utter a word of sympathy. But Saddam knew she was listening. It was a while before he spoke again.

"A few months after all this my mother, who was already unwell, died. I was left in the care of my uncle and my grandmother. I dropped out of school, stole some money from my uncle and came to Delhi. I arrived in Delhi with just a little money and the clothes I was wearing. I had only one ambition—I wanted to kill that bastard Sehrawat. Someday I will. I slept on the streets, worked as a truck cleaner, for a few months even as a sewage worker. And then my friend Neeraj, who is from my village, now he works in the Municipal Corporation, you've met him—"

"Yes," Anjum said, "that tall, beautiful-looking boy—"

"Yes, him. He tried to get into modeling but couldn't . . . even for that you have to pay pimps. Now he drives a truck for the Municipal Corporation . . . Anyway, Neeraj helped me to get a job here, in the mortuary, where we first met . . . A few years after I came to Delhi I was passing a TV showroom, and one of the TVs in the window was playing the evening news. That's when I first saw the video of the hanging of Saddam Hussein. I didn't know anything about him, but I was so impressed by the courage and dignity of that man in the face of death. When I got my first mobile phone, I asked the shopkeeper to find that video and download it for me. I watched it again and again. I wanted to be like him. I decided to become a Muslim and take his name. I felt it would give me the courage to do what I had to do and face the consequences, like him."

"Saddam Hussein was a bastard," Anjum said. "He killed so many people."

"Maybe. But he was brave . . . See . . . Look at this."

Saddam took out his fancy new smartphone with its fancy big screen and pulled up a video. He shaded the screen with a cupped palm to cut the glare. It was a TV clip that began with an advertisement for Vaseline Intensive Care moisturizing cream in which a pretty girl oiled her elbows and shins and seemed extremely pleased with the results. Next up was an advertisement by the Jammu & Kashmir Tourism Department—snowy landscapes and happy people in warm clothes sitting in snow sledges. The voice-over said, "Jammu & Kashmir. So White. So Fair. So Exciting." Then the TV announcer said something in English and Saddam Hussein, former President of Iraq, appeared, elegant, with a salt-and-pepper beard, in a black overcoat and white shirt. He towered over the group of murmuring men wearing peaked, black executioner's hoods who surrounded him and looked at him through eye-slits. His hands were tied behind his back. He stood still while one of the men tied a black scarf around his neck, making gestures that seemed to suggest that the scarf would help to prevent the skin on his neck getting chafed by the hangman's rope. Once it was knotted, the scarf made Saddam Hussein look even more elegant. Surrounded by the jabbering, hooded men, he walked to the gallows. The noose was looped over his head and tightened around his neck. He said his prayers. The last expression on his face before he fell through the trap-door was one of absolute disdain for his executioners.

"I want to be this kind of a bastard," Saddam said. "I want to do what I have to do and then, if I have to pay a price, I want to pay it like that."

"I have a friend who lives in Iraq," Anjum said, seemingly more impressed by Saddam's phone than with the execution video. "Guptaji. He sends me his photos from Iraq." She pulled out her phone and showed Saddam the pictures that D. D. Gupta sent her regularly—Guptaji in his flat in Baghdad, Guptaji and his Iraqi mistress on a picnic, and a series of portraits of the blast walls that Guptaji had constructed all over Iraq for the US Army. Some were new and some were already pockmarked with bullet holes and covered with graffiti. Across one of them, someone had scrawled an American army general's famous words: *Be professional, be polite and have a plan to kill everybody you meet.*

Anjum couldn't read English. Saddam could, if he paid careful attention. On this occasion he didn't.

Anjum finished her tea and then lay on her back with her forearms crossed over her eyes. She seemed to have dozed off, but she hadn't. She was worried.

"And in case you didn't know," she said after a while, as though she was continuing a conversation—actually she was, except that it was one she had been having with herself in her head. "Let me tell you that we Muslims are motherfuckers too, just like everyone else. But I suppose one additional murderer won't harm the reputation of our *badnaam qoam*, our name is mud already. Anyway, take your time, don't do anything in a hurry."

"I won't. But Sehrawat must die."

Saddam took off his glasses and closed his eyes, screwing them up against the light. He played an old Hindi film song on his phone and began to sing along tunelessly but confidently. Biroo slurped up the cold tea remaining in the saucepan and trotted off with boiled tea leaves on his nose.

When the sun grew hot, they returned indoors where they continued to float through their lives like a pair of astronauts, defying gravity, limited only by the outer walls of their fuchsia spaceship with its pale pistachio doors.

It isn't as though they didn't have plans.

Anjum waited to die.

Saddam waited to kill.

And miles away, in a troubled forest, a baby waited to be born . . .

In what language does rain fall
over tormented cities?

—PABLO NERUDA

3

THE NATIVITY

It was peacetime. Or so they said.

All morning a hot wind had whipped through the city streets, driving sheets of grit, soda-bottle caps and beedi stubs before it, smacking them into car windscreens and cyclists' eyes. When the wind died, the sun, already high in the sky, burned through the haze and once again the heat rose and shimmered on the streets like a belly dancer. People waited for the thunder-shower that always followed a dust storm, but it never came. Fire raged through a swathe of huts huddled together on the river-bank, gutting more than two thousand in an instant.

Still the Amaltas bloomed, a brilliant, defiant yellow. Each blazing summer it reached up and whispered to the hot brown sky, *Fuck You.*

She appeared quite suddenly, a little after midnight. No angels sang, no wise men brought gifts. But a million stars rose in the east to herald her arrival. One moment she wasn't there, and the next—there she was on the concrete pavement, in a crib of litter: silver cigarette foil, a few plastic bags and empty packets of Uncle

Chipps. She lay in a pool of light, under a column of swarming neon-lit mosquitoes, naked. Her skin was blue-black, sleek as a baby seal's. She was wide awake, but perfectly quiet, unusual for someone so tiny. Perhaps, in those first short months of her life, she had already learned that tears, *her* tears at least, were futile.

A thin white horse tethered to the railing, a small dog with mange, a concrete-colored garden lizard, two palm-striped squirrels who should have been asleep and, from her hidden perch, a she-spider with a swollen egg sac watched over her. Other than that, she seemed to be utterly alone.

Around her the city sprawled for miles. Thousand-year-old sorceress, dozing, but not asleep, even at this hour. Gray flyovers snaked out of her Medusa skull, tangling and untangling under the yellow sodium haze. Sleeping bodies of homeless people lined their high, narrow pavements, head to toe, head to toe, head to toe, looping into the distance. Old secrets were folded into the furrows of her loose, parchment skin. Each wrinkle was a street, each street a carnival. Each arthritic joint a crumbling amphitheater where stories of love and madness, stupidity, delight and unspeakable cruelty had been played out for centuries. But this was to be the dawn of her resurrection. Her new masters wanted to hide her knobby, varicose veins under imported fishnet stockings, cram her withered tits into saucy padded bras and jam her aching feet into pointed high-heeled shoes. They wanted her to swing her stiff old hips and re-route the edges of her grimace upwards into a frozen, empty smile. It was the summer Grandma became a whore.

She was to become supercapital of the world's favorite new superpower. *India! India!* The chant had gone up—on TV shows, on music videos, in foreign newspapers and magazines, at business conferences and weapons fairs, at economic conclaves and environmental summits, at book festivals and beauty contests. *India! India! India!*

Across the city, huge billboards jointly sponsored by an English newspaper and the newest brand of skin-whitening cream (selling by the ton) said: *Our Time Is Now*. Kmart was coming. Walmart and Starbucks were coming, and in the British Airways advertisement on TV, the People of the World (white, brown, black, yellow) all chanted the Gayatri Mantra:

Om bhur bhuvah svaha
Tat savitur varenyam
Bhargo devasya dhimahi
Dhiyo yo nah pracodayat

O God, thou art the giver of life,
Remover of pain and sorrow,
Bestower of happiness,
O Creator of the Universe,
May we receive thy supreme sin-destroying light,
May thou guide our intellect in the right direction.

(*And may everyone fly BA.*)

When they finished chanting, the People of the World bowed low and joined their palms in greeting. *Namaste*, they said in exotic accents, and smiled like the turbaned doormen with maharaja mustaches who greeted foreign guests in five-star hotels. And with that, in the advertisement at least, history was turned upside down. (Who was bowing now? And who was smiling? Who was the petitioner? And who the petitioned?) In their sleep India's favorite citizens smiled back. *India! India!* they chanted in their dreams, like the crowds at cricket matches. The drum major beat out a rhythm . . . *India! India!* The world rose to its feet, roaring its appreciation. Skyscrapers and steel factories sprang up where forests used to be, rivers were bottled and sold in supermarkets, fish were tinned, mountains mined and turned into shining missiles. Massive dams lit up the cities like Christmas trees. Everyone was happy.

Away from the lights and advertisements, villages were being emptied. Cities too. Millions of people were being moved, but nobody knew where to.

"People who can't afford to live in cities shouldn't come here," a Supreme Court judge said, and ordered the immediate eviction of the city's poor. "Paris was a slimy area before 1870, when all the slums were removed," the Lieutenant Governor of the city said, rearranging his last-remaining swatch of hair across his scalp, right to left. (In the evenings when he went for a swim it swam beside him in the chlorine in the Chelmsford Club pool.) "And look at Paris now."

So surplus people were banned.

In addition to the regular police, several battalions of the Rapid Action Force in strange, sky-blue camouflage uniforms (to flummox the birds perhaps) were deployed in the poorer quarters.

In slums and squatter settlements, in resettlement colonies and "unauthorized" colonies, people fought back. They dug up the roads leading to their homes and blocked them with rocks and broken things. Young men, old men, children, mothers and grandmothers armed with sticks and rocks patrolled the entrances to their settlements. Across one road, where the police and bulldozers had lined up for the final assault, a slogan scrawled in chalk said, *Sarkar ki Maa ki Choot.* The Government's Mother's Cunt.

"Where shall we go?" the surplus people asked. "You can kill us, but we won't move," they said.

There were too many of them to be killed outright.

Instead, their homes, their doors and windows, their makeshift roofs, their pots and pans, their plates, their spoons, their school-leaving certificates, their ration cards, their marriage certificates, their children's schools, their lifetime's work, the expression in their eyes, were flattened by yellow bulldozers imported from Australia. (Ditch Witch, they were called, the 'dozers.) They were State-of-the-Art machines. They could flatten history and stack it up like building material.

In this way, in the summer of her renewal, Grandma broke.

Fiercely competitive TV channels covered the story of the breaking city as "Breaking News." Nobody pointed out the irony. They unleashed their untrained, but excellent-looking, young reporters, who spread across the city like a rash, asking urgent, empty questions; they asked the poor what it was like to be poor, the hungry what it was like to be hungry, the homeless what it was like to be homeless. "Bhai Sahib, yeh bataaiye, aap ko kaisa lag raha hai . . . ?" Tell me, brother, how does it feel to be . . . ? The TV channels never ran out of sponsorship for their live telecasts of despair. They never ran out of despair.

Experts aired their expert opinions for a fee: *Somebody* has to pay the price for Progress, they said expertly.

Begging was banned. Thousands of beggars were rounded up and held in stockades before being shipped out of the city in batches. Their contractors had to pay good money to ship them back in.

Father John-for-the-Weak sent out a letter saying that, according to police records, almost three thousand unidentified dead bodies (human) had been found on the city's streets last year. Nobody replied.

But the food shops were bursting with food. The bookshops were bursting with books. The shoe shops were bursting with shoes. And people (who counted as people) said to one another, "You don't have to go abroad for shopping any more. Imported things are available here now. See, like Bombay is our New York, Delhi is our Washington and Kashmir is our Switzerland. It's like really like *saala* fantastic *yaar*."

All day long the roads were choked with traffic. The newly dispossessed, who lived in the cracks and fissures of the city, emerged and swarmed around the sleek, climate-controlled cars, selling cloth dusters, mobile phone chargers, model jumbo jets, business magazines, pirated management books (*How to Make Your First Million*, *What Young India Really Wants*), gourmet guides, interior design magazines with color photographs of country houses in Provence, and quick-fix spiritual manuals (*You Are Responsible for Your Own Happiness* . . . or *How to Be Your Own Best Friend* . . .). On Independence Day they sold toy machine guns and tiny national flags mounted on stands that said *Mera Bharat Mahan*, My India Is Great. The passengers looked out of their car windows and saw only the new apartment they planned to buy, the Jacuzzi they had just installed and the ink that was still wet on the sweetheart deal they had just closed. They were calm from their meditation classes and glowing from yoga practice.

On the city's industrial outskirts, in the miles of bright swamp tightly compacted with refuse and colorful plastic bags, where the evicted had been "re-settled," the air was chemical and the water poisonous. Clouds of mosquitoes rose from thick green ponds. Surplus mothers perched like sparrows on the debris of what used to be their homes and sang their surplus children to sleep.

Sooti rahu baua, bhakol abaiya
Naani gaam se angaa, siyait abaiya
Maama sange maami, nachait abaiya
Kara sange chara, labait abaiya

Sleep, my darling, sleep, before the demon comes
Your newly tailored shirt from mother's village comes
Your uncle and auntie, a-dancing they will comes
Your anklets and bracelets, a-bringing they will comes

The surplus children slept, dreaming of yellow 'dozers.

Above the smog and the mechanical hum of the city, the night was vast and beautiful. The sky was a forest of stars. Jet aircraft darted about like slow, whining comets. Some hovered, stacked ten deep over the smog-obscured Indira Gandhi International Airport, waiting to land.

DOWN BELOW, on the pavement, on the edge of Jantar Mantar, the old observatory where our baby made her appearance, it was fairly busy even at that time of the morning. Communists, seditionists, secessionists, revolutionaries, dreamers, idlers, crackheads, crackpots, all manner of freelancers, and wise men who couldn't afford gifts for newborns, milled around. Over the last ten days they had all been sidelined and driven off what had once been *their* territory—the only place in the city where they were allowed to gather—by the newest show in town. More than twenty TV crews, their cameras mounted on yellow cranes, kept a round-the-clock vigil over their bright new star: a tubby old Gandhian, former-soldier-turned-village-social-worker, who had announced a fast to the death to realize his dream of a corruption-free India. He lay fatly on his back with the air of an ailing saint, against a backdrop of a portrait of Mother India—a many-armed goddess with a map-of-India-shaped body. (Undivided British India, of course, which included Pakistan and Bangladesh.) Each sigh, each whispered instruction to the people around him, was being broadcast live through the night.

The old man was on to something. The summer of the city's resurrection had also been the summer of scams—coal scams, iron-ore scams, housing scams, insurance scams, stamp-paper scams, phone-license scams, land scams, dam scams, irrigation scams, arms and ammunition scams, petrol-pump scams, polio-vaccine scams, electricity-bill scams, school-book scams,

God Men scams, drought-relief scams, car-number-plate scams, voter-list scams, identity-card scams—in which politicians, businessmen, businessmen-politicians and politician-businessmen had made off with unimaginable quantities of public money.

Like a good prospector, the old man had tapped into a rich seam, a reservoir of public anger, and much to his own surprise had become a cult figure overnight. His dream of a society free of corruption was like a happy meadow in which everybody, including the most corrupt, could graze for a while. People who would normally have nothing to do with each other (the left-wing, the right-wing, the wingless) all flocked to him. His sudden appearance, as if from nowhere, inspired and gave purpose to an impatient new generation of youngsters that had been innocent of history and politics so far. They came in jeans and T-shirts, with guitars and songs against corruption that they had composed themselves. They brought their own banners and placards with slogans like *Enough Is Enough!* and *End Corruption Now!* written on them. A team of young professionals—lawyers, accountants and computer programmers—formed a committee to manage the event. They raised money, organized the massive canopy, the props (the portrait of Mother India, a supply of national flags, Gandhi caps, banners) and a digital-age media campaign. The old man's rustic rhetoric and earthy aphorisms trended on Twitter and swamped Facebook. TV cameras couldn't get enough of him. Retired bureaucrats, policemen and army officers joined in. The crowd grew.

Instant stardom thrilled the old man. It made him expansive and a little aggressive. He began to feel that sticking to the subject of corruption alone cramped his style and limited his appeal. He thought the least he could do was to share with his followers something of his essence, his true self and his innate, bucolic wisdom. And so the circus began. He announced that he was leading India's Second Freedom Struggle. He made stirring speeches in his old-man-baby-voice, which, although it sounded like a pair of balloons being rubbed together, seemed to touch the very soul of the nation. Like a magician at a children's birthday party, he performed tricks and conjured gifts out of thin air. He had something for everyone. He electrified Hindu chauvinists (who were already excited by the Mother India map) with their controversial old war cry, *Vande Mataram!* Salute the Mother! When some Muslims got upset, the committee arranged a visit from a Muslim film star from Bombay who sat on the dais next to the old man for more than an hour wearing a Muslim prayer cap (something he never usually did) to underline the message of Unity in Diversity. For traditionalists the old man quoted Gandhi. He said that the caste system was India's salvation. "Each caste must do the work it has been born to do, but all work must be respected." When Dalits erupted in fury, a municipal sweeper's little daughter was dressed up in a new frock and seated by his side with a bottle of water from which he sipped from time to time. For militant moralists the old man's slogan was *Thieves must have their hands cut off! Terrorists must be hanged!* For Nationalists of all stripes he roared, "Doodh maangogey to kheer dengey! Kashmir maangogey to chiir dengey!" Ask for milk, we'll give you cream! Ask for Kashmir, we'll rip you open seam to seam!

In his interviews he smiled his gummy Farex-baby smile and described the joys of his simple, celibate life in his room that was attached to the village temple, and explained how the Gandhian practice of *rati sadhana*—semen retention—had helped him to keep up his strength during his fast. To demonstrate this, on the third day of his fast, he got off his bed, jogged around the stage in his white kurta and dhoti and flexed his flappy biceps. People laughed and cried and brought their children to him to be blessed.

Television viewership skyrocketed. Advertising rolled in. Nobody had seen frenzy like this, at least not since twenty years ago, when, on the Day of the Concurrent Miracle, idols of Lord Ganesh in temples all over the world were reported to have simultaneously started drinking milk.

But now it was the ninth day of the old man's fast and, despite his stockpile of unspilled semen, he was noticeably weaker. Rumors about the rise in his creatinine levels and the deterioration of his kidneys had flown around the city that afternoon. Luminaries lined up by his bedside and had themselves photographed with him while they held his hand and (although nobody seriously believed it would come to that) urged him not to die. Industrialists who had been exposed in the scams donated money to his Movement and applauded the old man's unwavering commitment to non-violence. (His prescriptions for hand-chopping, hanging and disemboweling were accepted as reasonable caveats.)

The relatively well off among the old man's fans, who had been blessed with life's material needs, but had never experienced the adrenaline rush, the taste of the righteous anger that came with participating in a mass protest, arrived in cars and on motorcycles, waving national flags and singing patriotic songs. The Trapped Rabbit's government, once the messiah of India's economic miracle, was paralyzed.

In faraway Gujarat, Gujarat ka Lalla recognized the appearance of the old man–baby as a sign from the gods. With a predator's unerring instinct, he accelerated his March to Delhi. By the fifth day of the old man's fast, Lalla was (metaphorically speaking) camped outside the city gates. His army of belligerent janissaries flooded Jantar Mantar. They overwhelmed the old man with boisterous declarations of support. Their flags were bigger, their songs louder than anyone else's. They set up counters and distributed free food to the poor. (They were flush with funds from millionaire God Men who were supporters of Lalla.) They were under strict instructions not to wear their signature saffron headbands, not to carry saffron flags and never to mention Gujarat's Beloved by name even in passing. It worked. Within days they had pulled off a palace coup. The young profession-als who had worked so hard to make the old man famous were deposed before they, or even he, understood what had happened. The Happy Meadow fell. And nobody realized. The Trapped Rabbit was dead meat. Soon the Beloved would ride into Delhi. His people, wearing paper masks of his likeness, would carry him on their shoulders chanting his name—*Lalla! Lalla! Lalla!*—and place him on the throne. Wherever he looked, he would see only himself. The new Emperor of Hindustan. He was an ocean. He was infinity. He was humanity itself. But that was still a year away.

For now, in Jantar Mantar, his supporters shouted themselves hoarse about government corruption. (*Murdabad! Murdabad!* Down! Down! Down! Down!) At night they rushed home to watch themselves on TV. Until they returned in the morning the old man and his "core group" of a few supporters looked a little desolate under the billowing white canopy that was large enough to accommodate a crowd of thousands.

Right next to the anti-corruption canopy, in a clearly demar-cated space under the spreading branches of an old Tamarind tree, another well-known Gandhian activist had committed her-self to a fast to the death on behalf of thousands of farmers and indigenous tribespeople whose land had been appropriated by the government to be given to a petrochemicals corporation for a captive coal mine and thermal power plant in Bengal. It was the nineteenth indefinite hunger strike of her career. Even though she was a good-looking woman with a spectacular plait of long hair, she was far less popular with the TV cameras than the old man. The reason for this wasn't mysterious. The petrochemicals corporation owned most of the television channels and adver-tised hugely on the others. So angry commentators made guest appearances in TV studios denouncing her and insinuating that she was being funded by a "foreign power." A good number of the commentators as well as journalists were on the corporation's payroll too and did their best by their employers. But on the pavement, the people around her loved her. Grizzled farmers fanned mosquitoes from her face. Sturdy peasant women massaged her feet and gazed at her adoringly. Apprentice activists, some of them young students from Europe and America, dressed in loose hippy outfits, composed her convoluted press releases on their laptop computers. Several intellectuals and concerned citizens squatted on the pavement explaining farmers' rights to farmers who had been fighting for their rights for years. PhD students from foreign universities working on social movements (an extremely sought-after subject) conducted long interviews with the farmers, grateful that their fieldwork had come to the city instead of their having to trek all the way out to the countryside where there were no toilets and filtered water was hard to find.

A dozen hefty men in civil clothes but with uncivil haircuts (short back and sides) and uncivil socks and shoes (khaki socks, brown boots) had distributed themselves among the crowd, blatantly eavesdropping on conversations. Some of them pretended to be journalists and filmed conversations with small Handycams. They paid special attention to the young foreigners (many of whom would soon find their visas revoked).

The TV lights made the hot air hotter. Suicidal moths bombed the sun guns and the night smelled of charred insect. Fifteen severely disabled people, sullen and tired from a long, hot day's begging, hovered in the dark, just outside the circle of lights, resting their buckled backs and wasted limbs on government-issue, hand-operated cycle rickshaws. The displaced farmers and their famous leader had displaced them from the coolest, shadiest stretch of pavement where they usually lived. So their sympathies were entirely with the petrochemicals industry. They wanted the farmers' agitation to end as soon as possible so they could have their spot back.

Some distance away a bare-torsoed man, with yellow limes stuck all over his body with superglue, sucked noisily on a thick mango drink from a small carton. He refused to say why he had stuck limes to his skin or why he was drinking mango juice even though he seemed to be promoting limes, and grew abusive if anyone asked. Another freelancer, who called himself a "performance artist," wandered aimfully through the crowds wearing a suit and tie and an English bowler hat. From a distance his suit looked as though it had seekh kebabs printed all over it, but on closer inspection they turned out to be perfectly shaped turds. The wilted red rose pinned to his collar had turned black. A triangle of white handkerchief peeped out of his breast pocket. When asked what his message was, in refreshing contrast to the rudeness of the Lime Man, he patiently explained that his body was his instrument and he wanted the so-called civilized world to lose its aversion to shit and accept that shit was just processed food. And vice versa. He also explained that he wanted to take Art out of Museums and bring it to "The People."

Sitting near the Lime Man (who ignored them completely) were Anjum, Saddam Hussain and Ustad Hameed. With them was a striking-looking young Hijra, Ishrat, a guest at Jannat Guest House who was visiting from Indore. Of course it had been Anjum's idea—her long-standing desire to "help the poor"—which made her suggest they go to Jantar Mantar to see for themselves what the "Second Freedom Struggle" the TV channels had been broadcasting was all about. Saddam was dismissive: "You don't have to go all the way there to find out. I can tell you now—it's the motherfucker of all scams." But Anjum had been adamant and of course Saddam would not let her go alone. So they made up a little party, Anjum, Saddam (still in his sunglasses) and Nimmo Gorakhpuri. Ustad Hameed, who had dropped in to see Anjum, was dragooned into the expedition, as was young Ishrat. They decided to go at night when the crowds would be comparatively thinner. Anjum had dressed down, in one of her drabber Pathan suits, though she could not resist a hairclip, a dupatta and a touch of lipstick. Ishrat was dressed as though she was at her own wedding—in a lurid pink kurta with sequins and a green Patiala salwar. She ignored all advice to the contrary and wore bright pink lipstick and enough jewelry to light up the night. Nimmo had driven Anjum, Ishrat and Ustad Hameed in her car. Saddam had arranged to meet them there. He rode Payal to Jantar Mantar and tethered her to a railing some distance away (and promised a cheeky little shoe-shine boy two choco-bars and ten rupees to keep an eye on her). Sensing Nimmo Gorakhpuri's restlessness, Saddam had tried to entertain her with the animal videos he had on his phone—some that he had shot himself, of the stray dogs and cats and cows he came across on his daily treks across the city, and others he had received from friends on WhatsApp: *See, this fellow is called Chaddha Sahib. He never barks. Every day at 4 p.m. sharp he comes to this park to play with his girl-friend. This cow loves tomatoes. I take her some every day. This one has a bad case of itching. Have you seen this lion standing on two legs and kissing this woman . . . ? Yes, she's a woman. You can tell when she turns around . . .* Since none of them featured goats or Western women's fashion, they did nothing to alleviate Nimmo Gorakh-puri's boredom and she soon excused herself and left. Anjum on the other hand was fascinated by the bustle, the banners and the bits of conversation she overheard. She insisted they stay on and "learn something." So, like everybody else on the pavement, they settled into their own little huddle. Headquartered there, Anjum sent her envoy—His Excellency, Plenipotentiary, Sad-dam Hussain—from group to group to get a quick low-down on where they were from, what their protest was about and what their demands were. Saddam went obediently from stall to stall like a shopper in a political flea market, returning every now and then to brief Anjum about the insights he had gained. She sat cross-legged on the ground, leaning forward and listening intently, nodding, half smiling, but not looking at Saddam as he spoke because her head was turned and her shining eyes were fixed firmly on whichever group it was that he was talking about. Ustad Hameed was not remotely interested in the information Saddam brought. But the expedition was a welcome change from his daily routine so he was content to be part of it and hummed to himself as he looked around absent-mindedly. Ishrat, inappropriately dressed and absurdly vain, spent all her time taking selfies from various angles with different backgrounds. Though nobody paid much attention to her (it was a No-contest between her and the old man–baby) she was careful not to stray too far from base camp. At one point she and Ustad Hameed dissolved into a spasm of schoolgirl giggles. When Anjum asked what was so funny, Ustad Hameed told her how his grandchildren had tutored their grandmother to call him (her husband) a "bloody fucking bitch," which she had been given to understand was a term of endearment in English.

"She had no idea what she was saying, she looked so sweet when she said it," Ustad Hameed said, laughing. "Bloody fucking bitch! That's what my begum calls me . . ."

"What does it mean?" Anjum asked. (She knew what the English word "bitch" meant, but not "bloody" and "fucking.") Before Ustad Hameed could begin to explain (although even he wasn't all that sure himself, he just knew it was bad), they were interrupted by a long-haired, bearded young man in floaty, shabby clothes and an equally shabbily dressed girl with gorgeous, wild hair that she wore loose. They were making a documentary film about Protest and Resistance, they explained, and one of the recurring themes of the film was to have protesters say, "Another World Is Possible" in whatever language they spoke. For example, if their mother tongue was Hindi or Urdu, they could say, "Doosri duniya mumkin hai . . ." They set up their camera while they were talking and asked Anjum to look straight into the lens when she spoke. They had no idea what "Duniya" meant in Anjum's lexicon. Anjum, for her part, completely uncomprehending, stared into the camera. "Hum doosri Duniya se aaye hain," she explained helpfully, which meant: We've come from there . . . from the other world.

The young film-makers, who had a long night's work ahead of them, exchanged glances and decided to move on rather than try to explain what they meant because it would take too long. They thanked Anjum and crossed the road to the opposite pavement where several groups had their own separate canopies.

In the first, seven men with shaved heads, dressed in white dhotis, had taken a vow of silence, claiming they would not speak until Hindi was declared India's national language—its official mother tongue—over the twenty-two other official languages and hundreds of unofficial ones. Three of the bald men were asleep and the other four had slipped down their white hospital masks (their "vow of silence" prop) in order to drink their late-night tea. Since they could not speak, the film-makers gave them a small poster that said *Another World Is Possible* to hold up. They made sure that the banner with the demand for Hindi to be declared the national language was out of frame, because both film-makers agreed it was a somewhat regressive demand. But they felt that bald men with masks provided good visual texture for their film, and ought not to be passed over.

Occupying a substantial part of the pavement quite close to the bald men were fifty representatives of the thousands of people who had been maimed in the 1984 Union Carbide gas leak in Bhopal. They had been on the pavement for two weeks. Seven of them were on an indefinite hunger strike, their condition deteriorating steadily. They had walked to Delhi all the way from Bhopal, hundreds of kilometers in the searing summer sun, to demand compensation: clean water and medical care for themselves and the generations of deformed babies who were born after the gas leak. The Trapped Rabbit had refused to meet the Bhopalis. The TV crews were not interested in them; their struggle was too old to make the news. Photographs of deformed babies, misshapen aborted fetuses in bottles of formaldehyde and the thousands who had been killed, maimed and blinded in the gas leak were strung up like macabre bunting on the railings. On a small TV monitor (they had managed to get an electricity connection from a nearby church) grainy old footage played on a loop: a jaunty young Warren Anderson, the American CEO of the Union Carbide Corporation, arriving at Delhi airport days after the disaster. "I've just arrived," he tells the jostling journalists. "I don't know the details yet. So hey! Whaddya want me to say?" Then he looks straight into the TV cameras and waves, "Hi Mom!"

On and on through the night he went: "Hi Mom! Hi Mom! Hi Mom! Hi Mom! Hi Mom . . ."

An old banner, faded from decades of use, said, *Warren Anderson is a war criminal*. A newer one said, *Warren Anderson has killed more people than Osama bin Laden*.

Next to the Bhopalis was the Delhi Kabaadi-Wallahs' (Waste-recyclers') Association and the Sewage Workers' Union, protesting against the privatization and corporatization of the city's garbage and the city's sewage. The corporation that bid for and won the contract was the same one that had been given farmers' land for its power plant. It already ran the city's electricity and water distribution. Now it owned the city's shit and waste-disposal systems too.

Right next to the waste-recyclers and the sewage workers was the plushest part of the pavement, a glittering public toilet with float glass mirrors and a shiny granite floor. The toilet lights stayed on, night and day. It cost one rupee for a piss, two for a shit and three for a shower. Not many on the pavement could afford these rates. Many pissed outside the toilet, against the wall. So, though the toilet was spotlessly clean inside, from the outside it gave off the sharp smoky smell of stale urine. It didn't matter very much to the management; the toilet's revenue came from elsewhere. The exterior wall doubled up as a billboard that advertised something new every week.

This week it was Honda's newest luxury car. The billboard had its own personal guard. Gulabiya Vechania lived under a small blue plastic sheet right next to the billboard. This accommodation was a step up from where he'd begun. When he first arrived in the city a year ago, out of abject terror as well as necessity, Gulabiya had lived in a tree. Now he had a job, and some semblance of shelter. The name of the security agency he worked for was embroidered on the epaulettes of his stained blue shirt: TSGS Security. (A rival concern to Sangeeta Madam *Haramzaadi* Bitch's SSGS.) His job was to prevent vandalism, in particular, to thwart repeated attempts being made by certain miscreants to urinate right on to the billboard. He worked seven days a week, twelve hours a day. That night Gulabiya was drunk and had dropped off to sleep when someone sprayed *Inqilab Zindabad!* Long Live Revolution! right across the silver Honda City. Below that, someone else scrawled a poem.

Chheen li tumne garib ki rozi roti
Aur laga diye hain fees karne pe tatti

You've snatched poor folks' daily bread
And slapped a fee on their shit instead

Gulabiya would lose his job in the morning. Thousands like him would line up hoping to replace him. (One might even be the street poet himself.) But for now, Gulabiya slept soundly and dreamed deep. In his dream he had enough money to feed himself and send a little home to his family in his village. In his dream his village still existed. It wasn't at the bottom of a dam reservoir. Fish didn't swim through his windows. Crocodiles didn't knife through the high branches of the Silk Cotton trees. Tourists didn't go boating over his fields, leaving rainbow clouds of diesel in the sky. In his dream his brother Luariya wasn't a tour-guide at the dam-site whose job was to showcase the miracles the dam had wrought. His mother didn't work as a sweeper in a dam-engineer's house that was built on the land that she once owned. She didn't have to steal mangoes from her own trees. She didn't live in a resettlement colony in a tin hut with tin walls and a tin roof that was so hot you could fry onions on it. In Gulabiya's dream his river was still flowing, still alive. Naked children still sat on rocks, playing the flute, diving into the water to swim among the buffaloes when the sun grew too hot. There were leopard and sambar and sloth bear in the Sal forest that clothed the hills above the village, where during festivals his people would gather with their drums to drink and dance for days.

All he had left from his old life now were his memories, his flute and his earrings (which he was not allowed to wear to work).

Unlike the irresponsible Gulabiya Vechania, who had failed in his duty to protect the silver Honda City, Janak Lal Sharma, the toilet "in-charge," was wide awake and working hard. His dog-eared logbook was updated. The money in his wallet was organized carefully, by denomination. He had a separate pouch for coins. He supplemented his salary by allowing activists, journalists and TV cameramen to recharge their mobile phones, laptops and camera batteries from the power point in the toilet for the price of six showers and a shit (i.e., twenty rupees). Sometimes he allowed people to shit for the price of a piss and didn't enter it in the logbook. At first he was a little careful with the anti-corruption activists. (They were not hard to identify—they were less poor and more aggressive than everybody else. Though they were fashionably dressed in jeans and T-shirts, most of them wore white Gandhi caps stamped with a solarized print of the old man–baby smiling his Farex-baby smile.) Janak Lal Sharma took care to charge them the proper rates and log the nature of each one's ablution correctly and carefully. But some of them, especially the second batch of new arrivals, who were even more aggressive than the first, grew resentful that they were being charged more than the others. Soon, with them too, it became business as usual. With his extra income he subcontracted his toilet-cleaning duties, which were unthinkable for a man of his caste and background to perform (he was a Brahmin), to Suresh Balmiki who, as his name makes clear, belonged to what most Hindus overtly, and the government covertly, thought of as the shit-cleaning caste. With the increasing unrest in the country, the endless stream of protesters arriving on the pavement, and all the TV coverage, even after setting aside what he paid Suresh Balmiki, Janak Lal had earned enough to make a down payment on an LIG flat.

Opposite the toilet, back on the TV-crew side of the road (but some serious ideological distance away), was what people on the pavement called the Border: Manipuri Nationalists asking for the revocation of the Armed Forces Special Powers Act, which made it legal for the Indian Army to kill on "suspicion"; Tibetan refugees calling for a free Tibet; and, most unusually (and most dangerously, for them), the Association of Mothers of the Disappeared, whose sons had gone missing, in their thousands, in the war for freedom in Kashmir. (Spooky, then, to have a soundtrack that went "Hi Mom! Hi Mom! Hi Mom!" However, the Mothers of the Disappeared did not register this eeriness because they thought of themselves as Moj—"Mother" in Kashmiri—and not "Mom.")

It was the Association's first visit to the Super Capital. They weren't all mothers; the wives, sisters and a few young children of the Disappeared had come too. Each of them carried a picture of their missing son, brother or husband. Their banner said:

> *The Story of Kashmir*
> DEAD = 68,000
> DISAPPEARED = 10,000
> Is this Democracy or *Demon Crazy*?

No TV camera pointed at that banner, not even by mistake. Most of those engaged in India's Second Freedom Struggle felt nothing less than outrage at the idea of freedom for Kashmir and the Kashmiri women's audacity.

Some of the Mothers, like some of the Bhopal gas leak victims, had become a little jaded. They had told their stories at endless meetings and tribunals in the international supermarkets of grief, along with other victims of other wars in other countries. They had wept publicly and often, and nothing had come of it. The horror they were going through had grown a hard, bitter shell.

The trip to Delhi had turned out to be an unhappy experience for the Association. The women were heckled and threatened at their roadside press conference in the afternoon and eventually the police had had to intervene and throw a cordon around the Mothers. "Muslim Terrorists do not deserve Human Rights!" shouted Gujarat ka Lalla's undercover janissaries. "We have seen your genocide! We have faced your ethnic cleansing! Our people have been living in refugee camps for twenty years now!" Some young men spat at photographs of the dead and missing Kashmiri men. The "genocide" and "ethnic cleansing" they referred to was the mass exodus of Kashmiri Pandits from the Kashmir Valley when the freedom struggle had turned militant in the 1990s and some Muslim militants had turned on the tiny Hindu population. Several hundred Hindus had been massacred in macabre ways and when the government announced that it could not ensure their safety, almost the entire population of Kashmiri Hindus, almost two hundred thousand people, had fled the Valley and moved into refugee camps in the plains of Jammu where many of them still lived. A few of Lalla's janissaries on the pavement that day were Kashmiri Hindus who had lost their homes and families and all they had ever known.

Perhaps even more hurtful to the Mothers than the Spitters were the three beautifully groomed, pencil-thin college girls who walked past that morning on their way to shop at Connaught Place. "Oh wow! Kashmir! What *funnn*! Apparently it's completely normal now, *ya*, safe for tourists. Let's go? It's supposed to be stunning."

The Association of Mothers had decided to get through the night somehow and never come back to Delhi. Sleeping out on the street was a new experience for them. Back home they all had pretty houses and kitchen gardens. That night they had a meager meal (that was a new experience too), rolled up their banner and tried to sleep, waiting for day to break, longing to begin their journey back to their beautiful, war-torn valley.

It was there, right next to the Mothers of the Disappeared, that our quiet baby appeared. It took the Mothers a while to notice her, because she was the color of night. A sharply outlined absence in the shadows under the street light. More than twenty years of living with crackdowns, cordon-and-search operations and the midnight knock (Operation Tiger, Operation Serpent Destruction, Operation Catch and Kill) had taught the Mothers to read the darkness. But when it came to babies, the only ones they were used to looked like almond blossoms with apple cheeks. The Mothers of the Disappeared did not know what to do with a baby that had Appeared.

Especially not a *black* one
Kruhun kaal
Especially not a black *girl*
Kruhun kaal hish
Especially not one that was swaddled in litter
Shikas ladh

The whisper was passed around the pavement like a parcel. The question grew into an announcement: "Bhai baccha kiska hai?" Whose baby is this?

Silence.

Then someone said they had seen the mother vomiting in the park in the afternoon. Someone else said, "Oh no, that wasn't her."

Someone said she was a beggar. Someone else said she was a rapevictim (which was a word in every language).

Someone said she had come with the group that had been there earlier in the day organizing a signature campaign for the release of political prisoners. It was rumored to be a Front organization for the banned Maoist Party that was fighting a guerrilla war in the forests of Central India. Someone else said, "Oh no, that wasn't her. She was alone. She's been here for some days."

Someone said she was the former lover of a politician who had thrown her out after she got pregnant.

Everybody agreed that politicians were all bastards. That didn't help address the problem:

What to do with the baby?

Perhaps aware that she had become the center of attention, or perhaps because she was frightened, the quiet baby finally wailed. A woman picked her up. (Later, about her it was said that she was tall, she was short, she was black, she was white, she was beautiful, she was not, she was old, she was young, she was a stranger, she was often seen at Jantar Mantar.) A piece of paper folded many times into a small square pellet, taped down along one edge, was threaded on to the thick black string tied around the baby's waist. The woman (who was beautiful, who was not, who was tall, who was short) untaped it and handed it to someone to read. The message was written in English and was unambiguous: *I cannot look after this child. So I am leaving her here.*

Eventually, after a lot of murmured consultation, hesitantly, sadly, rather reluctantly, the people decided that the baby was a matter for the police.

Before Saddam could stop her, Anjum stood up and began to walk fast towards what seemed to have become a spontaneously constituted Baby Welfare Committee. She was a head taller than most people, so it wasn't hard to follow her. As she walked through the crowd, the bells on her anklets, not visible below her loose salwar, went *chhann-chhann-chhann*. To Saddam, suddenly terrified, each *chhann-chhann* sounded like a gunshot. The blue street light lit up the faint shadow of white stubble on Anjum's dark, pitted skin, shiny now with sweat. Her nose-pin flashed on her magnificent nose that curved downwards like the beak of a bird of prey. There was something unleashed about her, something uncalibrated and yet absolutely certain—a sense of destiny perhaps.

"Police? We're going to give her to the *police*?" Anjum said in both her voices, separate, yet joined, one rasping, one deep, distinct. Her white tusk shone out from between her betel-nut-red stumps.

The solidarity of her "We" was an embrace. Predictably, it was met with an immediate insult.

A wit from the crowd said, "Why? What will *you* do with her?

You can't turn her into one of you, can you? Modern technology has made great advances, but it hasn't got that far yet . . ." He was referring to the widely held belief that Hijras kidnapped male babies and castrated them. His waggishness earned him an eddy of spineless laughter.

Anjum didn't balk at the vulgarity of the comment. She spoke with an intensity that was as clear and as urgent as hunger.

"She's a gift from God. Give her to me. I can give her the love she needs. The police will just throw her in a government orphanage. She'll die there."

Sometimes a single person's clarity can unnerve a muddled crowd. On this occasion, Anjum's did. Those who could understand what she was saying were a little intimidated by the refinement of her Urdu. It was at odds with the class they assumed she came from.

"Her mother must have left her here thinking as I did, that this place is today's Karbala, where the battle for justice, the battle of good against evil, is being fought. She must have thought, 'These people are fighters, the best in the world, one of them will look after the child that I cannot'—and you want to call the *police*?" Though she was angry and though she was six feet tall and had broad, powerful shoulders, her manner was inflected with the exaggerated coquetry and the fluttering hand gestures of a 1930s Lucknow courtesan.

Saddam Hussain braced himself for a brawl. Ishrat and Ustad Hameed arrived to do what they could.

"Who gave these Hijras permission to sit here? Which of these Struggles do they belong to?"

Mr. Aggarwal, a slim, middle-aged man with a clipped mustache, wearing a safari shirt, terry cotton trousers and a printed Gandhi cap that said *I am against Corruption are You?* had the curt, authoritative air of a bureaucrat, which was indeed what he had been until recently. He had spent most of his working life in the Revenue Department, until one day, on a whim, sickened by his ringside view of the rot in the system, he had resigned his government job to "serve the nation." He had been tinkering on the periphery of good works and social service for a few years, but now, as the tubby Gandhian's chief lieutenant, he had shot to prominence and his picture was in the papers every day. Many believed (correctly) that the real power lay with him, and that the old man was just a charismatic mascot, a hireling who fitted the job-profile and had now begun to exceed his brief. The conspiracy theorists, who huddled on the edges of all political movements, whispered that the old man was deliberately being encouraged to promote himself, to paint himself into a corner, so that his own hubris would not allow a retreat. If the old man died of hunger publicly, on live TV, the rumor went, the Movement would have a martyr and that would kick-start the political career of Mr. Aggarwal in a way nothing else could. The rumor was unkind and untrue. Mr. Aggarwal *was* the man behind the Movement, but even he had been taken aback at the frenzy the old Gandhian evoked, and he was riding the tide, not plotting a stage-managed suicide. In a few months he would jettison his mascot and go on to become a mainstream politician—a veritable treasure house of many of the qualities he had once denounced—and a formidable opponent of Gujarat ka Lalla.

Mr. Aggarwal's singular advantage as an emerging politician was his unsingular looks. He looked like many people. Everything about him, the way he dressed, the way he spoke, the way he thought, was neat and tidy, clipped and groomed. He had a high voice and an understated, matter-of-fact manner, except when he stood before a microphone. Then he was transformed into a raging, almost uncontrollable, tornado of terrifying righteousness. By intervening in the matter of the baby, he hoped to deflect another public spat (like the one between the Kashmiri Mothers and the Spitting Brigade) that could distract media attention away from what he thought of as the Real Issues. "This is our Second Freedom Struggle. Our country is on the brink of a Revolution," he said portentously to the quickly growing audience. "Thousands have gathered here because corrupt politicians have made our lives unbearable. If we solve the problem of corruption we can take our country to new heights, right to the top of the world. This is a space for serious politics, not a circus ring." He addressed Anjum without looking at her: "Do you have police permission to be here? Everybody must have permission to be here." She towered over him. His refusal to meet her eye meant he was squarely addressing her breasts.

Mr. Aggarwal had misread the temperature, misjudged the situation completely. The people who had gathered were not wholly sympathetic to him. Many resented the way his "Freedom Struggle" had grabbed all the media attention and undermined everybody else. Anjum, for her part, was oblivious to the crowd. It didn't matter to her in which direction its sympathies lay. Something had lit up inside her and filled her with resolute courage.

"Police permission?" Never could two words have been pronounced with more contempt. "This is a *child*, not some illegal encroachment on your father's property. *You* apply to the police, Sahib. The rest of us will take the shorter route and apply straight to the Almighty." Saddam had just enough time to whisper a small prayer of gratitude that the word she used for the Almighty was the generic *Khuda* and not specifically *Allah mian* before the battle lines were drawn.

The adversaries squared off.

Anjum and the Accountant.

What a confrontation it was.

Ironically both of them were on the pavement that night to escape their past and all that had circumscribed their lives so far.

And yet, in order to arm themselves for battle, they retreated right back into what they sought to escape, into what they were used to, into what they really *were*.

He, a revolutionary trapped in an accountant's mind. She, a woman trapped in a man's body. He, raging at a world in which the balance sheets did not tally. She, raging at her glands, her organs, her skin, the texture of her hair, the width of her shoulders, the timbre of her voice. He, fighting for a way to impose fiscal integrity on a decaying system. She, wanting to pluck the very stars from the sky and grind them into a potion that would give her proper breasts and hips and a long, thick plait of hair that would swing from side to side as she walked, and yes, the thing she longed for most of all, that most well stocked of Delhi's vast stock of invectives, that insult of all insults, a *Maa ki Choot*, a mother's cunt. He, who had spent his days tracking tax dodges, pay-offs and sweetheart deals. She, who had lived for years like a tree in an old graveyard, where, on lazy mornings and late at night, the spirits of the old poets whom she loved, Ghalib, Mir and Zauq, came to recite their verse, drink, argue and gamble. He, who filled in forms and ticked boxes. She, who never knew which box to tick, which queue to stand in, which public toilet to enter (Kings or Queens? Lords or Ladies? Sirs or Hers?). He, who believed he was always right. She, who knew she was all wrong, always wrong. He, reduced by his certainties. She, augmented by her ambiguity. He, who wanted a law. She, who wanted a baby.

A circle formed around them: furious, curious, assessing the adversaries, picking sides. It didn't matter. Which tight-arsed Gandhian accountant stood a chance in hell in a one-to-one public face-off against an old, Old Delhi Hijra?

Anjum bent low and brought her face within kissing distance of Mr. Aggarwal's.

"*Ai Hai!* Why so angry, *jaan*? Won't you look at me?"

Saddam Hussain clenched his fists. Ishrat restrained him. She took a deep breath and waded into the battlefield, intervening in the practiced way that only Hijras knew how to when it came to protecting each other—by making a declaration of war and peace at the same time. Her attire, which had looked absurd only a few hours ago, could not have been more appropriate for what she needed to do now. She started the spread-fingered Hijra clap and began to dance, moving her hips obscenely, swirling her chunni, her outrageous, aggressive sexuality aimed at humiliating Mr. Aggarwal, who had never in all his life fought a fair street fight. Damp patches appeared in the armpits of his white shirt.

Ishrat began with a song she knew the crowd would know— from a film called *Umrao Jaan*, immortalized by the beautiful actress Rekha.

Dil cheez kya hai, aap meri jaan lijiye
Why just my heart, take my whole life too

Someone tried to hustle her off the pavement. She moved to the middle of the wide, empty road, enjoying herself now as she pirouetted on the zebra crossing under the street lights. From the opposite side of the road someone began beating out a rhythm on a dafli. People joined the singing. She was right. Everybody knew the song:

Bas ek baar mera kaha maan lijiye
But just this once, my love, grant me my wish

That courtesan's song, or at least that one line, could have been the anthem for almost everybody in Jantar Mantar that day. All those who were there were there because they believed that somebody cared, that somebody was listening. That somebody would grant them a hearing.

.   .   .

A fight broke out. Perhaps someone said something lewd. Perhaps Saddam Hussain hit him. It's not clear exactly what happened.

The policemen on duty at the pavement snapped out of their sleep and swung their lathis at anybody who was within their reach. Police patrol jeeps (*With You, For You, Always*) arrived with flashing lights and the Delhi Police special—*maader chod behen chod maa ki choot behen ka lauda.*[*]

The TV cameras crowded in. The activist on her nineteenth fast saw her chance. She waded into the crowd and turned to the cameras with her trademark, clenched-fist call and, with unerring political acumen, she appropriated the lathi charge for her people.

> *Lathi goli khaayenge!*
> Batons and bullets we will bear!

And her people answered:

> *Andolan chalaayenge!*
> With our struggle we'll persevere!

It didn't take the police long to restore order. Among those arrested and driven away in police vans were Mr. Aggarwal, Anjum, a quaking Ustad Hameed and the live art installation in his scatological suit. (The Lime Man had made himself scarce.) They were released the following morning with no charges.

By the time someone remembered how it had all begun, the baby was gone.

---

[*] Motherfucker sisterfucker your mother's cunt your sister's cock.

4

DR. AZAD BHARTIYA

The last person to see the baby was Dr. Azad Bhartiya, who had just entered, according to his own calculations, the eleventh year, third month and seventeenth day of his hunger strike. Dr. Bhartiya was so thin as to be almost two-dimensional. His temples were hollow, his dark, sunbaked skin slunk over the bones of his face and the prominent cartilage of his long, reedy neck and collarbone. Searching, fevered eyes stared out at the world from deep shadow bowls. One of his arms, from shoulder to wrist, was encased in a filthy white plaster cast supported by a sling looped around his neck. The empty sleeve of his grimy striped shirt flapped at his side like the desolate flag of a defeated country. He sat behind an old cardboard sign covered with a dim, scratched, plastic sheet. It said:

My Full Name:
Dr. Azad Bhartiya. (Translation: The Free Indian)

My Home Address:
Dr. Azad Bhartiya
Near Lucky Sarai Railway Station
Lucky Sarai Basti
Kokar
Bihar

My Current Address:
Dr. Azad Bhartiya
Jantar Mantar
New Delhi

My Qualifications: MA Hindi, MA Urdu (First Class First), BA
History, BEd, Basic Elementary Course in Punjabi, MA Punjabi
ABF (Appeared But Failed), PhD (pending), Delhi University
(Comparative Religions and Buddhist Studies), Lecturer, Inter
College, Ghaziabad, Research Associate, Jawaharlal Nehru
University, New Delhi, Founder Member *Vishwa Samajwadi
Sthapana* (World People's Forum) and Indian Socialist
Democratic Party (Against Price-rise).

I am fasting against the following issues: I am against the
Capitalist Empire, plus against US Capitalism, Indian and
American State Terrorism/ All Kinds of Nuclear Weapons and
Crime, plus against the Bad Education System/ Corruption/
Violence/ Environmental Degradation and All Other Evils.
Also I am against Unemployment. I am also fasting for the
complete obliteration of the entire Bourgeois class. Each day
I remember the poor of the world, Workers/ Peasants/ Tribals/
Dalits/ Abandoned Ladies and Gents/ including Children and
Handicapped People.

The yellow plastic *Jaycees Sari Palace* shopping bag that sat next to him upright, like a small yellow person, contained papers, typed as well as handwritten, in English and Hindi. Several copies of a document—a newsletter or a transcript of some sort—were laid out on the pavement, weighed down by stones. Dr. Azad Bhartiya said it was available for sale at cost price for normal people and at a discount for students:

"MY NEWS & VIEWS." (UPDATE)

My original name as given to me by my parents is Inder Y. Kumar. Dr. Azad Bhartiya is the name I have given myself. It was registered in court on October 13th 1997 along with the English translation i.e.: Free/Liberated Indian. My affidavit is attached. It is not the original; it is a copy attested by a Patiala House magistrate.

If you accept this name for me, then you have the right to think that this is no place for an Azad Bhartiya to be found, here in this public prison on the public footpath—see, it even has bars. You may think a real Azad Bhartiya should be a modern person living in a modern house with a car and a computer, or maybe in that tall building there, that five-star hotel. That one is called Hotel Meridian. If you look up at the twelfth floor you will be able to see the AC room with attached breakfast and bathroom where the US President's five dogs stayed when he came to India. Actually we are not supposed to call them dogs because they are officers of the American Army, of the rank of Corporal. Some people say those dogs can smell hidden bombs and that they know how to eat with knives and forks sitting at a table. They say the hotel manager has to salute them when they come out of the lift. I don't know if this information is true or false, I have not been able to verify it. You might have heard that the dogs went to visit Gandhi's memorial in Rajghat? That is confirmed, it was in the newspaper. But I don't care. I don't admire Gandhi. He was a reactionary. He should be happy about the dogs. They are better than all those World Killers who regularly place flowers at his memorial.

But why is this Dr. Azad Bhartiya here on the footpath while the American dogs are in the Five Star hotel? This must be the question uppermost on your mind.

The answer for that is that I am here because I'm a revolutionary. I have been on hunger strike for more than eleven years. This is my twelfth year running. How can a man survive for twelve years on hunger strike? The answer is that I have developed a scientific technique of fasting. I eat one meal (light, vegetarian) either every 48 or 58 hours. That is more than sufficient for me. You may wonder how an Azad Bhartiya with no job and no salary manages a meal every 48 or 58 hours. Let me tell you, here on the footpath, no day goes without somebody who has nothing offering to share it with me. If I wanted, just sitting here I could become a fat man like the Maharaja of Mysore. By God. That would be easy. But my weight is forty-two kilos. I eat only to live and I live only to struggle.

I try my best to tell the truth, so I should clarify that the Doctor part of my name is actually pending, like my PhD. I'm using that title a little bit in advance only in order to make people listen to me and believe what I say. If there were no urgency in our political situation, I would not do this because, technically speaking, it is dishonest. But sometimes, in politics, one has to cut poison with poison.

I have been sitting here in Jantar Mantar for eleven years. I only leave this place sometimes to attend seminars or meetings on subjects of my interest in Constitution Club or Gandhi Peace Foundation. Otherwise I am permanently here. All these people from every corner of India come here with their dreams and demands. There is nobody to listen. No one listens. The police beats them, the government ignores them. They cannot stay here these poor people, as they are mostly from villages and slums and they have to earn a living. They have to go back to their land, or to their landlords, to their moneylenders, to their cows and buffaloes who are more expensive than humans, or to their jhuggis. But I stay here on those people's behalf. I fast for their progress, for the acceptance of all their demands, for the realization of their dreams and for the hope that some day they will have their own government.

What caste am I? That is your question? With such a huge political agenda as mine, you tell me, what caste should I be? What caste were Jesus and Gautam Buddh? What caste was Marx? What caste was Prophet Mohammed? Only Hindus have this caste, this inequality contained in their scriptures. I am everything except for a Hindu. As an Azad Bhartiya, I can tell you openly that I have renounced the faith of the majority of the people in this country only for this reason. For that my family does not talk to me. But even if I was President of America, that world class Brahmin, still I would be here on hunger strike for the poor. I don't want dollars. Capitalism is like poisoned honey. People swarm to it like bees. I don't go to it. For this reason I have been put under twenty-four-hours surveillance. I am under twenty-four-hours remote control electronic surveillance by the American Government. Look behind you. Can you see that blinking red light? That's their camera battery light. They have installed their camera in that traffic light also. They have their control room for their cameras in the Meridian hotel, in the dogs' room. The dogs are still there. They never went back to America. Their visas were extended indefinitely. Now because the American Presidents come to India so often, they keep their dogs here, permanently stationed. At night when the lights are on they sit on the windowsills. I see their shadows, their outline. My distance vision is very good and getting better. Every day I can see further and further. Bush, Hitler, Stalin, Mao and Ceausescu are members of a one hundred member club of leaders that are plotting to destroy all the good governments in the world. All the American presidents are members, even this new one.

Last week I was hit by a white car, Maruti Zen DL 2CP 4362 belonging to an Indian TV Channel funded by Americans. It crashed through the iron railing and drove onto me. You can see that part of the railing is still broken. I was sleeping, but alert. I rolled to one side like a commando, and so I escaped that attempt on my life, only my arm was crushed. It is now under repair. The rest of me was saved. The driver tried to escape. The people stopped him and forced him to take me to Ram Manohar Lohia hospital. Two people sat in the car and slapped him all the way to the hospital. The government doctors treated me very well. In the morning when I came back, all the revolutionaries who were here that night, bought me samosas and a glass of sweet lassi. They all signed or put their thumb impressions on my plaster. See, here are Santhal tribals from Hazaribagh, displaced by East Parej coal mines, these are Union Carbide Gas victims who walked here all the way from Bhopal. It took them three weeks. That Gas-Leak company has a new name now, Dow Chemicals. But these poor people who were destroyed by them, can they buy new lungs, new eyes? They have to manage with their same old organs, which were poisoned so many years ago. But nobody cares. Those dogs just sit there on that Meridian Hotel windowsill and watch us die. This is Devi Singh Suryavanshi's signature; he is like me, a nonaligned. He has given his phone number also. He is fighting against corruption and the cheating of the nation by politicians. I don't know what his other demand is; you can phone him directly and ask. He has gone to visit his daughter in Nashik, but he will come back next week. He is a eighty-seven years old man, but for him, still, the nation comes first. This is the rickshaw union Rashtravadi Janata Tipahiya Chalak Sangh. This thumb impression belongs to Phoolbatti from Betul, Madhya

Pradesh. She's a very good lady. She was working in a field as a daily laborer when a BSNL—Bharat Sanchar Nigam Limited—telephone pole fell on her. Her left leg had to be amputated. The Nigam gave her money for the amputation, fifty thousand rupees, but how is she to work now, with only one leg? She is a widow, what will she eat, who will feed her? Her son doesn't want to keep her so he has sent her here to do a satyagraha to demand a sedentary job. She has been here for three months. No one comes to see her. No one will. She will die here.

You see this English signature? This is S. Tilottama. She is a lady who comes here and goes. I have seen her for many years. Sometimes she comes in the day. Sometimes she comes in the late night or in the early morning. She is always alone. She has no schedule. She has this very good handwriting. She is also a very good lady.

These are the Latur earthquake victims whose cash compensation has been eaten up by corrupt collectors and tehsildars. Out of three crore rupees only three lakh rupees reached the people, 3 percent. The rest was eaten by cockroach people on the way. They have been sitting here since 1999. Can you read Hindi? You can see what they have written, *Bharat mein gadhey, giddh aur sooar raj kartein hain.* It means India is ruled by donkeys, vultures and pigs.

This is the second assassination attempt on me. Last year on 8th April, Honda City DL 8C X 4850, drove onto me. That same car you see in the advertisement there on the toilet except that my car was maroon, not silver. Driven by an American agent. On 17th July, *Hindustan Times* city section, *HT City* reported it. My right leg was fractured in three places. Even now it's hard for me to walk. I have to limp. People joke and say that I should marry Phoolbatti so that we have one healthy left leg and one healthy right leg for two of us. I laugh with them even though I don't find it funny. But it is important to laugh sometimes. I am against the institution of marriage. It was invented to subjugate women. I was married one time. My wife eloped with my brother. They call my son their son now. He calls me Uncle. I never see them. After they eloped I came here.

Sometimes I cross the road and fast on the other side, with the Bhopalis. But it's much hotter there.

Do you know what this place is, this Jantar Mantar? In the old days it was a sun-dial. It was built by some Maharaja, I have forgotten his name, in the year 1724. Foreigners still come to see it with tour guides. They walk past us but they don't see us, sitting here on the side of the road, fighting for a better world in this Democracy Zoo. Foreigners only see what they want to see. Earlier it was snake charmers and sadhus, now it is the superpower things, the Bazaar Raj. We sit here like caged animals, and the government feeds us useless little pieces of hope through the bars of this iron railing. Not enough to live on, but just enough to prevent us from dying. They send their journalists to us. We tell our stories. For a while that lightens our burden. This is how they control us. Everywhere else in the city there is Section 144 of Criminal Procedure Code.

See this new toilet they have built? For us, they say. Separate for ladies and gents. We have to pay to go inside. When we see ourselves in those big mirrors, we get afraid.

DECLARATION

I do hereby declare that all the information given herein above are true to the best of my knowledge and no material has been concealed therefrom.

FROM HIS VANTAGE POINT on the pavement Dr. Azad Bhartiya had seen that far from being alone, the baby that had disappeared had three mothers on the pavement that night, all three stitched together by threads of light.

The police, who knew that he knew everything that happened at Jantar Mantar, descended on him to question him. They slapped him around a little—not seriously, just from habit. But all he would say was:

Mar gayee bulbul qafas mein
Keh gayee sayyaad se
Apni sunehri gaand mein
Tu thoons le fasl-e-bahaar

She died in her cage, the little bird,
These words she left for her captor—
Please take the spring harvest
And shove it up your gilded arse

The police kicked him over (as a matter of routine) and confiscated all the copies of his *News & Views* as well as his *Jaycees Sari Palace* bag and all the papers in it.

Once they left, Dr. Azad Bhartiya didn't lose a moment. He immediately set to work, starting the laborious process of documentation from scratch.

Though they didn't have a suspect (the name and address of S. Tilottama, publisher of Dr. Azad Bhartiya's *News & Views*, jumped out at them at a later stage), the police registered a case under Section 361 (Kidnapping from Lawful Guardianship), Section 362 (Abducting, Compelling, Forcing or Deceitfully Inducing a Person from a Place), Section 365 (Wrongful Confinement), Section 366A (a Crime Committed against a Minor Girl Who Has Not Attained Eighteen Years of Age), Section 367 (Kidnapping in Order to Cause Grievous Hurt, Place in Slavery or Subject the Kidnapped Person to Unnatural Lust), Section

369 (Kidnapping a Child under Ten Years of Age in Order to Steal from Them).

The offenses were cognizable, bailable and trialable by Magistrates of the First Class. The punishment was imprisonment for not more than seven years.

They had already registered one thousand one hundred and forty-six similar cases in the city that year. And it was only May.

5

THE SLOW-GOOSE CHASE

A horse's hooves echoed on an empty street.
Payal the thin day-mare clop-clipped through a part of the city she oughtn't to be in.

On her back, astride a red cloth saddle edged with gold tassels, two riders: Saddam Hussain and Ishrat-the-Beautiful. In a part of the city they oughtn't to be in. No signs said so, because everything was a sign that any fool could read: the silence, the width of the roads, the height of the trees, the unpeopled pavements, the clipped hedges, the low white bungalows in which the Rulers lived. Even the yellow light that poured from the tall street lights looked encashable—columns of liquid gold.

Saddam Hussain put on his sunglasses. Ishrat said it looked silly to wear goggles at night.

"You call this night?" Saddam asked. He explained that he wasn't wearing his sunglasses in order to look good. He said the glare from the lights hurt his eyes and that he'd tell her the story of his eyes later.

Payal pinned her ears back and twitched her hide even though there weren't any flies around. She sensed her transgression. But she liked this part of the city. There was air to breathe. She could have galloped, if they'd let her. But they wouldn't.

They were on a slow-goose chase, she and her riders. Their mission was to follow an autorickshaw and its passengers.

They kept their distance from it as it sputtered like a lost child around vast roundabouts landscaped with sculptures, fountains and flower beds, and down avenues that spiked off them, each lined with different kinds of trees—Tamarind, Jamun, Neem, Pakad, Arjun.

"Look, they even have gardens for their cars," Ishrat said as they circled a roundabout.

Saddam laughed, delighted, into the night.

"They have cars for their dogs and gardens for their cars," he said.

A cavalcade of black Mercedes with tinted, bulletproof windows appeared as if from nowhere and scorched past them like a serpent.

Past the Garden City the chasees and chasers approached a bumpy flyover. (Bumpy for vehicles, that is, not horses.) The row of lights running down the middle looked like mechanical cherubs' wings mounted on long poles. The rickshaw chugged uphill, then dipped down and disappeared from view. To keep up, Payal broke into a gentle, happy trot. A slim unicorn inspecting the cherub brigade.

Beyond the flyover the city grew less sure of itself.

The slow chase threaded past two hospitals so full of sickness that patients and their families had spilled out and were camped on the roads. Some were on makeshift beds and in wheelchairs. Some wore hospital gowns and had bandages and IV drips. Children, bald from chemotherapy, wore hospital masks and clung to their empty-eyed parents. People crowded the counters of the all-night chemists, playing Indian Roulette. (There was a 60:40 chance that the drugs they bought were genuine and not spuri-

ous.) Families cooked on the street, cutting onions, boiling pota-
toes gone gritty with dust on small kerosene stoves. They hung
their washing on tree guards and railings. (Saddam Hussain took
note of all this—for professional reasons.) A bunch of emaciated
twig-thighed villagers in dhotis squatted on their haunches in a
circle. In the center, perched like a wounded bird, was a wizened
old lady in a printed sari and enormous dark glasses that were
sealed along the edges with cotton wool. A thermometer angled
out of her mouth like a cigarette. They paid no attention to the
white horse and her riders as they cantered past.

Another flyover.

This time the goose-chase party went under it. It was packed
tight with sleeping people. A bare-bodied bald man with a purple
crust of congealed talcum powder on his head and a long, gray,
bushy beard beat out a rhythm on an imaginary drum, flinging
his head around like Ustad Zakir Hussain.

"Dha Dha Dhim Ti-ra-ki-ta Dhim!" Ishrat called out to him
as they went past. He smiled and rewarded her with a complicated flourish of percussion.

A shuttered market, a midnight egg-paratha stall. A Sikh
Gurdwara. Another market. A row of car-repair shops. The men
and dogs asleep outside were covered in car grease.

The rickshaw turned into a residential colony. And then
leftrightleftrightleft. A lane. Construction material stacked along
it. The houses were all three and four storeys high.

The rickshaw stopped outside a barred iron gate painted a
dull shade of lavender. Payal stopped in the shadows, many gates
away. A snuffling specter. A pale mare-ghost. The gold thread on
her saddle glinting in the night.

A woman got out, paid and went into the house. After the rickshaw left, Saddam Hussain and Ishrat-the-Beautiful approached
the lavender gate. Two black bulls with wobbling humps lolled
outside.

A light came on in the second-floor window.

Ishrat said, "Write down the house number." Saddam said he didn't need to because he never forgot places he'd been to. He'd be able to find it in his sleep.

She wriggled against him. "*Wah!* What a man!"

He squished her breast. She slapped his hand away. "Don't. They cost a lot. I'm still paying my installments."

The woman silhouetted against the rectangle of light on the second floor looked down and saw two people on a white horse. They looked up and saw her.

As though to acknowledge the glance that passed between them, the woman (who was beautiful, who was not, who was tall, who was short) inclined her head and kissed the stolen goods she held in her arms. She waved to them and they waved back. Of course she recognized them as the team from the scrum at Jantar Mantar. Saddam dismounted and held up a small white rectangle—his visiting card with the address of Jannat Guest House and Funeral Services. He dropped it into the tin letter box that said *S. Tilottama. Second Floor.*

The baby had fretted most of the way, but had finally fallen asleep. Tiny heartbeats and a black velvet cheek against a bony shoulder. The woman rocked her as she watched the horse and its riders exit the lane.

She could not remember when last she had been this happy. Not because the baby was hers, but because it wasn't.

6

SOME QUESTIONS FOR LATER

When the Baby Seal grew older, when she was (say) crowded around an ice-cream cart on a burning afternoon, one among a press of schoolgirls clamoring for an orange bar, might she get a sudden whiff of the heady scent of ripe Mahua that had infused the forest the day she was born? Would her body remember the feel of dry leaves on the forest floor, or the hot-metal touch of the barrel of her mother's gun that had been held to her forehead with the safety catch off?

Or had her past been erased forever?

Death flies in, thin bureaucrat, from the plains—

—AGHA SHAHID ALI

7

THE LANDLORD

It's cold. One of those dim, dirty winter days. The city is still stunned by the simultaneous explosions that tore through a bus stop, a café and the basement parking lot of a small shopping plaza two days ago, leaving five dead and very many more severely injured. It will take our television news anchors a little longer than ordinary folks to recover from the shock. As for myself, blasts evoke a range of emotions in me, but sadly, shock is no longer one of them.

I'm upstairs in this barsati, this small, second-floor apartment-on-the-roof. The Neem trees have shed their leaves; the rose-ringed parakeets seem to have moved to a warmer (safer?) place. The fog is hunched up against the windowpanes. A clot of blue rock pigeons huddles on the shit-crusted *chhajja*. Though it's the middle of the day, nearly lunchtime, I've had to switch the lights on. I notice that my experiment with the red cement floor has failed. I wanted a floor with a deep, soft shine, like those graceful old houses down South. But here, over the years, the summer heat has leached the color from the cement and the winter cold has caused the surface to contract and shatter into a pattern of hairline cracks. The apartment is dusty and run-down. Something about the stillness of this hastily abandoned space makes it look like a frozen frame in a moving picture. It seems to contain the geometry of motion, the shape of all that has happened and everything that is still to come. The absence of the person who lived here is so real, so palpable, that it's almost a presence.

The noise from the street is muted. The blades of the still ceiling fans are edged with grime, a paean to Delhi's famously filthy air. Fortunately for my lungs, I'm only visiting. Or at least that's what I hope. I have been sent home on leave. Though I don't feel unwell, when I look at myself in the mirror I can see that my skin is dull and my hair has thinned noticeably. My scalp shines through it (yes, shines). Almost nothing remains of my eyebrows. I'm told this is a sign of anxiety. The drinking, I admit, is worrying. I have tested the patience of both my wife and my boss in unacceptable ways and am determined to redeem myself. I am booked into a rehabilitation center where I will be for six weeks with no phone, no internet and no contact whatsoever with the world. I was supposed to check in today, but I'll do it on Monday.

I long to return to Kabul, the city where I will probably die, in some hackneyed, unheroic manner, perhaps while handing my Ambassador a file. BOOM. No more me. Twice they nearly got us; both times luck was on our side. After the second attack we received an anonymous letter in Pashtu (which I read as well as speak): *Nun zamong bad qismati wa. Kho yaad lara che mong sirf yaw waar pa qismat gatta kawo. Ta ba da hamesha dapara khush qismata ve.* That translates (more or less) as: Today we were unlucky. But remember we only have to be lucky once. You will need good luck all the time.

Something about those words rang a bell. I googled them. (That's a verb now, isn't it?) It was a close-to-verbatim translation of what the IRA said after Margaret Thatcher escaped their bomb attack on the Grand Hotel in Brighton in 1984. It's another kind of globalization, I suppose, this universal terrorspeak.

Every day in Kabul is a battle of wits and I'm addicted.

While I waited to be certified fit for service, I decided to visit my tenants and see how the house—I bought it fifteen years ago and more or less rebuilt it—was bearing up. At least that's what I told myself. When I got here I found myself avoiding the main entrance and going all the way to the end of the road and around to the back, to take the gate that opens on to the service lane that runs behind the row of townhouses.

It was a quiet, pretty lane once. Now it's like a construction site. Building material—steel reinforcement rods, slabs of stone and heaps of sand—occupies what little space parked cars do not. Two open manholes give off a stench that doesn't quite complement the soaring price of property here. Most of the older houses have been torn down and plush new developers' flats are coming up in their place. Some are on stilts, the ground floors given over to parking. It's a good idea in this car-maddened city, but somehow it saddens me. I'm not sure why. Nostalgia for an older, quieter time perhaps.

A posse of dusty children, some carrying infants on their hips, amuse themselves by ringing doorbells and skittering away hiccuping with delight. Their emaciated parents, hauling cement and bricks around in the deep pits dug for new basements, would not look out of place on a construction site in ancient Egypt, heaving stones for a pharaoh's pyramid. A small donkey with kind eyes walks past me carrying bricks in its saddlebags. The post-blast announcements being made in English and Hindi on the loudspeaker in the police booth in the market are fainter here: "Please report any unidentified baggage or suspicious-looking person to the nearest police post . . ."

Even in the few months since I was last here, the number of cars parked in the back lane has grown—and most are bigger, swisher. My neighbor Mrs. Mehra's new driver, his whole head wrapped in a brown muffler with a slit for his eyes, is hosing down a new cream Toyota Corolla as though it's a buffalo. It has a small saffron OM painted on its bonnet. Only a year ago Mrs. Mehra was flinging her garbage straight from her first-floor balcony on to the street. I wonder whether owning a Toyota has improved her sense of community hygiene.

I can see that most of the apartments on the second and third floors have been smartened up, glassed in.

The black bulls that lived around the concrete lamp post opposite my back gate for many years, fed and spoiled by Mrs. Mehra and her cow-worshipping cohorts, aren't around. Maybe they've gone for a jog.

Two young women in smart winter coats and clicking high heels walk past, both smoking cigarettes. They look like Russian or Ukrainian whores, the kind you can dial up for farmhouse parties. There were a few at my old friend Bobby Singh's stag party in Mehrauli last week. One of them, who walked around with a plate of tacos, was actually a Dip—she was topless, more or less—with hummus all over her chest. I thought it was a bit much, but the other guests seemed to enjoy it. The girl gave that impression too—although that may have been part of the job description. Hard to say.

Servants wearing their employers' expensive cast-offs are being walked by even better-dressed dogs—Labradors, German shepherds, Dobermans, beagles, dachshunds, cocker spaniels—with wool coats that say things like *Superman* and *Woof!* Even some of the street mongrels have coats and show traces of pedigreed lineage. Trickledown. Ha! Ha!

Two men—one white, one Indian—go past, holding hands. Their plump black Labrador is dressed in a red-and-blue jersey

that says *No. 7 Manchester United*. Like a genial holy man distrib-
uting his blessings, he bestows a little squirt of piss on to the tires
of the cars he waddles past.

The sheet-metal gate of the Municipal Primary School that
abuts the deer park is new. It's painted over with a dreadful ren-
dition of a happy baby in its happy mother's arms being given
a polio vaccination by a happy nurse in a white dress and white
stockings. The syringe is roughly the size of a cricket bat. I can
hear children's voices in their classrooms, shouting *Baa baa black
sheep*, rising to a shriek on *Wool!* and *Full!*

Compared to Kabul, or anywhere else in Afghanistan or Pakistan, or for that matter any other country in our neighborhood
(Sri Lanka, Bangladesh, Burma, Iran, Iraq, Syria—Good God!)
this foggy little back lane, with its everyday humdrumness, its
vulgarity, its unfortunate but tolerable inequities, its donkeys and
its minor cruelties, is like a small corner of Paradise. The shops in
the market sell food and flowers and clothes and mobile phones,
not grenades and machine guns. Children play at ringing doorbells, not at being suicide bombers. We have our troubles, our
terrible moments, yes, but these are only aberrations.

I feel a rush of anger at those grumbling intellectuals and professional dissenters who constantly carp about this great country.
Frankly, they can only do it because they are allowed to. And
they are allowed to because, for all our imperfections, we are a
genuine democracy. I would not be crass enough to say this too
often in public, but the truth is that it gives me great pride to be
a servant of the Government of India.

The back gate was open, as I expected it to be. (The ground-
floor tenants have painted it lavender.) I went straight up the
stairs to the second floor. The door was locked. The extent of
my disappointment unsettled me. The landing looked deserted.
There was mail and old newspapers piled up against the door. I
noticed a dog's paw-prints in the dust.

On my way down, the plump, pretty wife of my ground-floor tenant, who runs some sort of video production company, came out of her kitchen and accosted me on the stairs. She invited me in for a cup of tea (to what used to be my home when my wife and I were both posted in Delhi).

"I'm Ankita," she said over her shoulder as she led me in. Her long, chemically straightened hair streaked with blonde highlights was damp and I could smell her tangy shampoo. She wore solitaires in her ears and a fuzzy white wool sweater. The back pockets of her tight blue jeans—"jeggings," my daughters say they're called—stretched over her generous behind were embroidered with colorful forked-tongued Chinese dragons. My mother would have approved, if not of the clothes, then certainly of the plumpness. *Dekhte besh Rolypoly*, she'd have said. My poor mother, who spent all of her married life in Delhi, dreaming of her childhood in Calcutta.

The word set up an annoying buzz in my head. Rolypolyrolypolyrolypoly.

Three of the four walls in the room were painted watermelon pink. All the furniture including the dining table was a sort of flecked—*distressed*, I believe is the right word—rind green. The door and window frames were black (the seeds, I suppose). I began to regret having given them a free hand with the interior. Ankita and I sat facing each other, separated by the length of the sofa (my old sofa, re-upholstered now). At one point we had to clasp our knees and lift our feet off the floor while her maid passed below us, shuffling on her haunches like a small duck, swabbing the floor with something that smelled sharp, like citronella. Would it have been so difficult for Rolypoly to have had that section of her floor swabbed a little later? When will our people learn some basic etiquette?

The maid was obviously a Gond or a Santhal from Jharkhand or Chhattisgarh, or perhaps one of the aboriginal tribes in Orissa.

She looked like a child of maybe fourteen or fifteen. From where I sat I could see down her kurta to where a tiny silver crucifix nestled between her tiny breasts. My father, who had a reflexive hostility towards Christian missionaries and their flock, would have called her Hallelujah. For all his sophistication he possessed more than just a streak of impropriety.

Enthroned in her giant watermelon, looking radiantly out at me from under her halo of tinted hair, Rolypoly gave me a whispered, incoherent account of what had happened upstairs. "I think so she is not a normal person," she said, more than once. To be fair, perhaps she was coherent and I was hostile to the idea of hearing her out. She said something about a baby and the police ("I was dump-struck when police knocked on the door") and bringing disrepute to the house and the entire neighborhood. It all sounded a bit vicious and far-fetched. I thanked her and left with the gift she pressed into my hands—a DVD of her husband's latest documentary on the Dal Lake in Kashmir made for the Department of Tourism.

An hour or two later, here I am. I've had to bring in a locksmith from the market to fashion a key for me. In other words, I've had to break in. My second-floor tenant seems to have left. "Left," if Rolypoly is to be believed, may be something of a euphemism. But then "tenant" is a euphemism too. No, we were not lovers. At no point did she ever offer me a hint that she might be open to a relationship of that sort. Had she, I don't know myself well enough to say how things might have turned out. Because all my life, ever since I first met her all those years ago when we were still in college, I have constructed myself around her. Not around *her* perhaps, but around the memory of my love for her. She doesn't know that. Nobody does, except perhaps Naga, Musa and me, the men who loved her.

I use the word *love* loosely, and only because my vocabulary is unequal to the task of describing the precise nature of that maze, that forest of feelings that connected the three of us to her and eventually to each other.

The first time I saw her was almost exactly thirty years ago, in 1984 (who in Delhi can forget 1984?), at the rehearsals of a college play in which I was acting, called *Norman, Is That You?* Sadly, after rehearsing it for two months we never performed it. A week before it was meant to open, Mrs. G—Indira Gandhi—was assassinated by her Sikh bodyguards.

For a few days after the assassination, mobs led by her supporters and acolytes killed thousands of Sikhs in Delhi. Homes, shops, taxi stands with Sikh drivers, whole localities where Sikhs lived were burned to the ground. Plumes of black smoke climbed into the sky from the fires all over the city. From my window seat in a bus on a bright, beautiful day, I saw a mob lynch an old Sikh gentleman. They pulled off his turban, tore out his beard and necklaced him South Africa–style with a burning tire while people stood around baying their encouragement. I hurried home and waited for the shock of what I had witnessed to hit me. Oddly, it never did. The only shock I felt was shock at my own equanimity. I was disgusted by the stupidity, the futility of it all, but somehow, I was not shocked. It could be that my familiarity with the gory history of the city I had grown up in had something to do with it. It was as though the Apparition whose presence we in India are all constantly and acutely aware of had suddenly surfaced, snarling, from the deep, and had behaved exactly as we expected it to. Once its appetite was sated it sank back into its subterranean lair and normality closed over it. Maddened killers retracted their fangs and returned to their daily chores—as clerks, tailors, plumbers, carpenters, shopkeepers—life went on as before. Normality in our part of the world is a bit like a boiled egg: its humdrum surface conceals at its heart a yolk of egregious violence. It is our constant anxiety about that violence, our memory of its past labors and our dread of its future manifestations, that lays down the rules for how a people as complex and as diverse as we are continue to coexist—continue to live together, tolerate each other and, from time to time, murder one another. As long as the center holds, as long as the yolk doesn't run, we'll be fine. In moments of crisis it helps to take the long view.

We decided to postpone the opening of the play by a month in the hope that by then things would have settled down. But in early December tragedy struck again, this time even harder. The Union Carbide pesticide plant in Bhopal sprang a deadly gas leak that killed thousands of people. The newspapers were full of accounts of people trying to flee the poisonous cloud that pursued them, their eyes and lungs on fire. There was something almost biblical about the nature and the scale of the horror. News magazines published photographs of the dead, the ill, the dying, the mangled and the permanently blinded, their sightless eyes eerily turned towards the cameras. Eventually we decided that the gods weren't with us and that performing *Norman* would be inappropriate for the times, so the whole thing was shelved. If you'll pardon me for making this somewhat prosaic observation—maybe that's what life is, or ends up being most of the time: a rehearsal for a performance that never eventually materializes. In the case of *Norman*, though, we didn't need a final performance to change the course of our lives. The rehearsals turned out to be more than enough.

David Quartermaine, the director of the play, was a young Englishman who had moved to Delhi from Leeds. He was a lean, athletic and, if I may say so, devastatingly beautiful man. His blond hair fell to his shoulders, his eyes were an unreal, sapphire blue, like Peter O'Toole's. He was stoned most of the time, and was candidly homosexual, although he never brought it up in conversation. A parade of dusky adolescent boys—the turnover was high—passed through his book-lined rooms in Defense Colony. They lounged on his bed or curled up on his rocking chair, flipping through magazines they obviously couldn't read (he had a clear preference for proletarians). We had never seen anything remotely like it. The day we gathered in his two-room flat for the first play-reading, his silent, efficient maid had efficiently delivered her third child in his bathroom. We lived in awe of David Quartermaine, of his audacious sexuality, his collection of books, his moodiness, his mumbling and his sudden enigmatic silences, which we believed were the prerequisite characteristics of a true artist. Some of us tried to replicate that behavior in our free time, imagining we were preparing ourselves for a life in the theater. My classmate Naga, Nagaraj Hariharan, was cast as Norman. I was to play his lover, Garson Hobart. (In the early rehearsals we hammed it up more than just a little. I suppose in our young, stupid way we were trying to signal that we weren't really homosexual.) We were both finishing our master's in history at Delhi University. As a consequence of his parents and mine being friends (his father was in the Foreign Service, mine was a senior heart surgeon), Naga and I had been together through school and now university. Like most such children we were never close friends. We didn't dislike each other, but our relationship had always been more than a little adversarial.

Tilo was a third-year student at the Architecture School and was working on the sets and lighting design. She introduced herself to us as Tilottama. The moment I saw her, a part of me walked out of my body and wrapped itself around her. And there it still remains.

I wish I knew what it was about her that disarmed me so completely and made me behave like someone I am not—solicitous, a little overeager. She didn't look like any of the pale, well-groomed girls I knew at college. Her complexion was what the French might call *café au lait* (with very little *lait*), which, as far as most Indians were concerned, disqualified her straightaway from being considered good-looking. It's hard for me to describe someone who has been imprinted on me, on my soul, like a stamp or a seal of some sort for so many years. I see her as I see a limb of mine—a hand, or a foot. But let me try, if only in the broadest brushstrokes. She had a small, fine-boned face and a straight nose, with pert, flared nostrils. Her long, thick hair was neither straight nor curly, but tangled and uncared for. I could imagine small birds nesting in it. It would have easily made the Before part of a Before-and-After shampoo commercial. She wore it down her back in a plait and sometimes twisted into an untidy knot at the nape of her long neck with a yellow pencil stuck through it. She wore no make-up and did nothing—none of those delightful things girls do, with their hair, or their eyes, or their mouths—to augment her looks. She wasn't tall, but she was rangy, and she had a way of standing, with her weight on the balls of her feet, her shoulders squared, that was almost masculine, and yet wasn't. The day I first met her she was wearing white cotton pajamas and a hideous—the hideousness somehow deliberate—printed, oversized man's shirt that didn't seem to belong to her. (I was wrong about that: weeks later, when we got to know each other better, she told us that it was indeed hers. That she had bought it at the second-hand clothes market outside Jama Masjid for one rupee. Naga—typically—told her that he knew from reliable sources that the clothes sold there were taken off the bodies of people who died in train accidents. She said she didn't mind as long as there were no bloodstains.) The only jewelry she wore was a broad silver ring on a long, ink-stained middle finger and a silver toe-ring. She smoked Ganesh beedis that she kept in a scarlet Dunhill cigarette packet. She would look right through the disappointment on the faces of those who had tried to scam what they thought was an imported filter cigarette off her and ended up instead with a beedi that they were too embarrassed not to smoke, especially when she was offering to light it for them. I saw this happen a number of times, but her expression always remained impassive—there was never a smile or the exchange of an amused glance with a friend, so I never could tell whether she was playing a practical joke or whether this was just the way she did things. The complete absence of a desire to please, or to put someone at their ease, could, in a less vulnerable person, have been construed as arrogance. In her it came across as a kind of reckless aloneness. Behind her plain, unfashionable spectacles, her slightly slanting cat-eyes had the insouciant secretiveness of a pyromaniac. She gave the impression that she had somehow slipped off her leash. As though she was taking herself for a walk while the rest of us were being walked—like pets. As though she was watching considerately, somewhat absent-mindedly, from a distance, while we minced along, grateful to our owners, happy to perpetuate our bondage.

I tried to find out more about her, but she gave very little away. When I asked her what her surname was, she said her name was S. Tilottama. When I asked what S stood for she said, "S stands for S." She evaded my indirect questions about where home was, what her father did. She didn't speak much Hindi at the time. So I guessed South India. Her English was curiously unaccented, except that Z sometimes softened into S, so, for example, she would say "Sip" for "Zip." I guessed Kerala.

It turned out that I was right about that. About the rest—I learned that she wasn't being evasive; she genuinely did not have answers to those ordinary college-kid questions: Where are you from? What does your father do? Et cetera and so on. From stray wisps of conversation I gathered that her mother was a single woman whose husband had left her, or she had left him, or he was dead—it was all a bit of a mystery. Nobody seemed to be able to *place* her. There were rumors that she was an adopted child. And rumors that she was not. Later I learned—from a college junior, a fellow called Mammen P. Mammen, a gossipmonger from Tilo's home town—that both rumors were true. Her mother was indeed her real mother, but had first abandoned her and then adopted her. There had been a scandal, a love affair in a small town. The man, who belonged to an "Untouchable" caste (a "Paraya," Mammen P. Mammen whispered, as though even to say it aloud would contaminate him), had been dispensed with in the ways high-caste families in India—in this case Syrian Christians from Kerala—traditionally dispense with inconveniences such as these. Tilo's mother was sent away until the baby was born and placed in a Christian orphanage. In a few months she returned to the orphanage and adopted her own child. Her family disowned her. She remained unmarried. To support herself she started a small kindergarten school which, over the years, had grown into a successful high school. She never publicly admitted—understandably—that she was the real mother. That was about as much as I knew.

Tilottama never went home for her holidays. She never said why. Nobody came looking for her. She paid her fees by working in architects' offices as a draftsman after college hours and on weekends and holidays. She didn't live in the hostel—she said she couldn't afford it. Instead she lived in a shack in a nearby slum that was strung along the outer walls of an old ruin. None of us was invited to visit her.

During the rehearsals of *Norman*, she called Naga Naga, but me, for some reason, she only ever addressed as Garson Hobart. So there we were, Naga and I, students of history, wooing a girl who didn't seem to have a past, a family, a community, a people, or even a home. Actually Naga wasn't really wooing her. In those days he was mesmerized more by himself than anybody else. He noticed Tilo and switched on his (considerable) charm, like you might switch on the headlights of a car, only because she didn't pay attention to him. He wasn't used to that.

I was never entirely sure what the relationship between Musa—Musa Yeswi—and Tilo really was. They were quiet with each other in company, never demonstrative. Sometimes they seemed more like siblings than lovers. They were classmates in Architecture School. Both exceptionally gifted artists. I had seen some of their work, Tilo's charcoal and crayon portraits, Musa's watercolors of the ruins of the older cities of Delhi, Tughlakabad, Feroz Shah Kotla and Purana Qila, and his pencil drawings of horses—sometimes just parts of horses—a head, an eye, a wild mane, galloping hooves. I once asked him about those, whether he drew them from photographs or copied them from illustrations in books, or whether he had horses at home in Kashmir. He said he dreamed about them. I found that disquieting. I don't pretend to know much about art, but to my layman's eye, those drawings, both his and Tilo's, looked distinctive and dazzling. I remember they both had similar handwriting—that casual, angular calligraphy that used to be taught in architecture schools before everything came to be computerized.

I can't say that I knew Musa well. He was a quiet, conservatively dressed boy, compactly built and only about as tall as Tilo was. His reticence may have had something to do with the fact that his English wasn't fluent and he spoke it with a distinctly Kashmiri accent. He had a way of being in company without drawing any attention to himself, which was something of a skill, because he was striking-looking, in the way many young Kashmiri men can be. Though he wasn't tall, he was broad-shouldered, and there was a concealed sinewiness to his compactness. He had jet-black hair, which he wore cropped very short. His eyes were a dark browngreen. He was clean-shaven, his smooth, pale skin a sharp contrast to Tilo's complexion. I remember two things about him clearly: a chipped front tooth (which made him look ridiculously young when he smiled, which he seldom did) and his surprising hands—they were not the hands of an artist at all— they were a peasant's hands, big and strong, with stocky fingers.

There was a gentleness to Musa, a serenity, which I liked,

although it was probably those very qualities that coalesced into something dreadful later on. I'm certain he was aware of what I felt about Tilo, yet he showed no signs of feeling either threatened or triumphant. That, in my eyes, gave him tremendous dignity. In his relationship with Naga I think there was less equanimity, which in all probability had more to do with Naga than with Musa. Naga showed a peculiar insecurity and lack of grace when he was around Musa.

The contrast between the two of them was remarkable. If Musa was (or at least gave the impression of being) solid, dependable, a rock—Naga was breezy and mercurial. It was impossible to relax around him. He couldn't be in a room without directing all the attention towards himself. He was a great showman; boisterous, witty, a bit of a bully, and utterly, hilariously merciless with the people he chose to publicly pick on. He was nice-looking, slim, boyish, a good cricketer (off-spinner), with floppy hair and glasses—very much the cool, intellectual sportsman. But more than his looks, it was his roguish appeal that girls seemed to love. They flocked around him giddily, hanging on to his every word, giggling at his jokes even when they weren't funny. It was hard to keep track of his string of girlfriends. He had that chameleon-like quality that good actors have—the ability to alter his physical appearance, not superficially, but radically, depending on who he had decided to be at that particular moment in his life. When we were young, it was all very entertaining and exhilarating. Everybody looked forward to what Naga's newest avatar was going to be. But as we grew older it became a little hollow and tiresome.

After they graduated from Architecture School, Musa and Tilo seemed to have drifted apart. He returned to Kashmir. She got a job as a junior architect in an architectural firm. Her main responsibility at work, she told me, was to take the blame for other people's mistakes. With her meager salary (she was paid by the hour) she upgraded herself from the slum and rented a ramshackle room near the dargah of Hazrat Nizamuddin Auliya. I visited her there a few times.

On the last of those visits we sat by Mirza Ghalib's grave, in a pool of beedi and cigarette stubs, surrounded by the spectacular cripples, lepers, vagrants and freaks who always accumulate around holy places in India, and drank some thick, terrible tea.

"This is how we treat the memory of our greatest poet," I remember saying, somewhat pretentiously—at the time I knew nothing of Ghalib's poetry. (I do now. I have to. For professional reasons. Because nothing warms the subcontinental Muslim's heart more than a few well-chosen lines of Urdu verse.)

"Maybe he's happier this way," she said.

Later we walked through the beggar-lined lanes to the dargah for the Thursday-night qawwali. It wasn't the best qawwali I had ever heard, but the foreign tourists closed their eyes and swayed in ecstasy.

After the last song was sung, and the musicians packed away their battered instruments, we walked down the dark road that ran behind the colony, along the banks of a storm-water drain that smelled like a sewer, and climbed the steep, narrow stairs to her room. Her dusty terrace was stacked with someone's— probably her landlord's—discarded furniture, the wood bleached white by the sun. A ginger tomcat yowled in sexual desperation for the female who had barricaded herself inside a nest of loose wicker that had come undone from the seat of a broken chair. I probably remember him so clearly because he reminded me of myself.

The room was tiny, more like a storeroom than a room. It was bare except for a string cot, a terracotta *matka* for water and a cardboard carton with clothes and some books. An electric ring on an old jeep windscreen propped up on bricks functioned as the kitchen. A skillful, larger-than-life crayon drawing of an iridescent, purple-blue rooster took up one whole wall and regarded us with a stern yellow eye. It was as though, to make up for the lack of real ones, Tilo had conjured up a graffiti parent to keep an eye on her.

I was relieved to escape the rooster's irascible gaze when we went out on to the terrace. We smoked some hashish, got bitten by mosquitoes and laughed a lot at absolutely nothing. Tilo sat cross-legged, perched on top of the parapet wall, looking out at the darkness. A mottled moon rose, its other-worldly beauty at odds with the sharp, very worldly fumes from the open drain across the road. Suddenly a stone spun up at us from the street below, missing Tilo by a whisker. She jumped off the wall, but did not seem unduly perturbed.

"It's the crowd from the cinema hall. The last show must be over."

I looked down. I could hear sniggering, but couldn't see anybody in the shadows. I have to admit that I was a little unnerved. I asked her—it was a stupid question—what precautions she took to make sure she stayed safe. She said she didn't dispute the rumor in the neighborhood that she worked for a well-known drug dealer. That way, she said, people assumed she had protection.

I decided to brazen it out and ask about Musa, where he was, whether they were still together, whether they planned to get married. She said, "I'm not marrying anybody." When I asked her why she felt that way, she said she wanted to be free to die irresponsibly, without notice and for no reason.

At home that night I fell asleep thinking of the chasm that separated my life from hers. I still lived in the house I was born in. My parents were asleep in the next room. I could hear the familiar hum of our noisy refrigerator. All the objects—the carpets, the cupboards, the armchairs in the drawing room, the Jamini Roy paintings, the first editions of Tagore's books in Bengali as well as

English, my father's collection of mountaineering books (it was a hobby, he wasn't a climber), the family photo albums, the trunks in which our winter clothes were kept, the bed I had slept in since I was a boy—were like sentinels that had watched over me for so many years. True, my adult life lay ahead, but the foundations on which that life would be built seemed so immutable, so unassailable. Tilo, on the other hand, was like a paper boat on a boisterous sea. She was absolutely alone. Even the poor in our country, brutalized as they were, had families. How would she survive? How long would it be before her boat went down?

After I joined the Bureau and left for my training, I lost touch with her.

The next time I saw her was at her wedding.

I don't know what brought her and Musa together again all those years later, or how she came to be on that houseboat with him in Srinagar.

Given what I knew of him, I have never understood how that storm of dull, misguided vanity—the absurd notion that Kashmir could have "freedom"—swept him up as it did a whole generation of young Kashmiri men. It's true that he suffered the kind of tragedy that nobody ever should—but Kashmir was a war zone then. I can put my hand on my heart and swear that, whatever the provocation, I would never contemplate doing what he did.

But then he wasn't me, and I wasn't him. He did what he did. And he paid the price for it. As ye sow, so shall ye reap.

Within weeks of Musa's death, Tilo married Naga.

As for me, the least remarkable of us all—I loved her without pride. And without hope. Without hope, because I knew that even if by some remote chance she had reciprocated my feelings, my parents, my Brahmin parents, would never accept her—the girl without a past, without a caste—into the family. Had I persevered, it would have meant an upheaval of the sort that I simply did not have the stomach for. Even in the most uneventful of lives, we are called upon to choose our battles, and this one wasn't mine.

Now, these years later, my parents are both dead. And I'm what's known as a "family man." My wife and I tolerate each other and adore our children. Chitra—Chittaroopa—my wife (yes, my Brahmin wife), is in the Foreign Service and is posted to Prague. Our daughters, Rabia and Ania, are seventeen and fifteen. They stay with their mother and attend the French School. Rabia hopes to study English literature and young Ania is dead set on a career in human rights law. It's an unorthodox choice, and her determination, her refusal to even consider other options, is a little odd, especially for one so young. I was troubled about it at first. I wondered whether it was her way of staging a subtle version of a teenage rebellion against her father. But that doesn't seem to be the case at all. Over the last ten years or so the field of human rights has become a perfectly respectable and even lucrative profession. I have been nothing short of encouraging with her. In any case, a final decision is still a few years away. We'll see what happens. Both the girls are good students. Chitra and I have been promised a joint posting soon—hopefully in the country where the girls will be at university.

I never imagined I would ever do anything to upset or harm my family in any way. But when Tilo walked back into my life, those legal ties, those lofty, moral principles, atrophied and even seemed a little absurd. As it turned out my anxiety was irrelevant—she did not seem to even notice my dilemma or discomfort.

By renting these rooms to her when she needed them, I told myself I was making up for my trespasses tactfully and unobtrusively. I say "trespasses" because I have always felt that I had failed her in a nebulous and yet fundamental way. She didn't seem to see it like that at all—but then she wasn't that sort of person.

. . .

I had only seen her on and off since she married Naga. Their wedding in Delhi remains burned into my memory, and not because of what might seem to be the obvious reasons—heartbreak or thwarted love. That, in fact, was the least of it. I was reasonably happy at the time. My own marriage was less than two years old; there was still some semblance of real affection between me and my wife, if not love. The sapping brittleness that marks my relationship with Chitra now had not set in yet.

By the time Tilo and he got married, Naga had already made the many transitions from an irreverent, iconoclastic student to an unemployable intellectual on the radical Left, to being a passionate advocate of the Palestinian cause (his hero at the time was George Habash), and then on to mainstream journalism. Like many noisy extremists, he has moved through a whole spectrum of extreme political opinion. What has remained consistent is only the decibel level. Now Naga has a handler—though he may not see it quite that way—in the Intelligence Bureau. With a senior position at his paper, he is a valuable asset for us.

His journey to the dark side, if that's what you want to call it—I wouldn't—began with the usual bit of quid pro quo. His beat was the Punjab. The insurgency had more or less been crushed by then. But Naga spent his time digging up old stories, providing ammunition for those farcical parodies called "People's tribunals," after which they brought out even more farcical "People's charge-sheets" against the police and the paramilitary. An administration that was at war with a ruthless insurgency cannot be held to the same standards as one that is functioning in ordinary, peaceful conditions. But who was to explain that to a crusading journalist who wrote his copy with the sound of applause permanently ringing in his ears? On one of his vacations from this brand of performative radicalism, Naga went to Goa and, in typical Naga fashion, fell wildly in love and impulsively married a young Australian hippy. Lindy, I think she was called. (Or was it Charlotte? I'm not sure. It doesn't matter. I'll stay with Lindy.) Within a year of their marriage, Lindy was arrested in Goa for heroin trafficking. She faced the prospect of several years in prison. Naga was beside himself. His father was an influential man and could easily have helped, but Naga—a late arrival in his father's life—had always had a troubled relationship with him and didn't want him to know. So he called me and I pulled a few strings. The Director General of Police in Punjab spoke to his counterpart in Goa. We got Lindy out of custody and had the charges dropped. As soon as she was released, Lindy caught the first plane home to Perth. In a few months Naga and she were formally divorced. Naga continued his work in Punjab, needless to say, a considerably chastened man.

When we needed a journalist's help on a small matter, a case that human rights activists were making a noise about, though as usual many of their facts needed correcting, I called Naga. He helped. And so it went. A collaboration was born.

Gradually Naga began to enjoy the head start he had over his colleagues because of the briefings he received from us. It was a great irony—another kind of drug racket. This time around we were the drug dealers. He was our addict. In a few years he rose to become a star reporter and a sought-after security analyst in the media firmament. When his relationship with the Bureau promised to become more than a temporary association—a marriage and not just a one-night stand—I thought it prudent to step out of the way. A colleague of mine, R. C. Sharma—Ram Chandra Sharma—took over. R.C. and he got on very well. They shared the same cruel sense of humor and a love for rock 'n' roll and the blues. The one thing I will say for Naga is that not a rupee ever changed hands. About that he was—and continues to be—honest to a fault. Since his idea of professional integrity requires him to live by his principles, in order to remain a person of integrity, he has changed his principles, and now believes in us almost more than we believe in ourselves. What an irony for the schoolboy whose favorite taunt was to call me the "Running Dog of Imperialism" at an age when most of us were still reading *Archie* comics.

I'm not sure where and from whom Naga learned the fiery language of the Left. Perhaps from a relative who was communist. Whoever it was, he—or she—was a good teacher and Naga deployed what he learned spectacularly. It took him from conquest to conquest. I was once pitted against him in a school debate. We must have been thirteen or fourteen years old. The topic was "Does God Exist?" I was to speak for, and Naga against, the motion. I spoke first. Then Naga delivered his flaming speech, his skinny body taut as a whipcord, his voice quavering with indignation. Our mesmerized classmates took diligent notes of his blatant blasphemy: "The falsehood of our 330 million mute idols, the selfish deities we call Ram and Krishna are not going to save us from hunger, disease and poverty. Our foolish faith in monkeys and elephant-headed apparitions is not going to feed our starving masses . . ." I didn't stand a chance. Naga's speech made mine sound as though it had been written by a pious, elderly aunt. Oddly, though I have a clear, raw memory of my feeling of utter inadequacy, I have no memory of what I actually said. For months after that, I would secretly declaim Naga's sacrilege to myself in the mirror: "Our foolish faith in monkeys and elephant-headed apparitions is not going to feed our starving masses . . ." my atomized spit landing on my own reflection like rain.

Another of Naga's milestone performances came a few years later, at a college annual cultural event. Fresh from a summer trip to Bastar with two of his friends, where they had camped in the forest and walked through villages peopled by primitive tribes, Naga ambled on to the stage, long-haired, barefoot, bare-bodied, wearing only a loincloth, with a bow and a quiver of arrows slung over his shoulders. He made a great show of crunching what he claimed was termites on toast, eliciting breathless expressions of coy disgust from the girls in the audience, most of whom wanted to marry him. After swallowing the last morsel of toast, he went up to the microphone and performed the Stones' "Sympathy for the Devil," vocalizing the background score, simulating the chords on an imaginary guitar. He was a good, maybe even excellent, singer, but I found the whole thing distasteful, and thought it showed a deep disrespect for indigenous people as well as for Mick Jagger, who, at that point in my life, I believed was God. (I wish I had thought of that for my pro-God speech in school.) I actually took it upon myself to say so to him. Naga laughed and insisted that his performance was a tribute to both.

Today, as the saffron tide of Hindu Nationalism rises in our country like the swastika once did in another, Naga's "foolish faith" schoolboy speech would probably get him expelled, if not by the school authorities, then certainly by some sort of parents' campaign. In fact, in today's climate, to get away with just expulsion would be lucky. People are being lynched for far less. Even my colleagues in the Bureau don't seem to be able to see the difference between religious faith and patriotism. They seem to want a sort of Hindu Pakistan. Most of them are conservative, closet Brahmins who wear their sacred threads inside their safari suits, and their sacred ponytails dangling down the inside of their vegetarian skulls. They tolerate me only because I am a fellow Twice-born (actually, the caste I belong to is Baidya, but we count ourselves as Brahmin). Still, I keep my opinions to myself. Naga on the other hand has slid into the new dispensation in one smooth slither. His old irreverence has vanished without a trace. In his current avatar he wears a tweed blazer and smokes cigars. I haven't met him in years, but I see him playing the National Security expert on those excitable TV shows—he doesn't seem to even realize that he's not much more than a ventriloquist's bright puppet. It saddens me sometimes, to see him so housebroken. Naga is perpetually experimenting with his facial hair. Sometimes he sports a French goatee, sometimes a twirled, waxed, Daliesque mustache, sometimes he affects designer stubble, and sometimes he's clean-shaven. He can't seem to settle on a "look." It's the Achilles heel in his rig-out of opinionated self-importance. It gives him away. Or at least that's the way I see it.

Unfortunately of late he has begun to overplay his hand, and his intemperance is becoming a liability. Twice in two years the Bureau has had to intervene (discreetly of course) with the proprietors of his newspaper, to settle squabbles he has had with his editor that ended in impulsive resignations. The last time around we pulled off a coup. We had him reinstated with a raise.

If being together in kindergarten, school and university, and playing homosexual lovers in a play wasn't enough, during the years that I was posted to Srinagar, as Deputy Station Head for the Bureau, Naga was the Kashmir correspondent for his newspaper. He wasn't stationed in Kashmir, but lived there most days of the month. He had a permanent room at Ahdoos Hotel, where most reporters stayed. His relationship with the Bureau had been cemented by then, but was not as evident as it is now. It suited us much better that way. To his readers—and possibly even to himself—he was still the intrepid journalist who could be trusted to expose the so-called crimes of the Indian State.

It must have been well past midnight when the call came through on the Governor's hotline at the Forest Guest House in Dachigam National Park, about twenty kilometers out of Srinagar. I was there as part of His Excellency's entourage. (We were well into the Troubles by then. The civilian government had been dismissed; it was 1996, the sixth straight year of Governor's Rule in the State.)

His Excellency, a former Chief of the Indian Army, liked to get away from the bloodletting in the city as often as he could. He spent his weekends in Dachigam, strolling along a rushing mountain stream with his family and friends, while the children in the party, each shadowed by a tense, heavily armed security guard, mowed down imaginary militants (who shouted *Allah-hu-Akbar!* as they died) and chased long-tailed marmots into their holes. They usually had a picnic lunch, but dinner was always back at the guest house—rice and curried trout from the fish farm close by. The ponds in the hatchery were so thick with fish that you could put your hand in—if you could stand the close-to-freezing temperature—and pick out your own thrashing rainbow trout.

It was autumn. The forest was heart-stoppingly beautiful in the way only a Himalayan forest can be. The Chinar trees had begun to turn color. The meadows were a coppery gold. If you were lucky you might spot a black bear or a leopard or Dachigam's famous deer, the hangul. (Naga used to call one of Kashmir's famously randy ex–Chief Ministers the "well-hung ghoul." It was a clever pun, I have to admit, though of course most people didn't get it.) I had become something of a bird man—a passion that has remained with me—and could tell a Himalayan griffon from a bearded vulture and could identify the streaked laughing thrush, the orange bullfinch, Tytler's leaf warbler and the Kashmir flycatcher, which was threatened then, and must surely by now be extinct. The trouble with being in Dachigam was that it had the effect of unsettling one's resolve. It underlined the futility of it all. It made one feel that Kashmir really belonged to those creatures. That none of us who were fighting over it—Kashmiris, Indians, Pakistanis, Chinese (they have a piece of it too—Aksai Chin, which used to be part of the old Kingdom of Jammu and Kashmir), or for that matter Pahadis, Gujjars, Dogras, Pashtuns, Shins, Ladakhis, Baltis, Gilgitis, Purikis, Wakhis, Yashkuns, Tibetans, Mongols, Tatars, Mon, Khowars—none of us, neither saint nor soldier, had the right to claim the truly heavenly beauty of that place for ourselves. I was once moved to say so, quite casually, to Imran, a young Kashmiri police officer who had done some exemplary undercover work for us. His response was, "It's a very great thought, sir. I have the same love for animals as yourself. Even in my travels in India I feel the exact same feeling—that India belongs not to Punjabis, Biharis, Gujaratis, Madrasis, Muslims, Sikhs, Hindus, Christians, but to those beautiful creatures—peacocks, elephants, tigers, bears . . ."

He was polite to the point of being obsequious, but I knew what he was getting at. It was extraordinary; you couldn't—and still cannot—trust even the ones you assumed were on your side. Not even the damn *police*.

It had already snowed in the high mountains, but the border passes were still negotiable and small legations of fighters—gullible young Kashmiris and murderous Pakistanis, Afghans, even some Sudanese—who belonged to the thirty or so remaining terrorist groups (down from almost one hundred) were still making the treacherous journey across the Line of Control, dying in droves on the way. Dying. Maybe that's an inadequate description. What was that great line in *Apocalypse Now*? "Terminate with Extreme Prejudice." Our soldiers' instructions at the Line of Control were roughly similar.

What else should they have been? "Call their mothers"?

The militants who managed to make it through rarely survived in the Valley for more than two or at most three years. If they weren't captured or killed by the security forces, they slaughtered each other. We guided them along that path, although they didn't need much assistance—they still don't. The Believers come with their guns, their prayer beads and their own Destroy-Yourselves Manual.

Yesterday a Pakistani friend forwarded me this—it's making the mobile phone rounds, so you may have seen it already:

I saw a man on a bridge about to jump.

I said, "Don't do it!"

He said, "Nobody loves me."

I said, "God loves you. Do you believe in God?"

He said, "Yes."

I said, "Are you a Muslim or a non-Muslim?"

He said, "A Muslim."

I said, "Shia or Sunni?"

He said, "Sunni."

I said, "Me too! Deobandi or Barelvi?"

He said, "Barelvi."

I said, "Me too! Tanzeehi or Tafkeeri?"

He said, "Tanzeehi."

I said, "Me too! Tanzeehi Azmati or Tanzeehi Farhati?"

He said, "Tanzeehi Farhati."

I said, "Me too! Tanzeehi Farhati Jamia ul Uloom Ajmer, or Tanzeehi Farhati Jamia ul Noor Mewat?"

He said, "Tanzeehi Farhati Jamia ul Noor Mewat."

I said, "Die, kafir!" and I pushed him over.

Thankfully some of them still have a sense of humor.

The inbuilt idiocy, this idea of jihad, has seeped into Kashmir from Pakistan and Afghanistan. Now, twenty-five years down the line, I think, to our advantage, we have eight or nine versions of the "True" Islam battling it out in Kashmir. Each has its own stable of Mullahs and Maulanas. Some of the most radical among them—those who preach against the idea of nationalism and in favor of the great Islamic Ummah—are actually on our payroll.

One of them was recently blown up outside his mosque by a bicycle bomb. He won't be hard to replace. The only thing that keeps Kashmir from self-destructing like Pakistan and Afghanistan is good old petit bourgeois capitalism. For all their religiosity, Kashmiris are great businessmen. And all businessmen eventually, one way or another, have a stake in the status quo—or what we call the "Peace Process," which, by the way, is an entirely different kind of business opportunity from peace itself.

The men who came were young, in their teens or early twenties. A whole generation virtually committed suicide. By '96 the border-crossings had slowed to a trickle. But we hadn't managed to completely stem the flow. We were investigating some disturbing intelligence we had received about our soldiers at some border security posts selling windows of "safe passage" during which they would look away discreetly while Gujjar shepherds, who knew those mountains like the backs of their hands, guided the contingents through. Safe Passage was only one of the things on the market. There was also diesel, alcohol, bullets, grenades, army rations, razor wire and timber. Whole forests were disappearing. Sawmills had been set up inside army camps. Kashmiri labor and Kashmiri carpenters had been press-ganged into service. The trucks in the army convoy that brought supplies up to Kashmir from Jammu every day returned loaded with carved walnut-wood furniture. If not the best-equipped, we certainly had the best-furnished—if I may coin a phrase—army in the world. But who's to interfere with a victorious army?

The mountains around Dachigam were comparatively quiet. Still, in addition to the paramilitary pickets permanently stationed there, each time His Excellency visited, Area Domination Patrols would go in a day ahead to secure the hills that looked down on to the route his armored convoy took, and Mine Proof Armored Vehicles would check the road for landmines. The park was permanently closed to local people. To secure the guest house, more than a hundred men were stationed on the roof, in watchtowers around the property and in concentric circles a kilometer deep into the forest. Not many folks in India would believe the lengths to which we had to go in Kashmir just to get our boss a little fresh fish.

I was up late that night finalizing my daily report for His Excellency's morning briefing. The volume on my old Sony player was turned low. Rasoolan Bai was singing a Chaiti, "Yahin thaiyan motiya hiraee gaeli Rama." Kesar Bai was undoubtedly our most accomplished female Hindustani vocalist, but Rasoolan was surely our most erotic. She had a deep, gravelly, masculine voice, quite unlike the high-pitched, virginal, permanently adolescent voice that has come to dominate our collective imagination through Bollywood soundtracks. (My father, a scholar of Hindustani classical music, thought Rasoolan was profane. It remained one of our many unresolved differences.) I could picture the string of pearls she sang about being broken in the urgency of lovemaking, her voice languorously following the beads as they skittered around the bedroom floor. (Ah yes, there was a time when a Muslim courtesan could so hauntingly invoke a Hindu deity.)

There had been serious trouble in the city that morning. The government had announced elections in a few months' time. They would be the first in almost nine years. The militants had announced a boycott. It was pretty clear then (unlike now when the queues at the voting booths are unmanageable) that people were not going to come out and vote without some serious persuasion on our part. The "free" press would be there in all its glorious idiocy, so we would have to be careful. Our Ace of Spades was to be the Ikhwan-ul-Muslimoon, the Muslim Brotherhood, our counter-insurgency force, an opportunistic militant group that had surrendered as a group—lock, stock and barrel.

Gradually its ranks were expanded by other disaggregated individuals who began to surrender ("cylinder" as Kashmiris called it) in droves. We had regrouped and rearmed them, and returned them to the fray. The Ikhwanis were rough men, mostly extortionists and petty criminals who had joined the militancy when they saw profit in that endeavor, and were the first to cylinder when the going got rough. They had the kind of access to local intelligence that we could never hope for, and once they had been turned around, they had the advantage of an ambiguous provenance that allowed them to carry out operations that were outside the mandate of our regular forces. At first they had proved to be an invaluable asset, but then had become increasingly hard to control. The most feared of them all, the Prince of Darkness himself, was a man known locally as Papa, who had once been nothing more than a factory watchman. In his illustrious career as an Ikhwan he had killed scores of people. (I think the number now stands at one hundred and three.) The terror he evoked did, at first, weigh the balance in our favor, but by '96 he had begun to outlive his usefulness and we were considering reining him in. (He's in prison now.) In March that year, without instructions from us, Papa had bumped off the well-known editor of an Urdu daily—an irresponsible Urdu daily, I have to say. (Irresponsible, virulently anti-India dailies that exaggerated body counts and got their facts wrong had their uses too—they undermined the local media in general and made it easier for us to tar them all with the same brush. To tell you the truth, we even funded some of them.) In May Papa had enclosed a community graveyard in Pulwama, claiming it was his ancestral property. Then he killed a much-loved village schoolteacher in a border village and threw his body into a no man's land that had been mined with IEDs. So the body couldn't be approached, there could be no funeral prayers, and the dead man's students had to watch the corpse of their teacher being picked at by kites and vultures.

Impressed by Papa's gains, other Ikhwanis had begun to follow his example.

That morning a group of them had stopped an old Kashmiri couple at a security barrier in downtown Srinagar. When the man refused to hand over his wallet they abducted him and drove away. People gathered and chased them all the way to the camp the Ikhwanis shared with the Border Security Force. The old man was thrown out of the Gypsy just outside the camp. Once they were inside they—how should I put it—they completely lost their marbles. They lobbed a grenade over the walls and then fired into the crowd with a machine gun. A boy was killed and a dozen or so people injured, half of them seriously. The Ikhwanis then went to the police station, threatened the police and prevented them from lodging a report. In the afternoon they ambushed the boy's funeral procession and made off with the coffin. Which meant there was no body, and therefore there could be no murder charge. By evening public protests had turned violent. Three police stations were burned down. The security forces fired at the crowds and killed fourteen more people. Curfew was declared in all the larger towns—Sopore, Baramulla and Srinagar of course.

When I heard the phone ring and His Excellency's aide-de-camp answer it, I assumed the trouble had got out of hand and they were calling to ask for fresh orders. That did not turn out to be the case.

The caller said he was speaking from the Joint Interrogation Center, the JIC, which functioned out of the Shiraz Cinema.

It isn't what it sounds like. We hadn't shut down a functioning cinema hall and turned it into an interrogation center. The Shiraz had been shut down years ago by an outfit called the Allah Tigers. It ordered the closing of all cinema halls, liquor shops and bars as being un-Islamic and "vehicles of India's cultural aggression." The proclamation was signed by an Air Marshal Noor Khan. The Tigers plastered the city with threatening posters and put bombs in bars. When the Air Marshal was finally captured he turned out to be a barely literate peasant from a remote mountain village who had probably never set eyes on an airplane. I was a junior member of a team of interrogators (it was before my Srinagar posting) who visited him and several other senior militants in prison in the hope of turning them around. He answered our questions with slogans, which he shouted out as though he was addressing a mass rally: *Jis Kashmir ko khoon se seencha, woh Kashmir hamara hai!* The Kashmir we have irrigated with our blood, that Kashmir is ours! Or the war cry of the Allah Tigers: *La Sharakeya wa La Garabeya, Islamia, Islamia!*—roughly: Neither East nor West, Islam is best!

The Air Marshal was a brave man and I almost envied him his clear-hearted, simple-minded fervor. He remained impenitent, even after a stint in Cargo. He's out now, after serving a long sentence. We still keep an eye on him and others like him. He seems to have stayed out of trouble. He earns a meager living selling stamps outside a district court in Srinagar. I'm told he is not in his right mind, although I cannot confirm that. Cargo could be a pretty rough place.

The ADC who answered the phone told me that the caller had given his name as Major Amrik Singh and had asked for me not just by designation but, unusually, also by name—Biplab Dasgupta, Deputy Station Head, India Bravo (radio code in Kashmir for the Intelligence Bureau).

I knew the fellow, not personally—I'd never set eyes on him—but by reputation. He was known as Amrik Singh "Spotter"—for his uncanny ability to spot the snake in the grass, the militant hidden among a crowd of civilians. (He's famous now, by the way. Posthumously. He killed himself recently—shot his wife, his three young sons and put a bullet through his own head. I can't say I'm sorry. Shame about the wife and children though.) Major Amrik Singh was a bad apple. No, let me rephrase that—he was a putrid apple, and was, at the time of that midnight phone call, at the center of a pretty putrid storm. A couple of months after I arrived in Srinagar, which was in January of 1995, Amrik Singh had, on orders quite likely, apprehended a well-known lawyer and human rights activist, Jalib Qadri, at a checkpoint. Qadri was a nuisance, a brash, abrasive man who did not know the meaning of nuance. The night he was arrested, he was due to leave for Delhi from where he was going to Oslo to depose at an international human rights conference. His arrest was only meant to prevent that silly circus from taking place. Amrik Singh apprehended Qadri publicly, in the presence of Qadri's wife, but the arrest was not formally registered, which was not unusual. There was an outcry about Qadri's "abduction," a much bigger one than we expected, so after a few days we thought it prudent to release the man. But he was nowhere to be found. A great hue and cry arose. We set up a search committee and tried to calm nerves. A few days later Jalib Qadri's body showed up in a sack floating down the Jhelum. It was in a terrible condition—skull smashed in, eyes gouged out, and so on. Even by Kashmir's standards, this was somewhat excessive. The level of public anger went off the charts—naturally—so the local police were permitted to file a case. A high-level committee was set up to look into the whole thing. Witnesses to the abduction, people who saw Qadri in Amrik Singh's custody in an army camp, people who witnessed the altercation between the two that sent Amrik Singh into a rage, actually came forward to give written statements, which was rare. Even Amrik Singh's accomplices, Ikhwanis most of them, were willing to turn approvers and testify against him in court. But then one by one their bodies began to turn up. In fields, in forests, by the side of the road . . . he killed them all. The army and the administration had to at least pretend to do something, although they couldn't really act against him. He knew too much and he made it clear that if he went down he would take as many people as he could down with him. He was cornered, and dangerous. It was decided the best thing to do would be to get him out of the country and find him asylum somewhere. Which is eventually what happened. But it couldn't be done at once. Not while the spotlight was on him. There had to be a cooling-off period. As a first step he was taken off field operations and given a desk job. In the Shiraz JIC, out of trouble's way. Or so we thought.

So this was the man who was calling me. I can't say I was longing to speak to him. A pestilence like that is best kept quarantined.

When I answered the phone he sounded excited. He spoke so fast it took me a while to realize he was speaking English and not Punjabi. He said they had captured an A-Category Terrorist, a Commander Gulrez, a dreaded Hizb-ul-Mujahideen commander, in a massive cordon-and-search operation on a houseboat.

This was Kashmir; the Separatists spoke in slogans and our men spoke in press releases; their cordon-and-search operations were always "massive," everybody they picked up was always "dreaded," seldom less than "A-category," and the recoveries they made from those they captured were always "war-like." It wasn't surprising, because each of those adjectives had a corresponding incentive—a cash reward, an honorable mention in their service dossier, a medal for bravery or a promotion. So, as you can imagine, that piece of information didn't exactly get my pulse going.

He said that the terrorist had been killed while trying to escape. That didn't do much for me either. It happened several times a day on a good day—or a bad day, depending on your perspective. So why was I being called in the middle of the night about something so routine? And what did his zealousness have to do with my department or with me?

A "ladies" had been captured along with Commander Gulrez, he said. She wasn't Kashmiri.

Now that was unusual. Unheard of, actually.

The "ladies" had been handed over to ACP Pinky, for interrogation.

We all knew Assistant Commandant Pinky Sodhi of the peach complexion and the long black braid worn coiled under her cap. Her twin brother, Balbir Singh Sodhi, was a senior police officer who had been shot down by militants in Sopore when he was out on his morning jog. (Foolish thing for a senior officer to do, even one who prided himself on, or, as it turned out, deluded himself about, being "loved" by the locals.) ACP Pinky had been given a job in the CRPF—Central Reserve Police Force—on compassionate grounds, as compensation to the family for the death of her brother. Nobody had ever seen her out of uniform. For all her stunning looks, she was a brutal interrogator who often exceeded her brief because she was exorcizing demons of her own. She wasn't in the Amrik Singh league, but still—God help any Kashmiri who fell into her hands. As for those who didn't fall into her hands—many of them were busy writing love poems to her and even proposing marriage. Such was ACP Pinky's fatal charm.

The "ladies" whom they had arrested, I was told, had refused to divulge her name. Since the captured "ladies" wasn't a Kashmiri, I imagined ACP Pinky had exercised some restraint and had not unleashed herself completely. Had she, then neither Ladies nor Gents would have been able to withhold information. Anyway, I was getting impatient. I still could not fathom what any of it had to do with me.

Finally Amrik Singh came to the point: during the interrogation, *my* name had come up. The woman had asked for a message to be passed on to me. He said he couldn't understand the message, but she said I'd understand. He read it, or rather spelled it, aloud over the phone:

G-A-R-S-O-N H-O-B-A-R-T

Rasoolan's voice, still searching for her scattered pearls, filled my head: *Kahan vaeka dhoondhoon re? Dhoondhat dhoondhat baura gaeli Rama . . .*

Garson Hobart must have sounded like a secret code for a militant strike, or an acknowledgment of receipt for a weapons consignment. The mad brute on the other end of the phone was waiting for an explanation from me. I couldn't think of how to even begin.

Could Commander Gulrez have something to do with Musa? *Was* he Musa? I had tried to get in touch with him several times after moving to Srinagar. I wanted to offer my condolences to him for what had happened to his family. I had never succeeded, which in those days usually meant only one thing. He was underground.

Who else could Tilo have been with? Had they killed Musa in front of her? Oh God.

I told Amrik Singh as curtly as I could that I would call him back.

My first instinct was to put as great a distance as possible between the woman I loved and myself. Does that make me a coward? If it does, at least I'm a candid one.

Even if I did want to go to her, it wasn't possible. I was in the middle of a jungle in the middle of the night. Moving out would have meant sirens, alarms, at least four jeeps and an armored vehicle. It would have meant taking along sixteen men at the very least. That was the minimum protocol. That kind of circus would not have helped Tilo. Or me. And it would have compromised His Excellency's security in ways that could have led to unthinkable consequences. It could have been a trap to draw me out. After all, Musa knew about Garson Hobart. It was paranoid thinking, but in those days there wasn't much daylight between caution and paranoia.

I was out of options. I dialed Ahdoos Hotel and asked for Naga. Fortunately he was there. He offered to go to the Shiraz immediately. The more concerned and helpful he sounded, the more annoyed I became. I could literally hear him growing into the role I was offering him, seizing with both hands the opportunity to do what he loved most—grandstand. His eagerness reassured and infuriated me at the same time.

I called Amrik Singh and told him to expect a journalist called Nagaraj Hariharan. Our man. I said that if they had nothing on the woman, they were to release her immediately and hand her over to him.

A few hours later Naga called to say Tilo was in the room next to his at Ahdoos. I suggested he put her on the morning flight to Delhi.

"She's not freight, Das-Goose," he said. "She says she's going for this Commander Gulrez's funeral. Whoever the hell that is."

Das-Goose. He hadn't called me that since college. In college, in his ultra-radical days, he would mockingly call me (for some reason always in a German accent) "Biplab Das-Goose-*da*"—his version of Biplab Dasgupta. The Revolutionary Brother Goose.

I never forgave my parents for naming me Biplab, after my paternal grandfather. Times had changed. By the time I was born the British were gone, we were a free country. How could they name a baby "Revolution"? How was anybody supposed to go through life with a name like that? At one point I did consider changing my name legally, to something a little more peaceful like Siddhartha or Gautam or something. I dropped the idea because I knew that with friends like Naga, the story would clatter behind me like a tin can tied to a cat's tail. So there I was—here I am—a Biplab, in the innermost chamber of the secret heart of the establishment that calls itself the Government of India.

"Was it Musa?" I asked Naga.

"She won't say. But who else could it have been?"

By Monday morning the weekend body count had risen to nineteen; the fourteen demonstrators killed in the firing, the boy the Ikhwanis had shot, Musa or Commander Gulrez or whatever the hell he called himself, and three bodies of militants killed in a shoot-out in Ganderbal. Hundreds of thousands of mourners had gathered to carry those nineteen coffins (which included an empty one for the boy whose body had been stolen) on their shoulders to the Martyrs' Graveyard.

The Governor's office called to say that it would not be advisable for us to attempt to return to the city until the following day. In the afternoon my secretary called:

"Sir, *sun lijiye*, please listen, sir . . ."

Sitting on the verandah of the Dachigam Forest Guest House, over birdsong and the sounds of crickets, I heard the reverberating boom of a hundred thousand or more voices raised together calling for freedom: *Azadi! Azadi! Azadi!* On and on and on. Even on the phone it was unnerving. Quite unlike hearing the Air Marshal shouting slogans in his prison cell. It was as though the city was breathing through a single pair of lungs, swelling like a throat with that urgent, keening cry. I had seen my share of demonstrations by then, and heard more than my share of slogan-shouting in other parts of the country. This was different, this Kashmiri chant. It was more than a political demand. It was an anthem, a hymn, a prayer. The irony was—is—that if you put four Kashmiris in a room and ask them to specify what exactly they mean by *Azadi*, what exactly are its ideological and geographic contours, they would probably end up slitting each other's throats. And yet it would be a mistake to chalk this down to confusion. Their problem is not confusion, not really. It's more like a terrible clarity that exists outside the language of modern geopolitics. All the protagonists on all sides of the conflict, especially us, exploited this fault line mercilessly. It made for a perfect war—a war that can never be won or lost, a war without end.

The chant that I heard on the phone that morning was condensed, distilled passion—and it was as blind and as futile as passion usually is. During those (fortunately short-lived) occasions when it was in full cry, it had the power to cut through the edifice of history and geography, of reason and politics. It had the power to make even the most hardened of us wonder, even if momentarily, what the hell we were doing in Kashmir, governing a people who hated us so viscerally.

The so-called martyrs' funerals were always a game of nerves. The police and security forces had orders to remain alert, but out of sight. This was not just because on those occasions tempers naturally ran high and a confrontation would inevitably lead to another massacre—this we had learned from bitter experience. The thinking was that permitting the population to vent its feelings and shout its slogans from time to time would prevent that anger from accumulating and building into an unmanageable cliff of rage. So far, in this more than quarter-century-long conflict in Kashmir, it has paid off. Kashmiris mourned, wept, shouted their slogans, but in the end they always went back home. Gradually, over the years, as it grew into a habit, a predictable, acceptable cycle, they began to distrust and disrespect themselves, their sudden fervors and their easy capitulations. That was an unplanned benefit that accrued to us.

Nevertheless, to allow half a million, sometimes even a million, people to take to the streets in *any* situation, let alone during an insurgency, is a serious gamble.

. . .

The following morning, once the streets had been secured, we returned to the city. I drove straight to Ahdoos to find that Tilo and Naga had checked out. Naga didn't return to Srinagar for a while. I was told he was on leave.

A few weeks later, I received an invitation for their wedding. I went of course, how could I not? I felt responsible for the travesty. For driving Tilo into the arms of a man I felt sure had been less than honest with her. I didn't think she would have been made privy to the relationship between her soon-to-be husband and the Intelligence Bureau. She would have thought she was marrying a campaigning journalist, seeker of justice, scourge of the establishment that had killed the man she loved. The deception made me angry, but of course I couldn't be the one to disabuse her of that notion.

The reception was on the moonlit lawns of Naga's parents' big white Art Deco house in Diplomatic Enclave. It was a small, exquisite affair, very unlike the overblown extravaganzas that have become so popular these days. There were white flowers everywhere, lilies, roses, cascading strings of jasmine, arranged in the most artful ways by Naga's mother and older sister, neither of whom looked, or even pretended to look, happy. The driveway and the flower beds were lined with clay lamps. Japanese lanterns hung from trees. Fairy lights were threaded through the branches. Old-world bearers in liveried costumes with brass buttons, red-and-gold cummerbunds and starched white turbans rushed about with trays of food and drink. A posse of mop-haired dogs smelling of perfume and cigarette smoke ran amok among the guests, like a small army of yapping, motorized floor swabs.

On a raised platform covered with white sheets, a band of musicians from Barmer, in white dhotis and kurtas and bright, printed turbans, transported us to the Rajasthan desert. Muslim folk musicians were an odd choice for a wedding of this kind. But my friend Naga was eclectic and had discovered them on a trip he'd made to the desert. They were outstanding performers. Their raw, haunting music opened up the city sky and shook the dust off the stars. The greatest of them all, Bhungar Khan, sang of the coming of the monsoon. In his wild, high, almost-female voice he transformed a song about the parched desert's ache for rain into a song about a woman yearning for the return of her lover. My memory of Tilo's wedding has always been imbued with that song.

It had been more than ten years since I had seen Tilo and shared that joint with her on her terrace. She was thinner than I remembered. Her collarbones winged out from the base of her neck. Her gossamer sari was the color of sunset. Her head was covered, but through the sheer fabric I could see the smooth shape of her skull. She was bald, or almost. Her hair just a velvet stubble. My first thought was that she had been unwell, and was recovering from chemotherapy or some other dreadful affliction that caused hair loss. But her dense, almost-bushy eyebrows and thick eyelashes put that particular theory to rest. She certainly didn't look ill or unwell. She was barefaced and wore no make-up, no kajal, no bindi, no henna on her hands and feet. She looked like an understudy for the bride, temporarily standing in while the real one got dressed. *Desolate* I think is the word I'd use to describe her. She gave the impression of being utterly, unreachably alone, even at her own wedding. The insouciance was gone.

When I walked up to her, she looked straight at me, but I felt as though someone else was looking out through her eyes. I was expecting anger, but what I encountered was emptiness. It could have been my imagination, but as she held my gaze a tremor went through her. For the nine-thousandth time I noticed what a beautiful mouth she had. I was transfixed by the way it moved. I could almost see the effort it took for it to form words and a voice to attach to them:

"It's just a haircut."

The haircut—the shave—must have been ACP Pinky Sodhi's idea. A policewoman's therapy for what she saw as treason—sleeping with the enemy, her brother's killers. Pinky Sodhi liked to keep things simple.

I had never seen Naga look so disconcerted, so anxious. He held Tilo's hand right through the evening. Musa's ghost was wedged between them. I could almost see him—short, compact, with that chipped-tooth smile and that quiet air of his. It was as though the three of them were getting married.

That's probably how it turned out in the end.

Naga's mother was at the center of a clot of elegant ladies whose perfume I could smell from across the lawn. Auntie Meera was from a royal family, one of the minor principalities in Madhya Pradesh. She was a teenage widow, whose royal husband had developed an aggressive lung tumor and died three months after she married him. Unsure of what to do with her, her parents sent her to a finishing school in England, where she met Naga's father at a party in London. There could not have been a better position for a queen without a queendom than being the wife of a suave Foreign Service officer. She modeled herself into a perfect hostess—a modern Indian Maharani with a plummy British accent, acquired from a childhood governess and perfected at finishing school. She wore chiffon saris and pearls and always kept her head covered with her pallu, as Rajput royalty should. She was trying to put a brave face on the trauma that her new daughter-in-law's shocking complexion had visited upon her. She herself was the color of alabaster. Her husband, though Tamilian, was Brahmin and only a shade darker than her. As I walked past I heard her little granddaughter, her daughter's daughter, ask:

"Nani, is she a nigger?"

"Of course not, darling, don't be silly. And, darling, we don't use words like *nigger* any more. It's a bad word. We say *negro*."

"Negro."

"Good girl."

Auntie Meera, mortified, turned to her friends with a brave smile and said of the new member of her family, "But she has a beautiful neck, don't you think?" The friends all agreed enthusiastically.

"But, Nani, she looks like a servants."

The little girl was admonished and sent off on a pretend errand.

The other guests, Naga's old college friends—acolytes more than friends—none of whom had ever met Tilo, were bunched together on the lawn, already gossiping, trained by now in Naga's distinctive brand of cruel humor. One of them raised a toast.

"To Garibaldi." (That was Abhishek, who worked for his father's company, which sourced and sold sewage pipes.)

They laughed loudly, like men trying to be boys.

"Tried talking to her? She doesn't talk."

"Tried smiling? She doesn't smile."

"Where the hell did he find her?"

I'd had my last drink and was moving towards the gate when Naga's father, Ambassador Shivashankar Hariharan, called out to me. "Baba!"

He belonged to another era. He pronounced Baba the way an Englishman would—barber. (His own name he pronounced Shiver.) He never lost an opportunity to let people know that he was a Balliol man.

"Uncle Shiva, sir."

Retirement is rarely kind to powerful men. I could see he had aged suddenly. He looked gaunt and a little too small for his suit. He had a cigar clenched between his perfect, pearly dentures. Fat veins pushed through the pale skin on his temples. His neck was too thin for his collar. Pale rings of cataract had laid siege to his dark irises. He shook my hand with more affection than he had ever shown me in the past. He had a thin, reedy voice.

"Running away, are you? Leaving us to our own devices on this happy occasion?"

That was the only reference he made to his son's latest escapade.

"Where's your beautiful wife? Where're you posted these days?"

When I told him his face suddenly hardened. The change that came over him was almost frightening.

"Get them by the balls, Barber. Hearts and minds will follow."

Kashmir did this to us.

After that I dropped out of their lives. Between then and now, I met her only once, and quite by chance. I was with R.C.—R. C. Sharma—and another colleague. We were taking a walk in Lodhi Gardens, discussing some vexing office politics. I saw her from a distance. She was in a tracksuit, running full pelt, with a dog by her side. I couldn't tell if it was hers or just a Lodhi Garden stray that had decided to run with her. I think she saw us too, because she slowed her run to a walk. When we came face-to-face, she was soaked in sweat and still out of breath. I don't know what got into me. Maybe it was embarrassment at being seen with R.C. Or the usual confusion that came over me when I was with her. Whatever it was, it made me say something stupid—something I'd say to the wife of a colleague I happened to bump into somewhere—chummy, cocktail-party banter.

"Hello! Where's the hubby?"

I could have killed myself just after those words came out.

She held up the leash she was carrying in her hand (the dog was hers) and said, "The hubby? Oh sometimes he allows me to take myself for a walk."

It sounds terrible, but it wasn't. She said it with a smile. Her smile.

Four years ago, out of the clear blue sky, she rang to ask whether I was the Biplab Dasgupta (there are plenty of us, the absurdly named, in this world) who had advertised in the papers for a tenant for a second-floor apartment. I said indeed I was. She said she was working as a freelance illustrator and graphic designer and needed an office and could pay whatever the going rent was. I said I'd be more than delighted. A couple of days later, my doorbell rang and there she was. Much older of course, but in some essential way unchanged—as peculiar as ever. She wore a purple sari and a black-and-white-checked blouse, a shirt actually, with a collar and long sleeves rolled halfway up her forearms. Her hair was dead white and cropped close to her head, short enough for it to look spiky. She looked either much younger or much older than her years. I couldn't decide which.

I was on deputation to the Ministry of Defense at the time, and was living downstairs (in what is now the watermelon). It was a Saturday, Chitra and the girls were out. I was alone at home.

Instinct told me to be more formal than friendly, not to reminisce about the past. So I took her up straightaway, to have a look at the apartment. I showed her around the two rooms—a tiny bedroom and a larger workroom. It was an improvement on her Nizamuddin storeroom for sure, but no comparison to her home of many years in Diplomatic Enclave. She barely looked around before saying she would like to move in as soon as possible.

She walked through the empty rooms and sat at the bay window, looking down at the street below. She seemed enthralled by what she saw, but somehow when I looked out at the same view I didn't think we were seeing the same things.

She made no attempt at conversation and appeared at ease with the silence. She still wore the same plain silver ring on the middle finger of her right hand. I could see she was having some kind of conversation with herself. Suddenly she became practical.

"May I give you a check? A deposit of some sort?"

I said I was in no hurry, that I would draw up an agreement in the next few days.

She asked if she could smoke. I said of course she could, this was her space now and she could do what she pleased in it. She took out a cigarette and lit it, cupping the flame in her palms like a man.

"Given up beedis?" I asked.

Her smile made the lights come on in the room.

I left her to finish her cigarette, and checked the lights, the fans, the water connections in the kitchen and bathroom. As she stood up to leave, she said, as though she was continuing a conversation we'd been having, "There's so much data, but no one really wants to know anything, don't you think?"

I had no idea what she meant. Then she was gone. Then too, her absence filled the apartment, like it does now.

She moved in a day or two later. She had almost no furniture. She did not tell me at the time that she had left Naga and that she intended not just to work, but to actually live upstairs. The rent was deposited straight into my account on the first of every month without fail.

Her arrival in my life, her presence upstairs, unlocked something inside me.

It worries me that I use the past tense.

. . .

Even a casual glance around the room—at the photographs (numbered, captioned) pinned up on the noticeboards, the little towers of documents stacked neatly on the floor and in labeled cartons and box files, the yellow Post-its stuck on bookshelves, cupboards, doors—tells me that there's something unsafe here, something best left untouched, turned over to Naga perhaps, or even the police. But can I bring myself to do that? Must I, should I, can I resist this invitation to intimacy, this opportunity to share these confidences?

At the far end of the room there's a long, thick plank of wood supported on two metal stands that serves as a table. It's piled with papers, old videotapes, a stack of DVDs. Pinned to the noticeboards, together with the photographs, are notes and sketches. Next to an old desktop computer is a tray full of labels, visiting cards, brochures and letterheads—probably the graphic design work with which she earned (*earns*, for God's sake!) her living—the only things in the room that look reassuringly normal. There are printouts of what appear to be several versions of a shampoo label, in various typefaces:

Naturelle Ultra Doux Nourishing Conditioner
With Walnut Oil and Peach Leaf

Naturelle Ultra Doux has combined the nourishing and relaxing virtues of walnut oil and the soothing qualities of peach leaf in a rich detangling cream that melts instantly in your hair.

Results: Very easy to comb. Your hair regains its irresistible softness, without heaviness. Deeply nourished, your hair is perfectly flowing and smooth.
A DEIGHTFUL EXPERIENCE.

"Delightful" is missing an "l" in all the versions. Trust her, at this stage of her life, to be designing misspelled shampoo labels. What about a shampoo for rapidly disappearing hair?

On the wall just above the computer there are two smallish, framed photographs. One is a picture of a child, maybe four or five years old. Her eyes are closed and her body is wrapped in a shroud. Blood from a wound on her temple has seeped through the white cloth, a rose-shaped stain. She's laid out on the snow. A pair of hands pillows her head, lifting it slightly. Along the top edge of the photograph is a row of feet, clad in all manner of winter shoes. It occurs to me that the child could be Musa's daughter. What an odd photograph to choose to frame and hang on your wall.

The other photograph is less distressing. It's been taken on the porch of a houseboat. One of the smaller, shabbier ones. You can see the lake dotted with a few shikaras in the background and the mountains beyond. It's a picture of an unusually short, bearded young man in a worn, brown Kashmiri pheran. His big head is disproportionate to the size of the rest of his body. He has a bunch of tiny wild flowers tucked behind each ear. He's laughing, his green eyes sparkle and his teeth are crooked. Something about the unguardedness, the sheer abandon of his smile, makes him look like a child. Crouching in the bowl of his large hands are two tiny kittens, one has a smoky gray coat streaked with black, and the other is a harlequin, with a black eyepatch. He's holding them out, as though he's offering them to the photographer to touch or stroke. The kittens are peering over the barricade of his thick fingers, their liquid eyes alert and apprehensive.

Who could he be? I have no idea.

I pick up a fat green file from a pile of files on the table and open it at a random page. Two photographs are glued on to a sheet of paper. In the first one, a blurred, out-of-focus cyclist rides past a barred metal doorway set in a six- or seven-foot-high pink boundary wall, the entrance to what looks like a public men's toilet. It is located in a crowded neighborhood and is surrounded by one- and two-storeyed brick buildings with balconies. There's an advertisement for "Roxy Photocopier" painted directly on to the wall in large green letters. The second photograph has been taken inside the toilet. The weathered pink walls are streaked with moss and moisture and have rusty pipes running along them, horizontally as well as vertically. There is a grimy white sink on the wall, and a row of three uncovered manholes in the concrete floor. Metal covers with handles, like the lids of enormous saucepans, lie next to them. An old, broken window frame and a plank of wood are propped up on one wall. They are the most unexceptional photographs I have ever seen. Who has taken them? Why would anybody take pictures like that? And why would anybody file them away so carefully?

The next page explains it:

GHAFOOR'S STORY

This place is called Nawab Bazaar. See that public toilet? Where it says Roxy Photocopier? That's where it happened. It was 2004. Must have been April. It was cold and raining heavily. We were sitting in my friend's shop, New Electronics, right next to Rafiq Tailor Shop, drinking tea. Tariq and me. It was around eight at night. Suddenly we heard the screech of brakes. Across the road about four or five vehicles drove up and cordoned off the toilet. They were STF vehicles. STF, you know, is Special Task Force. Eight soldiers came to the shop and forced us to cross the street with them at gunpoint. When we reached the toilet they told us to go in and search it. They said an Afghan terrorist had escaped and had run into the toilet. They wanted us to go in and ask him to surrender. We didn't want to go in because we thought that the mujahid would have a gun. The STF men put pistols to our heads. We went in. It was absolutely dark. We could see nothing. There was no person there. We came out and told them that there was nobody there. They asked us to go back in. They gave us a torch. We had never seen such a huge torch. One of them showed us how it works, switching it on and off on and off on and off. Another kept staring at us, clicking the safety catch of his gun on and off on and off on and off. They sent us back into the toilet with the torch. We flashed it around but found nobody. We called out, but nobody replied. We were completely drenched.

The STF soldiers had taken position in the next-door building. Two were on the first-floor balcony. They said they could see someone in the drain. How could that be? It was so dark, how could they see anything from so far away? I shone the torch down on the row of three man-holes. I saw a man's head. I was so afraid. I thought he had a gun, I moved away to one side. The soldiers asked me to ask him to come out. Tariq, who was standing behind me, whispered, "They're making a film. Do what they say." By "film" he did not mean really a "film" in that sense. He meant they were setting up the scene, to make a story.

I asked the man in the manhole to come out. He didn't reply. I could tell he was a Kashmiri. Not an Afghan. He just stared back. He couldn't speak. We stood around the man with the STF torch. It was still raining. The smell from the manhole was unbearable. Maybe an hour and a half went by. We did not dare to speak to each other. We switched the torch on and off. Then the man's head fell sideways. He had died. Buried in shit.

The STF men gave us crowbars and spades. We had to

break the concrete edges around the manhole to pull him out. All of us were wet, shivering, stinking. When we pulled out the body we found that his legs were tied together and weighted down with a rock.

Only later we learned what had happened earlier in the STF film.

First a few of them had come quietly in one car. They tied up the man and stuffed him into the manhole. He had been badly tortured and was about to die. When they came in they found another young man in one of the booths. They arrested him and took him away—maybe he refused to do what we agreed to do. Then they came back in their vehicles and staged the rest of the film in which there were roles for us too.

Their officer asked us to sign a paper. If we hadn't signed they would have killed us. We signed as witnesses to an encounter in which the STF had tracked down and killed a dreaded Afghan terrorist who was cornered in a public toilet in Nawab Bazaar. It was in the news.

The man they killed was a laborer from Bandipora. The young man they arrested because he was pissing at a weird and inconvenient hour has disappeared.

And Tariq and I have lies and treachery on our conscience.

Those eyes that stared at us for one and a half hours—they were forgiving eyes, understanding eyes. We Kashmiris do not need to speak to each other any more in order to understand each other.

We do terrible things to each other, we wound and betray and kill each other, but we understand each other.

BAD STORY. Terrible actually. If it's true, that is. How does one verify these things? People aren't reliable. They're forever exaggerating. Kashmiris especially. And then they begin to believe in their own exaggeration as if it's God's truth. I can't imagine what Madam Tilottama is doing, collecting this pointless stuff. She should stick to her shampoo labels. Anyway, it isn't a one-way street. The other side has its repertory of horror too. Some of those militants were maniacs. If one *has* to choose, then give me a Hindu fundamentalist any day over a Muslim one. It's true we did—we do—some terrible things in Kashmir, but . . . I mean what the Pakistan Army did in East Pakistan—now *that* was a clear case of genocide. Open and shut. When the Indian Army liberated Bangladesh, the good old Kashmiris called it—still call it—the "*Fall* of Dhaka." They aren't very good at other people's pain. But then, who is? The Baloch, who are being buggered by Pakistan, don't care about Kashmiris. The Bangladeshis whom we liberated are hunting down Hindus. The good old communists call Stalin's Gulag a "necessary part of revolution." The Americans are currently lecturing the Vietnamese about human rights. What we have on our hands is a species problem. None of us is exempt. And then there's that other business that's become pretty big these days. People—communities, castes, races and even countries—carry their tragic histories and their misfortunes around like trophies, or like stock, to be bought and sold on the open market. Unfortunately, speaking for myself, on that count I have no stock to trade, I'm a tragedy-less man. The upper-caste, upper-class oppressor from every angle.

Cheers to that.

What else do we have here?

There's an open carton, an old Hewlett-Packard printer cartridge carton lying open on the table. I'm relieved to see that its contents are somewhat sunnier—two yellow photo sachets, one labeled "Otter Pics" and the other "Otter Kills." Nice. I had no idea that she had an interest in otters. It suddenly makes her less—how should I say it—less hazardous. The idea of her walking on a beach, or a riverbank, with the wind in her hair . . . relaxed, unguarded . . . looking for otters . . . makes me glad for her. I love otters. I think they might be my favorite creatures. I once spent a whole week watching them when we were on a family holiday, a Pacific cruise along the west coast of Canada. Even when it was stormy and the ocean was dangerously choppy, there they were, those cheeky little bastards, floating nonchalantly on their backs, looking for all the world as though they were reading the morning papers.

I tip the photos out of one of the sachets.

None of them are pictures of otters.

I should have known. I feel like the victim of a prank.

The one on the top of the pile is a photo taken on the promenade around Dal Gate in Srinagar. A swarthy Sikh soldier wearing a flak jacket and holding a rifle is on his haunches. One knee up, one knee down, posing triumphantly over the corpse of a young man. From the way his body lies, it's clear the young man is dead. He's propped up on his chin, which is jammed up on the one-foot-high concrete verge that runs around the lake, the rest of his body is slumped in a downward arc. His legs are splayed, one knee bent at a right angle. He's in trousers and a beige polo shirt. He's been shot through his throat. There's not much blood. There are blurred silhouettes of houseboats in the background. The soldier's head has been circled with a purple marker. Judging from the dead man's clothes and the weapon the soldier is holding, it's a pretty old picture. In each of the other less dramatic photographs of groups of soldiers taken in marketplaces, at checkpoints, or on a highway while they are waving down vehicles, a soldier has been singled out with the same purple marker. There's no obvious connection between them. Some are clean-shaven, some are Sikh, some are obviously Muslim. In all but one of the photographs the setting is Kashmir. In the one that isn't, a bored-looking soldier is sitting on a blue plastic chair in a sandbagged bunker in what looks like the middle of a desert. His helmet is on his lap and he's holding an orange fly swatter and looking away into the distance. There's something about his eyes, something blank and expressionless that holds your attention. His head too is circled with that purple marker.

Who are these men?

And then, when I spread them out on the table, I get it—they're all the same soldier. He looks different in each photograph, except for his eyes. He's a shape-shifter. Maybe one of our counter-intelligence boys. Why does he have a purple noose around his head?

There's a file in the carton that says "Otter." The first document in it looks like someone's CV. The letterhead says Ralph M. Bauer, LCSW, Licensed Clinical Social Worker, followed by a long list of his educational qualifications. A word jumped out at me. *Clovis*. Ralph Bauer's street address was East Bullard Avenue, Clovis, California.

Clovis was where Amrik Singh shot himself and his family. In their home, in a small suburban residential colony. And then I get it. Spotter. Otter. Of course. The man in the photographs is Amrik Singh "Spotter." I never actually came face-to-face with him in Kashmir. I didn't know what he looked like as a younger man (those were pre-Google days). These pictures of him bear almost no resemblance to the photograph of him as an older man, pudgy, clean-shaven and looking completely disoriented, that appeared in the papers after his suicide.

My veins feel as though they're flooded with some kind of chemical, something other than blood. How did she get hold of these documents? And why? *Why?* What use did she have for them? What was this now? Some sort of voodoo revenge fantasy?

The first few pages in the file are a sort of questionnaire—a series of those typically corny, psychobabble types of questions: *Have you ever had distressing dreams of the event? Have you been unable to have sad or loving feelings? Have you found it hard to imagine a long lifespan and fulfilling your goals?* That sort of thing. Attached to the questionnaire are two written testimonies signed by Amrik Singh and his wife (hers long, his very brief), and photocopies of two thick, neatly filled-out application forms for asylum in the US, also signed by them.

I need to sit down. I need a drink. I have a bottle of Cardhu that I shouldn't have picked up in the Duty Free on my way in from Kabul, and shouldn't have brought up here with me. Especially not when I have promised Chitra that I will never touch another drink. Not a peg. Not a drop. Especially not when I know my job is at risk. Especially not when I know that my boss has given me this one last chance to—in his hackneyed words—"shape up or ship out."

I'd like some ice, but there's none. The whole freezer has turned into a block of ice and needs defrosting. The fridge is empty but the kitchen is stacked with fruit cartons. Maybe she was—is—on one of those trendy detox diets where you eat only fruit. Maybe that's where she's gone. To a yoga retreat or something.

Of course she hasn't.

I'll have to drink the Cardhu neat. It's really cold and those damn pigeons really ought to stop fornicating on the windowsill. Why won't they stop?

Date: April 16th, 2012
Re: Loveleen Singh née Kaur and Amrik Singh

This is a request for a Psycho-Social Evaluation of Amrik Singh and his wife, Loveleen Singh née Kaur, to determine if they were victims of persecution as a result of the abuse, police corruption and extortion they suffered in India, their native country. Do they have a genuine "well-founded fear" of being tortured or killed by their government? They are seeking asylum as they claim that Amrik Singh will be tortured or killed if he returns to India. During the course of the interview I administered a Trauma Symptom Inventory-2 (TSI-2), Mental Status Checklist, Post-Traumatic Stress Disorder (PTSD) Screening Interview, and a Davidson Trauma Scale. A lengthy history was taken during a two-hour face-to-face interview with each of them to complete a narrative of the actual events that they actually experienced in Kashmir, India.

Background:

Mr. and Mrs. Amrik Singh reside in Clovis, California. Loveleen Singh née Kaur was born in Kashmir, India, on November 19th 1972. Amrik Singh, born in Chandigarh, India, on June 9th 1964. The couple has three children, the youngest of whom was born in the US. The couple fled from India to Canada with their two older children. They entered the United States by foot on October 1st 2005. They first entered Blaine, Washington, but now live in Clovis, California, where Mr. Amrik Singh works as a truck driver. Loveleen Kaur is a home-maker. They are constantly anxious about their family's safety.

Loveleen's Narrative:
This is a Narrative based on a paraphrase of Loveleen's interview.

My husband Amrik Singh was a military major posted in Srinagar, Kashmir. While he was on the post I did not live with him on the base, I lived with our son in a private accommodation, in a second-floor flat in Jawahar Nagar, Srinagar. In that colony many Sikh families and only few

Muslims live. In 1995 a human rights lawyer by the name of Jalib Qadri was kidnapped and killed and my husband was blamed by the local police and we felt that Muslims were framing him. My husband did not accept bribes and he did not like Muslim terrorists. He was an honorable man. In his own words: "I will not cheat on my country and you cannot bribe me."

My friend Manpreet was at that time a journalist in Srinagar. She found out who was framing my husband and who had killed Jalib Qadri. She and my mother went to the police station to tell them the information. The police did not listen to her because she was a woman and a relative of the accused. And because JK Police are mostly Kashmiri Muslims. The leading police investigator said, "If I want I can make you ladies burn alive here. I have that power."

After one year police units encircled Jawahar Nagar colony where I lived without my husband to do a cordon-and-search. Then they banged on my door and came inside. They grabbed me by my hair and dragged me from the second floor to the first floor. One policeman took my son. They stole all my jewelry. All the while they kicked and beat me and said, "This is the family of Amrik Singh who killed our leader." In the police headquarters they tied me to a wood plank and kicked and slapped and beat me. They beat me on my head with a rubber plank. They told me, "We will make you a mad vegetable for the rest of your life." A man with metal shoes kicked and crushed my chest and stomach. Then they rolled wooden poles down my legs. Then they attached sticky things on my body and thumbs and gave me electric shocks again and again. They wanted me to give a false statement about my husband. I was kept there for two days. They kept my son in another room and said I will get him back only after I make a false statement. Finally they let me go. I saw my son then. We were both crying. I could not walk to him because my feet were hurting. A rickshaw driver picked me up and took me to my mother's home.

No doctor would treat me because they were scared that the Muslim terrorists would kill them. Me and my husband were being watched all the time. We lived a very stressful life.

We left Kashmir after three years and lived in Jammu. In 2003 we left our country for Canada. We applied for asylum and they denied us. It was heartless. We needed help. We showed them all our evidences, still they denied us. In October 2005 we came to Seattle. My husband got a job as a truck driver and in 2006 we moved to Clovis, California. We have no protection. We don't go anywhere, we have no outings or happy life. If we go out we don't know if we will come home alive. All the time we feel we are watched by the terrorists. With every noise I think I am going to die. I get scared easily with loud noises. Last year, in 2011, when my husband was just verbally disciplining our children, I got so scared I thought they were here to kill us. I ran to the phone to call 911. I hurt myself badly on my head, chest and legs while I was running. I thought I was going to die even though he was only verbally disciplining the children. My heartbeat goes so fast I feel like a crazy woman. I often react dramatically to yelling and loud noises. Even though my husband was only verbally disciplining our children I called the police and I don't know what I told them. They arrested my husband and they released him on bail. I am still unsure what happened. The news came in the papers that my husband was so and so and had served in Kashmir. They showed my husband's picture and our house and told everyone we lived here. That news came on the internet and in Kashmir too. Again the Muslim terrorists began to ask for my husband to be sent back. After a few days a journalist called and told us a magazine writer from India was looking for us. But we knew he wasn't who he said he was. I saw him drive past our house. I saw him many times. I told my husband that we must leave. He said, "We don't have money to keep moving. I don't want to run. I want to live." The man is always around. Other men too. All Muslim terrorists. I am constantly scared. I keep all the curtains closed and watch from behind the curtain. They stand on the street and stare at our house. Now I keep everything locked. Before I used to run a small beauty parlor from my house, doing eyebrows threading and legs waxing for ladies. Now I feel it is unsafe to let strangers come to my house.

Seventeen years have gone passed and the Kashmiri Muslim terrorists still celebrate that lawyer man's death. In the newspapers and on internet they still blame my husband. My children are scared. They always ask, "Mom when can we enjoy our lives?" I tell them, "I'm trying, but it's not in my hands."

SHE HURT HER LEGS, head and chest while running to the telephone. That's a feat. What did her husband do to make her withdraw her complaint, I wonder? Maybe she and her children would be alive today if she hadn't. I particularly love the part in which local police do a cordon-and-search operation in Jawahar Nagar of all places and then arrest and torture a serving army major's wife. That's peerless. In Kashmir this story would be received as slapstick comedy. The "scared doctors" bit was a good touch too. Verisimilitude is everything. As for her detailed and knowledgeable account of torture, I hope her husband only tutored her in his techniques and didn't actually use them on her. "He was only verbally disciplining the children," repeated three times in a single paragraph sounds dire to me.

Amrik Singh's own testimony was soldier-like. Brief and to the point:

> I served in the Indian Army as a commissioned officer. I was posted in various counter-insurgency and peacekeeping duties within India and abroad. In 1995 I was posted in Kashmir where insurgency is ongoing since 1990. In 1995 a human rights worker who I later came to know belonged to a banned terrorist outfit was kidnapped and killed. The Kashmir police and Indian Government is putting this blame on me. I am being made an escape goat. I had no choice but to flee from India along with my family. If I return Government of India would not like me to face any court where I can put up my view. I would be tortured by beating, shocks, waterboarding, food and sleep deprivation or else be killed and never to be seen or heard again.

The application forms were filled in by hand. Amrik Singh had neat, almost girlish handwriting and a neat, girlish signature to match. It's eerie looking at his handwriting. It feels oddly intimate.

They certainly knew how to go about their business, those two. How was poor old Ralph Bauer, LCSW, to know that their story rang so true because it *was* true, except that the victims and the perpetrators had swapped roles? Small wonder that he came to this hilarious conclusion:

Findings:

Based on the data presented above there is no doubt in my mind that Mrs. Loveleen Singh and Mr. Amrik Singh both suffer from severe Post-Traumatic Stress Disorder. This degree of stress is definitely indicative of individuals that have suffered destructive and traumatic events such as torture, indefinite periods of incarceration and separation from family. They deeply fear that if they return to India these events will be repeated. There is no question that there are persons at large who still seek revenge and carry out their vendetta in various blogs of the World Wide Web.

Given these facts I highly recommend that Mr. and Mrs. Amrik Singh and their family be given protection and asylum here in the United States of America so that they can begin to lead a normal life to the extent that it is possible for them.

So they had nearly pulled it off, Mr. and Mrs. Singh. They were on the verge of becoming legal citizens of the United States. And yet, a couple of months later Amrik Singh chose to shoot himself and his whole family.

What sense did that make?

Could it have been something other than suicide?

Who was the drive-by artist that the wife mentioned in her testimony? And who were the others?

Does it matter any more?

Not to me.

Not to the Government of India.

Surely not to the California Police, who must have other things on their minds.

Shame about the wife and kids though.

Why does my tenant Madam S. Tilottama have this file?
And where the hell is she?

My phone beeps. Strange. No one has this number. As far as the world is concerned I'm in rehab. Or on study leave, which is the other way of putting it. Who's texting me? Oh. THYROCARE, whatever that is:

> Dear Client please attend our health camp.
> VitD+B12, Sugar, Lipid, LFT, KFT,
> Thyroid, Iron, CBC, Urine test for Rs 1800/-

Dear Thyrocare. I think I'd rather die.

I've already drunk a quarter of the bottle. It's time for a forbidden afternoon snooze. Working men shouldn't snooze. I shouldn't take the Cardhu into the bedroom. But I must. It insists.

There's no bed. Just a mattress on the floor. There are books, notebooks, dictionaries arranged in neat towers.

I switch on the tall standard lamp. I can see a piece of colored paper Scotch-taped to the wide-brimmed lampshade of the standard lamp. A reminder? A note to herself? It says:

> *As for their death, need I tell you about it? It will be, for*
> *all of them, the death of him who, when he learned of his*
> *from the jury, merely mumbled in a Rhenish accent, "I'm*
> *already way beyond that."*
> *Jean Genet*

P.S. This lampshade is made of some kind of animal skin. If you look carefully you will find some hairs growing out of it.

Thankyou.

These rooms seem to have witnessed some sort of unraveling. The unraveling of any human being is probably horrifying to witness. But *this* human being? It has an edge of danger, like the faint, acrid smell of gunpowder hanging in the air at the scene of a crime.

I have not read Genet, should I have? Have you?

It's good whisky, Cardhu. And bloody expensive. I'll have to drink it respectfully. I'm already a bit woozy—"oozy," as my old friend Golak would have put it. In Orissa they tend to drop their W's.

IT'S PITCH-DARK.

I dreamed of a tower of stacked saucepan lids and open manholes stuffed with strange things—files mostly, and Musa's drawings of horses. And long bolts of very dry snow that look like bones.

Who finished the whisky?

Who brought the vodka and the crate of beer from my car up to the apartment?

Who turned the day into night?

How many days have been turned into how many nights?

And who is at the door? I can hear the key turning.

Is it her?

No it's not.

. . .

It's two people with three voices. Strange. They come in and switch on the lights as though they own the place. And now we're face-to-face. A young man in dark glasses and an older man. Older woman. Man. Woman-man. Whatever. Some sort of freak dressed in a Pathan suit and a cheap plastic anorak. Very tall. With a red mouth and a bright, shining tooth. Or maybe it's just me still dreaming. My senses are weirdly heightened and blunted at the same time. There are bottles everywhere, crashing around our feet, rolling under the furniture and into the open manholes.

Since we don't seem to have much to say to each other and I'm unsteady on my feet—I can feel myself swaying like corn in a cornfield—I go back into the bedroom and lie down. What else is there for me to do?

They follow me in. That strikes me as unusual behavior, even in a dream sequence, if that's what's going on here. The woman-man speaks to me in a voice that sounds like two voices. She speaks the most beautiful Urdu. She says her name is Anjum, that she's a friend of Tilottama, who is living with her for the moment, and that she and her friend Saddam Hussain had come because Tilo needed some things from her cupboard. I said I was a friend of Tilo's too and they should go right ahead and take what they needed. The young man produces a key and opens the cupboard.

A cloud of balloons floats out.

The young man produces a sack and begins to fill it. In goes—at least from what I can tell—a rubber duck, an inflatable baby's bathtub, a large, stuffed zebra, some blankets, books and warm clothes. When they are done they thank me for my patience. They ask if I want to send a message to Tilo. I say I do.

I tear a page out of one of her notebooks and write GARSON HOBART. The letters come out much larger than I intend them to be. Like some sort of declaration. I hand the note to them.

And then they are gone.

I move to the window to watch them exit the building. One of them—the older one—gets into an autorickshaw, the other, I swear on my children, leaves on a *horse*. A pair of freaks with a swag bag full of stuffed toys trotting off into the mist on a frigging white horse.

My mind is in a shambles. My hallucinations are so pitiful. It was all so real. I could smell it. I can't remember when I last ate. Where's my phone? What's the time? What day is it, or what night?

I look back at the room. The balloons are floating around like a screensaver. The cupboard doors have swung open. The inside of one is marked up. From where I'm standing it looks like a chart of some kind . . . a parents' record of the height of their growing child—we used to do that with Ania and Rabia when they were growing up. What child could she have been measuring, I wonder. From up close I realize it's not that at all. How could I have imagined, however briefly, that it would be something so domestic and endearing?

It's some kind of dictionary, a work in progress—the entries are in uneven handwriting and in different colors:

Kashmiri-English Alphabet

A: Azadi/army/Allah/America/Attack/AK-47/
Ammunition/Ambush/Aatankwadi/Armed Forces Special
Powers Act/Area Domination/Al Badr/Al Mansoorian/Al
Jehad/Afghan/Amarnath Yatra

B: BSF/body/blast/bullet/battalion/barbed wire/brust (burst)/
border cross/booby trap/bunker/byte/begaar (forced labor)

C: Cross-border/Crossfire/camp/civilian/curfew/
Crackdown/Cordon-and-Search/CRPF/Checkpost/

Counter-insurgency/Ceasefire/Counter-Intelligence/
Catch and Kill/Custodial Killing/Compensation/Cylinder
(surrender)/Concertina wire/Collaborator

D: Disappeared/Defense Spokesman/Double Cross/
Double Agent/Disturbed Areas Act/Dead body

E: Encounter/EJK (extrajudicial killing)/Ex Gratia/
Embedded journalists/Elections/enforced disappearance

F: Funerals/Fidayeen/Foreign Militant/FIR (First Information
Report)/Fake Encounter

G: Grenade Blast/Gunbattle/G Branch (General branch–
BSF intelligence)/Graveyard/Gun culture

H: HM (Hizb-ul-Mujahideen)/HRV (human rights
violations)/HRA (human rights activist)/Hartal/Harkat-
ul-Mujahideen/Honeymoon/Half-widows/Half-orphans/
Human shields/Healing Touch/Hideout

I: Interrogation/India/Intelligence/Insurgent/Informer/I-card/
ISI/intercepts/Ikhwan/Information Warfare/IB/Indefinite
Curfew

J: Jail/Jamaat/JKP/JIC (Joint Interrogation Center)/JKLF
(Jammu & Kashmir Liberation Front)/jihad/jannat/
jahannum/Jamiat ul Mujahideen/Jaish-e-Mohammed

K: Kills/Kashmir/Kashmiriyat/Kalashnikov (see also AK)/
Kilo Force/Kafir

L: Lashkar-e-Taiba/LMG/Launcher/Love letter/Lahore/
Landmine

M: Mujahideen/Military/Mintree/Media/Mines/MPV
(mine proof vehicle)/Militant (also Milton, Mike)/
Muslim Mujahideen/Mistaken Identity/Martyrs/Mukhbir
(Informer)/Misfire (Accidental death)/Muskaan (army
orphanage)/Massacre/Mout/Moj

N: NGO/New Delhi/Nizam-e-Mustapha/Nabad (see also Ikhwan)/Night Patrolling/NTR (Nothing To Report)/nail parade/normalcy

O: Occupation/Ops/OGW (overground worker)/overground/ official version/Operation Tiger/Operation Sadbhavana

P: Pakistan/PSA (Public Security Act)/POTA (Prevention of Terrorism Act)/Picked Up/Prima Facie/Peace/Police/ Papa I, Papa II (interrogation centers)/Psyops (psychological warfare)/Pandits/Press Conference/Peace Process/ Paramilitary/PTSD (Post-Traumatic Stress Disorder)/Paar/ press release

Q: Quran/Questioning

R: RR (Rashtriya Rifles)/Regular Army/rape/rigging/ Road Opening Patrol/RDX/RAW/Renegades/RPG (rocket propelled grenade)/razor wire/referendum

S: Separatists/Surveillance/Spy/SOG/STF/Suspected/ Shaheed/Shohadda (martyrs)/Sources/Security/Sadbhavana (Goodwill)/Surrender (aka cylinder)/SRO 43 (Special Relief Order-1 lakh)

T: Third Degree/Torture/Terrorist/tip-off/tourism/TADA (Terrorist and Disruptive Activities Act)/threats/target/task force

U: Unidentified gunmen/unidentified body/Ultras/ underground

V: violence/Victor Force/Village Defense Committee/ Version (local/official/police/army)/victory

W: Warnings/wireless/waza/wazwaan

X: X gratia

Y: Yatra (Amarnath)

Z: Zulm (oppression)/Z plus Security

There's no Musa, so who has been filling her head with this trash?

Why is she still wallowing in this old story?

Everyone's moved on.

I thought she had too.

I'm lying on her bed.

My head is killing me.

And the room is full of balloons.

Why do I always end up like this around her?

I open the notebook I've torn a page out of. On the first page it says:

> *Dear Doctor,*
> *Angels hover over me as I write. How can I tell them that*
> *their wings smell like the bottom of a chicken coop?*

Honestly, it's so much simpler in Kabul.

Then, as she had already died four or five times, the apartment had remained available for a drama more serious than her own death.

—JEAN GENET

8

THE TENANT

The spotted owlet on the street light ducked and bobbed with the delicacy and immaculate manners of a Japanese businessman. He had an unobstructed view through the window of the small, bare room and the odd, bare woman on the bed. She had an unobstructed view of him too. Some nights she bobbed back and said, *Moshi Moshi*, which was all the Japanese she knew.

Even indoors the walls radiated a bullying, unyielding heat. The slow ceiling fan stirred the scorched air, layering it with fine, cindery dust.

The room showed signs of celebration. The balloons tied to the window grille bumped into each other desultorily, softened and shriveled by the heat. In the center, on a low, painted stool, was a cake with bright strawberry icing and sugar flowers, a candle with a charred wick, a matchbox and a few used matchsticks. On the cake it said *Happy Birthday Miss Jebeen*. The cake had been cut, a small piece eaten. The icing had melted and dribbled on to the silver-foil-covered cardboard cake-base. Ants were making off with crumbs larger than themselves. Black ants, pink crumbs.

The baby, whose birthday and baptism ceremonies had been simultaneously celebrated and successfully concluded, was fast asleep.

Her kidnapper, who went by the name of S. Tilottama, was awake and concentrating. She could hear her hair growing. It sounded like something crumbling. A burnt thing crumbling. Coal. Toast. Moths crisped on a light bulb. She remembered reading somewhere that even after people died, their hair and nails kept growing. Like starlight, traveling through the universe long after the stars themselves had died. Like cities. Fizzy, effervescent, simulating the illusion of life while the planet they had plundered died around them.

She thought of the city at night, of cities at night. Discarded constellations of old stars, fallen from the sky, rearranged on Earth in patterns and pathways and towers. Invaded by weevils that have learned to walk upright.

A weevil-philosopher with a grave manner and a sharp mustache was teaching a class, reading aloud from a book. Admiring young weevils strained to catch each word that spilled from his wise weevil lips. "Nietzsche believed that if Pity were to become the core of ethics, misery would become contagious and happiness an object of suspicion." The youngsters scratched away on their little notepads. "Schopenhauer on the other hand believed that Pity is and ought to be the supreme weevil virtue. But long before them, Socrates asked the key question: Why should we be moral?"

He had lost a leg in Weevil World War IV, this professor, and carried a cane. His remaining five (legs) were in excellent condition. Airbrush graffiti sprayed on the back wall of his classroom said:

Evil Weevils Always Make the Cut.

Other creatures crowded into the already-crowded classroom.

> An alligator with a humanskin purse
> A grasshopper with good intentions
> A fish on a fast
> A fox with a flag
> A maggot with a manifesto
> A neocon newt
> An icon iguana
> A communist cow
> An owl with an alternative
> A lizard on TV. *Hello and welcome, you're watching*
> *Lizard News at Nine. There's been a blizzard on lizard*
> *island.*

The baby was the beginning of something. This much the kidnapper knew. Her bones had whispered this to her that night (the *said* night, the concerned night, the aforementioned night, the night hereinafter referred to as "the night") when she made her move on the pavement. And her bones were nothing if not reliable informants. The baby was Miss Jebeen returned. Returned, that is, not to her (Miss Jebeen the First was never hers), but to the world. Miss Jebeen the Second, when she was grown to be a lady, would settle accounts and square the books. Miss Jebeen would turn the tide.

There was hope yet, for the Evil Weevil World.

True, the Happy Meadow had fallen. But Miss Jebeen was come.

NAGA ASKED TILO for one good reason why she was leaving him. Did he not love her? Had he not been caring? Considerate? Generous? Understanding? Why now? After all these years? He said fourteen years was enough time for anyone to get over anything. Provided they wanted to get over it. People had been through much worse.

"Oh *that*," she said. "I got over all that long ago. I'm happy and well adjusted now. Like the people of Kashmir. I've learned to love my country. I may even vote in the next election."

He let that pass. He said she should think about seeing a psychiatrist.

Thinking made her throat ache. That was a good reason not to think about seeing a psychiatrist.

Naga had started wearing tweed coats and smoking cigars. Like his father did. And talking to servants in the imperious way that his mother did. Termites on toast, khadi loincloths and the Rolling Stones were a forgotten fever dream from a past life.

Naga's mother, who lived alone on the ground floor of the big house (his father, Ambassador Shivashankar Hariharan, had died), advised him to let Tilo go. "She won't be able to manage on her own, she'll beg you to take her back." Naga knew otherwise. Tilo would manage. And even if she didn't, there would be no begging. He sensed she was drifting on a tide that neither he nor she could do much about. He couldn't tell whether her restlessness, her compulsive and increasingly unsafe wandering through the city, marked the onset of an unsoundness of mind or an acute, perilous kind of sanity. Or were they both the same thing?

The only thing he could attribute her newfound restiveness to was her mother's bizarre passing, which he thought odd, given that it was a relationship that had barely existed. True, Tilo had been at her bedside during the last two weeks in hospital. But other than that, she had seen her mother only a few times in the past several years.

Naga was right in one sense but wrong in another. Her

mother's death (she died in the winter of 2009) had released Tilo from an internment that nobody, including she herself, had been aware of because it had passed itself off as something quite the opposite—a peculiar, insular independence. For all of her adult life Tilo had defined and shaped herself by marking off and maintaining a distance between herself and her mother—her real foster-mother. When that was no longer necessary, something frozen began to thaw and something unfamiliar began to take its place.

Naga's pursuit of Tilo had not turned out as planned. She was meant to be just another easy conquest, yet another woman who succumbed to his irreverent brilliance and edgy charm and had her heart broken. But Tilo had crept up on him, and become a kind of compulsion, an addiction almost. Addiction has its own mnemonics—skin, smell, the length of the loved one's fingers. In Tilo's case it was the slant of her eyes, the shape of her mouth, the almost-invisible scar that slightly altered the symmetry of her lips and made her look defiant even when she did not mean to, the way her nostrils flared, announcing her displeasure even before her eyes did. The way she held her shoulders. The way she sat on the pot stark naked and smoked cigarettes. So many years of marriage, the fact that she was not young any more—and did nothing to pretend otherwise—didn't change the way he felt. Because it had to do with more than all that. It was the haughtiness (despite the question mark over her "stock," as his mother had not hesitated to put it). It had to do with the way she lived, in the country of her own skin. A country that issued no visas and seemed to have no consulates.

True, it had never been a particularly friendly country even at the best of times. But its borders were sealed and the regime of more or less complete isolationism began only after the trainwreck at the Shiraz Cinema. Naga married Tilo because he was never really able to reach her. And because he couldn't reach her he couldn't let her go. (Of course that raises another question: Why did Tilo marry Naga? A generous person would say it was because she needed shelter. A less generous view would be that it was because she needed cover.)

Although his was only a small part in the story, in Naga's mind, "Before" and "After" Shiraz sometimes took on the overtones of BC and AD.

AFTER THE MIDNIGHT CALL from Biplab Das-Goose-*da* in Dachigam, it took Naga a few hours and several discreet phone calls to make the necessary arrangements to get from Ahdoos to the Shiraz. Curfew had been declared. Srinagar was locked down. Security was being put in place for the funeral procession for the people who had been killed over the weekend, which would rage through the streets the next morning. There were shoot-on-sight orders. Moving around the city that night was next to impossible. By the time Naga managed to organize a vehicle, a curfew pass, checkpoint waivers and an entry-permit to the Shiraz, it was almost dawn.

An orderly was waiting for him outside the cinema lobby, near what had once been the ticket booth and was now a sentry post. He said the Major Sahib (Amrik Singh) had left, but that his deputy would meet him in his office. The orderly escorted Naga to the back of the building, up the fire escape to a dim, makeshift office on the first floor. He asked Naga to take a seat, saying that "Sahib" would be there in a minute. When he entered the room Naga had no means of knowing that the figure in a pheran and balaclava sitting on a chair with her back to the door was Tilo. He hadn't seen her in a while. When she turned around, what alarmed him more than the look in her eyes was the effort she made to smile and say hello. That, to him, was a sign of breakage. It wasn't her. She wasn't a woman who smiled and said hello. Her close friends had learned over time that with Tilo the absence of a greeting was actually a brusque declaration of intimacy. Thanks to the balaclava, what they later came to call "the haircut" wasn't immediately evident. Naga assumed the balaclava was just a South Indian's exaggerated response to the cold. (He had a cache of jokes about South Indians and monkey caps that he used to tell with accents and aplomb, without fear of causing offense, because he was half South Indian himself.) As soon as Tilo saw him she stood up and moved quickly to the door.

"It's you! I thought Garson—"

"He called me. He's in Dachigam with the Governor. I happened to be in town. Are you OK? And Musa . . . ? Was it . . . ?"

He put an arm around her shoulder. She wasn't shivering so much as vibrating, as though there was a motor just underneath her skin. A pulse jumped on the side of her mouth.

"Can we go now? Shall we leave . . . ?"

Before Naga could reply, Ashfaq Mir, Deputy Commandant of the Shiraz Cinema JIC, walked in, heralded by the overpowering scent of his cologne. Naga dropped his arm from Tilo's shoulder, feeling guilty for an imagined misdemeanor. (In Kashmir in those days, the difference between what constituted guilt and innocence lay in the realm of the occult.)

Ashfaq Mir was startlingly short, startlingly strong-looking and startlingly white even for a Kashmiri. His ears and nostrils were shell pink. He exuded an almost metallic radiance. He was smartly turned out, khaki trousers creased, brown boots polished, buckles gleaming, hair gelled and raked back off his smooth, shining forehead. He could have been Albanian, or a young army officer from the Balkans, but when he spoke, it was with the manner of an old-world houseboat owner, steeped in generations of legendary Kashmiri hospitality, greeting an old customer.

"Welcome, sir! Welcome! Welcome! I must tell you, I am

your biggest fan, sir! We need people like you to keep people like me on the right track!" The smile that spread across his fresh, boyish face was a pennant. His amazed, baby-blue eyes lit up with what looked like real pleasure. He sandwiched Naga's hand between both his hands and pumped it warmly for a good length of time before taking his place behind his desk and gesturing to Naga to sit down opposite him. "I'm sorry I am a little late. I was out all night. There's trouble in the city—you must have heard—protests, firings, killings, funerals . . . Our usual Srinagar Special. I just got back. My CO Sir asked me to come and hand over Ma'am personally."

Though he called her "Ma'am," he behaved as though Tilo wasn't there. (Which allowed Tilo to behave as though she wasn't there either.) Even when he referred to her he didn't look at her. Whether that was a gesture of respect, disrespect or just local tradition was not clear.

Not much about what happened in that room that day was clear. Ashfaq Mir's performance could either have been carefully scripted, including the manner and timing of his entrance, or it could have been a kind of practiced improvisation. The only thing that was unambiguous was the undertone of bustling, smiling menace: "Ma'am" would be personally handed over, but Sir and Ma'am could leave only when Ashfaq Mir said they could. Yet he conducted himself as though he was a humble minion merely carrying out, in the most gracious way possible, a duty he had been assigned. He gave the impression that he had absolutely no idea what had happened, what Tilo was doing in the JIC or why she needed to be "handed over."

It was obvious from, if nothing else, the quality of the air in the room (it trembled) that something heinous had happened. It wasn't clear what, or who the sinner was and who the sinned against.

Ashfaq Mir rang a bell and ordered tea and biscuits without asking his guests if they wanted any. While they waited for it to be served, he followed Naga's gaze to a framed poster on the wall:

We follow our own rules

Ferocious we are

Lethal in any form

Tamer of tides

We play with storms

U guessed it right

We are

Men in Uniform

"Our in-house poetry . . ." Ashfaq Mir threw his head back and guffawed.

Either the tea—or the script—made him talkative. Oblivious to the disquiet (as well as the quiet) of his audience he chattered amiably about his college days, his politics, his job. He had been a student leader, he said, and like most young men of his generation, a hard-core Separatist. But having lived through the bloodshed of the early 1990s, having lost a cousin and five close friends, he had come to see the light. He now believed Kashmir's struggle for Azadi had lost its way and that nothing could be achieved without the "Rule of Law." And so he joined the Jammu and Kashmir Police and had been deputed to the SOG, the Special Operations Group. Holding a biscuit in the air, delicately between his thumb and forefinger, he recited a poem by Habib Jalib that he said had simply *come* to him—at the very moment of his change of heart:

Mohabbat goliyon se bo rahe ho
Watan ka chehra khoon se dho rahe ho

Gumaan tum ko ke rasta katt raha hai
Yaqeen mujhko ke manzil kho rahe ho

Bullets you sow instead of love
Our homeland you wash with blood
You imagine you're showing the way
But I believe you've gone astray

Without waiting for a reaction he switched from his declamatory tone to a conspiratorial one:

"And after Azadi? Has anyone thought? What will majority
do to the minority? Kashmiri Pandits have already gone. Only
us Muslims remain. What will we do to each other? What will
Salafis do to Barelvis? What will Sunnis do to Shias? They say
they will go to Jannat more surely if they kill a Shia than if they
kill a Hindu. What will be the fate of Ladakhi Buddhists? Jammu
Hindus? J&K is not just Kashmir. It's Jammu and Kashmir, and
Ladakh. Has any Separatist thought of this? The answer, I can
tell you, is a big 'No.'"

Naga agreed with what Ashfaq Mir said, and he knew how
carefully this seed of self-doubt had been sown by an administration that had clawed its way back into control from the brink
of utter chaos. Listening to Ashfaq Mir was like watching the
season change and the crop mature. It gave Naga a momentary
rush, a cultish sense of omniscience. But he didn't want to do
anything that would prolong the meeting. So he said nothing.
He made a show of craning his neck to read the list of the "Most
Wanted"—about twenty-five names—written with green Magic
Marker on the whiteboard behind the desk. Next to more than
half the names it said (killed) (killed) (killed).

"They are all Pakistanis and Afghanis," Ashfaq Mir said, not
turning around, keeping his gaze on Naga. "Their shelf-life is
not more than six months. By the year-end they will all be elimi-

nated. But we never kill Kashmiri boys. NEVER. Never unless they are hard-core."

The barefaced lie hung in the air unchallenged. That was its purpose—to test the air.

Ashfaq Mir sipped his tea, continuing to stare at Naga with those amazed, unblinking eyes. Suddenly—or perhaps not so suddenly—an idea seemed to occur to him. "Would you like to see a milton? I have a wounded one with me here in custody. A Kashmiri. Shall I order for him?"

He rang the bell once again. Within seconds a man answered it and took the "order" as though it were an additional snack that was being ordered with the tea.

Ashfaq Mir grinned mischievously. "Don't tell my boss, please. He will scold me. This type of thing is not allowed. But you— and Ma'am—will find it very interesting."

While he waited for the new snack to be served he turned his attention to the papers on his desk, signing his name rapidly on several of them, with an air of cheerful triumph, the scratch of his pen on paper amplified by the silence. Tilo, who had been sitting on a chair at the back of the room, stood up and walked to the window that looked out on to a bleak parking lot full of military trucks. She didn't want to be the audience for Ashfaq Mir's show. It was an instinctive gesture of solidarity with a prisoner against a jailer—regardless of the reasons that had made the prisoner a prisoner and the jailer a jailer.

From being someone who had been trying to turn her presence in the room into an absence, her unpresent form now turned thermal, emitting a flux that both the men in the room were acutely aware of, although in very different ways.

In a few minutes a burly policeman entered, carrying a thin boy in his arms. One leg of the boy's trousers was rolled up, exposing a matchstick-thin calf held together by a splint from ankle to knee. His arm was in a plaster cast and his neck was bandaged. Though his face was drawn with pain, he didn't grimace when the soldier deposited him on the floor.

To refuse to show pain was a pact the boy had made with himself. It was a desolate act of defiance that he had conjured up in the teeth of absolute, abject defeat. And that made it majestic. Except that nobody noticed. He stayed very still, a broken bird, half sitting, half lying, propped up on one elbow, his breath shallow, his gaze directed inward, his expression giving nothing away. He showed no curiosity about his surroundings or the people in the room.

And Tilo, with her back to the room, in an equally desolate act of defiance, refused to show curiosity about him.

Ashfaq Mir broke up the tableau with the same declamatory tone in which he had recited his poem. What he said this time was a kind of recital too:

"The average age of a milton is between seventeen and twenty years. He is brainwashed, indoctrinated and given a gun. They are mostly poor, low-caste boys—yes, for your kind information even we Muslims happily practice caste. They don't know what they want. They are simply being used by Pakistan to bleed India. It's what we can call their 'Prick and Bleed' policy. This boy's name is Aijaz. He was captured in an operation in an apple orchard near Pulwama. You can talk to him. Ask him any questions. He was with a new *tanzeem* that has recently started operations here. Lashkar-e-Taiba. His commander, Abu Hamza, was a Pakistani. He has been neutralized."

The game became clear to Naga. He was being offered a deal in Kashmir's special currency. An interview with a captured militant from a relatively new and—according to the intelligence reports he was privy to—deadly outfit, in exchange for peace over the night's events—for whatever had happened with Tilo and whatever horror she might have witnessed.

Ashfaq Mir walked over to his quarry and spoke to him in

Kashmiri, in a tone one might use for someone who was hard of hearing.

"*Yi chui* Nagaraj Hariharan Sahib. He is a famous journalist from India." (Sedition was a contagion in Kashmir—sometimes it involuntarily slipped into the vocabulary of Loyalists too.) "He writes against us openly, but still we respect and admire him. This is the meaning of democracy. Some day you will understand what a beautiful thing it is." He turned to address Naga, switching to English (which the boy understood, but could not speak). "After being with us and coming to know us well, this boy has seen the error of his ways. Now he thinks of us as his family. He has renounced his past and denounced his colleagues and those who forcibly indoctrinated him. He has himself requested us to keep him in custody for two years so that he can be safe from them. His parents are being allowed to visit him. In a few days he will be transferred to jail, to judicial custody. There are many boys like him who are with us here, ready to work with us. You can speak with him—ask him anything. It's no problem. He will talk."

Naga said nothing. Tilo remained at the window. It was cool outside, but the air rumbled and smelled of diesel. She watched soldiers escort a young woman with a baby in her arms through the maze of trucks and soldiers. The woman seemed reluctant to go. She kept turning around to look back at something. The soldiers deposited her outside the tall metal gates of the Shiraz, beyond the coiled razor-wire fence that barricaded the torture center from the main road. The woman remained standing where she had been deposited. A small, desperate, frightened figure, a traffic island on the crossroads to nowhere.

For a moment the silence in the room grew awkward.

"Oh I see I understand . . . you would like to speak with him one on one? Shall I go out? It's no problem. I can easily go out." Ashfaq Mir rang a bell. "I'm going out," he informed the puzzled orderly who answered the bell. "We are going out. We will sit in the outside room."

Having ordered himself out of his own office, he left and shut the door. Tilo turned around briefly to watch him leave. Through the gap between the bottom of the door and the floor she could see his brown shoes blocking the light. Within a second he came back in with a man who carried a blue plastic chair. It was positioned facing the boy on the floor.

"Please have a seat, sir. He will talk. You need not worry. He will not harm you. I'm going now, OK? You can speak in private."

He left, closing the door behind him. He returned almost immediately.

"I forgot to tell you that his name is Aijaz. Ask him anything." He looked at Aijaz and his tone became slightly peremptory. "Answer whatever he asks you. Urdu is no problem. You can speak in Urdu."

"*Ji*, sir," the boy said, not looking up.

"He's a Kashmiri, I'm a Kashmiri, we're brothers—and just look at us! OK. I'll go out."

Ashfaq Mir left the room once again. And once again his shoes paced up and down just outside the door.

"Would you like to say anything?" Naga asked Aijaz, ignoring the chair and crouching on the floor in front of him. "You don't have to. Only if you want to. On or off the record."

Aijaz held Naga's gaze for a moment. The mortification of being described as a renegade clean outstripped the physical pain he was in. He knew who Naga was. He didn't recognize his face, obviously, but Naga's name was well known in militant circles as a fearless journalist—not a fellow traveler by any means, but someone who could be useful—a member of the "human right-wing," as some militants jokingly called Indian journalists who wrote even-handedly and equally conscientiously about the excesses committed by the security forces as well as the militants. (Naga's political shift had still not manifested itself as a discernible pattern, not even to himself.) Aijaz knew he had only moments within which to decide what to do. Like a goalkeeper in a penalty shoot-out, he had to commit himself one way or another. He was young—he chose the riskier option. He began to speak, quietly and clearly, in Kashmiri-accented Urdu. The incongruity between his appearance and his words was almost as shocking as the words themselves.

"I know who you are, sir. Struggling people, people fighting for their freedom and dignity, know Nagaraj Hariharan as an honest, upright journalist. If you write about me you must write the truth. It's not true what he—Ashfaq Sahib—said. They tortured me, they gave me electric shocks and made me sign a blank sheet. This is what they do here with everybody. I don't know what they wrote on it later. I don't know what they have made me say in it. The truth is that I have not denounced anybody. The truth is that I honor those who trained me in jihad more than I honor my own parents. They didn't force me to join them. It was I who went looking for them."

Tilo turned around.

"I was in Class Twelve in a government school in Tangmarg. It took me one whole year to get recruited. They—Lashkar—were very suspicious of me because I didn't have any family member who had been killed, tortured or made to disappear. I did it for Azadi and for Islam. They took one year to believe me, to check me out, to see if I was an army agent, or if my family would be left without a breadwinner if I became a militant. They are very careful about—"

Four policemen burst into the room with trays of omelettes, bread, kebabs, onion rings, chopped carrots and more tea. Ashfaq Mir appeared behind them like a charioteer driving his horses. He personally served the food on to the plates, taking his time to arrange the carrots on the outer rim, the onions inside, like an impenetrable military formation. The room fell silent. There were only two plates. Aijaz returned his gaze to the floor. Tilo turned back to the window. The trucks came and went. The woman with the baby was still standing in the middle of the road. The sky was a flaming rose. The mountains in the distance were ethereally beautiful, but it had been another terrible year for tourism.

"Please go ahead. Help yourself. Will you like kebab? Now or later? Please, keep talking. No problem. OK, I'm going." And for the fourth time in ten minutes Ashfaq Mir left his office and stood outside the door.

Naga was pleased by what Aijaz had said about him and delighted that it had been said in front of Tilo. He could not resist a small performance.

"You crossed over? You were trained in Pakistan?" Naga asked Aijaz once he was sure Ashfaq Mir was out of earshot.

"No. I was trained here. In Kashmir. We have everything here now. Training, weapons . . . We buy our ammunition from the army. It's twenty rupees for a bullet, nine hundred for—"

"From the *army*?"

"Yes. They don't want the militancy to end. They don't want to leave Kashmir. They are very happy with the situation as it is. Everybody on all sides is making money on the bodies of young Kashmiris. So many of the grenade blasts and massacres are done by them."

"You're a Kashmiri. Why did you choose the Lashkar instead of Hizb or JKLF?"

"Because even the Hizb has respect for certain political leaders in Kashmir. In Lashkar we have no respect for these leaders. I have no respect for any leader. They have cheated and betrayed us. They have made their political careers on the bodies of Kashmiris. They have no plan. I joined Lashkar because I wanted to die. I am supposed to be dead. I did not ever think I would be caught alive."

"But first—before you died—you wanted to kill . . . ?"

Aijaz looked Naga in the eye.

"Yes. I wanted to kill the murderers of my people. Is that wrong? You can write that."

Ashfaq Mir burst in, smiling broadly, but his unsmiling eyes darted from person to person, trying to assess what had passed between them.

"Enough? Happy? Did he cooperate? Before publication you can please reconfirm with me any facts he gave you. He's a terrorist, after all. My terrorist brother."

And once again he guffawed happily and rang his bell. The burly policeman returned, gathered Aijaz in his arms and carried him away.

Once the snack had been cleared away on its burly tray, Naga and Tilo were given cheerful (but unspoken) permission to leave. The food on the plates remained untouched, the military formation unbreached.

On their way to Ahdoos, sitting in the claustrophobic back seat of an armored Gypsy, Naga held Tilo's hand. Tilo held his hand back. He was acutely aware of the circumstances in which that tentative exchange of tenderness was taking place. He could feel the tremor, the motor under her skin. Still, of all the women in the world, to have this woman's hand in his made him indescribably happy.

The smell inside the jeep was overpowering—a rank cocktail of sour metal, gunpowder, hair oil, fear and treachery. Its customary passengers were masked informers, known as "Cats." During cordon-and-search operations, the adult men of the cordoned neighborhood would be rounded up and paraded past the armored Gypsy, that ubiquitous symbol of dread in the Kash-mir Valley. From the depths of his metal cage, the concealed Cat would nod, or blink, and a man would be taken out of the line to be tortured, "disappeared," or to die. Naga knew all this of course, but it did nothing to lessen the intensity of his contentment.

The sullen city was wide awake but feigning sleep. Empty streets, closed markets, shuttered shops and locked houses slid past the jeep's slit windows—"death windows," local people called them, because what peered out of them were either soldiers' guns or informers' eyes. Packs of street dogs slouched about like small bears, their burred coats thickening in anticipation of the approaching winter. Other than tense soldiers on hair-trigger alert, there was not a human in sight. By mid-morning the cur-few would be lifted and the security withdrawn to allow people to reclaim their city for a few hours. They would swarm out of their homes in their hundreds of thousands and march to the graveyard, unaware that even the outpouring of their grief and fury had become part of a strategic, military, management plan.

Naga waited for Tilo to say something. She didn't. When he tried to initiate a conversation she said, "Please. Can we . . . is it . . . possible . . . to not talk?"

"Garson said they had killed a man, a Commander Gulrez . . . they think, or I don't know who thinks . . . Garson thinks . . . or maybe they told him it was Musa. Was it? Just that. Tell me just that?"

She said nothing for a moment. Then she turned and looked straight at him. Her eyes were broken glass.

"It was impossible to tell."

When he covered the conflict in Punjab, Naga had seen, often enough, the condition of bodies when they came out of interro-gation centers. So he took what Tilo said as confirmation of his suspicions. He understood that it would take Tilo a while to get over what she had been through. He was prepared to wait. He thought he knew enough—or at least all that he really needed to know—about what had happened. He forgave himself for the fact that Tilo's anguish was, for him, the source of exquisite contentment.

Tilo's answer to Naga's question wasn't an outright lie. But it certainly wasn't the truth. The truth was that given the condition of the body she saw, had she not known who it was, it would have been impossible to tell. But she did know who it was. She knew very well that it wasn't Musa.

With that untruth or half-truth or one-tenth truth (or whatever other fraction of the truth it was), the barriers came down and the borders of the country without consulates were sealed. The episode at the Shiraz was filed away as a closed subject.

When they returned to Delhi, since Tilo was in no condition to be left alone in what Naga called her "storeroom" in the Nizamuddin basti, he invited her to stay for a while in his little flat on the roof of his parents' house. When he finally saw her "haircut" he told her that it really suited her and that whoever had done it should become a hairdresser. That made her smile.

A few weeks later he asked her if she would marry him. She delighted him by saying that she would. Very soon, to his parents' utter dismay, the ceremony was, as they say, solemnized. They were married on Christmas Day, 1996.

If cover was what Tilo needed, she couldn't have done better than becoming the daughter-in-law of Ambassador Shivashankar Hariharan with a home address in Diplomatic Enclave.

She held that life together for fourteen years and then suddenly, she couldn't any more. There were a number of explanations for why this was so, but chief among them was exhaustion. She grew tired of living a life that wasn't really hers at an address she oughtn't to be at. Ironically, when the drift began, she was fonder of Naga than she had ever been. It was herself she was exhausted by. She had lost the ability to keep her discrete worlds discrete—a skill that many consider to be the cornerstone of sanity. The traffic inside her head seemed to have stopped believing in traffic lights. The result was incessant noise, a few bad crashes and eventually gridlock.

Looking back now, Naga realized that for years he had lived with the subconscious dread that Tilo was just passing through his life, like a camel crossing a desert. That she would surely leave him one day.

Still, when it actually happened, it took him a while to believe it.

His old friend R.C., who had always maintained that working in the Intelligence Bureau and reading interrogation transcripts gave a man an unparalleled understanding of human nature, more profound than any preacher, poet or psychiatrist could ever hope to attain, took him in hand.

"What she needs, I'm sorry to say, is two tight slaps. This modern approach of yours doesn't always work. At the end of the day we're all animals. We need to be shown our pee ell a see ee. A little clarity will go a long way towards helping all the concerned parties. You will be doing her a favor for which she will, one day, be grateful. Believe me, I speak from experience." R.C. often dropped his voice mid-sentence and spelled out random words, as though he was hoodwinking an imaginary eavesdropper who didn't know how to spell. He always referred to people as "parties." "At the end of the day" was his favorite launching pad for all his advice and insights, just as when he wanted to belittle someone he always began by saying, "With all due respect."

R.C. chastised Naga for allowing Tilo to refuse to have children. Children, he said, would have bound her to their marriage like nothing else could. He was a small, soft, effeminate man with a salt-and-pepper mustache. He had a small, soft wife and a small, soft teenaged daughter who was studying molecular biology. They looked like a model family of small, soft toys. So coming from him, this masculine advice was startling even to Naga, who had known him for years. Naga fell to wondering about the nature and frequency of tight slaps that had kept Mrs. R.C. in place. Outwardly she looked placid and perfectly content with her lot—with her houseful of mementoes and her collection of somewhat tasteless jewelry and expensive Kashmiri shawls. He couldn't imagine that she was really a volcano of hidden furies that needed to be disciplined and slapped from time to time.

R.C., who loved the blues, played a song for Naga. Billie Holiday's "No Good Man."

I'm the one who gets
The run-around,
I oughta hate him
And yet
I love him so
For I require
Love that's made of fire

R.C. heard "I oughta hate him" as "All the hittin'."
"Women," he said. "*All* women. No exceptions. Get it?"

Tilo had always reminded Naga of Billie Holiday. Not the woman so much as her voice. If it was possible for a human being to evoke a voice, a sound, then for Naga, Tilo evoked Billie Holiday's voice—she had that same quality of limbering, heart-stopping, fucked-up unexpectedness to her. R.C. had no idea what he had set off when he used Billie Holiday to illustrate the point he was making.

One morning, Naga, who, whatever his other faults, was physically the gentlest of men, hit his wife. Not very convincingly, they both realized. But he did hit her. Then he held her and wept. "Don't go. Please don't go."

That day Tilo stood at the gate and watched him being driven away in his office car, by his office driver. She couldn't see that he cried in the back seat all the way to work. Naga was not a crying man. (When he appeared as a guest on a prime-time TV debate about national security later that night, he showed no signs of personal distress. He was sharp with his repartee and made quick work of the Human Rights woman who said that New India was sliding towards fascism. Naga's laconic response raised a titter from the carefully picked studio audience of nattily dressed students and ambitious young professionals. Another guest, a retired, geriatric army general, all mustache and medals, who was trundled out regularly by TV studios to supply venom and stupidity to all discussions on national security, laughed and applauded.)

Tilo took a bus to the edge of the city. She walked through miles of city waste, a bright landfill of compacted plastic bags with an army of ragged children picking through it. The sky was a dark swirl of ravens and kites competing with the children, pigs and packs of dogs for the spoils. In the distance, garbage trucks wound their way slowly up the garbage mountain. Partly collapsed cliffs of refuse revealed the depth of what had accumulated.

She took another bus to the riverfront. She stopped on a bridge and watched a man row a circular raft built with old mineral-water bottles and plastic jerry cans across the thick, slow, filthy river. Buffaloes sank blissfully into the black water. On the pavement vendors sold lush melons and sleek green cucumbers grown in pure factory effluent.

She spent an hour on a third bus and got off at the zoo. For a long time she watched the little gibbon from Borneo in his vast, empty enclosure, a furry dot hugging a tall tree as though his life depended on it. The ground underneath the tree was littered with things visitors had thrown at him to attract his attention. There was a gibbon-shaped cement trashcan outside the gibbon's cage and a hippo-shaped trashcan outside the hippo's cage. The cement hippo's mouth was open and crammed with trash. The real hippo was wallowing in a scummy pond, her slick, wide, ballooning bottom the color of a wet tire, her tiny eyes set inside their pink, puffy eyelids, watchful, above the water. Plastic bottles and empty cigarette packets floated around her. A man bent down to his little daughter dressed in a bright frock, her eyes smudged with kohl. He pointed to the hippo and said, "Crocodile." "Cockodie," his little girl said, cranking up the cuteness. A knot of noisy young men flicked razor blades across the barred enclosure and down the cement banks of the hippo pond. When they ran out of blades they asked Tilo if she would take a photograph of them. One of them, with rings on every finger and faded red threads around his wrists, composed the picture for her, handed her his phone and ran back into the frame. He put his arms around his companions' shoulders and made the victory sign. When Tilo returned the phone she congratulated them for the courage it must require to feed a caged hippo razor blades. It took a while for the insult to register. When it did, they followed her around the zoo with that leering Delhi yodel "Oye! Hapshie madam!" Hey! Nigger madam! They taunted her not because the color of her skin was unusual in India, but because they saw in her bearing and demeanor a "hapshie"—Hindi for Abyssinian—who had risen above her station. A "hapshie" who was clearly not a maidservant or a laborer.

There was an Indian rock python in every cage in the snake house. Snake scam. There were cows in the sambar stag's enclosure. Deer scam. And there were women construction workers carrying bags of cement in the Siberian tiger enclosure. Siberian tiger scam. Most of the birds in the aviary were ones you could see on the trees anyway. Bird scam. At the cage of the sulphur-crested cockatoo one of the young men insinuated himself next to Tilo and sang to the cockatoo, setting his own lyrics to the tune of a popular Bollywood song:

Duniya khatam ho jayegi
Chudai khatam nahi hogi

The world will end,
But fucking never will.

It was intended to be doubly insulting because Tilo was at least double his age.

Outside the enclosure of the rosy pelicans she received a text message on her phone:

Organic Homes on NH24 Ghaziabad
1 BHK 15L*
2 BHK 18L*
3 BHK 31L*
Booking starting at Rs 35000
For Discount call 91-103-957-9-8

The dusty old Nicaraguan jaguar had his chin on the dusty ledge of his cage. He stayed like that, supremely indifferent, for hours. Maybe years.

Tilo felt like him. Dusty, old and supremely indifferent.

Maybe she *was* him.

Maybe some day she would have an expensive city car named after her.

WHEN SHE MOVED OUT, she didn't take much with her. At first it wasn't clear to Naga or, for that matter, even to her that she had moved out. She told him she had rented an office space, she didn't say where. (Garson Hobart didn't tell him either.) For a few months she came and went. Over time she went more than she came, and then gradually she stopped returning home.

Naga began his life as a newly unmarried man by plunging into work and into a string of gloomy affairs. Being on TV as often as he was had made him what magazines and newspapers called a "celebrity," which people seemed to think was a profession in and of itself. At restaurants and airports strangers often approached him for an autograph. Many of them weren't even sure who he was, or what exactly he did or why he looked familiar. Naga was too bored to even bother to refuse. Unlike most men of his age, he was still slim, and had a full head of hair. Being seen as "successful" gave him the pick of a range of women, some single and far younger than him, and some his age or older, married and looking for variety, or divorced and looking for a second chance. The front runner among them was a slender, stylish widow in her mid-thirties with milk-white skin and glossy hair—minor royalty from a small principality—in whom Naga's mother saw her younger self, and coveted more than her son did. She invited the lady and Prince Charles, her Chihuahua, to stay with her downstairs as a house guest, from where they could jointly plan the capture of the summit.

A few months into their affair, the Princess began to call Naga "jaan"—Beloved. She taught the servants in the house to call her Bai Sa in the tradition of Rajput royalty. She cooked Naga dishes made with secret family recipes from her family's royal kitchen. She ordered new curtains, embroidered cushions and lovely dhurries for the floor. She brought a sweet, sunny, feminine touch to an egregiously neglected apartment. Her attentions were balm to Naga's injured pride. Though he didn't reciprocate her feelings with the same intensity with which they were offered, he accepted them with a tired grace. He had almost forgotten what it was like to be the doted-on one in a couple. Notwithstanding his general prejudice towards small dogs, he grew inordinately fond of Prince Charles. He took him to the neighborhood park regularly, where he threw a tiny, saucer-sized frisbee for him that he had sourced and bought online. Prince Charles would retrieve his saucer-frisbee, lolloping back to Naga through weeds that were almost as tall as he was. The Princess played hostess at a few dinners that Naga threw. R.C. was entranced by her and impressed upon Naga that he should lose no time and marry her while she was still of childbearing age.

Naga, still distraught and still vulnerable to R.C.'s disastrous advice, asked the Princess if she would like to move in for a trial run. She reached across and tenderly neatened his unruly eyebrows, pressing the hairs into a ridge between her forefinger and her thumb. She said nothing would make her happier, but that before she moved in she would need to liberate Tilo's *chi* that still hung about the house. With Naga's permission she dry-roasted whole red chilies and carried the smoking copper pot from room to room, coughing delicately and turning her glossy head away from the acrid smoke with her eyes screwed shut. When the chilies stopped smoking she said a prayer and buried them in the garden along with the pot. Then she tied a red thread around Naga's wrist and lit expensive scented candles, one in each room, and left them to burn down to the wick. She bought a dozen large cardboard cartons for Naga to pack Tilo's things into and take down to the basement. It was while he was cleaning out Tilo's cupboard (that smelled so unashamedly of her) that Naga came upon Tilo's mother's thick medical file from Lakeview Hospital in Cochin.

. . .

In all the years he and Tilo had been married, Naga had never met Tilo's mother. Tilo never talked about her. He knew the broad contours of course. Her name was Maryam Ipe. She belonged to an old, aristocratic Syrian Christian family that had fallen on bad times. Two generations of the family—her father and her brother—had graduated from Oxford and she herself had been educated at a convent school in Ootacamund, a hill station in the Nilgiris, and then at a Christian college in Madras, after which her father's illness forced her to return to her home town in Kerala. Naga knew that she had been an English teacher in a local school before she started her own school, which grew to be an extremely successful high school known for its innovative teaching methods—the school that Tilo had attended before she came to college in Delhi. He had read a few newspaper articles about Tilo's mother in which Tilo was never named, but always referred to as her adopted daughter who lived in Delhi. R.C. (whose job it was to know everything about everybody and to let everybody know that he knew everything about everybody) had once made a file of clippings for him, saying, "Your Foster-Mother-in-Law is a cool chick, *yaar*." The articles spanned a period of several years—some were about her school, its teaching methods and its beautiful campus, some were about the social and environmental campaigns that she had led or the awards she had won. They told the story of a woman who had overcome great adversity in her early life to become what she was—an iconic feminist who never moved to a big city, but chose instead to take the hard path and continue to live and fight her battles in the conservative little town she belonged to. They described how she had struggled against cabals of bullying men, how she eventually won the respect and admiration of those who had tormented her and how she had inspired a whole generation of young women to follow their dreams and desires.

It was obvious to anybody who knew Tilo that she was not the foster-daughter of the woman in the photographs in those articles. Although their complexions were dramatically different, their features were strikingly similar.

From what little he knew, Naga sensed there was a substantial piece of the puzzle that had gone missing in the newspaper stories—a sort of epic Macondo madness, the stuff of literature, not journalism. Although he never said so, he felt Tilo's attitude towards her mother was punitive and unreasonable. In his opinion, even if it was true that Tilo was her real child whom she would not publicly acknowledge, it was equally true that for a young woman who belonged to a traditional community, to have chosen a life of independence, chosen to eschew marriage in order to claim a child born to her out of wedlock—even if it meant masking it as benevolence and masquerading as the baby's foster-mother—was an act of immense courage and love.

Naga noticed that in all the newspaper articles, the paragraph concerning Tilo was always a set piece: "Sister Scholastica called me to say that a coolie woman had left a newborn baby in a basket outside the Mount Carmel orphanage. She asked if I wanted to take her. My family was dead against it, but I thought that if I adopted her I could give her a new life. She was a jet-black baby, like a little piece of coal. She was so small she almost fitted in the palm of my hand so I called her Tilottama, which means 'sesame seed' in Sanskrit."

Hurtful as this might have been for Tilo, Naga thought she should be able to look at it from her mother's point of view—she needed to distance herself from her baby if only in order to be able to claim her, own her and love her.

According to Naga, the credit for Tilo's individuality, her quirkiness and unusualness—regardless of which school you subscribed to, nature or nurture—went straight to her mother.

But nothing he could say, directly or indirectly, led to a rapprochement.

So Naga was puzzled when, having kept away from her mother for so many years, Tilo so readily agreed to go to Cochin and look after her in hospital. He imagined (even though he couldn't recall Tilo ever having betrayed any curiosity on the subject) that it could have been in the hope of gaining some information, a deathbed revelation perhaps, about herself and who her father really was. He was right. But it turned out to be a little late for that sort of thing.

BY THE TIME Tilo reached Cochin, her mother's deteriorating lungs had led to a build-up of carbon dioxide in her bloodstream, which in turn led to the inflammation of her brain, which made her severely disoriented. To add to that, her medication and her extended stay in the ICU had induced a form of psychosis which doctors said particularly affected powerful, self-willed people who suddenly found themselves helpless and at the mercy of those they had once treated as minions. Other than the hospital staff, her anger and bewilderment were directed at her faithful old servants and the teachers from her school who took turns to be on hospital duty. They hovered around in the hospital corridor and were allowed to visit their beloved Ammachi in the ICU for a few minutes every couple of hours.

On the day Tilo arrived, her mother's face lit up.

"I'm scratching all the time," she said by way of greeting. "He says it's good to scratch, but I couldn't stand it any more, so I took the scratching medicine. How are you?"

She held up her dark purple arms, one of them attached to a drip, to show Tilo what had happened to her skin from having been prodded and poked with needles by the doctors' endless search for veins that were still open. Most of her veins had collapsed and closed down and formed a darker purple web underneath the already-purple skin.

"Then will he strip his sleeve and show his scars and say, 'These wounds had I on Crispin's day.' Remember? I taught you that."

"Yes."

"What's the next line?"

"Old men forget. Yet all shall be forgot. But he'll remember with advantages what feats he did that day."

Tilo had forgotten that she remembered. Shakespeare came back to her not as a feat of memory so much as music, as an old tune remembered. She was taken aback by her mother's condition, but the doctors were pleased and said the fact that her mother had recognized her was a remarkable improvement. That day they moved her to a private room with a window that overlooked the saltwater lagoon and the Coconut trees that bent into it and the monsoon storms that blew across it.

The improvement didn't last. In the days that followed the old lady drifted in and out of lucidity and didn't always recognize Tilo. Each day was an unpredictable new chapter in the course her illness took. She developed new quirks and irrational preoccupations. The hospital staff, the doctors, nurses and even the attendants were kind, and seemed not to take anything she said to heart. They too called her Ammachi, sponged her, changed her nappies and combed her hair with no sign of annoyance or rancor. In fact, the more havoc she created, the more they seemed to love her.

A few days after Tilo arrived, her mother developed a weird fixation. She turned into a sort of caste-inquisitor. She began to insist on knowing the caste and subcaste and sub-subcaste of everybody who attended to her. It wasn't enough if they said they were "Syrian Christian"—she had to know whether they were

Marthoma, Yacoba, Church of South India or C'naah. If they were "Hindu," it wasn't enough if they said Ezhava, she had to know if they were Theeyas or Chekavars. If they said "Scheduled Caste," she had to know if they were Parayas, Pulayas, Paravans, Ulladans. Were they originally of the coconut-picker caste? Or were their ancestors designated corpse-carriers, shit-cleaners, clothes-washers or rat-catchers? She insisted on specifics and only once she knew would she permit herself to be handled by them. If they were Syrian Christian, then what was their family name? Whose nephew was married to whose sister-in-law's niece? Whose grandfather had been married to whose great-grandfather's sister's daughter?

"COPD," the smiling nurses said to Tilo when they saw the expression on her face. "Don't worry. It happens like this always." She looked it up. Chronic Obstructive Pulmonary Disease. The nurses told Tilo it was a disease that could give harmless old grandmothers the manners of brothel-owners and make bishops swear like drunks. It was best not to take anything personally. They were fabulous girls, those nurses, precise and professional. Each of them was waiting for a job that would take her to a Gulf country, or to England or the US, where they would join that elite community of Malayali nurses. Until then, they fluttered around the patients in Lakeview Hospital like butterfly healers. They became friends with Tilo and exchanged phone numbers and email addresses. For years after that she'd receive WhatsApp Christmas greetings and round-robin Malayali nurse jokes from them.

As her illness intensified, the old lady became restless and almost impossible to manage. Sleep forsook her and she stayed awake, night after night, her pupils dilated, her eyes terrified, talking continuously to herself and to anybody who would listen. It was as though she thought she could outsmart death by remaining constantly vigilant. So she talked continuously, sometimes belligerent, sometimes pleasant and amusing. She sang snatches of old songs, hymns, Christmas carols, Onam boat-race songs. She recited Shakespeare in her impeccable convent-school English. When she got upset she insulted everybody around her in a hard-core dialect of guttersnipe Malayalam that nobody could work out how (and from where) in the world a woman of her class and breeding had picked up. As the days wore on, she grew more and more aggressive. Her appetite increased dramatically and she downed soft-boiled eggs and pineapple upside-down pastries with the urgency of a convict on parole. She tapped into reserves of physical strength that were nothing short of superhuman for a woman of her age. She fought off nurses and doctors, pulled ports and syringes out of her veins. She could not be sedated because sedatives suppressed lung function. Finally she was moved back to the ICU.

That made her furious and pushed her further into psychosis. Her eyes turned sly and hunted and she constantly plotted her escape. She offered bribes to nurses and attendants. She promised a young doctor that she would sign over her school and its grounds to him if he would help her to get out. Twice she made it all the way down the corridor in her hospital gown. After that episode two nurses had to keep constant vigil, and occasionally even hold her down in her bed. When she had exhausted everybody around her the doctors said the hospital could not afford to give her round-the-clock nursing care and that she would need to be physically restrained, strapped to her bed. They asked Tilo, as her next of kin, to sign the forms that gave them permission to do so. Tilo asked them for one last chance to try to calm her mother down. The doctors agreed, if a little reluctantly.

The last time she called Naga from the hospital, Tilo told him that she had been given special permission to stay by her mother's side in the ICU because she had finally found a way of soothing her. He thought he detected a hint of laughter and even affection in her voice. She said she had found a simple, workable solution. She sat on a chair by her mother's bed with a notebook and her mother dictated endless notes to her. Sometimes they were letters: *Dear Parent comma next line . . . it has been brought to my notice that . . . did you put a comma after Dear Parent?* Mostly they were pure gibberish. Somehow the idea of dictating things, Tilo said, seemed to make her mother feel that she was still the captain of the ship, still in charge of something, and that calmed her down considerably.

Naga had no idea what Tilo was talking about and told her she sounded a little delirious herself. She laughed and said he'd understand when he saw the notes. He remembered wondering at the time what kind of person it was that got on best with her mother when she was hallucinating on her deathbed in an ICU while she, the daughter, masqueraded as her stenographer.

Eventually, though, things didn't turn out well in Lakeview Hospital. Tilo returned after her mother's funeral, gaunt and more uncommunicative than ever. Her description of her mother's passing was brief and almost clinical. Within weeks of returning to Delhi she began her restless wandering.

Naga never did see the notes.

THAT MORNING, as he leafed aimlessly through the medical file in Tilo's cupboard, he found some of them. They were in Tilo's writing, on ruled pages torn out of a notebook, folded up and tucked between hospital bills, medicine prescriptions, oxygen-saturation charts and blood-gas test results. As he read them, Naga realized how little he knew about the woman he had married. And how little he would ever know:

9/7/2009

Take care of the potted plants they may fall.

And that fold—the crumple in the blanket—I might
have to trump them all.

What does that say about you Madam Ambassador
Master Builder Paraya Girl?

Those people in blue, they handle the shit. Are they
your relatives?

As far as I know Paulose doesn't get on with the
orchids, he's killing them. It could be a Paraya
problem.

Ask Biju or Reju to take over.

Have you heard the dogs at night? They come to
take away the legs from the diabetes people that are
cut off and thrown away. I can hear them howling
and they run off with people's arms and legs. Nobody
tells them not to.

Are they your dogs? Are they boys or girls? They
seem to like sweet things.

Can you get me a good-quality jujube?

The blue people must stop hanging around us.

We must be very careful, you and I. You know that,
don't you?

They have measured my tears and they are OK in
terms of salt and water. I have dry eyes and must
keep bathing them and eating sardines to make tears.
Sardines are full of tears.

This girl in checks will do stunning deeds with the
lottery.

Let's go.

Ask Reju to get the car. I just can't. I don't want to.

Hello! How nice to meet you! This is my
granddaughter. She cannot be controlled. Please see
that this place is cleaned out.

As soon as Reju comes let's take the car and make a
run for it. Carry the potty. Leave the shit.

You come here now. Give me a whisper. I'm in a jam.
Are you in a jam too?

We'll sit on the potty and make a jump for it.

I'll have a Johnnie Walker. Is he up there on top
of us?

I'll just take two sheets. But what should our legs do?

Will there be a horse?

A great war has started between me and the
butterflies.

Will you get out as soon as possible with Princey, Nicey and friends? Take the brass vase, the violin and the stitches. Leave the shit and darkglasses and forget about the broken chairs, they're always hanging around, they come and go.

She'll help you with your shit this girl in checks. Her father is going to be here soon to take out the rubbish. I don't want him to be caught with you. I think we should just clear out.

When you look out behind those curtains, do you feel there's a crowd of people? I feel there is. There's definitely a smell. A crowd smell. A bit rotten, like the sea.

I think you should leave your poems and all your plans with Alicekutty. She is hideously ugly. I'd like a photograph of her for me to laugh at. That's how nasty I am.

The bishop will want to see me in my coffin. It's quite a relief because it's for my funeral. I never thought I'd get there. Is it raining, is it shining, is it dark is it day is it night? Can't somebody please tell me?

Now BUNK.

And get these horses out.

I think it's mean to take this girl and empty out her everything.

Get up!!!

I'm going out. You can do what you want. You'll get such a thrashing.

Most shameful you are to stand around saying you are Tilottama Ipe when you are not. I won't tell you anything about myself or yourself either.

I'm just going to stand here and say, "Do this and do that." And you'll jolly well do it. No salary for you from tomorrow. Have you written that? I'll fine you every time.

Go and tell everybody that "This is my mother, Ms Maryam Ipe, and she's one hundred and fifty years old."

Do they have medicine for all the horses?

Have you noticed how people look like horses when they yawn?

Look after your teeth viciously and don't let anyone take them out.

Sometimes they offer you a discount and that's stupid.

Check everything and let's go.

And then there's Hannah. I owe her money and I have to jump over all the children with catheters.

There are so many catheters and everybody was rather pleased that Mrs. Ipe was getting her onions. But she's been so good this child. You didn't remove my catheter. She did. She's a proper Paraya. You've forgotten how to be one.

Somebody came up and then somebody and somebody.

The shock of it all is that YOU are giving your rules to everybody. But I expect people to obey me.

But I AM in charge. It is very difficult to get out of charge as you will no doubt find. Annamma is the quietest creature in our community.

Who is the Annamma who plays Sherlock Holmes and Sherlock Holmes? She does both with grace. She was my head teacher who died so beautifully. She went home and brought me a cough.

Hello Doctor this is my daughter who is homeschooled. She's pretty nasty. She was awful today at the races. But I was pretty awful too. We gave everybody a kicking.

I spent my life doing ridiculous things. I produced a baby. Her.

And that boy with dirty clothes and a dirty catheter and I sat for hours in the dirty river.

I feel I am surrounded by eunuchs. Am I?

Music . . . what's wrong with it? I just can't remember any more.

Listen to that . . . it's oxygen. Bubbling to its death. I am running out of oxygen. But I don't care whether I'm running out or running in.

I want to sleep. I'd love to die. Wrap my feet in warm water.

I'd like to go to sleep. I'm not asking for permission.

It's like hpsf hpsf hpsf . . . CUK! CUK! CUK!

This is my engine.

When you die you can hook on to a cloud and we can have all your information. Then they give you your bill.

WHERE'S MY MONEY?

The arterial port is Jesus Christ's screw. It doesn't hurt.

I'm just a wee mannequin.

I like my bum. I don't know why Dr. Verghese wants to cut it out of the picture.

The frozen flowers never go away. They hang around somewhere all the time. I think we need to talk about vases.

Did you hear the sound of the white flower?

What Naga found was just a sampling. The compiled notes, if they hadn't gone out with the hospital waste, would have made up several volumes.

ONE MORNING, after a week of non-stop stenography, Tilo, worn out, was standing by her mother's bedside, leaning her arms on the back of the chair she usually sat in. It was the busiest time of the day in the ICU, doctors were on their rounds, the nurses and attendants were busy, the ward was being cleaned. Maryam Ipe was having a particularly vile morning. Her face was flushed and her eyes had a feverish glitter. She had pulled up her hospital gown and lay in her nappy, her legs ramrod straight and splayed apart. When she shouted, her voice was deep enough to be a man's.

"Tell the Parayas that it's time to clean my shit!"

Tilo's blood left the highway and steamed along mad forest paths. Without warning, the chair she had been leaning on picked itself up and smashed itself down. The sound of splintering wood echoed through the ward. Needles jumped out of veins. Medicine bottles rattled in their trays. Weak hearts missed a beat. Tilo watched the sound travel through her mother's body, from her feet upwards, like a shroud being pulled over a corpse.

She had no idea how long she continued to stand there or who took her to Dr. Verghese's office.

Dr. Jacob Verghese, Head of the Department of Critical Care, had, until four years ago, been a medic with the US Army. He was second-in-command of critical care in his unit in the Kuwait war and had returned to Kerala when his tenure ended. Even though he had lived most of his life abroad, his speech did not bear even a trace of an American accent, which was remarkable, because in Kerala people joked that applying for a US visa was enough for people to affect an American accent. Nothing about Dr. Verghese suggested that he was anything other than an absolutely local Syrian Christian who had lived in Kerala all his life. He smiled at Tilo kindly and ordered coffee. He came from the same town as Maryam Ipe and was probably well aware of all the old rumors and whispers. The air conditioning in his office was being serviced and the clatter of that took away the awkwardness in the room. Tilo watched the mechanic carefully, as though her life depended on it. Men and women in green tunics and trousers, wearing surgical masks, floated around soundlessly in the corridor in operation-theater slippers. Some of them had blood on their surgeons' gloves. Dr. Verghese looked at Tilo over his reading glasses, studying her as though he was trying to make a diagnosis. Perhaps he was. In a while he reached across the table and took her hand in his. He could not have known that he was trying to comfort a building that had been struck by lightning. There wasn't much left of it to comfort. After his coffee had been drunk and hers left untouched, he suggested they go back to the ICU and that she apologize to her mother.

"Your mother is a remarkable woman. You must understand that it isn't she who is uttering those ugly words."

"Oh. Who is it, then?"

"Someone else. Her illness. Her blood. Her suffering. Our conditioning, our prejudices, our history . . ."

"So to whom will I be apologizing? To prejudice? Or to history?"

But she was already following him down the corridor, back to the ICU.

By the time they arrived her mother had slipped into a coma. She was beyond hearing, beyond history, beyond prejudice, beyond apology. Tilo curled up on the bed and put her face on her mother's feet until they went cold. The broken chair watched over them like a melancholy angel. Tilo wondered how her mother had known what the chair would do. How could she have known?

Forget about the broken chairs, they're always hanging around.

Maryam Ipe died early the next morning.

The Syrian Christian church would not forgive her her trespasses and flat out refused to bury her. So the funeral, attended mostly by schoolteachers and a few of her pupils' parents, took place in the government crematorium. Tilo brought her mother's ashes back to Delhi. She told Naga that she needed to think very carefully about what to do with them. She didn't tell him much else. The pot containing the ashes sat on her worktable for as long as he could remember. Lately Naga noticed that it had disappeared. He was not sure whether Tilo had found an appropriate place to immerse the ashes (or scatter them, or bury them), or whether they had simply moved with her to her new home.

THE PRINCESS CAME UPON NAGA sitting on the floor looking through a fat medical file. She stood behind him and read the notes aloud over his shoulders.

" 'The arterial port is Jesus Christ's screw' . . . 'Did you hear the sound of the white flower?' What's this rubbish you're reading, jaan? Since when did flowers start making sounds?"

Naga remained sitting and said nothing for a long time. He appeared to be deep in thought. Then he stood up and cupped her beautiful face in his hands.

"I'm so sorry . . ."

"For what, jaan?"

"It's not going to work . . ."

"What?"

"Us."

"But she's gone! She's left you!"

"She has. She has, yes . . . But she'll come back. She has to. She will."

The Princess looked at Naga pityingly and moved on. She was soon married to the Chief Editor of a TV news channel. They made a handsome, happy couple and went on to have many healthy, happy children.

THE ROOMS TILO RENTED were on the second floor of a town-house overlooking a government primary school full of relatively poor children and a Neem tree full of reasonably well-off parakeets. Every morning at assembly the children shouted out the whole of "Hum Hongey Kaamyaab"—the Hindi version of "We Shall Overcome." She sang with them. On weekends and holidays she missed the children and the school assembly, so she sang the song to herself at exactly 7 a.m. On the days that she didn't, she felt the morning was just the previous day extended, that a new day hadn't dawned. On most mornings, anyone who put an ear to her door would have heard her.

No one put an ear to her door.

Miss Jebeen's birthday and baptism ceremony marked Tilo's fourth year and last night in the second-floor apartment. She wondered what she should do with the rest of the birthday cake. Perhaps the ants would invite their relatives in the neighborhood to partake of the feast and either finish it or remove every last crumb into storage.

The heat stood up and paced around the room. Traffic growled in the distance. City thunder.

No rain.

The spotted owlet flitted away to duck and bob and practice

his good manners on some other woman through some other window.

When she noticed that the owl had left, Tilo felt unutterably sad. She knew she would soon be leaving too, and might never see him again. The owl was *someone*. She wasn't sure who. Musa maybe. That was always how it was with Musa. Each time he left, after his brief, mysterious visits, in his peculiar disguises, looking like Mr. Nobody from District Nowhere, she knew she might never see him again. Usually it was he who disappeared and she who waited. This time it was her turn to disappear. She had no means of letting him know where she was. He did not use a mobile phone, and the only calls he made to her were on her landline, which would now go unanswered. She was overcome by the desire to communicate the uncertain nature of their farewell to the spotted owlet that night. She scribbled a line on a piece of paper and stuck it on the window, facing outwards for the owl to read:

Who can know from the word goodbye *what kind of parting is in store for us.*

She returned to her mattress, pleased with herself and the borrowed clarity of her communication. But then, in no time at all, she felt ashamed. Osip Mandelstam had had more serious things on his mind when he wrote that line. He was negotiating Stalin's Gulag. He wasn't talking to owls. She retrieved her note and once again returned to bed.

A few miles away from where she lay awake, three men had been crushed to death the previous night by a truck that had careened off the road. Perhaps the driver had fallen asleep. On TV they said that that summer homeless people had taken to sleeping on the edges of roads with heavy traffic. They had discovered that diesel exhaust fumes from passing trucks and buses were an effective mosquito repellent and protected them from the outbreak of dengue fever that had killed several hundred people in the city already.

She imagined the men: new immigrants to the city, stone-workers, come home to their pre-booked, pre-paid-for spot whose rent was calculated by calibrating the optimum density of exhaust fumes and dividing it by the acceptable density of mosquitoes. Precise algebra; not easily found in textbooks.

The men were tired from their day's work on the building site, their eyelashes and lungs pale with stone-dust from cutting stone and laying floors in the multi-story shopping centers and housing estates springing up around the city like a fast-growing forest. They spread their soft, frayed *gamchha*s on the poky grass of the sloping embankment dotted with dogshit and stainless-steel sculptures—public art—sponsored by the Pamnani Group that was promoting cutting-edge artists who used stainless steel as a medium, in the hope that the cutting-edge artists would promote the steel industry. The sculptures looked like clusters of steel spermatozoa, or perhaps they were meant to be balloons. It wasn't clear. Either way, they looked cheerful. The men lit a last beedi. Smoke rings curled into the night. The neon street lights made the grass look metal blue and the men look gray. There was teasing and some laughter, because two of them could blow smoke rings and the third couldn't. He was bad at things, always the last to learn.

Sleep came to them, quick and easy, like money to millionaires.

If they hadn't died of truck, they would have died of:

(a) Dengue fever
(b) The heat
(c) Beedi smoke
or
(d) Stone-dust

Or maybe not. Maybe they would have risen to become:

(a) Millionaires
(b) Supermodels
or
(c) Bureau chiefs

Did it matter that they were mashed into the grass they slept on? To whom did it matter? Did those to whom it mattered matter?

> *Dear Doctor,*
>   *We have been crushed. Is there a cure?*
> *Regards,*
> *Biru, Jairam, Ram Kishore*

Tilo smiled and closed her eyes.

Careless motherfuckers. Who asked them to get in the way of the truck?

She wondered how to un-know certain things, certain specific things that she knew but did not wish to know. How to un-know, for example, that when people died of stone-dust, their lungs refused to be cremated. Even after the rest of their bodies had turned to ash, two lung-shaped slabs of stone remained behind, unburned. Her friend Dr. Azad Bhartiya, who lived on the pavement of Jantar Mantar, had told her about his older brother, Jiten Y. Kumar, who had worked in a granite quarry and died at the age of thirty-five. He described how he had had to break up his brother's lungs with a crowbar on the funeral pyre to release his soul. He did it, he said, even though he was a communist and didn't believe in souls.

He did it to please his mother.

He said his brother's lungs glittered, because they were speckled with silica.

> *Dear Doctor,*
> *Nothing, really. I just wanted to say hello. Actually—*
> *there is something. Imagine having to smash your*
> *brother's lungs to please your mother. Would you call that*
> *normal human activity?*

She wondered what an unreleased soul, a soul-shaped stone on a funeral pyre, might look like. Like a starfish maybe. Or a millipede. Or a dappled moth with a living body and stone wings—poor moth—betrayed, held down by the very things that were meant to help it to fly.

Miss Jebeen the Second stirred in her sleep.

Concentrate, the kidnapper told herself as she stroked the baby's damp, sweaty forehead. *Otherwise things could get completely out of hand.* She had no idea why she of all people, who never wanted children, had picked up the baby and run. But now it was done. Her part in the story had been written. But not by her. By whom, then? Someone.

> *Dear Doctor,*
> *If you like you can change every inch of me. I'm just a*
> *story.*

Miss Jebeen was a good-natured baby and seemed to like the saltless soup and mashed vegetables that Tilo made for her. For a woman who had very little experience with children, Tilo was surprisingly easy with her and confident in the way she handled her. On the few occasions that Miss Jebeen cried, she was able to comfort her in no time at all. The best course of action, Tilo found (a feed being the exception), was to lay her down on the floor with the litter of five gun-colored puppies that Comrade Laali, a red-haired mongrel, had birthed on the landing outside her door five weeks ago. Both parties (the puppies and Miss Jebeen) seemed to have plenty to say to each other. Both mothers were great friends. So the get-togethers were usually a success. When everybody was tired, Tilo would return the puppies to their burlap sack on the landing, and give Comrade Laali a little bowl of milk and bread.

Earlier in the day, Tilo had just lit the candle on the cake and was waltzing the newly named Miss Jebeen around the room humming "Happy Birthday," when Ankita, the ground-floor tenant, phoned. She said that a constable had come by that morning inquiring about her (Tilo) and asking her (Ankita) whether she knew anything about a new baby in the building. He was in a hurry and had left a newspaper with her in which the police had published a routine notice. Ankita sent it up with her little Adivasi child-slave. It said:

KIDNAPPING NOTICE DP/1146

NEW DELHI 110001

General Public is hereby informed that one unknown baby, s/o UNKNOWN, r/o UNKNOWN, without clothes was abandoned at Jantar Mantar, New Delhi. After Police was informed but before police-force arrived on the scene the said baby was kidnapped by an unknown person/persons. First Information Report has been registered under Sections 361, 362, 365, 366A, Sections 367 & 369. For all or any infor-

mation please contact Station House Officer,
Parliament Street Police Station, New Delhi. The
description of the baby is as under:

Name: UNKNOWN, Father's Name: UNKNOWN,
Address: UNKNOWN, Age: UNKNOWN, Wearing:
NO CLOTHES.

Ankita sounded superior and disapproving on the phone. But
that was just her usual manner with Tilo. She tended to assume
that somewhat smug, triumphant air of a woman-with-a-husband
speaking to a woman-without-a-husband. It didn't have anything
to do with the baby. She did not know about Miss Jebeen. (Fortunately Garson Hobart had seen to it that the construction of
his house was solid and the walls soundproof.) Nobody in the
neighborhood did. Tilo had not taken her out. She hadn't been
out much herself, except for occasional, essential trips to the
market when the baby was asleep. The shopkeepers might have
wondered about the uncharacteristic purchases of baby food. But
Tilo did not think the police would take the investigation that far.

When she first read the police notice in the newspaper, Tilo
didn't take it seriously. It looked like a routine, bureaucratic
requirement that was being mindlessly fulfilled. On a second
reading, however, she realized it could spell serious trouble. To
give herself time to think, she copied the notice carefully into a
notebook, word for word, in olde-worlde calligraphy, and decorated it with a margin of vines and fruit as though it were the
Ten Commandments. She couldn't imagine how the police had
traced her and come knocking. She knew she needed a plan. But
she didn't have one. So she called the only person in the world
that she trusted would understand the problem and give her
sound counsel.

They had been friends for more than four years, she and Dr.

Azad Bhartiya. They met for the first time while they were both waiting for their sandals to be mended by a street-side cobbler in Connaught Place who was famous for his skill and his smallness. In his hands, each shoe or slipper he was mending looked as though it belonged to a giant. While they stood around with one shoe on and one shoe off, Dr. Bhartiya surprised Tilo by asking her (in English) if she had a cigarette. She surprised him back by replying (in Hindi) that she had no cigarettes but could offer him a beedi. The little cobbler lectured them both at length about the consequences of smoking. He told them how his father, a chain-smoker, had died of cancer. He drew the outline of his father's lung tumor with his finger in the dust. "It was this big." Dr. Bhartiya assured him that he smoked only on the occasions when he was having his shoes mended. The conversation switched to politics. The cobbler cursed the current climate, bad-mouthed the gods of every creed and religion, and ended his diatribe by bending down and kissing his iron last. He said it was the only God he believed in. By the time their soles had been mended, the cobbler and his clients had become friends. Dr. Bhartiya invited both his new friends to his pavement home in Jantar Mantar. Tilo went. From then on there was no looking back.

She visited him twice a week or more, often arriving in the evening and leaving at dawn. Occasionally she brought him a deworming pill, which, for some reason, she deemed essential for everybody's well-being, and he deemed ethical to consume even while on hunger strike. She considered him to be a man of the world, among the wisest, sanest people she knew. In time she became the translator/transcriber as well as printer/publisher of his single-page broadsheet: *My News & Views*, which he revised and updated every month. They managed to sell as many as eight or nine copies of each edition. All in all it was a thriving media partnership—politically acute, uncompromising, and wholly in the red.

The media partners had not met for more than eight days—since the coming of Miss Jebeen the Second. When Tilo called Dr. Bhartiya to tell him about the police notice, he dropped his voice to a whisper. He said they should speak as little as possible on the mobile phone, because they were under constant surveillance by International Agencies. But after that initial moment of caution, he chatted away sunnily. He told her how the police had beaten him and confiscated all his papers. He said it was quite likely that they had picked up the trail from there (because the publisher's name and address were given at the bottom of the pamphlet). It was either that or her flamboyant signature on his plaster cast, which they had forcibly photographed from several angles. "No one else signed in green ink and put their address," he told her. "So you must be the first person on their list. It must be just a routine check-up." Still, he suggested that she immediately transfer Miss Jebeen and herself, at least temporarily, to a place called Jannat Guest House and Funeral Services in the old city. The person to contact there, he said, was Saddam Hussain, or the proprietor herself, Dr. Anjum, who, Dr. Bhartiya said, was an extremely good person and had met him several times after the incident (of the *said* night), inquiring about the baby. Due to the honorific he had arbitrarily bestowed on himself (even though his PhD was still "pending"), Dr. Bhartiya often called people he liked "Doctor" for no real reason other than that he liked and respected them.

Tilo recognized the name of the guest house as well as the name Saddam Hussain from the visiting card that the man on the white horse who had followed her home from Jantar Mantar had dropped into her letter box (on the *said* night). When she phoned him, Saddam told her that Dr. Bhartiya had been in touch, and that he (Saddam) had been waiting for her call. He said he was of the same opinion as Dr. Bhartiya, and that he would come back to her with a plan of action. He advised her that she should on no account leave her house with the baby until she heard from him. The police could not enter her house without a search warrant, he said, but if they were watching the house, as they might well be, and they caught her with the baby on the street, they could do anything they liked. Tilo was reassured by his voice and his friendly, efficient manner on the phone. And Saddam, for his part, was reassured by hers.

He called her a few hours later to say that arrangements had been made. He would pick her up from her home at dawn, probably between 4 and 5 a.m., before "Truck Entry" closed in the area. If the house *was* being watched, it would be easy to tell at that hour, when the streets were empty. He would come with a friend who drove a pickup for the Municipal Corporation of Delhi. They had to pick up the carcass of a cow that had died—burst—from eating too many plastic bags at the main garbage dump in Hauz Khas. Her address would not be much of a detour. It was a foolproof plan, he said. "No policeman ever stops an MCD garbage truck," he said, laughing. "If you keep your window open you'll be able to smell us before you see us."

So, once again she was moving.

Tilo surveyed her home like a thief, wondering what to take. What should the criterion be? Things that she might need? Or things that ought not to be left lying around? Or both? Or neither? It vaguely occurred to her that if the police were to make a forced entry, kidnapping might turn out to be the least of her crimes.

Most incriminating of all the things in her apartment was the stack of bright fruit cartons that had been delivered to her doorstep, one at a time, over a few days, by a Kashmiri fruit-seller. They contained what Musa called his "recoveries" from the flood that had inundated Srinagar a year ago.

When the Jhelum rose and breached its banks, the city disappeared. Whole housing colonies went underwater. Army camps, torture centers, hospitals, courthouses, police stations—all went down. Houseboats floated over what had once been market-places. Thousands of people huddled precariously on sharply sloping rooftops and in makeshift shelters set up on higher ground, waiting for rescues that never happened. A drowned city was a spectacle. A drowned civil war was a phenomenon. The army performed stunning helicopter rescues for TV crews. In live round-the-clock bulletins news anchors marveled at how much brave Indian soldiers were doing for ungrateful, surly Kashmiris who did not really deserve to be rescued. When the flood receded, it left behind an uninhabitable city, encased in mud. Shops full of mud, houses full of mud, banks full of mud, refrigerators, cupboards and bookshelves full of mud. And an ungrateful, surly people who had survived without being rescued.

During the weeks the flood lasted, Tilo had no news of Musa. She did not even know whether he was in Kashmir or not. She did not know whether he had survived or drowned, his body washed up on some distant shore. On those nights, while she waited for news of him, she put herself to sleep with heavy doses of sleeping pills, but during the day while she was wide awake she dreamed of the flood. Of rain and rushing water, dense with coils of razor wire masquerading as weeds. The fish were machine guns with fins and barrels that ruddered through the swift current like mermaids' tails, so you could not tell who they were really pointed at, and who would die when they were fired. Soldiers and militants grappled with each other underwater, in slow motion, like in the old James Bond films, their breath bubbling up through the murky water, like bright silver bullets. Pressure cookers (separated from their whistles), gas heaters, sofas, bookshelves, tables and kitchen utensils spun through the water, giving it the feel of a lawless, busy highway. Cattle, dogs, yaks and chickens swam around in circles. Affidavits, interrogation transcripts and army press releases folded themselves into paper boats and rowed themselves to safety. Politicians and TV anchors, both men and women, from the Valley as well as the mainland went prancing past in sequined bathing suits, like a chorus line of seahorses, executing beautifully choreographed aqua-ballet routines, diving, surfacing, twirling, pointing their toes, happy in the debris-filled water, smiling broadly, their teeth glimmering like barbed wire in the sun. One politician in particular, whose views were not dissimilar to those of the Schutzstaffel of Nazi Germany, cartwheeled in the water, looking triumphant, in a starched white dhoti that gave the impression of being waterproof.

It recurred, day after day, this day-mare, each time with new embellishments.

A month went by before Musa finally called. Tilo was furious with him for sounding cheerful. He said there was no safe house left in Srinagar where he could store his "recoveries" from the flood, and asked whether he could keep them in her flat until the city got back on its feet.

He could. Of course he could.

They were excellent quality, the Kashmiri apples that were delivered in custom-made cartons, red ones, less-red ones, green, and almost-black ones—Delicious, Golden Delicious, Ambri, Kaala Mastana—all individually packed in shredded paper. Each carton had Musa's calling card—a small sketch of a horse's head—tucked into a corner. And each carton had a false bottom. And each false bottom contained his "recoveries."

Tilo reopened the cartons to remind herself what was in them and work out what to do with them—take them or leave them behind? Musa had the only other key to the apartment. Garson Hobart was safely parked in Afghanistan. In any case he did not have a key. So leaving them where they were was no great risk. Unless, unless, unless—was there an off-chance that the police would break in?

The "recoveries" were few and had obviously been hurriedly dispatched. When they first arrived some of them were caked with mud—thick, dark river silt. Some were in fine shape and had obviously escaped the flood waters. There was a ruined album of water-stained family photographs, most of them barely recognizable, of Musa's daughter, Miss Jebeen the First, and her mother, Arifa. There was a stack of passports in a plastic Ziploc— seven altogether, two Indian and five other nationalities—Iyad Khareef (Musa the Lebanese pigeon), Hadi Hassan Mohseni (Musa the Iranian wise man and guide), Faris Ali Halabi (Musa the Syrian horseman), Mohammed Nabil al-Salem (Musa the Qatari nobleman), Ahmed Yasir al-Qassimi (Musa the rich man from Bahrain). Musa clean-shaven, Musa with a salt-and-pepper beard, Musa with long hair and no beard, Musa with close-cropped hair and a clipped beard. Tilo recognized the first name, Iyad Khareef, as a name that Musa had always loved, and which they had both laughed about during their college days, because it meant "the pigeon who was born in the autumn." Tilo had a variation on the theme for people she was annoyed with— Gandoo Khareef. The asshole who was born in autumn. (She had been exceptionally foul-mouthed as a young woman, and when she first started learning Hindi, took pleasure in using newly learned expletives as the foundation on which she built a working vocabulary.)

In another plastic packet there were mud-crusted credit cards with names that matched the passports, boarding passes and a few airline tickets—relics from the days when airline tickets existed. There were old telephone diaries, with names, addresses and numbers crammed into them. Diagonally, across the back of one of them, Musa had scrawled a fragment of a song:

Dark to light and light to dark
Three black carriages, three white carts,

What brings us together is what pulls us apart,
Gone our brother, gone our heart.

Who was he mourning? She didn't know. A whole generation
maybe.

There was a half-written letter, on a blue inland letter-form.
It wasn't addressed to anybody. Perhaps he was writing it to himself . . . or to her, because it began with an Urdu poem that he
had tried to translate, something he often did for her:

Duniya ki mehfilon se ukta gaya hoon ya Rab
Kya lutf anjuman ka, jab dil hi bujh gaya ho
Shorish se bhagta hoon, dil dhoondta hai mera
Aisa sukoot jis pe taqreer bhi fida ho

I am weary of worldly gatherings, O Lord
What pleasure in them, when the light in my heart is gone?
From the clamor of crowds I flee, my heart seeks
The kind of silence that would mesmerize speech itself

Underneath he had written:

I don't know where to stop, or how to go on.
I stop when I shouldn't. I go on when I should
stop. There is weariness. But there is also defiance.
Together they define me these days. Together they
steal my sleep, and together they restore my soul.
There are plenty of problems with no solutions
in sight. Friends turn into foes. If not vocal ones,
then silent, reticent ones. But I've yet to see a foe
turning into a friend. There seems to be no hope.
But pretending to be hopeful is the only grace we
have . . .

She didn't know which friends he meant.

She knew that it was nothing short of a miracle that Musa was still alive. In the eighteen years that had gone by since 1996, he had lived a life in which every night was potentially the night of the long knives. "How can they kill me again?" he would say if he sensed worry on Tilo's part. "You've already been to my funeral. You've already laid flowers on my grave. What more can they do to me? I'm a shadow at high noon. I don't exist." The last time she met him he said something to her, casually, jokingly, but with heartbreak in his eyes. It made her blood freeze.

"These days in Kashmir, you can be killed for surviving."

In battle, Musa told Tilo, enemies can't break your spirit, only friends can.

In another carton there was a hunting knife and nine mobile phones—a lot, for a man who did not use mobiles—old ones the size of small bricks, tiny Nokia ones, a Samsung smartphone and two iPhones. When they were delivered, covered in mud, they looked like slabs of fossilized chocolate. Now, minus the mud, they just looked old and unusable. There was a sheaf of stiff, yellowed newspaper clippings, the first of which contained a statement made by the then Chief Minister of Kashmir. Someone had underlined it:

> We can't just go on digging all the graveyards
> up. We need at least general directions from the
> relatives of the Missing, if not pointedly specific
> information. Where could be the greater pos-
> sibility of their disappeared kin being buried?

A third carton contained a pistol, a few loose bullets, a vial of pills (she didn't know *what* pills, but was in a position to make an educated guess—something beginning with C) and a notebook that seemed not to have suffered the depredations of the flood. Tilo recognized the book and the writing in it as hers, but she read through its contents curiously, as though it had been written by someone else. These days her brain felt like a "recovery"—encased in mud. It wasn't just her brain, she herself, *all* of her, felt like a recovery—an accumulation of muddy recoveries, randomly assembled.

Long before she became stenographer to her mother and to Dr. Azad Bhartiya, Tilo had been a weird, part-time stenographer to a full-time military occupation. After the episode at the Shiraz, after she came back to Delhi and married Naga, she had traveled back to Kashmir obsessively, month after month, year after year, as though she was searching for something she had left behind. She and Musa seldom met on those trips (when they met, they met in Delhi, mostly). But while she was in Kashmir, he watched over her from his hidden perch. She knew that the friendly souls that appeared as if from nowhere, to hang about with her, to travel with her, to invite her to their homes, were Musa's people. They welcomed her and told her things they would hardly tell themselves, only because they loved Musa—or at least their idea of him, the man whom they knew as a shadow among shadows. Musa didn't know what she was searching for, neither did she. Yet she spent almost all the money she earned from her design and typography assignments on these trips. Sometimes she took odd pictures. She wrote strange things down. She collected scraps of stories and inexplicable memorabilia that appeared to have no purpose. There seemed to be no pattern or theme to her interest. She had no set task, no project. She was not writing for a newspaper or magazine, she was not writing a book or making a film. She paid no attention to things that most people would have considered important. Over the years, her peculiar, ragged archive grew peculiarly dangerous. It was an archive of recoveries, not from a flood, but from another kind of disaster. Instinctively she kept it hidden from Naga, and ordered it according to some elaborate logic of her own that she intuited but did not understand. None of it amounted to anything in the cut and thrust of real argument in the real world. But that didn't matter.

The truth is that she traveled back to Kashmir to still her troubled heart, and to atone for a crime she hadn't committed.

And to put fresh flowers on Commander Gulrez's grave.

The notebook that Musa sent back with his "recoveries" was hers. She must have left it behind on one of her trips. The first few pages were filled with her writing, the rest were blank. She grinned when she saw the opening page:

The Reader's Digest Book
of English Grammar
and Comprehension
for Very Young Children

By

S. Tilottama

She got herself an ashtray, settled down cross-legged on the floor, and chain-smoked her way to the end of her book. It contained stories, press clippings and some diary entries:

THE OLD MAN & HIS SON

When Manzoor Ahmed Ganai became a militant, soldiers went to his home and picked up his father, the handsome, always dapper Aziz Ganai. He was kept in the Haider Baig Interrogation Center. Manzoor Ahmed Ganai worked as a militant for one and a half years. His father remained imprisoned for one and a half years.

On the day Manzoor Ahmed Ganai was killed, smiling soldiers opened the door of his father's cell. "*Jenaab*, you wanted Azadi? *Mubarak ho aapko.* Congratulations! Today your wish has come true. Your freedom has come."

The people of the village cried more for the shambling wreck who came running through the orchard in rags with wild eyes and a beard and hair that hadn't been cut in a year and a half than they did for the boy who had been murdered.

The shambling wreck was just in time to be able to lift the shroud and kiss his son's face before they buried him.

Q 1: Why did the villagers cry more for the shambling wreck?
Q 2: Why did the wreck shamble?

NEWS

Kashmir Guideline News Service
Dozens of Cattle Cross Line of Control (LoC) in Rajouri
At least 33 cattle including 29 buffaloes have crossed over to Pakistan side in Nowshera sector of Rajouri district in Jammu and Kashmir.

According to KGNS, the cattle crossed the LoC in Kalsian sub-sector. "The cattle which belong to Ram Saroop, Ashok Kumar, Charan Das, Ved Prakash and others were grazing near LoC when they crossed over to other side," locals told KGNS.

Tick the Box:
Q 1: Why did the cattle cross the LoC?
    (a) For training
    (b) For sneak-in ops
    (c) Neither of the above

THE PERFECT MURDER (J's story)

This happened a few years ago, before I resigned from the service. Maybe in 2000 or 2001. I was at the time DySP, Deputy Superintendent of Police, posted in Mattan.

One night at about 11:30 p.m. we got a call from a neighboring village. The caller was a villager, but he wouldn't reveal his name. He said there had been a murder. So we went. I, along with my boss, the SP. It was in January. Very cold. Snow everywhere.

We arrived in the village. The people were all inside their houses. Doors were locked. Lights were off. It had stopped snowing. The night was clear. Full moon. The moonlight was reflecting off the snow. You could see everything very clearly.

We saw the body of a person, a big strong man. He was lying in the snow. He had been freshly killed. His blood had flooded on to the snow. It was still warm. It had melted the snow. The snow was still steaming. He lay there as though he was being cooked . . .

You could tell that after his throat had been slit he had dragged himself about thirty meters to knock on the door of a house. But out of fear nobody had opened the door, so he had bled to death. As I said, he was a big strong man, so there was a lot of blood. He was dressed in Pathan clothes—salwar kameez—he wore a camouflage bulletproof vest, and an ammunition belt full of ammunition. An AK-47 was lying near him. We had no doubt he was a militant—but who had killed him? If it had been the army of course they would have removed the body and claimed the Kill immediately. If it had been a rival militant group they would have taken his weapon. This was a big puzzle for us.

We rounded up the villagers and questioned them. Nobody admitted to seeing or hearing or knowing anything. We took the body back with us to the Mattan police station. There my SP called the Commanding Officer of the Rashtriya Rifle (RR) camp—the army camp—nearby to ask if he knew anything about it. Nothing.

It wasn't hard to identify the body. He was a well-known, very senior militant commander. He belonged to the Hizb. Hizb-ul-Mujahideen. But nobody claimed the Kill. So eventually the army CO and my SP decided to claim it. They announced that he had been killed in an encounter following a Search-and-Cordon operation conducted jointly by the RR and JKP (Jammu and Kashmir Police).

The story appeared in the national press as follows: *In a fierce gun battle that lasted several hours a dreaded militant was killed in a joint operation by the Rashtriya Rifles and the Jammu and Kashmir Police led by Major XX and Superintendent of Police YY.*

Both of us, the RR and JKP, were given citations and we shared the cash reward. We handed the militant's body over to his family and made discreet inquiries about whether they had any idea who killed him. We made no headway.

Seven days later, in another village, another Hizb militant was found beheaded. He was the second-in-command of the first man whose body we had found. The Hizb owned up to the killing. Privately they let it be known that he was killed for having murdered his commander and stolen twenty-five lakhs in cash that was meant for distribution among the cadre.

The story in the national press appeared as follows:
Gruesome Beheading of Innocent Civilian by Militants

Q 1: Who is the hero of this story?

THE INFORMER—I

In the notified area of Tral. A village called Nav Dal. It's 1993. The village is bristling with militants. It's a "liberated" village. The army is camped on the outskirts, but soldiers daren't enter the village. It's a complete stand-off. No villagers approach the army camp. There is no exchange of any sort between soldiers and villagers.

And yet, the officer commanding the camp knows every move the militants make. Which villagers support the Movement, which ones don't, who offers militants food and lodging willingly, who doesn't.

For days a close watch is mounted. Not a single person goes to the camp. Not a single soldier enters the village. And yet, the information gets to the army.

Finally the militants notice a sleek black bull from the village who regularly visits the camp. They intercept the bull. Tied to his horns, along with an assortment of *taveez* (to keep him from illness, from the evil eye, from impotence), are little notes with information.

The next day the militants attach an IED to the bull's horns. They detonate it as he approaches the camp. No one dies. The bull is severely injured. The village butcher offers to do "halal" so the villagers can at least feast on the meat.

The militants pass a fatwa. It's an Informer Bull. Nobody is allowed to eat the meat.

Amen.

Q 1: Who is the hero of the story?

THE INFORMER—II

He liked selling out on people, for this
dehumanized him. Dehumanizing myself
is my own most fundamental tendency.

Jean Genet

I'm not yet cured of happiness.

Anna Akhmatova

Q 1: Who is the hero of the story?

THE VIRGIN

The fidayeen attack that had been planned on the army
camp was aborted at the last minute by none other than the
fidayeen themselves. They took this decision because Abid
Ahmed alias Abid Suzuki, the driver of the Maruti Suzuki
they were in, was driving really badly. The little car veered
sharply to the left, then sharply to the right, as though it was
dodging something. But the road was empty and there was
nothing to dodge. When Abid Suzuki's companions (none
of whom knew how to drive) asked him what the matter
was, he said it was the houris who had come to take them
all to heaven. They were naked and dancing on the bonnet,
distracting him.

There's no way to ascertain whether the naked houris
were virgins or not.

But Abid Suzuki certainly was one.

Q 1: Why was Abid Suzuki driving badly?
Q 2: How do you establish a man's virginity?

THE BRAVEHEART

Mehmood was a tailor in Budgam. His greatest desire was to have himself photographed posing with guns. Finally a school friend of his who had joined a militant group took him to their hideout and made his dream come true. Mehmood returned to Srinagar with the negatives and took them to Taj Photo Studio to have prints made. He negotiated a 25-paisa discount for each print. When he went to pick up his prints the Border Security Force laid a cordon around Taj Photo Studio and caught him red-handed with the prints. He was taken to a camp and tortured for many days. He did not give away any information. He was sentenced to ten years in jail.

The militant commander who facilitated the photography session was arrested a few months later. Two AK-47s and several rounds of ammunition were recovered from him. He was released after two months.

Q 1: Was it worth it?

THE CAREERIST

The boy had always wanted to make something of himself. He invited four militants for dinner and slipped sleeping pills into their food. Once they had fallen asleep he called the army. They killed the militants and burned down the house. The army had promised the boy two canals of land and one hundred and fifty thousand rupees. They gave him only fifty thousand and accommodated him in quarters just outside an army camp. They told him that if he wanted a permanent job with them instead of being just a daily wage worker he would have to get them two foreign militants.

He managed to get them one "live" Pakistani but was having trouble finding another. "Unfortunately these days business is bad," he told PI. "Things have become such that you cannot any longer just kill someone and pretend he's a foreign militant. So my job cannot be made permanent."

PI asked him, if there was a referendum whom he would vote for, India or Pakistan?

"Pakistan of course."

"Why?"

"Because it is our Mulk (country). But Pakistan militants can't help us in this way. If I can kill them and get a good job it helps me."

He told PI that when Kashmir became a part of Pakistan, he (PI) would not be able to survive in it. But he (the boy) would. But that, he said, was just a theoretical matter. Because he would be killed shortly.

Q 1: Who did the boy expect to be killed by?
  (a) The army
  (b) Militants
  (c) Pakistanis
  (d) Owners of the house that was burned

THE NOBEL PRIZE WINNER

Manohar Mattoo was a Kashmiri Pandit who stayed on in the Valley even after all the other Hindus had gone. He was secretly tired of and deeply hurt by the barbs from his Muslim friends who said that all Hindus in Kashmir were actually, in one way or another, agents of the Indian Occupation Forces. Manohar had participated in all the anti-India protests, and had shouted *Azadi!* louder than everybody else.

But nothing seemed to help. At one point he had even contemplated taking up arms and joining the Hizb, but eventually he decided against it. One day an old school friend of his, Aziz Mohammed, an intelligence officer, visited him at home to tell him that he was worried for him. He said that he had seen his (Mattoo's) surveillance file. It suggested that he be put under watch because he displayed "anti-national tendencies."

When he heard the news Mattoo beamed and felt his chest swell with pride.

"You have given me the Nobel Prize!" he told his friend.

He took Aziz Mohammed out to Café Arabica and bought him coffee and pastries worth Rs 500.

A year later he (Mattoo) was shot by an unknown gunman for being a kafir.

Q 1: Why was Mattoo shot?
  (a) Because he was a Hindu
  (b) Because he wanted Azadi
  (c) Because he won the Nobel Prize
  (d) None of the above
  (e) All of the above

Q 2: Who could the unknown gunman have been?
  (a) An Islamist militant who thought all kafirs should be killed
  (b) An agent of the Occupation who wanted people to think that all Islamist militants thought that all kafirs should be killed
  (c) Neither of the above
  (d) Someone who wanted everyone to go crazy trying to figure it out

KHADIJA SAYS . . .

In Kashmir when we wake up and say "Good Morning" what we really mean is "Good Mourning."

THE TIMES THEY ARE A-CHANGIN'

Begum Dil Afroze was a well-known opportunist who believed, quite literally, in changing with the times. When the Movement seemed to be on the up and up, she would set the time on her wristwatch half an hour ahead to Pakistan Standard Time. When the Occupation regained its grip she would reset it to Indian Standard Time. In the Valley the saying went, "Begum Dil Afroze's watch isn't really a watch, it's a newspaper."

Q 1: What is the moral of this story?

APRIL FOOL'S DAY 2008: Actually it's April Fool's night. All night the news comes in sporadically, relayed from mobile phone to mobile phone: *"Encounter" in a village in Bandipora.* The BSF and STF say they received specific information that there were militants—the Chief of Operations of the Lashkar-e-Taiba and some others—in a house in the village of Chithi Bandi. There was a crackdown. The encounter went on all night. Past midnight the army announced that the operation had been successful. They said that two militants had been killed. But the police said there were no bodies.

I went with P to Bandipora. We left at dawn.

From Srinagar to Bandipora the road winds

through mustard fields. Wular Lake is glassy, inscrutable. Slim boats preen on it like fashion models. P tells me that recently, as part of "Operation Good Will," the army took twenty-one children on a picnic in a navy boat. The boat overturned. All twenty-one children drowned. When the parents of the drowned children protested they were shot at. The luckier ones died.

Bandipora is "liberated," they say. Like Sopore once was. Like Shopian still is. Bandipora is backed up against the high mountains. When we reached we found that the crackdown hadn't ended.

The villagers said it had begun at 3:30 p.m. the previous day. People were forced out of their homes at gunpoint. They had to leave their houses open, hot tea not yet drunk, books open, homework incomplete, food on the fire, the onions frying, the chopped tomatoes waiting to be added.

There were more than a thousand soldiers, the villagers said. Some said four thousand. At night terror is magnified, the leaves in the Chinar trees must have looked like soldiers. As the crackdown wore on, and dawn broke, it was not just the occasional gunshots that tore through people, but also the softer sounds, of their cupboards being opened, their cash and jewelry being stolen, their looms being smashed. Their cattle being barbecued alive in their pens.

A big house belonging to a poet's brother had been razed. It was a heap of rubble. No bodies had been found. The militants had escaped. Or perhaps they were never there.

But why was the army still there? Soldiers

with machine guns, shovels and mortar launchers controlled the crowd.

More news:

Two young men have been picked up from a petrol pump nearby.

The crowd goes rigid.

The army has already announced that they've killed two militants here in Chithi Bandi. So now it has to produce bodies. The people know how real life works. Sometimes the script is written in advance.

"If the bodies of those boys are freshly burned we won't accept the army story."

Go India! Go Back!

People catch sight of a soldier standing in the village mosque, looking down at them. He hasn't taken his boots off in the holy place. A howl goes up. Slowly the barrel of the gun rises and takes aim. The air shrinks and grows hard.

A shot rings out from the poet's brother's ex-house. It's an announcement. The army is going to withdraw. The village road isn't wide enough for us and them, so to make room for them we flatten ourselves against the walls of houses. The soldiers file through. Hooting pursues them like the wind whistling down the village road. You can sense the soldiers' anger and shame. You can sense their helplessness too. That could change in a second.

All they have to do is to turn around and shoot.

All the people have to do is to lie down and die.

When the last soldier has gone, the people climb over the debris of the burnt house. The tin sheets that were once the roof are still smoldering. A scorched trunk lies open, flames still leaping out of it. What was in it that burns so beautifully?

On the small, smoky mountain of rubble, the people stand and chant:

Hum Kya Chahtey?

Azadi!

And they call for the Lashkar:

Aiwa Aiwa!

Lashkar-e-Taiba!

More news comes.

Mudasser Nazir has been picked up by the STF.

His father arrives. His breathing is shallow. His face is ashen. An autumn leaf in spring.

They've taken his boy to the camp.

"He's not a militant. He was injured in a protest last year."

"They're saying if you want your son back, then send us your daughter. They say she's an OGW—an overground worker. That she helps a Hizb Man transport his things."

Maybe she does, maybe she doesn't. Either way, she's a goner.

I'll help a Hizb Man transport his things.

And then he'll kill me for being me.

Bad, uncovered woman.

Indian

Indian?

Whatever

So it goes.

NOTHING

I would like to write one of those sophisticated stories in which even though nothing much happens there's lots to write about. That can't be done in Kashmir. It's not sophisticated, what happens here. There's too much blood for good literature.

Q 1: Why is it not sophisticated?
Q 2: What is the acceptable amount of blood for good literature?

THE LAST ENTRY in the notebook was an army press release, pasted on to one of the pages:

PRESS INFORMATION BUREAU (DEFENSE WING)
GOVERNMENT OF INDIA PUBLIC RELATIONS OFFICE,
MINISTRY OF DEFENSE, SRINAGAR
GIRLS OF BANDIPORA LEFT FOR EXCURSION

Bandipora 27 September: Today was an important day in the life of 17 girls of village Erin and Dardpora of Bandipora district when their 13 days SADHBHAVANA Tour to Agra, Delhi and Chandigarh was flagged off by Mrs. Sonya Mehra and Brigadier Anil Mehra, Commander, 81 Mountain Brigade from Fishery grounds of Erin Village. These girls accompanied by two elderly women and two panches from the area along with officials of 14 Rashtriya Rifles. They will visit places of historical and educational interest at Agra, Delhi and Chandigarh. They would have a privilege of interacting with Governor of Punjab and of their own state.

Brig Anil Mehra, Commander 81 Mountain Brigade, while addressing the tour participants, told them to make full use of the excellent opportunity provided to them. He also asked them to keenly observe the progress made by other states and to see themselves as ambassadors of peace. Also present on the occasion to give a warm send off were Colonel Prakash Singh Negi, Commanding Officer, 14 Rashtriya Rifles, elected sarpanches of the two villages and parents of all the participants along with a gathering of local populace.

The Reader's Digest Book of English Grammar and Comprehension for Very Young Children was two beedis and four cigarettes long. Adjusting of course for reading/smoking speed, both of which are variables.

Tilo smiled to herself, remembering another Good Will excursion like the one described in the press release that the army had very kindly organized for the boys from Muskaan, the army orphanage in Srinagar. Musa had sent a message asking her to meet him at the Red Fort. It must have been about ten years ago. She was still living with Naga at the time.

On that occasion, Musa, at his most audacious, was one of the civilian escorts to the group. They were passing through Delhi on their way to Agra to see the Taj Mahal. While they were in Delhi the orphans were taken to see the Qutb Minar, Red Fort, India Gate, Rashtrapati Bhavan, Parliament House, Birla House (where Gandhi was shot), Teen Murti (where Nehru had lived) and 1 Safdarjung Road (where Indira Gandhi was shot by her Sikh bodyguards). Musa was unrecognizable. He called himself Zahoor Ahmed, smiled more often than he needed to and had cultivated a bent, slightly oafish, obsequious air.

He and Tilo met as strangers who sat next to each other by chance, on a bench in the dark at the Sound and Light Show at the Red Fort. Most of the rest of the audience were foreign tourists. "This is a collaborative venture between us and the Security

Forces," Musa whispered to her. "Sometimes, in these kinds of collaborations, the partners don't know that they are partners. The army thinks it is teaching the children love for their Motherland. And we think we are teaching them to know their Enemy, so that when it is their generation's turn to fight, they won't end up behaving like Hassan Lone."

One of the orphans, a tiny boy with huge ears, climbed on to Musa's lap, gave him a thousand kisses and then sat very still, regarding Tilo from a distance of about three inches, with intense, expressionless eyes. Musa was gruff with him, unresponsive. But Tilo saw his face muscles twitch and, for a moment, his eyes grow bright. She let the moment pass.

"Who's Hassan Lone?"

"He was my neighbor. Great guy. A brother."

"Brother" was Musa's highest form of praise.

"He wanted to join the militancy, but on his first trip to India, to Bombay, he saw the crowds at VT station and he gave up. When he returned he said, 'Brothers, have you seen how many of them there are? We have no chance! I surrender.' He *actually* gave up! He's doing some small textile business now."

Musa, smiling broadly in the dark, gave the child on his lap a smacking kiss on his head in memory of his friend Hassan Lone. The little fellow stared straight ahead, glowing like a lamp.

On the soundtrack the year was 1739. Emperor Mohammed Shah Rangeela had been on the Peacock Throne in Delhi for almost thirty years. He was an interesting emperor. He watched elephant fights dressed in ladies' clothes and jeweled slippers. Under his patronage a new school of miniature painting depicting explicit sex and bucolic landscapes was born. But it wasn't all sex and debauchery. Great kathak dancers and qawwals performed in his court. The scholar-mystic Shah Waliullah translated the Quran into Persian. Khwaja Mir Dard and Mir Taqi Mir recited their verse in the teahouses of Chandni Chowk:

Le saans bhi ahista ki nazuk hai bahut kaam
Afaq ki iss kargah-e-shishagari ka

Breathe gently here, for with fragility all is fraught,
Here, in this workshop of the world, where wares of glass are
wrought

But then, the sound of horses' hooves. The tiny boy stood
up on Musa's lap and turned around to see where the sound was
coming from. It was Nadir Shah's cavalry galloping from Persia to Delhi, pillaging cities that lay on its route. The Emperor
on the Peacock Throne was unperturbed. Poetry, music and literature, he believed, ought not to be interrupted by the banality
of war. The lights in the Diwan-e-Khas changed color. Purple,
red, green. On the soundtrack the laughter of women in the
zenana. Bells on the ankles of dancing girls. The unmistakable,
deep, coquettish giggle of a court eunuch.

After the show the orphans and their escorts spent the night in
a dormitory in the Vishwa Yuvak Kendra in Diplomatic Enclave.
It happened to be just down the road from Tilo's (and Naga's)
home.

When Tilo got home, Naga was asleep with the TV on. She
switched it off and lay down next to him. That night she dreamed
of a winding desert road that had no reason to wind. She and
Musa were walking down it. There were buses parked along one
side and shipping containers on the other—each with an entrance
door and a tattered, gauze curtain. There were whores in some
of the doorways and soldiers in the others. Long Somali soldiers.
Badly harmed people were being brought out and chained people
taken in. Musa stopped to speak to a man in white. He seemed
to be an old friend. Musa followed him into a shipping container
while Tilo waited outside. When he didn't come out she went in
looking for him. The light in the room was red. A man and woman

were having sex on a bed in a corner of the container. There was
a big dressing table with a mirror. Musa wasn't in the room, but
his image was reflected in the mirror. He was hanging from the
roof by his arms, swinging around and around. There was a lot of
talcum powder in the room, including in Musa's armpits.

Tilo woke up wondering how she came to be on a boat. She
looked at Naga for a long time and was briefly overcome by
something that felt like love. She didn't understand it and didn't
do anything about it.

SHE CALCULATED that it had been thirty years since all of them—
Naga, Garson Hobart, Musa and she—had first met on the set
of *Norman, Is That You?* And still they continued to circle around
each other in these peculiar ways.

The last box wasn't a fruit carton and wasn't a "recovery" from
the flood. It was a small Hewlett-Packard printer-cartridge carton that contained the Amrik Singh documents that Musa had
left with her after he returned from one of his trips to the US.
She opened it to double-check that her memory served her right.
It did. There was a sachet of old photographs, a folder of press
clippings reporting Amrik Singh's suicide. One of the reports
had a photograph of the Singhs' house in Clovis with police cars
parked outside it and policemen milling around inside the No
Go zone they had marked off with the yellow tape you saw in TV
serials and crime films. There was an inset photograph of Xerxes,
the robot with a camera mounted on to it that the California
police had sent into the house before they went in to make sure
nobody was lurking around waiting to ambush them. Other than
the press clippings there was a file with copies of Amrik Singh's
and his wife's applications for asylum in the US. Musa had given
her a long, comical account of how he had got the file. He, along

with a lawyer who had argued hundreds of asylum cases on the West Coast—the friend of a "brother"—visited the American social worker in Clovis who had been dealing with Amrik Singh's case. The social worker was a wonderful man, Musa said, old and infirm, but dedicated to his job. He had socialist leanings and was furious with his government's immigration policy. His small office was lined with files—the legal records of the hundreds of people he had helped to get asylum in the US, most of them Sikhs who had fled India after 1984. He was familiar with the stories of police atrocities in Punjab, the army invasion of the Golden Temple and the 1984 massacre of Sikhs that followed the assassination of Indira Gandhi. He lived in a time warp and wasn't up to date on current affairs. So he had conflated Punjab and Kashmir and viewed Mr. and Mrs. Amrik Singh through that prism—as yet another persecuted Sikh family. He had leaned across his desk and whispered that he believed the tragedy occurred because neither Amrik Singh nor his wife had come to terms with the rape that Mrs. Amrik Singh was bound to have suffered while she was in police custody. He had tried to convince her that mentioning it would greatly enhance their chances of getting asylum. But she wouldn't admit to it and had grown agitated when he suggested that there was no shame in talking about it.

"They were simple good folks, those two, all they needed was some counseling, they and their little ones," he said, handing over copies of their papers to Musa. "Some counseling and some good friends. Just a little help and they would still have been alive. But that's too much to expect from this great country, isn't it?"

Right at the bottom of the printer-cartridge carton was a fat, old-fashioned legal file that Tilo didn't remember having seen before. It was a set of loose, unbound pages, perhaps fifty or sixty pages, stacked on a piece of cardboard and tied down with red straps and white string. Witness testimonies in the Jalib Qadri case from nearly twenty years ago:

Memorandum of Statement by Ghulam Nabi Rasool s/o Mushtaq Nabi Rasool, r/o Barbarshah. Occupation— Service in Tourism Department. Age 37 years. Statement recorded under Section 161/CrPC

The witness states as under:
I am a resident of Barbarshah in Srinagar. On 8.03.1995 I saw a military contingent positioned at Parraypora. They were frisking vehicles there. An army truck and armored vehicle were also parked there. One tall Sikh army officer surrounded by many military personnel in uniform was conducting the frisking. A private taxi was also parked there. In the taxi there were some civilian personnel wrapped in a red blanket. On account of fear I remained some distance away from this scene. Then I saw a white Maruti car coming. Jalib Qadri was driving and his wife was in the passenger seat. On seeing Jalib Qadri the tall army officer stopped his vehicle and made him to get out. They pushed him in the armored vehicle and all the vehicles including the private taxi went away in a convoy via the Bypass.

Memorandum of Statement by Rehmat Bajad s/o Abdul Kalam Bajad, r/o Kursoo Rajbagh, Srinagar. Occupation— Agriculture Department. Age 32 years. Statement recorded under Section 161/CrPC

The witness states as under:
I am the inhabitant of Kursoo Rajbagh and work in the Agriculture Department as field assistant officer. Today, on 27.03.1995, I was at my home when I heard noise coming from outside. I came out and found people were gathered around a dead body which was tucked into a sack-

bag. The dead body had been recovered by local youth from the Jhelum Flood Channel. The youth removed the body from the sack-bag. I found it to be the body of Jalib Qadri. I recognized him because he had been living in my neighborhood for the past twelve years. After inspection I identified the following apparel:

1. Woolen sweater khaki colored
2. White shirt
3. Gray pants
4. White undershirt.

Besides this both eyes were missing. His forehead was bloodstained. Body was shrunk and decomposed. Police came and took custody and prepared a custody memo which I signed.

Memorandum of Statement by Maroof Ahmed Dar s/o Abdul Ahad Dar, r/o Kursoo Rajbagh, Srinagar. Occupation—Business. Age 40 years. Statement recorded under Section 161/CrPC

The witness states as under:
I am a resident of Kursoo Rajbagh and deal with business. On 27.03.1995 I heard noise coming from the bank of the Jhelum Flood Channel. I went to the spot and found that the dead body of Jalib Qadri was lying on the bund tucked in a sack bag. I could identify the deceased because he was residing in my neighborhood for a period of twelve years and we offered prayers in the same local mosque. On the deceased body the following apparels were seen:

1. Woolen sweater khaki colored
2. White shirt
3. Gray pants
4. White undershirt.

Besides this both eyes were missing. His forehead was bloodstained. Body was shrunk and decomposed. Police came and took custody and prepared a custody memo which I signed.

Memorandum of Statement by Mohammed Shafiq Bhat s/o Abdul Aziz Bhat, r/o Ganderbal. Occupation—Mason. Age 30 years. Statement recorded under Section 161/CrPC

The witness states as under:
I hail from Ganderbal. I am a mason by profession and presently I am working in the house of Mohammed Ayub Dar in Kursoo Rajbagh. Today, on 27.03.1995 at about 6:30 a.m. in the morning I went to the Jhelum Flood Channel for washing my face. I saw a dead body in a sack-bag floating in the river. One leg and one arm was visible from outside. On account of fear I did not report this to anybody. Later I went to Mohammed Shabir War's house to perform my labor as a mason. I found the same dead body in a sack-bag which was recovered by the locals from the Jhelum Flood Channel. The dead body was decomposed and soaked. The apparel on the body was as follows:

1. Woolen sweater khaki colored
2. White shirt
3. Gray pants
4. White undershirt.

Besides this both eyes were missing. His forehead was bloodstained. Body was shrunk and decomposed. Police came and took custody and prepared a custody memo which I signed.

Memorandum of Statement by brother of the deceased, Parvaiz Ahmed Qadri s/o Altaf Qadri, r/o Awantipora. Occupation—Service in Academy of Arts, Culture and Languages. Age 35 years. Statement recorded under Section 161/CrPC

The witness states as under:
I am a resident of Awantipora and the brother of the deceased Jalib Qadri. Today after the identification and Postmortem I took the dead body of my brother Jalib Qadri from the Police. The police separately filed an injury memo and receipt for the dead body. The contents of the memos were read to me which I acknowledge to be correct.

Memorandum of Statement by Mushtaq Ahmed Khan alias Usman alias Bhaitoth, r/o Jammu City. Age 30 years. Statement recorded on 12.06.95 under Section 164/CrPC

The witness states as under:
Sir, I am a baker. I had a shop at Rawalpora and used to supply bread to the army personnel from 1990–91. Then the situation in Kashmir deteriorated and the militants threatened me for supplying bread to army personnel. Since that was the only lifeline for my business, as such I closed down my bakery and went to my native village in Uri. After three months of my stay there militants started to victimize my

wife. Not only this, they forcibly kidnapped my 15 years old sister and forced her to marry one of their companions. On this account I left my native village and returned to Srinagar where I stayed in a rented house in Magarmal Bagh. In some time militants of the Jammu Kashmir Liberation Front (JKLF) reached there and forced me to join their cadre. Later on during the mutual conflicts among different militant factions the militants of Al-Umar outfit picked me up and I got associated with it for two years. Then the security forces started troubling me and picked up my children. As such I surrendered before India Bravo IB and handed over my AK-47 rifle to them. I was kept in custody for 8 months in Baramulla and then released but was bound to report to IB every fifteen days. I did this for three months but then ran away on account of fear because if anybody would have seen me with IB it would have been fatal to my life. In Srinagar, one person, namely Ahmed Ali Bhat alias Cobra met me and introduced me to the DySP of Kothi Bagh police station who took me and sent me for work with the Special Operations Group SOG in the Rawalpora camp. Cobra and Parwaz Bhat were Ikhwanis and used to work in the camp along with Major Amrik Singh. They provoked Major Amrik Singh against me and told him I knew all the militants and should help him in their arrest. One day Major Amrik Singh took me along with him for purpose of raid on militants' hideout at Wazir Bagh wherein two militants were captured and released after payment of Rs 40,000. I worked with Major Amrik Singh for many months and was witness to the elimination by him of the following people:

1. Ghulam Rasool Wani.
2. Basit Ahmed Khanday who was working in Century Hotel.

3. Abdul Hafeez Pir.
4. Ishfaq Waza.
5. One Sikh tailor whose name was Kuldeep Singh.

All they have been registered as disappeared since then.

Afterwards on one occasion in March 1995 Major Amrik Singh and his friend Salim Gojri who was also like me a surrendered militant and frequent visitor to the camp picked up one person who was wearing a coat, white shirt and tie and gray pant. At that time Sukhan Singh, Balbir Singh and Doctor were also there. The coat-pant man was a very learned person. He argued with them in the camp saying "Why did you got me arrested and brought me here?" Upon which Major Amrik Singh got furious and beat him ruthlessly and took him to a separate room. After confining him he came out and said, "Do you know that person is the famous advocate Jalib Qadri. We have arrested him because whosoever maligns the army and helps militants will not be spared whatever may be his status." That evening I heard cries and shouting from the same room in which Jalib Qadri was confined. I further heard sounds of gunshots in that room. Later I observed one sack-bag was loaded into a vehicle.

Few days later when the dead body of Jalib Qadri was recovered and news were published in the papers in this regard, Major Amrik Singh in regret said to me that he did wrong, and that he should not have killed Jalib Qadri but he was helpless in this regard because other officers had entrusted that job to him and Salim Gojri. When he said this to me I felt a threat to my life.

Then Salim Gojri and his associates, Mohammed Ramzan who was illegal immigrant from Bangladesh, Muneer Nasser Hajam and Mohammed Akbar Laway, stopped coming to the camp. Major Amrik Singh sent me along with Sukhan Singh and Balbir Singh in vehicles to find them and bring them to the camp. We found Salim Gojri sitting in a shop in Budgam and asked him why he had not come to the camp for one week. He said he was busy with raids and he would come the next day. Next day he came with his three associates. They came in an Ambassador taxi. Their weapons were held at the gate. Major Amrik Singh told them this was due to the impending visit of the CO of the camp. After that Major Amrik Singh, Salim Gojri and his associates sat in chairs at the compound and started drinking. After two hours Major Amrik Singh took Salim Gojri and his associates to the dining room. I was in the verandah. Sukhan Singh, Balbir Singh, one Major Ashok and Doctor tied Salim Gojri and his associates with ropes and closed the door. The next day their bodies were recovered in a field in Pampore along with the body of the taxi driver Mumtaz Afzal Malik. Afterwards I moved my wife and children to the house of my friend who was residing at Bypass. Then I escaped to Jammu. Further I do not know.

TILO PUT THE FILES and the sachet of photographs back into the carton and left it on the table. They were legal papers and contained nothing incriminating.

She packed Musa's "recoveries"—the gun, the knife, the phones, the passports, boarding passes and everything else—into airtight plastic food containers and stacked them in her freezer. Inside one of the containers she put Saddam Hussain's visiting card, so that Musa would know where to come. Her refrigerator was an old one—the kind that iced up if it wasn't regularly defrosted. She knew that if she turned the temperature down before she left, the incriminating evidence would turn into a block of ice. Her reasoning was that Recoveries that had survived a devastating flood surely had special powers. They would survive a mini-blizzard too.

She packed a small bag. Clothes, books, baby things, computer, toothbrush. The pot with her mother's ashes.

The only decision that remained to be made was what to do with the cake and the balloons.

She lay in her bed, fully dressed and ready to leave.

It was 3 a.m.

Still no sign (nor scent) of Saddam Hussain.

Reading the Otter papers was a mistake. A bad one. She felt as though she had been sealed into a barrel of tar, with him and all the people he had killed. She could smell him. And see his cold, flat eyes as he sat across from her on the boat and stared at her. She could feel his hand on her scalp.

The bed she lay on wasn't really a bed, just a mattress on the red cement floor. Ants hurried around with cake crumbs. The heat seeped through the mattress and the sheet felt coarse against her skin. A baby gecko walked unsteadily across the floor. It stopped a few feet away, lifted its big head and regarded her with bright, oversized eyes. She watched it back.

"Hide!" she whispered. "The vegetarians are coming."

She offered it a dead mosquito from the pile of dead mosquitoes she had collected on a sheet of blank paper. She put the mosquito carcass down, halfway between herself and the gecko. The gecko ignored it at first, and then ate it in a flash, while she looked away.

What I should have been, she thought, *is a gecko-feeder*.

. . .

Harsh neon light masquerading as the moon streamed through the window. A few weeks ago, walking across a steep, over-lit fly-over at night, she eavesdropped on a conversation between two men wheeling their bicycles: "Is sheher mein ab raat ka sahaara bhi nahin milta." In this city we've even lost the shelter of the night.

She lay very still, like a corpse in a morgue.

Her hair was growing.

Her toenails too.

The hair on her head was dead white.

The triangle of hair between her legs was jet black.

What did that *mean*?

Was she old or still young?

Was she dead or still alive?

And then, even without turning her head, she knew they had come. The bulls. Massive heads with perfect horns silhou-etted sickle-shaped against the light. Two of them. The color of night. The stolen color of what-used-to-be-night. Rough curls embossed into their damp foreheads like damask headscarves. Their moist, velvet noses glistened, and they pursed their purple lips. They made no sound. They never harmed her, only stared. The whites of their eyes as they looked around the room were crescent moons. They didn't seem curious or particularly grave. They were like doctors looking in on a patient, trying to agree on a diagnosis.

Did you forget to bring your stethoscopes again?

Time had a different quality in their presence. She couldn't tell for how long they watched her. She never looked back at them. She knew they were gone only when the light they had blocked returned to illuminate the room.

When she was sure they were gone, she went to the window and saw them shrink to street level and walk away. City-slickers. A pair of thugs. One of them lifted its leg like a dog and pissed on the window of a car. A very tall dog. She put on the light and looked up the word *insouciant*. The dictionary said: *Cheerfully unconcerned or unworried about something*. She kept dictionaries near her bed, piled up into a tower.

She picked a sheet of paper from a ream, and a pencil from a coffee mug full of sharpened blue pencils, and began to write:

Dear Doctor,
I am witness to a curious scientific phenomenon. Two bulls live in the service lane outside my flat. In the daytime they appear quite normal, but at night they grow tall—I think the word might be "elevate"—and stare at me through my second-floor window. When they piss, they lift their legs like dogs. Last night (at about 8 p.m.), when I was returning from the market, one growled at me. This I'm sure of. My question is: Is there any chance that they could be genetically modified bulls, with dog-growth or wolf-growth genes implanted in them, that might have escaped from a lab? If so, are they bulls or dogs? Or wolves?
I have not heard of any such experiments being done on cattle, have you? I am aware of human growth genes being used on trout, making them gigantic. The people who breed these giant trout say they're doing it to feed people in poor countries. My question is who will feed the giant trout? Human growth genes have also been used in pigs. I've seen the result of that experiment. It's a cross-eyed mutant that is so heavy that it cannot stand up or bear its own weight. It needs to be propped up on a board. It's pretty disgusting.
These days one is never really sure whether a bull is a dog, or an ear of corn is actually a leg of pork or

a beef steak. But perhaps this is the path to genuine
modernity? Why, after all, shouldn't a glass be a
hedgehog, a hedge an etiquette manual, and so on?

Yours truly,
Tilottama

P.S. I have learned that scientists working in the
poultry industry are trying to excise the mothering
instinct in hens in order to mitigate or entirely
remove their desire to brood. Their goal, apparently,
is to stop chickens wasting time on unnecessary
things and thereby to increase the efficiency of egg
production. Even though I am personally and in
principle completely against efficiency, I wonder
whether conducting this sort of intervention (by
which I mean excising the mothering instinct)
on the Maaji—The Mothers of the Disappeared
in Kashmir—would help. Right now they are
inefficient, unproductive units, living on a mandatory
diet of hopeless hope, pottering about in their
kitchen gardens, wondering what to grow and what
to cook, in case their sons return. I'm sure you agree
this is a bad business model. Could you propose
a better one? A doable, realistic (although I'm
against realism too) formula to arrive at an efficient
Quantum of Hope? The three variables in their case
are Death, Disappearance and Familial Love. All
other forms of love, assuming that they do indeed
exist, do not qualify and should be disregarded.
Barring of course the Love of God. (That goes
without saying.)

P.P.S. I'm moving. I don't know where I'm going.
This fills me with hope.

When she finished her letter she folded it carefully and put it
into her bag. She cut the cake, packed it into a box file and put
it into the fridge. She untied the balloons one by one and locked
them in the cupboard. She switched on the TV with the volume
off. A man was selling his eyebrows. He had turned down the
initial offer of five hundred dollars. Eventually, for one thousand
four hundred dollars he agreed to have them shaved off with an
electric shaver. He had a funny, sheepish smile on his face. He
looked like Elmer Fudd in *The Wacky Wabbit*.

Predawn.
Still no Saddam Hussain.
The kidnapper looked down from her window a little
impatiently.
A text message on her phone:

> Let's unite on International Yoga Day for
> poolside candlelight yoga and meditation by
> Guru Hanumant Bhardwaj

She tapped out a reply:

> Please let's not.

Right beside the school gate on which a painted nurse was giving a painted baby a painted polio vaccination, a circle of sleepy
women, migrant workers from roadworks nearby, stood around
a tiny boy as he squatted like a comma on the edge of an open
manhole. The women leaned on their shovels and pickaxes as

they waited for their star to perform. The comma had his eyes fixed on one of the women. His mother. The spirit moved him. He made a pool. A yellow leaf. His mother put down her ax and washed his bottom with muddy water from an old Bisleri bottle. With the leftover water she washed her hands, and washed the yellow leaf into the manhole. Nothing in the city belonged to the women. Not a tiny plot of land, not a hovel in a slum, not a tin sheet over their heads. Not even the sewage system. But now they had made a direct, unorthodox deposit, an express delivery straight into the system. Maybe it marked the beginning of a foothold in the city. The comma's mother gathered him in her arms, slung her ax across her shoulder, and the little contingent left.

The street was empty.

And then, as though he had been waiting for the women to leave before making his entry, Saddam Hussain appeared. In the following order:

Sound

Sight

Smell (stench).

The yellow municipal truck turned into the little service lane and parked a few houses away. Saddam Hussain swung out of the passenger seat (with the same flamboyance with which he usually swung off his horse), his gaze already scanning the second-floor window of Tilo's building. Tilo put her head out and signaled that the gate was open and that he should come up.

She met him at the door with a packed suitcase, a baby and a box file full of strawberry cake. Comrade Laali greeted Saddam on the landing as though she was being reunited with a lost lover. She held her head steady and wagged the rest of her body from side to side, her ears flattened, her eyes slanting coquettishly.

"Is she yours?" Saddam asked Tilo after they had introduced

themselves to each other. "We can take her, there's plenty of room where we are going."

"She has puppies."

"*Arre*, where's the problem . . . ?"

He gently pushed the puppies off the sack they lay on, opened it and dropped them in—a bunch of squealing, squirming brinjals. Tilo locked her door and the little procession trooped down the stairs and into the street.

Saddam with a packed suitcase and a sack full of puppies.

Tilo with a baby and a box file.

And Comrade Laali trailing her newfound love with unashamed devotion.

The driver's cabin was as big as a small hotel room. Neeraj Kumar the driver and Saddam Hussain were old friends. Saddam (master of forethought and attention to detail) placed a wooden fruit crate near the door of the truck. A makeshift step. Comrade Laali jumped in, followed by Tilo and Miss Jebeen the Second. They sat at the back, on a red Rexine bunk bed that truck drivers slept on during long-haul drives when they were tired and the stand-in driver took the wheel. (Municipal garbage trucks never went on long-haul drives, but they had the bunk beds anyway.) Saddam sat in front, on the passenger seat. He placed the puppy sack between his feet, opened it up for air, put on his sunglasses, rapped the passenger door twice, like a bus conductor, and they were off.

The yellow truck blazed a trail through the city, leaving the stench of burst cow in its wake. This time, unlike the last journey Saddam had made with similar cargo, he was in a municipal truck in the capital of the country. Gujarat ka Lalla was still a year away from taking the throne, the saffron parakeets were still biding their time, waiting in the wings. So temporarily, it was safe.

The truck rattled past the row of car-repair shops, the men and dogs covered in grease, still asleep outside.

Past a market, a Sikh Gurdwara, another market. Past a hospital with patients and their families camped on the road outside. Past jostling crowds at the 24x7 chemists. Over a flyover, the street lights still on.

Past the Garden City with lush, landscaped roundabouts.

As it drove on, the gardens disappeared, the roads grew bumpy and potholed, the pavements grew crowded with sleeping bodies. Dogs, goats, cows, humans. Parked cycle rickshaws stacked one behind the other like the vertebrae in a serpent's skeleton.

The truck stank its way under crumbling stone arches and past the ramparts of the Red Fort. It skirted the old city and arrived at Jannat Guest House and Funeral Services.

Anjum was waiting for them—an ecstatic smile shining out from among the tombstones.

She was splendidly dressed, in the sequins and satin of her glory days. She wore make-up and lipstick, she had dyed her hair and pinned on a thick, long, black plait with a red ribbon woven into it. She enveloped both Tilo and Miss Jebeen in a bear hug, kissing both of them several times.

She had organized a Welcome Home party. Jannat Guest House was decorated with balloons and streamers.

The guests, all splendidly dressed, were: Zainab, a plump eighteen-year-old now, studying fashion design at a local polytechnic, Saeeda (soberly dressed in a sari, in addition to being Ustad of the Khwabgah, she headed an NGO that worked on transgender rights), Nimmo Gorakhpuri (who had driven in from Mewat with three kilos of fresh mutton for the party), Ishrat-the-Beautiful (who had extended her visit), Roshan Lal (who remained poker-faced), Imam Ziauddin (who tickled Miss Jebeen with his beard, and then blessed her and said a prayer).

Ustad Hameed played the harmonium and welcomed her in Raag Tilak Kamod:

Ae ri sakhi mora piya ghar aaye
Bagh laga iss aangan ko

O my companions, my love has come home
This bare yard has blossomed into a garden

Saddam and Anjum showed Tilo to the room they had readied for her on the ground floor. She would share it with Comrade Laali and family, Miss Jebeen and Ahlam Baji's grave. Payal-the-mare was tethered outside the window. The room was festooned with streamers and balloons. Unsure of what arrangements to make for a woman, a real woman, from the Duniya—and not just the Duniya but the South Delhi Duniya—they had opted for a hairdressing-salon type of décor—a dressing table from a second-hand furniture market fitted out with a large mirror. A metal trolley on which there was a range of bottles of different shades of Lakmé nail polish and lipstick, a comb, a hairbrush, rollers, a hairdryer and a bottle of shampoo. Nimmo Gorakh-puri had brought her lifetime's collection of fashion magazines from her home in Mewat and arranged them in tall piles on a large coffee table. Next to the bed was a baby cot with a big teddy bear propped up on the pillow. (The controversial subject of where Miss Jebeen the Second would sleep and who would be called Mummy—not *"badi* Mummy" or *"chhoti* Mummy," but Mummy—would be raised later. It would be easily resolved because Tilo conceded to Anjum's demands quite happily.) Anjum introduced Tilo to Ahlam Baji as though Ahlam Baji were still alive. She recounted her accomplishments and achievements and listed the names of some of Shahjahanabad's luminaries that she had helped bring into the world—Akbar Mian the baker, maker of the best *sheermal* in the walled city, Jabbar Bhai the tailor, Sabiha Alvi, whose daughter had just started a Benarasi Sari Emporium in the first-floor room of their house. Anjum spoke as though it was a world that Tilo was familiar with, a world that everybody ought to be familiar with; in fact, the only world *worth* being familiar with.

For the first time in her life, Tilo felt that her body had enough room to accommodate all its organs.

The first ever hotel that had come up in the small town she grew up in was called Hotel Anjali. The street hoardings that advertised this exciting new development said *Come to Anjali for the Rest of Your Life.* The pun had been unintentional, but as a child she had always imagined that Hotel Anjali was full of the corpses of its unsuspecting guests who had been murdered in their sleep and would remain there for the rest of their (dead) lives. In the case of Jannat Guest House, Tilo felt that that tagline would have been not just appropriate, but comforting. Instinct told her that she may finally have found a home for the Rest of Her Life.

Dawn had just broken when the feasting began. Anjum had shopped all day (for meat and toys and furniture) and cooked all night.

On the menu was:

Mutton Korma
Mutton Biryani
Brain Curry
Kashmiri Rogan Josh
Fried Liver
Shami Kebab
Nan
Tandoori Roti
Sheermal

Phirni

Watermelon with black salt.

The addicts and homeless people from the periphery of the graveyard gathered in the yard to partake of the feast and merriment. Payal snuffled up a substantial serving of phirni. Dr. Azad Bhartiya arrived a little late, but to great applause and affection for having coordinated the escape and homecoming. His indefinite fast had entered its eleventh year, third month and twenty-fifth day. He would not eat, but settled for a deworming pill and a glass of water.

A few kebabs and some biryani were kept aside for the municipal officers who would surely come by later in the day.

"Those fellows are just like us Hijras," Anjum said and laughed affectionately. "Somehow they smell a celebration and arrive to demand their share."

Biroo and Comrade Laali feasted on bones and leftovers. As a matter of abundant caution, Zainab sequestered the pups in a place that was inaccessible to Biroo and spent hours delighting in them and flirting outrageously with Saddam Hussain.

Miss Jebeen the Second was passed from arm to arm, hugged, kissed and overfed. In this way she embarked on her brand-new life in a place similar to, and yet a world apart from where, over eighteen years ago, her young ancestor Miss Jebeen the First had ended hers.

In a graveyard.

Another graveyard, just a little further north.

And they would not believe me precisely because they would know that what I said was true.

—JAMES BALDWIN

9

THE UNTIMELY DEATH OF MISS JEBEEN THE FIRST

Ever since she was old enough to insist, she had insisted on being called Miss Jebeen. It was the only name she would answer to. Everyone had to call her that, her parents, her grandparents, the neighbors too. She was a precocious devotee of the "Miss" fetish that gripped the Kashmir Valley in the early years of the insurrection. All of a sudden, fashionable young ladies, especially in the towns, insisted on being addressed as "Miss." Miss Momin, Miss Ghazala, Miss Farhana. It was only one of the many fetishes of the times. In those blood-dimmed years, for reasons nobody fully understood, people became what can only be described as fetish-prone. Other than the "Miss" fetish, there was a nurse fetish, a PT (Physical Training) instructor fetish and a roller-skating fetish. So, in addition to checkposts, bunkers, weapons, grenades, landmines, Casspirs, concertina wire, soldiers, insurgents, counter-insurgents, spies, special operatives, double agents, triple agents and suitcases of cash from the Agencies on both sides of the border, the Valley was also awash with nurses, PT instructors and roller-skaters. And of course Misses.

Among them Miss Jebeen, who didn't live long enough to become a nurse, nor even a roller-skater.

In the Mazar-e-Shohadda, the Martyrs' Graveyard, where she was first buried, the cast-iron signboard that arched over the main gate said (in two languages): *We Gave Our Todays for Your Tomorrows*. It's corroded now, the green paint faded, the delicate calligraphy flecked with pinholes of light. Still, there it is, after all these years, silhouetted like a swatch of stiff lace against the sapphire sky and the snowy, saw-toothed mountains.

There it still is.

Miss Jebeen was not a member of the Committee that decided what should be written on the signboard. But she was in no position to argue with its decision. Also, Miss Jebeen hadn't notched up very many Todays to trade in for Tomorrows, but then the algebra of infinite justice was never so rude. In this way, without being consulted on the matter, she became one of the Movement's youngest martyrs. She was buried right next to her mother, Begum Arifa Yeswi. Mother and daughter died by the same bullet. It entered Miss Jebeen's head through her left temple and came to rest in her mother's heart. In the last photograph of her, the bullet wound looked like a cheerful summer rose arranged just above her left ear. A few petals had fallen on her *kaffan*, the white shroud she was wrapped in before she was laid to rest.

Miss Jebeen and her mother were buried along with fifteen others, taking the toll of their massacre to seventeen.

At the time of their funeral the Mazar-e-Shohadda was still fairly new, but was already getting crowded. However, the Intiza-miya Committee, the Organizing Committee, had its ear to the ground from the very beginning of the insurrection and had a realistic idea of things to come. It planned the layout of the graves carefully, making ordered, efficient use of the available space. Everyone understood how important it was to bury martyrs' bodies in collective burial grounds and not leave them scattered (in their thousands), like birdfeed, up in the mountains, or in the forests around the army camps and torture centers that had mushroomed across the Valley. When the fighting began and the Occupation tightened its grip, for ordinary people the consolidation of their dead became, in itself, an act of defiance.

The first to be laid to rest in the graveyard was a *gumnaam shaheed*, an anonymous martyr, whose coffin was brought out at midnight. He was buried in the graveyard-which-wasn't-yet-a-graveyard with full rites and honors before a solemn knot of mourners. The next morning, while candles were lit and fresh rose petals scattered on the fresh grave, and fresh prayers were said in the presence of thousands of people who had gathered following the post-Friday-prayer announcements in the mosques, the Committee began the business of fencing off a large swathe of land the size of a small meadow. A few days later the sign went up: Mazar-e-Shohadda.

Rumor had it that the unidentified martyr who was buried that night—the founder-corpse—was not a corpse at all, but an empty duffel bag. Years later, the (alleged) mastermind of this (alleged) plan was questioned by a young *sang-baaz*, a rock-thrower, a member of the new generation of freedom fighters, who had heard this story and was troubled by it: "But *jenaab*, *jenaab*, does this not mean that our Movement, our *tehreek*, is based on a lie?" The grizzled mastermind's (alleged) reply was, "This is the trouble with you youngsters, you have absolutely no idea how wars are fought."

Many of course maintained that the rumor about the martyr-bag was just another of those endless rumors generated and disseminated by the Rumours Wing in Badami Bagh, Military HQ, Srinagar; just another ploy by the occupation forces to undermine the *tehreek* and keep people destabilized, suspicious and racked by self-doubt.

Rumor had it that there really was a Rumours Wing with an officer of the rank of Major in charge of it. There was a rumor that a dreaded battalion from Nagaland (themselves subjects of another occupation in the east), legendary eaters of pigs and dogs, occasionally enjoyed a snack of human flesh as well, especially the meat of "oldies," those in the know said. There was a rumor that anybody who could deliver (to somebody, address unknown) an owl in good health that weighed three or more kilos (owls in the region weighed only half that, even the fat ones) would win a million-rupee prize. People took to snaring hawks, falcons, small owls and raptors of all kinds, feeding them rats, rice and raisins, injecting them with steroids and weighing them on the hour, every hour, even though they were not quite sure whom to deliver the birds to. Cynics said it was the army again, always looking for ways to keep gullible people busy and out of trouble. There were rumors and counter-rumors. There were rumors that might have been true, and truths that ought to have been just rumors. For instance, it really was true that for many years the army's Human Rights Cell was headed by a Lieutenant Colonel Stalin—a friendly fellow from Kerala, son of an old communist. (The rumor was that it was his idea to set up Muskaan—which means "smile" in Urdu—a chain of military "Good Will" centers for the rehabilitation of widows, half-widows, orphans and half-orphans. Infuriated people, who accused the army of creating the supply of orphans and widows, regularly burned down the "Good Will" orphanages and sewing-centers. They were always rebuilt, bigger, better, plusher, friendlier.)

In the matter of the Martyrs' Graveyard, however, the question of whether the first grave contained a bag or a body turned out to be of no real consequence. The substantive truth was that a relatively new graveyard was filling up, with real bodies, at an alarming pace.

. . .

Martyrdom stole into the Kashmir Valley from across the Line of Control, through moonlit mountain passes manned by soldiers. Night after night it walked on narrow, stony paths wrapped like thread around blue cliffs of ice, across vast glaciers and high meadows of waist-deep snow. It trudged past young boys shot down in snowdrifts, their bodies arranged in eerie, frozen tableaux under the pitiless gaze of the pale moon in the cold night sky, and stars that hung so low you felt you could almost touch them.

When it arrived in the Valley it stayed close to the ground and spread through the walnut groves, the saffron fields, the apple, almond and cherry orchards like a creeping mist. It whispered words of war into the ears of doctors and engineers, students and laborers, tailors and carpenters, weavers and farmers, shepherds, cooks and bards. They listened carefully, and then put down their books and implements, their needles, their chisels, their staffs, their plows, their cleavers and their spangled clown costumes. They stilled the looms on which they had woven the most beautiful carpets and the finest, softest shawls the world had ever seen, and ran gnarled, wondering fingers over the smooth barrels of Kalashnikovs that the strangers who visited them allowed them to touch. They followed the new Pied Pipers up into the high meadows and alpine glades where training camps had been set up. Only after they had been given guns of their own, after they had curled their fingers around the trigger and felt it give, ever so slightly, after they had weighed the odds and decided it was a viable option, only then did they allow the rage and shame of the subjugation they had endured for decades, for centuries, to course through their bodies and turn the blood in their veins into smoke.

The mist swirled on, on an indiscriminate recruitment drive. It whispered into the ears of black marketeers, bigots, thugs and confidence-tricksters. They too listened intently before they reconfigured their plans. They ran their sly fingers over the cold-metal bumps on their quota of grenades that was being distributed so generously, like parcels of choice mutton at Eid. They grafted the language of God and Freedom, Allah and Azadi, on to their murders and new scams. They made off with money, property and women.

Of course women.

Women of course.

In this way the insurrection began. Death was everywhere. Death was everything. Career. Desire. Dream. Poetry. Love. Youth itself. Dying became just another way of living. Graveyards sprang up in parks and meadows, by streams and rivers, in fields and forest glades. Tombstones grew out of the ground like young children's teeth. Every village, every locality, had its own graveyard. The ones that didn't grew anxious about being seen as collaborators. In remote border areas, near the Line of Control, the speed and regularity with which the bodies turned up, and the condition some of them were in, wasn't easy to cope with. Some were delivered in sacks, some in small polythene bags, just pieces of flesh, some hair and teeth. Notes pinned to them by the quartermasters of death said: *1 kg, 2.7 kg, 500 g.* (Yes, another of those truths that ought really to have been just a rumor.)

Tourists flew out. Journalists flew in. Honeymooners flew out. Soldiers flew in. Women flocked around police stations and army camps holding up a forest of thumbed, dog-eared, passport-sized photographs grown soft with tears: *Please sir, have you seen my boy anywhere? Have you seen my husband? Has my brother by any chance passed through your hands?* And the Sirs swelled their chests and bristled their mustaches and played with their medals and narrowed their eyes to assess them, to see which one's despair would be worth converting into corrosive hope (*I'll see what I can do*), and what that hope would be worth to whom. (*A fee? A feast? A fuck? A truckload of walnuts?*)

Prisons filled up, jobs evaporated. Guides, touts, pony own-ers (and their ponies), bellboys, waiters, receptionists, toboggan-pullers, trinket-sellers, florists and the boatmen on the lake grew poorer and hungrier.

Only for gravediggers there was no rest. It was just workwork-work. With no extra pay for overtime or night shifts.

In the Mazar-e-Shohadda, Miss Jebeen and her mother were buried next to each other. On his wife's tombstone, Musa Yeswi wrote:

ARIFA YESWI
12 September 1968–22 December 1995
Wife of Musa Yeswi

And below that:

Ab wahan khaak udhaati hai khizaan
Phool hi phool jahaan thay pehle

Now dust blows on autumn's breeze
Where once were flowers, only flowers

Next to it, on Miss Jebeen's tombstone it said:

MISS JEBEEN
2 January 1992–22 December 1995
Beloved d/o Arifa and Musa Yeswi

And then right at the bottom, in very small letters, Musa asked the tombstone-engraver to inscribe what many would consider an inappropriate epitaph for a martyr. He positioned it in a place where he knew that in winter it would be more or less hidden under the snow and during the rest of the year tall grass and wild narcissus would obscure it. More or less. This is what he wrote:

Akh daleela wann
Yeth manz ne kahn balai aasi
Na aes soh kunni junglas manz roazaan

It's what Miss Jebeen would say to him at night as she lay next to him on the carpet, resting her back on a frayed velvet bolster (washed, darned, washed again), wearing her own pheran (washed, darned, washed again), tiny as a tea cozy (ferozi blue with salmon-pink paisleys embroidered along the neck and sleeves) and mimicking precisely her father's lying-down posture—her left leg bent, her right ankle on her left knee, her very small fist in his big one. *Akh daleela wann*. Tell me a story. And then she would begin the story herself, shouting it out into the somber, curfewed night, her raucous delight dancing out of the windows and rousing the neighborhood. *Yeth manz ne kahn balai aasi! Na aes soh kunni junglas manz roazaan!* There *wasn't* a witch, and she *didn't* live in the jungle. Tell me a story, and can we cut the crap about the witch and the jungle? Can you tell me a *real* story?

Cold soldiers from a warm climate patrolling the icy highway that circled their neighborhood cocked their ears and uncocked the safety catches of their guns. *Who's there? What's that sound? Stop or we'll shoot!* They came from far away and did not know the words in Kashmiri for *Stop* or *Shoot* or *Who*. They had guns, so they didn't need to.

The youngest of them, S. Murugesan, barely adult, had never been so cold, had never seen snow and was still enchanted by the shapes his breath made as it condensed in the frozen air. "Look!" he said on his first night patrol, two fingers to his lips, pulling on an imaginary cigarette, exhaling a plume of blue smoke. "Free cigarette!" The white smile in his dark face floated through the night and then faded, deflated by the bored disdain of his mates. "Go ahead, Rajinikant," they said to him, "smoke the whole pack. Cigarettes don't taste so good once they've blown your head off."

They.

They *did* get him eventually. The armored jeep he was riding in was blown up on the highway just outside Kupwara. He and two other soldiers bled to death by the side of the road.

His body was delivered in a coffin to his family in his village in Thanjavur district, Tamil Nadu, along with a DVD of the documentary film *Saga of Untold Valor* directed by a Major Raju and produced by the Ministry of Defense. S. Murugesan wasn't in the film, but his family thought he was because they never saw it. They didn't have a DVD player.

In his village the Vanniyars (who were not "untouchable") would not allow the body of S. Murugesan (who was) to be carried past their houses to the cremation ground. So the funeral procession took a circuitous route that skirted the village to the separate Untouchables' cremation ground right next to the village dump.

One of the things that S. Murugesan had secretly enjoyed about being in Kashmir was that fair-skinned Kashmiris would often taunt Indian soldiers by mocking their dark skins and calling them "Chamar nasl" (Chamar breed). He was amused by the rage it provoked among those of his fellow soldiers who considered themselves upper caste and thought nothing of calling *him* a Chamar, which was what North Indians usually called all Dalits, regardless of which of the many Untouchable castes they belonged to. Kashmir was one of the few places in the world where a fair-skinned people had been ruled by a darker-skinned one. That inversion imbued appalling slurs with a kind of righteousness.

To commemorate S. Murugesan's valor, the army contributed towards building a cement statue of Sepoy S. Murugesan, in his soldier's uniform, with his rifle on his shoulder, at the entrance to the village. Every now and then his young widow would point it out to their baby, who was six months old when her father died. "Appa," she'd say, waving at the statue. And the baby would smile, mimicking precisely her mother's wave, a fold of babyfat spilling over her babywrist like a bracelet. "Appappappappap-pappappa," she'd say, smiling.

Not everyone in the village was happy with the idea of having an Untouchable man's statue put up at the entrance. Particularly not an Untouchable who carried a weapon. They felt it would give out the wrong message, give people ideas. Three weeks after the statue went up, the rifle on its shoulder went missing. Sepoy S. Murugesan's family tried to file a complaint, but the police refused to register a case, saying that the rifle must have fallen off or simply disintegrated due to the use of substandard cement—a fairly common malpractice—and that nobody could be blamed. A month later the statue's hands were cut off. Once again the police refused to register a case, although this time they sniggered knowingly and did not even bother to offer a reason. Two weeks after the amputation of its hands, the statue of Sepoy S. Murugesan was beheaded. There were a few days of tension. People from nearby villages who belonged to the same caste as S. Murugesan organized a protest. They began a relay hunger strike at the base of the statue. A local court said it would con-stitute a magisterial committee to look into the matter. In the meanwhile it ordered a status quo. The hunger strike was discon-tinued. The magisterial committee was never constituted.

In some countries, some soldiers die twice.

The headless statue remained at the entrance of the village. Though it no longer bore any likeness to the man it was supposed to commemorate, it turned out to be a more truthful emblem of the times than it would otherwise have been.

S. Murugesan's baby continued to wave at him.

"Appappappappa . . ."

As the war progressed in the Kashmir Valley, graveyards became as common as the multi-story parking lots that were springing up in the burgeoning cities in the plains. When they ran out of space, some graves became double-deckered, like the buses in Srinagar that once ferried tourists between Lal Chowk and the Boulevard.

Fortunately, Miss Jebeen's grave did not suffer that fate. Years later, after the government declared that the insurrection had been contained (although half a million soldiers stayed on just to make sure), after the major militant groups had turned (or been turned) on each other, after pilgrims, tourists and honeymooners from the mainland began to return to the Valley to frolic in the snow (to be heaved up and whisked down steep snow banks—shrieking—in sledges manned by former militants), after spies and informers had (for reasons of tidiness and abundant caution) been killed by their handlers, after renegades were absorbed into regular day jobs by the thousands of NGOs working in the Peace Sector, after local businessmen who had made fortunes supplying the army with coal and walnut wood began to invest their money in the fast-growing Hospitality Sector (otherwise known as giving people "Stakes in the Peace Process"), after senior bank managers had appropriated the unclaimed money that remained in dead militants' bank accounts, after the torture centers were converted into plush homes for politicians, after the martyrs' graveyards grew a little derelict and the number of martyrs had reduced to a trickle (and the number of suicides rose dramatically), after elections were held and democracy was declared, after the Jhelum rose and receded, after the insurrection rose again and was crushed again and rose again and was crushed again and rose again—even after all this, Miss Jebeen's grave remained single-deckered.

She drew a lucky straw. She had a pretty grave with wildflowers growing around it and her mother close by.

Her massacre was the second in the city in two months.

Of the seventeen who died that day, seven were by-standers like Miss Jebeen and her mother (in their case, they were technically by-sitters). They had been watching from their balcony, Miss Jebeen, running a slight temperature, sitting on her mother's lap, as thousands of mourners carried the body of Usman Abdullah, a popular university lecturer, through the streets of the city. He had been shot by what the authorities declared to be a "UG"—an unidentified gunman—even though his identity was an open secret. Although Usman Abdullah was a prominent ideologue in the struggle for Azadi, he had been threatened several times by the newly emerging hard-line faction of militants who had returned from across the Line of Control, fitted out with new weapons and harsh new ideas that he had publicly disagreed with. The assassination of Usman Abdullah was a declaration that the syncretism of Kashmir that he represented would not be tolerated. There was to be no more of that folksy, old-world stuff. No more worshipping of home-grown saints and seers at local shrines, the new militants declared, no more addle-headedness. There were to be no more sideshow saints and local God Men. There was only Allah, the one God. There was the Quran. There was Prophet Mohammed (Peace Be Upon Him). There was one way of praying, one interpretation of divine law and one definition of Azadi—which was this:

Azadi ka matlab kya?
La ilaha illallah

What does freedom mean?

There is no God but Allah

There was to be no debate about this. In future, all arguments would be settled with bullets. Shias were not Muslim. And women would have to learn to dress appropriately.

Women of course.

Of course women.

Some of this made ordinary people uncomfortable. They loved their shrines—Hazratbal in particular, which housed the Holy relic, the *Moi-e-Muqaddas*, a hair of Prophet Mohammed. Hundreds of thousands had wept on the streets when it went missing one winter in 1963. Hundreds of thousands rejoiced when it turned up a month later (and was certified as genuine by the concerned authority). But when the Strict Ones returned from their travels, they declared that worshipping local saints and enshrining hair were heresy.

The Strict Line plunged the Valley into a dilemma. People knew that the freedom they longed for would not come without a war, and they knew the Strict Ones were by far the better warriors. They had the best training, the better weapons and, as per divine regulation, the shorter trousers and the longer beards. They had more blessings and more money from the other side of the Line of Control. Their steely, unwavering faith disciplined them, simplified them, and equipped them to take on the might of the second-biggest army in the world. The militants who called themselves "secular" were less strict, more easy-going. More stylish, more flamboyant. They wrote poetry, flirted with the nurses and the roller-skaters, and patrolled the streets with their rifles slung carelessly on their shoulders. But they did not seem to have what it took to win a war.

People loved the Less Strict Ones, but they feared and

respected the Strict Ones. In the battle of attrition that took place between the two, hundreds lost their lives. Eventually the Less Strict Ones declared a ceasefire, came overground and vowed to continue their struggle as Gandhians. The Strict Ones continued the fight and over the years were hunted down man by man. For each one that was killed, another took his place.

A few months after the murder of Usman Abdullah, his assassin (the well-known UG) was captured and killed by the army. His body was handed over to his family, pockmarked with bullet-holes and cigarette burns. The Graveyard Committee, after discussing the matter at length, decided that he was a martyr too and deserved to be buried in the Martyrs' Graveyard. They buried him at the opposite end of the cemetery, hoping perhaps that keeping Usman Abdullah and his assassin as far apart as possible would prevent them from quarreling in the afterlife.

As the war went on, in the Valley the soft line gradually hardened and the hard line further hardened. Each line begot more lines and sub-lines. The Strict Ones begot even Stricter Ones. Ordinary people managed, quite miraculously, to indulge them all, support them all, subvert them all, and go on with their old, supposedly addle-headed ways. The reign of the *Moi-e-Muqaddas* continued unabated. And even as they drifted on the quickening currents of Strictness, ever-larger numbers of people continued to flock to the shrines to weep and unburden their broken hearts.

From the safety of their balcony, Miss Jebeen and her mother watched the funeral procession approach. Like the other women and children who were crowded into the wooden balconies of the old houses all the way down the street, Miss Jebeen and Arifa too had readied a bowl of fresh rose petals to shower on the body of Usman Abdullah as it passed below them. Miss Jebeen was bundled up against the cold in two sweaters and woolen mittens. On her head she wore a little white hijab made of wool. Thousands of people chanting *Azadi! Azadi!* funneled into the narrow lane. Miss Jebeen and her mother chanted it too. Although Miss Jebeen, always naughty, sometimes shouted *Mataji!* (Mother) instead of *Azadi!*—because the two words sounded the same, and because she knew that when she did that, her mother would look down at her and smile and kiss her.

The procession had to pass a large bunker of the 26th Battalion of the Border Security Force that was positioned less than a hundred feet from where Arifa and Miss Jebeen sat. The snouts of machine guns protruded through the steel mesh window of a dusty booth made up of tin sheets and wooden planks. The bunker was barricaded with sandbags and concertina wire. Empty bottles of army-issue Old Monk and Triple X Rum dangled in pairs from the razor wire, clinking against each other like bells—a primitive but effective alarm system. Any tinkering with the wire would set them off. Booze bottles in the service of the Nation. They came with the added benefit of being callously insulting to devout Muslims. The soldiers in the bunker fed the stray dogs that the local population shunned (as devout Muslims were meant to), so the dogs doubled as an additional ring of security. They sat around, watching the proceedings, alert, but not alarmed. As the procession approached the bunker, the men caged inside it fused into the shadows, cold sweat trickling down their backs underneath their winter uniforms and bulletproof vests.

Suddenly, an explosion. Not a very loud one, but loud enough and close enough to generate blind panic. The soldiers came out of the bunker, took position and fired their light machine guns straight into the unarmed crowd that was wedged into the narrow street. They shot to kill. Even after people turned to flee, the bullets pursued them, lodging themselves in receding backs and heads and legs. Some frightened soldiers turned their weapons on those watching from windows and balconies, and emptied their magazines into people and railings, walls and windowpanes. Into Miss Jebeen and her mother, Arifa.

Usman Abdullah's coffin and coffin-bearers were hit. His coffin broke open and his re-slain corpse spilled on to the street, awkwardly folded, in a snow-white shroud, doubly dead among the dead and injured.

Some Kashmiris die twice too.

The shooting stopped only when the street was empty, and when all that remained were the bodies of the dead and wounded. And shoes. Thousands of shoes.

And the deafening slogan there was nobody left to chant:

Jis Kashmir ko khoon se seencha! Woh Kashmir hamara hai!

The Kashmir we have irrigated with our blood! That Kashmir is ours!

The post-massacre protocol was quick and efficient—perfected by practice. Within an hour the dead bodies had been removed to the morgue in the Police Control Room, and the wounded to hospital. The street was hosed down, the blood directed into the open drains. Shops reopened. Normalcy was declared. (Normalcy was always a declaration.)

Later it was established that the explosion had been caused by a car driving over an empty carton of Mango Frooti on the next street. Who was to blame? Who had left the packet of Mango Frooti (*Fresh 'n' Juicy*) on the street? India or Kashmir? Or Pakistan? Who had driven over it? A tribunal was instituted to inquire into the causes of the massacre. The facts were never established. Nobody was blamed. This was Kashmir. It was Kashmir's fault.

Life went on. Death went on. The war went on.

⚭

ALL THOSE WHO WATCHED Musa Yeswi bury his wife and daughter noticed how quiet he had been that day. He displayed no grief. He seemed withdrawn and distracted, as though he wasn't really there. That could have been what eventually led to his arrest. Or it could have been his heartbeat. Perhaps it was too quick or too slow for an innocent civilian. At notorious checkposts soldiers sometimes put their ears to young men's chests and listened to their heartbeats. There were rumors that some soldiers even carried stethoscopes. "This one's heart is beating for Freedom," they'd say, and that would be reason enough for the body that hosted the too-quick or too-slow heart to make a trip to Cargo, or Papa II, or the Shiraz Cinema—the most dreaded interrogation centers in the Valley.

Musa was not arrested at a checkpost. He was picked up from his home after the funeral. Over-quietness at the funeral of your wife and child would not have passed unnoticed in those days.

At first of course everybody had been quiet, fearful. The funeral procession snaked its way through the drab, slushy little city in dead silence. The only sound was the *slap-slap-slap* of thousands of sockless shoes on the silver-wet road that led to the Mazar-e-Shohadda. Young men carried seventeen coffins on their shoulders. Seventeen plus one, that is, for the re-murdered Usman Abdullah, who obviously could not be entered twice in the books. So, seventeen-plus-one tin coffins wove through the streets, winking back at the winter sun. To someone looking down at the city from the ring of high mountains that surrounded it, the procession would have looked like a column of brown ants carrying seventeen-plus-one sugar crystals to their anthill to feed their queen. Perhaps to a student of history and human conflict, in relative terms that's all the little procession really amounted to: a column of ants making off with some crumbs that had fallen from the high table. As wars go, this was only a small one. Nobody paid much attention. So it went on and on. So it folded and unfolded over decades, gathering people into its unhinged embrace. Its cruelties became as natural as the changing seasons, each came with its own unique range of scent and blossom, its own cycle of loss and renewal, disruption and normalcy, uprisings and elections.

Of all the sugar crystals carried by the ants that winter morning, the smallest crystal of course went by the name of Miss Jebeen.

Ants that were too nervous to join the procession lined the streets, standing on slippery banks of old brown snow, their arms crossed inside the warmth of their pherans, leaving their empty sleeves to flap in the breeze. Armless people at the heart of an armed insurrection. Those who were too scared to venture out watched from their windows and balconies (although they had been made acutely aware of the perils of that too). Each of them knew that they were being tracked in the gunsights of the soldiers who had taken position across the city—on roofs, bridges, boats, mosques, water towers. They had occupied hotels, schools, shops and even some homes.

It was cold that morning; for the first time in years the lake had frozen over and the forecast predicted more snow. Trees raised their naked, mottled branches to the sky like mourners stilled in attitudes of grief.

In the graveyard, seventeen-plus-one graves had been readied. Neat, fresh, deep. The earth from each pit piled up next to it, a dark chocolate pyramid. An advance party had brought in the bloodstained metal stretchers on which the bodies had been returned to their families after the post-mortems. They were propped up, arranged around the trunks of trees, like bloodied steel petals of some gigantic flesh-eating mountain blossom.

As the procession turned in through the gates of the grave-yard, a scrum of pressmen, quivering like athletes on their start-ing blocks, broke rank and rushed forward. The coffins were laid down, opened, arranged in a line on the icy earth. The crowd made room for the press respectfully. It knew that without the journalists and photographers the massacre would be erased and the dead would truly die. So the bodies were offered to them, in hope and anger. A banquet of death. Mourning relatives who had backed away were asked to return into frame. Their sorrow was to be archived. In the years to come, when the war became a way of life, there would be books and films and photo exhibitions curated around the theme of Kashmir's grief and loss.

Musa would not be in any of those pictures.

On this occasion Miss Jebeen was by far the biggest draw. The cameras closed in on her, whirring and clicking like a worried bear. From that harvest of photographs, one emerged a local classic. For years it was reproduced in papers and magazines and on the covers of human rights reports that no one ever read, with captions like *Blood in the Snow*, *Vale of Tears* and *Will the Sorrow Never End?*

In the mainland, for obvious reasons, the photograph of Miss Jebeen was less popular. In the supermarket of sorrow, the Bhopal Boy, victim of the Union Carbide gas leak, remained well ahead of her in the charts. Several leading photographers claimed copyright of that famous photograph of the dead boy buried neck deep in a grave of debris, his staring, opaque eyes blinded by poison gas. Those eyes told the story of what had happened on that terrible night like nothing else could. They stared out of the pages of glossy magazines all over the world. In the end it didn't matter of course. The story flared, then faded. The battle over the copyright of the photograph continued for years, almost as ferociously as the battle for compensation for the thousands of devastated victims of the gas leak.

The worried bear dispersed, and revealed Miss Jebeen intact, un-mauled, fast asleep. Her summer rose still in place.

As the bodies were lowered into their graves the crowd began to murmur its prayer.

Rabbish rahlee sadree; Wa yassir lee amri
Wahlul uqdatan min lisaanee; Yafqahoo qawlee

My Lord! Relieve my mind. And ease my task for me
And loose a knot from my tongue. That they may understand my saying

The smaller, hip-high children in the separate, segregated section for women, suffocated by the rough wool of their mothers' garments, unable to see very much, barely able to breathe, conducted their own hip-level transactions: *I'll give you six bullet casings if you give me your dud grenade.*

A lone woman's voice climbed into the sky, eerily high, raw pain driven through it like a pike.

Ro rahi hai yeh zameen! Ro raha hai asmaan . . .

Another joined in and then another:

This earth, she weeps! The heavens too . . .

The birds stopped their twittering for a while and listened, beady-eyed, to humansong. Street dogs slouched past checkposts unchecked, their heartbeats rock steady. Kites and griffons circled the thermals, drifting lazily back and forth across the Line of Control, just to mock the tiny clot of humans gathered down below.

When the sky was full of keening, something ignited. Young men began to leap into the air, like flames kindled from smoldering embers. Higher and higher they jumped, as though the ground beneath their feet was sprung, a trampoline. They wore their anguish like armor, their anger slung across their bodies like ammunition belts. At that moment, perhaps because they were thus armed, or because they had decided to embrace a life of death, or because they knew they were already dead, they became invincible.

The soldiers who surrounded the Mazar-e-Shohadda had clear instructions to hold their fire, no matter what. Their informers (brothers, cousins, fathers, uncles, nephews), who mingled with the crowd and shouted slogans as passionately as everybody else (and even meant them), had clear instructions to submit photographs and if possible videos of each young man who, carried on the tide of fury, had leapt into the air and turned himself into a flame.

Soon each of them would hear a knock on his door, or be taken aside at a checkpoint.

Are you so-and-so? Son of so-and-so? Employed at such-and-such?

Often the threat went no further than that—just that bland, perfunctory inquiry. In Kashmir, throwing a man's own bio-data at him was sometimes enough to change the course of his life.

And sometimes it wasn't.

THEY CAME FOR MUSA at their customary visiting hour—four in the morning. He was awake, sitting at his desk writing a letter. His mother was in the next room. He could hear her crying and the comforting murmurs of her sisters and relatives. Miss

Jebeen's beloved stuffed (and leaking) green hippopotamus—with a V-shaped smile and a pink patchwork heart—was in his usual place, propped up against a bolster waiting for his little mother and his usual bedtime story. (*Akh daleela wann . . .*) Musa heard the vehicle approach. From his first-floor window he saw it turn into the lane and stop outside his house. He felt nothing, neither anger nor trepidation, as he watched the soldiers get out of the armored Gypsy. His father, Showkat Yeswi (Godzilla to Musa and his friends), was awake too, sitting cross-legged on the carpet in the front room. He was a building contractor who worked closely with the Military Engineering Services, supplying building materials and doing turnkey projects for them. He had sent his son to Delhi to study architecture in the hope that he would help him expand his line of business. But when the *tehreek* began in 1990, and Godzilla continued to work with the army, Musa shunned him altogether. Torn between filial duty and the guilt of enjoying what he saw as the spoils of collaboration, Musa found it harder and harder to live under the same roof as his father.

Showkat Yeswi seemed to have been expecting the soldiers. He did not appear alarmed. "Amrik Singh called. He wants to talk to you. It's nothing, don't worry. He will release you before daylight."

Musa did not reply. He did not even glance at Godzilla, his disgust apparent in the way he held his shoulders and in the erectness of his back. He walked out of the front door escorted by two armed men on either side of him and got into the vehicle. He was not handcuffed or headbagged. The Gypsy slid through the slick, frozen streets. It had begun to snow again.

The Shiraz Cinema was the centerpiece of an enclave of barracks and officers' quarters, cordoned off by the elaborate trappings of paranoia—two concentric rings of barbed wire sandwiching a shallow, sandy moat; the fourth and innermost ring was a high boundary wall topped with jagged shards of broken glass. The corrugated-metal gates had watchtowers on either side, manned by soldiers with machine guns. The Gypsy carrying Musa made it through the checkposts quickly. Clearly it was expected. It drove straight through the compound to the main entrance.

The cinema lobby was brightly lit. A mosaic of tiny mirrors that sequined the fluted white plaster-of-Paris false ceiling, whipped up like icing on a gigantic, inverted wedding cake, dispersed and magnified the light from cheap, flashy chandeliers. The red carpet was frayed and worn, the cement floor showing through in patches. The stale, recirculated air smelled of guns and diesel and old clothes. What had once been the cinema snack bar now functioned as a reception-cum-registration counter for torturers and torturees. It continued to advertise things it no longer stocked—Cadbury's Fruit & Nut chocolate and several flavors of Kwality ice cream, Choco Bar, Orange Bar, Mango Bar. Faded posters of old films (*Chandni*, *Maine Pyar Kiya*, *Parinda* and *Lion of the Desert*)—from the time before films were banned and the cinema hall shut down by the Allah Tigers—were still up on the wall, some of them spattered with red betel juice. Rows of young men, bound and handcuffed, squatted on the floor like chickens, some so badly beaten that they had keeled over, barely alive, still in squatting position, their wrists secured to their ankles. Soldiers milled around, bringing prisoners in, taking others away for interrogation. The faint sounds that came through the grand wooden doors leading to the auditorium could have been the muted soundtrack of a violent film. Cement kangaroos with mirthless smiles and garbage-bin pouches that said *Use Me* supervised the kangaroo court.

Musa and his escort were not detained by the formalities of reception or registration. Followed by the gaze of the chained, beaten men, they swept like royalty straight up the grand, curving staircase that led to the balcony seats—the Queen's Circle—and then further up a narrower staircase to the projection room that had been expanded into an office. Musa was aware that even the staging of this piece of theater was deliberate, not innocent.

Major Amrik Singh stood up from behind a desk that was cluttered with his collection of exotic paperweights—spiky, speckled seashells, brass figurines, sailing ships and ballerinas imprisoned in glass orbs—to greet Musa. He was a swarthy, exceptionally tall man—six foot two, easily—in his mid-thirties. His chosen avatar that night was Sikh. The skin on his cheeks above his beardline was large-pored, like the surface of a soufflé. His dark green turban, wound tight around his ears and forehead, pulled the corners of his eyes and his eyebrows upward, giving him a sleepy air. Those who were even casually acquainted with him knew that to be taken in by that sleepy air would be a perilous misreading of the man. He came around the desk and greeted Musa solicitously, with concern and affection. The soldiers who had brought Musa in were asked to leave.

"As *salaam aleikum huzoor* . . . Please sit down. What will you have? Tea? Or coffee?"

His tone was somewhere between a query and an order.

"Nothing. *Shukriya.*"

Musa sat down. Amrik Singh picked up the receiver of his red intercom and ordered tea and "officers' biscuits." His size and bulk made his desk look small and out of proportion.

It was not their first meeting. Musa had met Amrik Singh several times before, at, of all places, his (Musa's) own home, when Amrik Singh would drop in to visit Godzilla, upon whom he had decided to bestow the gift of friendship—an offer that Godzilla was not exactly free to turn down. After Amrik Singh's first few visits, Musa became aware of a drastic change in the home atmosphere. It became quieter. The bitter political arguments between himself and his father ebbed away. But Musa sensed that

Godzilla's suddenly suspicious eyes were constantly on him, as though trying to assess him, gauge him, fathom him. One afternoon, coming down from his room, Musa slipped on the staircase, righted himself mid-slide, and landed on his feet. Godzilla, who had been watching this performance, accosted Musa. He did not raise his voice, but he was furious and Musa could see a pulse throbbing near his temple.

"How did you learn to fall like that? Who taught you to fall like this?"

He examined his son with the finely honed instincts of a worried Kashmiri parent. He looked for unusual things—for a callus on a trigger finger, for horny, tough-skinned knees and elbows and any other signs of "training" that might have been received in militant camps. He found none. He decided to confront Musa with the troubling information Amrik Singh had given him— about boxes of "metal" being moved through his family's orchards in Ganderbal. About Musa's journeys into the mountains, about his meetings with certain "friends."

"What do you have to say about all this?"

"Ask your friend the Major Sahib. He'll tell you that non-actionable intelligence is as good as garbage," Musa said.

"Tse chhui marnui assi sarnei ti marnavakh," Godzilla said.

You're going to die and take us all with you.

The next time Amrik Singh dropped in, Godzilla insisted that Musa be present. On that occasion they sat cross-legged on the floor around a flowered, plastic *dastarkhan* as Musa's mother served the tea. (Musa had asked Arifa to make sure that she and Miss Jebeen did not come downstairs until the visitor had left.) Amrik Singh exuded warmth and camaraderie. He made himself at home, sprawling back against the bolsters. He told a few bawdy Stupid Sikh jokes about Santa Singh and Banta Singh, and laughed at them louder than anybody else. And then, on the pretext that it was preventing him from eating as much as he would like to, he unbuckled his belt with his pistol still in its holster. If the gesture was meant to signal that he trusted his hosts and felt at ease with them, it had the opposite effect. The murder of Jalib Qadri was still to come, but everyone knew about the string of other murders and kidnappings. The pistol lay balefully among the plates of cakes and snacks and Thermos flasks of salted *noon chai*. When Amrik Singh finally stood up to leave, burping his appreciation, he forgot it, or appeared to have forgotten it. Godzilla picked it up and handed it to him.

Amrik Singh looked straight at Musa and laughed as he buckled it back on.

"A good thing your father remembered. Imagine if it had been found here during a cordon-and-search. Forget me, even God wouldn't have been able to help you. Imagine."

Everybody laughed obediently. Musa saw that there was no laughter in Amrik Singh's eyes. They seemed to absorb light but not reflect it. They were opaque, depthless black discs with not a hint of a glimmer or a glint.

Those same opaque eyes now looked at Musa across a desk full of paperweights in the projection room of the Shiraz. It was an extraordinary sight—Amrik Singh sitting at a desk. It was clear that he had absolutely no idea what to do with it other than use it as a coffee table for mementoes. It was placed in such a way that he had only to lean back in his chair and peer through the tiny rectangular opening in the wall—once the projectionist's viewing portal, now a spyhole—to keep an eye on whatever was happening in the main hall. The interrogation cells led off from there, through the doorways over which red, neon-lit signs said (and sometimes meant): *EXIT*. The screen still had an old-fashioned red velvet tasseled curtain—the kind that used to go up in the old days to piped music: "Popcorn" or "Baby Elephant Walk." The cheaper seats in the stalls had been removed and piled up in a heap in a corner, to make space for an indoor badminton court where stressed-out soldiers could let off steam. Even at this hour, the faint *thwack thwack* of a shuttlecock meeting a racquet made its way into Amrik Singh's office.

"I brought you here to offer my apologies and my deepest personal condolences for what has happened."

The corrosion in Kashmir ran so deep that Amrik Singh was genuinely unaware of the irony of picking up a man whose wife and child had just been shot and bringing him forcibly, under armed guard, to an interrogation center at four in the morning, only in order to offer his commiseration.

Musa knew that Amrik Singh was a chameleon and that underneath his turban he was a "Mona"—he didn't have the long hair of a Sikh. He had committed that ultimate sacrilege against the Sikh canon by cutting his hair many years ago. Musa had heard him boast to Godzilla about how when he was out on a counter-insurgency operation he could pass himself off as a Hindu, a Sikh or a Punjabi-speaking Pakistani Muslim, depending on what the operation demanded. He guffawed as he described how, in order to identify and flush out "sympathizers," he and his men dressed in salwar kameez—"Khan Suits"—and knocked on villagers' doors in the dead of night, pretending to be militants from Pakistan asking for shelter. If they were welcomed, the next day the villagers would be arrested as OGWs (overground workers).

"How are unarmed villagers supposed to turn away a group of men with guns who knock on their doors in the middle of the night? Regardless of whether they are militants or military?" Musa could not help asking.

"Oh, we have ways of assessing the warmth of the welcome," Amrik Singh said. "We have our own thermometers."

Maybe. But you have no understanding of the depths of Kashmiri duplicity, Musa thought but did not say. *You have no idea how a people like us, who have survived a history and a geography such as ours, have learned to drive our pride underground. Duplicity is the only weapon we have. You don't know how radiantly we smile when our hearts are broken. How ferociously we can turn on those we love while we graciously embrace those whom we despise. You have no idea how warmly we can welcome you when all we really want is for you to go away. Your thermometer is quite useless here.*

That was one way of looking at it. On the other hand, it may have been Musa who was, at that point in time, the naive one. Because Amrik Singh certainly had the full measure of the dystopia he operated in—one whose populace had no borders, no loyalties and no limits to the depths to which it would fall. As for the Kashmiri psyche, if there was indeed such a thing, Amrik Singh was seeking neither understanding nor insight. For him it was a game, a hunt, in which his quarry's wits were pitted against his own. He saw himself more as a sportsman than a soldier. Which made for a sunny soul. Major Amrik Singh was a gambler, a daredevil officer, a deadly interrogator and a cheery, cold-blooded killer. He greatly enjoyed his work and was constantly on the lookout for ways to up the entertainment. He was in touch with certain militants who would occasionally tune into his wireless frequency, or he into theirs, and they would taunt each other like schoolboys. "*Arre yaar*, what am I but a humble travel agent?" he liked to say to them. "For you jihadis Kashmir is just a transit point, isn't it? Your real destination is *jannat* where your houris are waiting for you. I'm only here to facilitate your journey." He referred to himself as *Jannat Express*. And if he was speaking English (which usually meant he was drunk), he translated that as Paradise Express.

One of his legendary lines was: *Dekho mian, mein Bharat Sarkar ka lund hoon, aur mera kaam hai chodna.*

Look, brother, I am the Government of India's dick and it's my job to fuck people.

In his relentless quest for amusement, he was known to have

released a militant whom he had tracked down and captured with the greatest difficulty, only because he wanted to relive the exhilaration of recapturing him. It was in keeping with that spirit, with the perverse rubric of his personal hunting manual, that he had summoned Musa to the Shiraz to apologize to him. Over the last few months Amrik Singh had, correctly perhaps, identified Musa as a potentially worthy antagonist, someone who was his polar opposite and yet had the nerve and the intelligence to raise the stakes and perhaps change the nature of the hunt to a point where it would be hard to tell who was the hunter and who the hunted. For this reason Amrik Singh was extremely upset when he learned of the death of Musa's wife and daughter. He wanted Musa to know that he had nothing to do with it. That it was an unexpected and, as far as he was concerned, below-the-belt blow, never part of his plan. In order for the hunt to go on, he needed to clarify this to his quarry.

Hunting was not Amrik Singh's only passion. He had expensive tastes and a lifestyle that he couldn't support on his salary. So he exploited other avenues of entrepreneurial potential that being on the winning side of a military occupation offered. In addition to his kidnapping and extortion concerns, he owned (in his wife's name) a sawmill in the mountains and a furniture business in the Valley. He was as impetuously generous as he was violent, and distributed extravagant gifts of carved coffee tables and walnut-wood chairs to people he liked or needed. (Godzilla had a pair of bedside tables pressed on him.) Amrik Singh's wife, Loveleen Kaur, was the fourth of five sisters—Tavleen, Harpreet, Gurpreet, Loveleen and Dimple—famous for their beauty—and two younger brothers. They belonged to the small community of Sikhs who had settled in the Valley centuries ago. Their father was a small farmer with little or no means to feed his large family. It was said that the family was so poor that when one of the girls tripped on her way to school and dropped the tiffin carrier that contained their packed lunch, the hungry sisters ate the spilled food straight off the pavement. As the girls grew up, all manner of men began to circle around them like hornets, with all manner of proposals, none of them for marriage. So their parents were more than delighted to be able to give away one of their daughters (for no dowry) to a Sikh from the mainland—an army officer, no less. After they were married Loveleen did not move into Amrik Singh's officer's quarters in the various camps he was posted to in and around Srinagar. Because, it was said (rumored), at work he had another woman, another "wife," a colleague from the Central Reserve Police, an ACP Pinky who usually partnered him in field operations as well as in interrogation sessions at the camps. On weekends, when Amrik Singh visited his wife and their infant son in their first-floor flat in Jawahar Nagar, the little Sikh enclave in Srinagar, neighbors whispered about domestic violence and her muffled screams for help. Nobody dared to intervene.

Though Amrik Singh hunted down and eliminated militants ruthlessly, he actually regarded them—the best of them at least—with a sort of grudging admiration. He had been known to pay his respects at the graves of some, including a few whom he himself had killed. (One even got an unofficial gun salute.) The people he didn't just disrespect but truly despised were human rights activists—mostly lawyers, journalists and newspaper editors. To him, they were vermin who spoiled and distorted the rules of engagement of the great game with their constant complaints and whining. Whenever Amrik Singh was given permission to pick one of them up or "neutralize" them (these "permissions" never came in the form of orders to kill, but usually as an absence of orders *not* to kill) he was never less than enthusiastic in carrying out his duties. The case of Jalib Qadri was different. His orders had been merely to intimidate and detain the man. Things had gone wrong. Jalib Qadri had made the mistake of being unafraid. Of talking back. Amrik Singh regretted having lost control of himself and regretted even more that he had had to eliminate his friend and fellow traveler, the Ikhwan Salim Gojri, as a consequence of that. They had shared good times and many grand escapades, he and Salim Gojri. He knew that had things been the other way around, Salim would surely have done the same thing. And he, Amrik Singh, would surely have understood. Or so he told himself. Of all the things he had done, killing Salim Gojri was the one thing that had given him pause. Salim Gojri was the only person in the world, his wife Loveleen included, for whom Amrik Singh had felt something that vaguely resembled love. In acknowledgment of this, when the moment came, he pulled the trigger on his friend himself.

He was not a brooder though, and got over things quickly. Sitting across the table from Musa, the Major was his usual self, cocky and sure of himself. He had been pulled out of the field and given a desk job, yes, but things had not begun to unravel for him yet. He did still go out on field trips occasionally, on operations in which he was familiar with the particular case history of a militant or OGW. He was reasonably sure he had contained the damage, and was out of the woods.

The "officers' biscuits" and tea arrived. Musa heard the faint rattle of teacups on a metal tray before the bearer of the biscuits appeared from behind him. Musa and the bearer recognized each other at once, but their expressions remained passive and opaque. Amrik Singh watched them closely. The room ran out of air. Breathing became impossible. It had to be simulated.

Junaid Ahmed Shah was an Area Commander of the Hizb-ul-Mujahideen who had been captured a few months ago when he made that most common, but fatal, mistake of paying a midnight visit to his wife and infant son at their home in Sopore where soldiers lay in wait for him. He was a tall, lithe man, well known, much loved for his good looks and for his real, as well as apocryphal, acts of bravery. He had once had shoulder-length hair and a thick black beard. He was clean-shaven now, his hair close-cropped, Indian Army–style. His dull, sunken eyes looked out from deep, gray hollows. He was wearing worn tracksuit bottoms that ended halfway down his shins, woolen socks, army-issue canvas Keds and a scarlet, moth-eaten waiter's jacket with brass buttons that was too small for him and made him look comical. The tremor in his hands caused the crockery to dance on the tray.

"All right, get lost now. What are you hanging around for?" Amrik Singh said to Junaid.

"Ji Jenaab! Jai Hind!"

Yes sir! Victory to India!

Junaid saluted and left the room. Amrik Singh turned to Musa, the picture of commiseration.

"What happened to you is something that ought not to happen to any human being. You must be in shock. Here, have a Krackjack. It's very good for you. Fifty-fifty. Fifty percent sugar, fifty percent salt."

Musa did not reply.

Amrik Singh finished his tea. Musa left his untouched.

"You have an engineering degree, is that not so?"

"No. Architecture."

"I want to help you. You know the army is always looking for engineers. There is a lot of work. Very well paid. Border fencing, orphanage building, they are planning some recreation centers, gyms for young people, even this place needs doing up . . . I can get you some good contracts. We owe you that much at least."

Musa, not looking up, tested the spike of a seashell with the tip of his index finger.

"Am I under arrest, or do I have your permission to leave?"

Since he wasn't looking up, he did not see the translucent film of anger that dropped across Amrik Singh's eyes, as quietly and quickly as a cat jumping off a low wall.

"You can go."

Amrik Singh remained seated as Musa stood up and left the room. He rang a bell and told the man who answered it to escort Musa out.

Downstairs in the cinema lobby there was a torture-break. Tea was being served to the soldiers, poured out from big steaming kettles. There were cold samosas in iron buckets, two per head. Musa crossed the lobby, this time holding the gaze of one of the bound, beaten, bleeding boys whom he knew well. He knew the boy's mother had been going from camp to camp, police station to police station, desperately looking for her son. That could have lasted a whole lifetime. *At least some horrible good has come of this night*, Musa thought.

He had almost walked out of the door when Amrik Singh appeared at the head of the stairs, beaming, exuding bonhomie, an entirely different person from the one Musa had left in the projection room. His voice boomed across the lobby.

"Arre huzoor! Ek cheez main bilkul bhool gaya tha!"

There's something I completely forgot!

Everybody—torturers and torturees alike—turned their gaze on him. Wholly aware that he had the attention of his audience, Amrik Singh trotted athletically down the steps, like a joyful host saying goodbye to a guest whose visit he has greatly enjoyed. He hugged Musa affectionately and pressed on him a package he was carrying.

"This is for your father. Tell him I ordered it especially for him."

It was a bottle of Red Stag whiskey.

The lobby fell silent. Everybody, the audience as well as the protagonists of the play that was unfolding, understood the script. If Musa spurned the gift, it would be a public declaration of war with Amrik Singh—which made him, Musa, as good as dead. If he accepted it, Amrik Singh would have outsourced the death sentence to the militants. Because he knew that the news would get out, and that every militant group, whatever else they disagreed about, agreed that death was the punishment for collaborators and friends of the Occupation. And whiskey-drinking—even by non-collaborators—was a declared un-Islamic activity.

Musa walked over to the snack bar and put the bottle of whiskey down on it.

"My father does not drink."

"*Arre*, what is there to hide? There's no shame in it. Of course your father drinks! You know that very well. I bought this bottle especially for him. Never mind, I'll give it to him myself."

Amrik Singh, still smiling, ordered his men to follow Musa and see that he got home safe. He was pleased with the way things had turned out.

DAWN WAS BREAKING. A hint of rose in a pigeon-gray sky. Musa walked home through the dead streets. The Gypsy followed him at a safe distance, the driver instructing checkpost after checkpost on his walkie-talkie to let Musa through.

He entered his home with snow on his shoulders. The cold of that was nothing compared to the cold that was gathering inside him. When they saw his face his parents and sisters knew better than to approach him or ask what had happened. He went straight back to his desk and resumed the letter he had been writing before the soldiers came for him. He wrote in Urdu. He wrote quickly, as though it was his last task, as though he was racing against the cold and had to finish it before the warmth seeped out of his body, perhaps forever.

It was a letter to Miss Jebeen.

Babajaana
Do you think I'm going to miss you? You are wrong. I will never miss you, because you will always be with me.

You wanted me to tell you real stories, but I don't know what is real any more. What used to be real sounds like a silly fairy story now—the kind I used to tell you, the kind you wouldn't tolerate. What I know for sure is only this: in our Kashmir the dead will live forever; and the living are only dead people, pretending.

Next week we were going to try and make you your own ID card. As you know, *jaana*, our cards are more important than we ourselves are now. That card is the most valuable thing anyone can have. It is more valuable than the most beautifully woven carpet, or the softest, warmest shawl, or the biggest garden, or all the cherries and all the walnuts from all the orchards in our Valley. Can you imagine that? My ID card number is M 108672J. You told me it was a lucky number because it has an M for Miss and a J for Jebeen. If it is, then it will bring me to you and your Ammijaan quickly. So get ready to do your homework in heaven. What sense would it make to you if I told you that there were a hundred thousand people at your funeral? You who could only count to fifty-nine? Count did I say? I meant shout—you who could only shout to fifty-nine. I hope that wherever you are you are not shouting. You must learn to talk

softly, like a lady, at least sometimes. How shall I
explain one hundred thousand to you? Such a huge
number. Shall we try and think about it seasonally?
In spring think of how many leaves there are on
the trees, and how many pebbles you can see in the
streams once the ice has melted. Think of how many
red poppies blossom in the meadows. That should
give you a rough idea of what a hundred thousand
means in spring. In autumn it is as many Chinar
leaves as crackled under our feet in the university
campus the day I took you for a walk (and you were
angry with the cat who wouldn't trust you and
refused the piece of bread you offered him. We're
all becoming a bit like that cat, *jaana*. We can't trust
anyone. The bread they offer us is dangerous because
it turns us into slaves and fawning servants. You'd
probably be angry with us all). Anyway. We were
talking about a number. One hundred thousand. In
winter we'll have to think of the snowflakes falling
from the sky. Remember how we used to count
them? How you used to try and catch them? That
many people is a hundred thousand. At your funeral
the crowd covered the ground like snow. Can you
picture it now? Good. And that's only the people. I'm
not going to tell you about the sloth bear that came
down the mountain, the hangul that watched from
the woods, the snow leopard that left its tracks in the
snow and the kites that circled in the sky, supervising
everything. On the whole, it was quite a spectacle.
You'd have been happy, you love crowds, I know. You
were always going to be a city girl. That much was
clear from the beginning. Now it's your turn. Tell me
about—

Mid-sentence he lost the race against the cold. He stopped writing, folded the letter and put it in his pocket. He never completed it, but he always carried it with him.

He knew he didn't have much time. He would have to preempt Amrik Singh's next move, and quickly. Life as he once knew it was over. He knew that Kashmir had swallowed him and he was now part of its entrails.

He spent the day settling what affairs he could—paying the cigarette bills he had accumulated, destroying papers, taking the few things he loved or needed. The next morning when the Yeswi household woke up to its grief, Musa was gone. He had left a note for one of his sisters about the beaten boy he had seen in the Shiraz with his mother's name and address.

Thus began his life underground. A life that lasted precisely nine months—like a pregnancy. Except that in a manner of speaking at least, its consequence was the opposite of a pregnancy. It ended in a kind of death, instead of a kind of life.

During his days as a fugitive, Musa moved from place to place, never the same place on consecutive nights. There were always people around him—in forest hideouts, in businessmen's plush homes, in shops, in dungeons, in storerooms—wherever the *tehreek* was welcomed with love and solidarity. He learned everything about weapons, where to buy them, how to move them, where to hide them, how to use them. He developed real calluses in the places where his father had imagined phantom ones—on his knees and elbows, on his trigger finger. He carried a gun, but never used it. With his fellow travelers, who were all much younger than him, he shared the love that hot-blooded men who would gladly give their lives for each other share. Their lives were short. Many of them were killed, jailed or tortured until they lost their minds. Others took their place. Musa survived purge after purge. His ties to his old life were gradually (and deliberately) erased. Nobody knew who he really was. Nobody asked. His family did not know that. He did not belong to any one particular organization. In the heart of a filthy war, up against a bestiality that is hard to imagine, he did what he could to persuade his comrades to hold on to a semblance of humanity, to not turn into the very thing they abhorred and fought against. He did not always succeed. Nor did he always fail. He refined the art of merging into the background, of disappearing in a crowd, of mumbling and dissembling, of burying the secrets he knew so deep that he forgot he knew them. He learned the art of ennui, of enduring as well as inflicting boredom. He hardly ever spoke. At night, fed up with the regime of silence, his organs murmured to each other in the language of night crickets. His spleen contacted his kidney. His pancreas whispered across the silent void to his lungs:

Hello
Can you hear me?
Are you still there?

He grew colder, and quieter. The price on his head went up very quickly—from one lakh to three lakhs. When nine months had gone by, Tilo came to Kashmir.

TILO WAS WHERE SHE WAS most evenings, at a tea stall in one of the narrow lanes around the dargah of Hazrat Nizamuddin Auliya, on her way back home from work, when a young man approached her, confirmed that her name was S. Tilottama, and handed her a note. It said: *Ghat Number 33, HB Shaheen, Dal Lake. Please come 20th.* There was no signature, only a tiny pencil sketch of a horse's head in one corner. When she looked up, the messenger had vanished.

She took two weeks off from her job in an architecture firm in Nehru Place, caught a train to Jammu, and an early-morning bus from Jammu to Srinagar. Musa and she had not been in touch for a while. She went, because that was how it was between them.

She had never been to Kashmir.

It was late afternoon when the bus emerged from the long tunnel that bored through the mountains, the only link between India and Kashmir.

Autumn in the Valley was the season of immodest abundance. The sun slanted down on the lavender haze of zaffran crocuses in bloom. Orchards were heavy with fruit, the Chinar trees were on fire. Tilo's co-passengers, most of them Kashmiri, could dis-aggregate the breeze and tell not merely the scent of apples from the scent of pears and ripe paddy that wafted through the bus windows, but *whose* apples, *whose* pears and *whose* ripe paddy they were driving past. There was another scent they all knew well. The smell of dread. It soured the air and turned their bodies to stone.

As the noisy, rattling bus with its still, silent passengers drove deeper into the Valley the tension grew more tangible. Every fifty meters, on either side of the road, there was a heavily armed soldier, alert and dangerously tense. There were soldiers in the fields, deep inside orchards, on bridges and culverts, in shops and marketplaces, on rooftops, each covering the other, in a grid that stretched all the way up into the mountains. In every part of the legendary Valley of Kashmir, whatever people might be doing—walking, praying, bathing, cracking jokes, shelling wal-nuts, making love or taking a bus-ride home—they were in the rifle-sights of a soldier. And because they were in the rifle-sights of a soldier, whatever they might be doing—walking, praying, bathing, cracking jokes, shelling walnuts, making love or taking a bus-ride home—they were a legitimate target.

At every checkpoint the road was blocked with movable horizontal barriers mounted with iron spikes that could shred a tire to ribbons. At each checkpost the bus had to stop, all the passengers had to disembark and line up with their bags to be searched. Soldiers riffled through the luggage on the bus roof. The passengers kept their eyes lowered. At the sixth or perhaps the seventh checkpost, an armored Gypsy with slits for windows was parked on the side of the road. After conferring with a hidden person in the Gypsy, a gleaming, strutting young officer pulled three young men out of the passenger line-up—*You, You and You*. They were pushed into an army truck. They went without demur. The passengers kept their eyes lowered.

By the time the bus arrived in Srinagar, the light was dying.

In those days the little city of Srinagar died with the light. The shops closed, the streets emptied.

At the bus stop a man sidled up to Tilo and asked her her name. From then on, she was passed from hand to hand. An autorickshaw took her from the bus stand to the Boulevard. She crossed the lake in a shikara on which there was no sitting option, only a lounging one. So she lounged on the bright, floral cushions, a honeymooner without a husband. It was to make up for that, she thought, that the bright flanges of the boatman's oars which pushed through the weeds were heart-shaped. The lake was deadly quiet. The rhythmic sound of oars in the water might well have been the uneasy heartbeat of the Valley.

Plif

Plif

Plif

The houseboats anchored next to each other cheek by jowl on the opposite shore—HB *Shaheen*, HB *Jannat*, HB *Queen Victoria*, HB *Derbyshire*, HB *Snow View*, HB *Desert Breeze*, HB *Zam-Zam*,

HB *Gulshan*, HB *New Gulshan*, HB *Gulshan Palace*, HB *Mandalay*, HB *Clifton*, HB *New Clifton*—were dark and empty.

HB, the boatman told Tilo when she asked, stood for House Boat.

HB *Shaheen* was the smallest and shabbiest of them all. As the shikara drew up, a little man, lost inside his worn brown pheran that almost touched his ankles, came out to greet Tilo. Later she learned his name was Gulrez. He greeted her as though he knew her well, as though she had lived there all her life and had just returned from buying provisions in the market. His large head and oddly thin neck rested on broad, sturdy shoulders. As he led Tilo through the small dining room and down a narrow carpeted corridor to the bedroom, she heard kittens mewling. He threw a sparkling smile over his shoulder, like a proud father, his emerald, wizard eyes shining.

The cramped room was only slightly larger than the double bed covered with an embroidered counterpane. On the bedside table there was a flowered plastic tray with a filigreed bell-metal water jug, two colored glasses and a small CD player. The threadbare carpet on the floor was patterned, the cupboard doors were crudely carved, the wooden ceiling was honeycombed, the waste-paper bin was intricately patterned papier mâché. Tilo looked for a space that was not patterned, embroidered, carved or filigreed, to rest her eyes on. When she didn't find one, a tide of anxiety welled up in her. She opened the wooden windows but they looked directly on to the closed wooden windows of the next houseboat a few feet away. Empty cigarette packets and cigarette stubs floated in the few feet of water that separated them. She put her bag down and went out to the porch, lit a cigarette and watched the glassy surface of the lake turn silver as the first stars appeared in the sky. The snow on the mountains glowed for a while, like phosphorus, even after darkness had fallen.

She waited on the boat the whole of the next day, watching Gulrez dust the undusty furniture and talk to purple brinjals and big-leaved *haakh* in his vegetable garden on the bank just behind the boat. After clearing away a simple lunch, he showed her his collection of things that he kept in a big yellow airport duty-free shopping bag that said *See! Buy! Fly!* He laid them out on the dining table one by one. It was his version of a Visitors' Book: an empty bottle of Polo aftershave lotion, a range of old airline boarding passes, a pair of small binoculars, a pair of sunglasses from which one lens had fallen out, a well-thumbed *Lonely Planet* guidebook, a Qantas toilet bag, a small torch, a bottle of herbal mosquito repellent, a bottle of suntan lotion, a silver-foil card of expired diarrhea pills, and a pair of blue Marks & Spencer ladies' knickers stuffed into an old cigarette tin. He giggled and made his eyes sly as he rolled the knickers into a soft cigar and put them back in the tin. Tilo searched her sling bag and added a small strawberry-shaped eraser and a vial that used to contain clutch-pencil leads to the collection. Gulrez unscrewed the little cap of the vial and screwed it back on, thrilled. After contemplating the matter for a while, he put the eraser in the plastic bag and pocketed the vial. He went out of the room and came back with a postcard-sized print of a photograph of himself holding the kittens in the palms of his hands that the last visitor on the boat had given him. He gave it to Tilo formally, holding it out with both hands as though it were a certificate of merit being awarded to her. Tilo accepted it with a bow. Their barter was complete.

In a conversation in which her hesitant Hindi encountered his halting Urdu, Tilo figured out that the "Muzz-kak" that Gulrez kept referring to was Musa. He brought out a clipping of an Urdu newspaper which had published photographs of all those who had been shot on the same day as Miss Jebeen and her mother. He kissed the cutting several times over, pointing to a little girl and a young woman. Gradually Tilo pieced together the semblance of a narrative: the woman was Musa's wife and the child was their daughter. The photos were so badly printed it was impossible to decipher their features and tell what they looked like. To make sure Tilo understood his meaning, Gulrez laid his head down on a pillow made of his palms, closed his eyes like a child and then pointed to the sky.

They've gone to heaven.

Tilo didn't know that Musa was married.

He hadn't told her.

Should he have?

Why should he have?

And why should she mind?

It was she who had walked away from him.

But she did mind.

Not because he was married, but because he hadn't told her.

For the rest of the day a Malayalam nonsense rhyme looped endlessly in her head. It had been the monsoon anthem of an army of tiny, knickered children—she, one among them—who stomped in mud puddles and streaked down the creepered, over-greened riverbank in the pouring rain, shrieking it.

Dum! Dum! Pattalam
Saarinde veetil kalyanam
Aana pindam choru
Atta varthadu upperi
Kozhi theetam chamandi

Bang! Bang! Here's the army band
A wedding in the house of the lord of the land
Elephant dung rice!
Fried millipedes, nice!
Minced hen-shit for spice!

She couldn't understand. Could there be a more inappropriate response to what she had just learned? She hadn't thought of this verse since she was five years old. Why now?

Perhaps it was raining inside her head. Perhaps it was the survival strategy of a mind that might shut down if it was foolish enough to attempt to make sense of the intricate fretwork that connected Musa's nightmares to hers.

There was no tour guide on hand to tell her that in Kashmir nightmares were promiscuous. That they were unfaithful to their owners, they cartwheeled wantonly into other people's dreams, they acknowledged no precincts, they were the greatest ambush artists of all. No fortification, no fence-building could keep them in check. In Kashmir the only thing to do with nightmares was to embrace them like old friends and manage them like old enemies. She would learn that of course. Soon.

She sat on the upholstered, built-in bench in the entrance porch of the houseboat and watched her second sunset. A gloomy nightfish (no relative of the nightmare) rose from the bottom of the lake and swallowed the reflection of the mountains in the water. Whole. Gulrez was laying the table for dinner (for two, clearly he knew something) when Musa arrived suddenly, quietly, entering from the back of the boat.

"Salaam."

"Salaam."

"You came."

"Of course."

"How are you? How was the journey?"

"OK. You?"

"OK."

The rhyme in Tilo's head swelled into a symphony.

"I'm sorry I'm so late."

He didn't give any further explanation. Other than looking a little gaunt, he hadn't changed very much, and yet he was almost unrecognizable. He had grown a stubble that was almost a beard. His eyes seemed to have lightened and darkened at once, as though they'd been washed, and one color had faded and the other had not. His browngreen irises were circumscribed with a ring of black that Tilo did not remember. She saw that his outline—the shape he made in the world—had grown indistinct, smudged, somehow. He merged into his surroundings even more than he used to. It had nothing to do with the ubiquitous brown Kashmiri pheran that flapped around him. When he took off his wool cap Tilo saw that his hair had thick streaks of silver. He noticed that she noticed and ran self-conscious fingers through his hair. Strong, horse-drawing fingers, with a callus on the trigger finger. He was the same age as her. Thirty-one.

The silence between them swelled and subsided like the bellows of an accordion playing a tune that only they could hear. He knew that she knew that he knew that she knew. That's how it was between them.

Gulrez brought in a tray of tea. With him too, there was no great exchange of greetings, although it was clear that there was familiarity, even love. Musa called him Gul-kak and sometimes *"Mout"* and had brought him eardrops. The eardrops broke the ice as only eardrops can.

"He has an ear infection, and he's scared. Terrified," Musa explained.

"Is he in pain? He seemed fine all day."

"Not of the pain, there's no pain. Of being shot. He says he can't hear properly and he's worried that he might not hear them at the checkposts when they say 'Stop!' Sometimes they first let you go through and then stop you. So if you don't hear that . . ."

Gulrez, sensing the strain (and the love) in the room and alert to the fact that he could play a part in easing it, knelt on the floor theatrically, and rested his cheek on Musa's lap with a big cauliflower ear turned upwards to receive eardrops. After ministering to both cauliflowers and stopping them up with wads of cotton wool, Musa gave him the bottle.

"Keep it carefully. When I'm not here ask her, she'll do it," he said. "She's my friend."

Gulrez, much as he coveted the tiny bottle with its plastic nozzle, much as he felt its rightful place was in his *See! Buy! Fly!* Visitors' Book, entrusted it to Tilo and beamed at her. For a moment they became a spontaneously constituted family. Father bear, mother bear, baby bear.

Baby bear was by far the happiest. For dinner he produced five meat dishes: *gushtaba, rista, martzwangan korma, shami kebab, chicken yakhni.*

"So much food . . ." Tilo said.

"Cow, goat, chicken, lamb . . . only slaves eat like this," Musa said, heaping an impolite amount on to his plate. "Our stomachs are graveyards."

Tilo would not believe that baby bear had cooked the feast single-handedly.

"He was talking to brinjals and playing with the kittens all day. I didn't see him doing any cooking."

"He must have done it before you came. He's a wonderful cook. His father is a professional, a *waza*, from Godzilla's village."

"Why is he here all alone?"

"He's not alone. There are eyes and ears and hearts around him. But he can't live in the village . . . it's too dangerous for him. Gul-kak is what we call a *'mout'*—he lives in his own world, with his own rules. A bit like you, in some ways." Musa looked up at Tilo, serious, unsmiling.

"You mean a fool, a village fool?" Tilo looked back at him, not smiling either.

"I mean a special person. A blessed person."

"Blessed by whom? Twisted fucking way to bless someone."

"Blessed with a beautiful soul. Here we revere our *maet*."

It had been a while since Musa had heard a laconic profanity of this nature, especially from a woman. It landed lightly, like a cricket on his constricted heart, and stirred the memory of why, and how and how much, he had loved Tilo. He tried to return that thought to the locked section of the archive it had come out of.

"We nearly lost him two years ago. There was a cordon-and-search operation in his village. The men were asked to come out and line up in the fields. Gul ran out to greet the soldiers, insisting they were the Pakistani army, come to liberate them. He was singing, shouting *Jeevey! Jeevey! Pakistan!* He wanted to kiss their hands. They shot him in his thigh, beat him with rifle butts and left him bleeding in the snow. After that incident he became hysterical, and would try to run away whenever he saw a soldier, which is of course the most dangerous thing to do. So I brought him to Srinagar to live with us. But now since there's hardly anybody in our home—I don't live there any more—he didn't want to stay there either. I got him this job. This boat belongs to a friend; he's safe here, he doesn't need to go out. He just has to cook for the few visitors that come, hardly any do. Provisions are delivered to him. The only danger is that the boat is so old it might sink."

"Seriously?"

Musa smiled.

"No. It's quite safe."

The house with "hardly anybody" in it took its place at the dinner table, a third guest, with the ravenous appetite of a slave.

"Almost all the *maet* in Kashmir have been killed. They were the first to be killed, because they don't know how to obey orders. Maybe that's why we need them. To teach us how to be free."

"Or how to be killed?"

"Here it's the same thing. Only the dead are free."

Musa looked at Tilo's hand resting on the table. He knew it better than he knew his own. She still wore the silver ring he had given her, years ago, when he was someone else. There was still ink on her middle finger.

Gulrez, keenly aware that he was being spoken about, hovered around the table, refilling glasses and plates, with a mewling kitten in each pocket of his pheran. During a break in the conversation, he introduced them as Agha and Khanum. The streaky gray one was Agha. The black-and-white harlequin was Khanum.

"And Sultan?" Musa asked him with a smile. "How is he?"

As if on cue, Gulrez's face clouded over. His reply was a long profanity in a mixture of Kashmiri and Urdu. Tilo understood only the last sentence: *Arre uss bewakoof ko agar yahan mintree ke saath rehna nahi aata tha, to phir woh saala is duniya mein aaya hi kyuun tha?*

If that fool didn't know how to live here with the military, why did he have to come into this world in the first place?

It was no doubt something Gulrez had heard a worried parent or neighbor say about him, and had filed away to use as a complaint against Sultan, whoever Sultan was.

Musa laughed out loud, grabbed Gulrez and kissed him on his head. Gul smiled. A happy imp.

"Who's Sultan?" Tilo asked Musa.

"I'll tell you later."

After dinner they went out on to the porch to smoke and listen to the news on the transistor.

Three militants had been killed. Despite the curfew in Baramulla there had been major protests.

It was a no-moon night, pitch-dark, the water black as an oil slick.

The hotels on the boulevard that ran along the lakeshore had been turned into barracks, wrapped in razor wire, sandbagged and boarded up. The dining rooms were soldiers' dormitories, the receptions daytime lock-ups, the guest rooms interrogation centers. Thick, painstakingly embroidered crewelwork drapes and exquisite carpets muffled the screams of young men having their genitals prodded with electrodes and petrol poured into their anuses.

"D'you know who's here these days?" Musa said. "Garson Hobart. Have you been in touch with him at all?"

"Not for some years."

"He's Deputy Station Head, IB. It's a pretty important post."

"Good for him."

There was no breeze. The lake was calm, the boat steady, the silence unsteady.

"Did you love her?"

"I did. I wanted to tell you that."

"Why?"

Musa finished his cigarette and lit another.

"I don't know. Something to do with honor. Yours, mine and hers."

"Why didn't you tell me earlier, then?"

"I don't know."

"Was it an arranged marriage?"

"No."

Sitting next to Tilo, breathing next to her, he felt like an empty house whose locked windows and doors were creaking open a little, to air the ghosts trapped inside it. When he spoke again he spoke into the night, addressing the mountains, entirely invisible now, except for the winking lights of army camps that were strung across the range, like meager decorations for some dreadful festival.

"I met her in the most horrible way...horrible yet beautiful . . . it could have only happened here. It was the spring of '91, our year of chaos. We—everybody except Godzilla, I think—thought Azadi was around the corner, just a heartbeat away. Every day there were gun battles, explosions, encounter killings. Militants walked openly in the streets, flaunting their weapons . . ."

Musa trailed off, unsettled by the sound of his own voice. He wasn't used to it. Tilo did nothing to help him out. A part of her shied away from the story that Musa had begun to tell her, and was grateful for the diversion into generalities.

"Anyway. That year—the year I met her—I had just got a job. It should have been a big deal, but it wasn't, because in those days everything had shut down. Nothing worked . . . not courts, not colleges, not schools . . . there was a complete breakdown of normal life . . . how can I tell you how it was . . . how crazy . . . it was a free-for-all . . . there was looting, kidnapping, murder . . . mass cheating in school exams. That was the funniest thing. Suddenly, in the middle of war, everyone wanted to be a Matric Pass because it would help them to get cheap loans from the government . . . I actually know a family in which three generations, the grandfather, father and son, all sat for the school final exam together. Imagine that. Farmers, laborers, fruit-sellers, all of them Class Two and Three pass, barely literate, sat for the exam, copied from the guidebook and passed with flying colors. They even copied that 'Please Turn Over' sign at the bottom of the page—the pointing finger—remember? It used to be at the bottom of our school textbooks? Even today, when we want to insult someone who's being stupid, we say, 'Are you a *namtuk pass*?'"

Tilo understood he was deliberately digressing, circling around a story that was as hard—harder—for him to tell as it was for her to hear.

"Are you the batch of '91?" Musa's soft laugh was full of affection for the foibles of his people.

She had always loved that about him, the way he belonged so completely to a people whom he loved and laughed at, complained about and swore at, but never separated himself from. Maybe she loved it because she herself didn't—couldn't—think of anybody as "her people." Except perhaps the two dogs that arrived at 6 a.m. sharp in the little park outside her house where she fed them, and the hobos she drank tea with at the tea stall near the Nizamuddin dargah. But not even them, not really.

Long ago she had thought of Musa as "her people." They had been a strange country together for a while, an island republic that had seceded from the rest of the world. Since the day they decided to go their own ways, she had had no "people."

"We were fighting and dying in our thousands for Azadi, and at the same time we were trying to secure cheap loans from the very government we were fighting. We're a valley of idiots and schizophrenics, and we are fighting for the freedom to be idiotic and—"

Musa stopped mid-chuckle, cocking his head. A patrol boat chugged past some distance away, the soldiers in it sweeping the surface of the water with beams of light from powerful torches. Once they had gone, he stood up. "Let's go in, Babajaana. It's getting cold."

It slipped out so naturally, that old term of endearment. *Babajaana*. My love. She noticed. He didn't. It wasn't cold. But still, they went in.

Gulrez was asleep on the carpet in the dining room. Agha and Khanum were wide awake, playing on him as though his body were an amusement park constructed entirely for their pleasure. Agha hid in the crook of his knee, Khanum staged an ambush from the strategic heights of his hip.

Musa stood at the door of the carved, embroidered, patterned, filigreed bedroom and said, "May I come in?" and that hurt her.

"Slaves don't necessarily have to be stupid, do they?" She sat on the edge of the bed and flipped backwards, her palms under her head, her feet remaining on the floor. Musa sat next to her and put his hand on her stomach. The tension slipped out of the room like an unwanted stranger. It was dark except for the light from the corridor.

"Can I play you a Kashmiri song?"

"No, thanks, man. I'm not a Kashmiri Nationalist."

"You soon will be. In three or maybe four days' time."

"Why's that?"

"You will be, because I know you. When you see what you see and hear what you hear, you won't have a choice. Because you are you."

"Is there going to be a convocation? I'll get a degree?"

"Yes. And you'll pass with flying colors. I know you."

"You don't really know me. I'm a patriot. I get goosebumps when I see the national flag. I get so emotional I can't think straight. I love flags and soldiers and all that marching around stuff. What's the song?"

"You'll like it. I carried it through the curfew for you. It was written for us, for you and me. By a fellow called Las Kone, from my village. You'll love it."

"I'm pretty sure I won't."

"Come on. Give me a chance."

Musa took out a CD from the pocket of his pheran and put it into the player. Within seconds of the opening chords of the guitar, Tilo's eyes snapped open.

Trav'ling lady, stay awhile
until the night is over.
I'm just a station on your way,
I know I'm not your lover.

"Leonard Cohen."

"Yes. Even he doesn't know that he's really a Kashmiri. Or that his real name is Las Kone . . ."

Well I lived with a child of snow
when I was a soldier,
and I fought every man for her
until the nights grew colder.

She used to wear her hair like you
except when she was sleeping,
and then she'd weave it on a loom
of smoke and gold and breathing.

And why are you so quiet now
standing there in the doorway?
You chose your journey long before
you came upon this highway.

"How did he know?"

"Las Kone knows everything."

"Did she wear her hair like mine?"

"She was a civilized person, Babajaana. Not a *mout*."

Tilo kissed Musa, and while she held him to her and would not let him go she said, "Get away from me, you filthy mountain man."

"Overwashed river woman."

"How long since you bathed?"

"Nine months."

"No, seriously."

"A week maybe? I don't know."

"Filthy bastard."

· · ·

Musa's shower lasted an inordinately long time. She could hear him humming along with Las Kone. He came out bare-bodied, with a towel around his hips, smelling of her soap and shampoo. It made her chortle.

"You're smelling like a summer rose."

"I'm feeling really guilty," Musa said, smiling.

"Right. You really look it."

"After weeks of generous hospitality to lices and leeches I've turned them out of the house."

"Lices" made her love him a little more.

They had always fitted together like pieces of an unsolved (and perhaps unsolvable) puzzle—the smoke of her into the solidness of him, the solitariness of her into the gathering of him, the strangeness of her into the straightforwardness of him, the insouciance of her into the restraint of him. The quietness of her into the quietness of him.

And then of course there were the other parts—the ones that wouldn't fit.

What happened that night on the HB *Shaheen* was less lovemaking than lament. Their wounds were too old and too new, too different, and perhaps too deep, for healing. But for a fleeting moment, they were able to pool them like accumulated gambling debts and share the pain equally, without naming the injuries or asking which was whose. For a fleeting moment they were able to repudiate the world they lived in and call forth another one, just as real. A world in which *maet* gave the orders and soldiers needed eardrops so they could hear them clearly and carry them out correctly.

Tilo knew there was a gun underneath the bed. She made no comment about it. Not even afterwards, when Musa's calluses had been counted. And kissed. She lay stretched out on top of him, as though he were a mattress, her chin resting on her intertwined fingers, her distinctly un-Kashmiri bottom vulnerable to the Srinagar night. In a way Musa's journey to where he was now did not entirely surprise her. She clearly remembered a day years ago, in 1984 (who could forget 1984), when the newspapers reported that a Kashmiri called Maqbool Butt, jailed for murder and treason, had been hanged in Tihar Jail in Delhi, his remains interred in the prison yard, for fear his grave would become a monument, a rallying point in Kashmir, where trouble had already begun to simmer. The news had not mattered to even one other person in their college, neither student nor professor. But that night Musa had said to her, quietly, matter-of-factly, "Some day you'll understand why, for me, history began today." Though she had not fully comprehended the import of his words at the time, the intensity with which they had been uttered had remained with her.

"How's the Queen Mother in Kerala keeping?" Musa inquired into the bird's nest that passed off as his lover's hair.

"Don't know. Haven't visited."

"You should."

"I know."

"She's your mother. She's you. You are her."

"That's only the Kashmiri view. It's different in India."

"Seriously. It's not a joke. This is not a good thing on your part, Babajaana. You *should* go."

"I know."

Musa ran his fingers down the ridges of muscle on either side of her spine. What began as a caress turned into a physical examination. For a moment he became his suspicious father. He checked out her shoulders, her lean, muscled arms.

"Where's all this from?"

"Practice."

There was a second of silence. She decided against telling him about the men who stalked her, who knocked on her door at odd hours of the day and night, including Mr. S. P. P. Rajendran, a retired police officer who held an administrative post in the architectural firm she worked for. He had been hired more for his contacts in the government than for his skills as an administrator. He was openly lecherous towards her in the office, making lewd suggestions, often leaving gifts on her desk, which she ignored. But late at night, bolstered perhaps by alcohol, he would drive to Nizamuddin and hammer on her door, shouting to be let in. His brazenness came from knowing that if matters came to a head, in the public eye, as well as in a court of law, his word would prevail against hers. He had a record of exemplary public service, a medal for bravery, and she was a lone woman who was immodestly attired and smoked cigarettes, and there was nothing to suggest that she came from a "decent" family who would rise to her defense. Tilo was aware of this and had taken precautionary measures. If Mr. Rajendran pushed his luck she could have him pinned to the floor before he knew what had happened.

She said nothing of all this because it seemed sordid and trivial compared to what Musa was living through. She rolled off him.

"Tell me about Sultan . . . the *bewakoof* person that Gulrez was so upset with. Who's he?"

Musa smiled.

"Sultan? Sultan wasn't a person. And he wasn't *bewakoof*. He was a very clever fellow. He was a rooster, an orphan rooster that Gul had raised since he was a little chick. Sultan was devoted to him, he would follow him around wherever he went, they would have long conversations with each other that no one else understood, they were a team . . . inseparable. Sultan was famous in the region. People from nearby villages would come to see him. He had beautiful plumage, purple, orange, red, he would strut around the place like a real sultan. I knew him well . . . we all knew him. He was so . . . lofty, he always acted as though you owed him something . . . you know? One day an army captain came to the village with some soldiers . . . Captain Jaanbaaz he called himself, I don't know what his real name was . . . they always give themselves these filmy names these guys . . . they weren't there for a cordon-and-search or anything . . . just to speak to the villagers, threaten them a little, mistreat them a bit . . . the usual stuff. The men of the village were all made to assemble in the chowk. The well-known firm of Gul-kak and Sultan were there too, Sultan listening attentively as though he were a human being, a village elder. The captain had a dog with him. A huge German shepherd, on a leash. After he finished delivering his threats and his lecture, he let the dog off the leash, saying, 'Jimmy! Fetch!' Jimmy pounced on Sultan, killed him, and the soldiers took him for their dinner. Gul-kak was devastated. He cried for days, like people cry for their relatives who have been killed. For him Sultan *was* a relative . . . nothing less. And he was upset with Sultan for letting him down, for not fighting back, or escaping—almost as though he was a militant who should have known these tactics. So Gul would curse Sultan and wail, 'If you didn't know how to live with the military, why did you come into this world?'"

"So why were you reminding him about it? That was mean . . ."

"Gul is my little brother, *yaar*. We wear each other's clothes, we trust each other with our lives. I can do anything with him."

"This is not a good thing on your part, Musakuttan. In India we don't do these things . . ."

"We even share the same name . . ."

"Meaning?"

"That's what I'm known as. Commander Gulrez. No one knows me as Musa Yeswi."

"It's all a fucking mindfuck."

"Shhh . . . in Kashmir we don't use such language."

"In India we do."

"We should sleep, Babajaana."

"We should."

"But before that we should get dressed."

"Why?"

"Protocol. This is Kashmir."

After that casual intervention, sleep was no longer a realistic option. Tilo, fully dressed, a little apprehensive about what the "protocol" implied, but fortified by love and sated by lovemaking, propped herself up on an elbow.

"Talk to me . . ."

"And what do we call what we've been doing all this time?"

"We call it 'pre-talk.'"

She rubbed her cheek against his stubble and then lay back, her head on the pillow beside Musa's.

"What shall I tell you?"

"Every single thing. No omissions."

She lit two cigarettes.

"Tell me the other story . . . the one that's horrible and beautiful . . . the love story. Tell me the real story."

Tilo did not understand why what she said made Musa hold her tighter and turned his eyes bright with what might have been tears. She didn't know what he meant when he murmured "Akh daleela wann . . ."

And then, holding her as though his life depended on it, Musa told her about Jebeen, about how she insisted on being called Miss Jebeen, about her specific requirements from bedtime stories and all her other naughtinesses. He told her about Arifa and how he first met her—in a stationery shop in Srinagar:

"I'd had a huge fight with Godzie that day. Over my new boots. They were lovely boots—Gul-kak wears them now. Anyway . . . I was going out to buy some stationery, and I was wearing them. Godzie told me to take them off and wear normal shoes, because young men wearing good boots were often arrested as militants—those days that was evidence enough. Anyway, I refused to listen to him, so finally he said, 'Do what you want, but mark my words, those boots will bring trouble.' He was right . . . they did bring trouble—big trouble, but not the kind he was expecting. The stationery shop I used to go to, JK Stationery, was in Lal Chowk, the center of the city. I was inside when a grenade exploded on the street just outside. A militant had thrown it at a soldier. My eardrums nearly burst. Everything inside the shop shattered, there was glass everywhere, chaos in the market, everyone screaming. The soldiers went crazy—obviously. They smashed up all the shops, came in and beat everyone in sight. I was on the floor. They kicked me, beat me with rifle butts. I remember just lying there, trying to protect my skull, watching my blood spreading on the floor. I was hurt, not too badly, but I was too scared to move. A dog was staring at me. He seemed quite sympathetic. When I got over the initial shock, I felt a weight on my feet. I remembered my new boots and wondered if they were OK. As soon as I thought it was safe I lifted my head slowly, as carefully as I could, to take a look. And I saw this beautiful face resting on them. It was like waking up in hell and finding an angel on my shoe. It was Arifa. She too was frozen, too scared to move. But she was absolutely calm. She didn't smile, didn't move her head. She just looked at me and said, 'Asal boot'—'Nice boots'—I couldn't believe the coolness of that. No wailing, screaming, sobbing, crying—just absolutely cool. We both laughed. She had just done a degree in veterinary medicine. My mother was shocked when I said I wanted to get married. She thought I never would. She had given up on me."

It was possible for Tilo and Musa to have this strange conversation about a third loved one, because they were concurrently sweethearts and ex-sweethearts, lovers and ex-lovers, siblings and ex-siblings, classmates and ex-classmates. Because they trusted each other so peculiarly that they knew, even if they were hurt by it, that whoever it was that the other person loved had to be worth loving. In matters of the heart, they had a virtual forest of safety nets.

Musa showed Tilo a photograph of Miss Jebeen and Arifa that he carried in his wallet. Arifa wore a pearl-gray pheran with silver embroidery and a white hijab. Miss Jebeen was holding her mother's hand. She was dressed in a denim jumpsuit with an embroidered heart on its pinafore. A white hijab was pinned around her smiling, apple-cheeked face. Tilo looked at the photograph for a long time before she gave it back. She saw Musa suddenly look drawn and haggard. But he recovered his poise in a while. He told her about how Arifa and Miss Jebeen had died. About Amrik Singh and the murder of Jalib Qadri, and the string of murders that followed. About his ominous apology at the Shiraz.

"I'll never take what happened to my family personally. But I'll never *not* take it personally. Because that is important too."

They talked into the night. Hours later, Tilo circled back to the photograph.

"Did she like wearing a headscarf?"

"Arifa?"

"No, your daughter."

Musa shrugged. "It's the custom. Our custom."

"I didn't know you were such a customs man. So if I had agreed to marry you, you'd have wanted me to wear one?"

"No, Babajaana. If you had agreed to marry me, *I'd* have ended up wearing a hijab and you would have been running around the underground with a gun."

Tilo laughed out loud.

"And who would have been in my army?"

"I don't know. No humans for sure."

"A moth squadron and a mongoose brigade . . ."

Tilo told Musa about her boring job and her exciting life in her storeroom near the Nizamuddin dargah. About the rooster she had drawn on her wall—"So weird. Maybe Sultan visited me telepathically—is that a word?" (It was the pre-mobile-phone era, so she didn't have a photograph to show him.) She described her neighbor, the fake sex-hakim with waxed mustaches who had endless queues of patients outside his door, and her friends, the tramps and mendicants she drank tea with on the street every morning, who all believed she worked for a drug lord.

"I laugh, but I don't deny it. I leave it ambiguous."

"Why's that? That's dangerous."

"No. Opposite. It's free security for me. They think I have gangster protection. No one bothers me. Let's read a poem before we sleep." It was an old habit, from their college days. One of them would open the book at a random page. The other would read the poem. It often turned out to have uncanny significance for them and the particular moment they were living through. Poetry roulette. She scrambled out of bed and returned with a slim, worn volume of Osip Mandelstam. Musa opened the book. Tilo read:

I was washing at night in the courtyard,
Harsh stars shone in the sky.
Starlight, like salt on an ax-head—
The rain-butt was brim-full and frozen.

"What's a rain-butt? Don't know . . . must check."

The gates are locked,
And the earth in all conscience is bleak.
There's scarcely anything more basic and pure
Than truth's clean canvas.

A star melts, like salt, in the barrel
And the freezing water is blacker,
Death cleaner, misfortune saltier,
And the earth more truthful, more awful.

"Another Kashmiri poet."

"Russian Kashmiri," Tilo said. "He died in a prison camp, during Stalin's Gulag. His ode to Stalin wasn't considered sincere enough."

She regretted reading the poem.

They slept fitfully. Before dawn, still half asleep, Tilo heard Musa splashing in the bathroom again, washing, brushing his teeth (with her toothbrush of course). He came out with his hair slicked down and put on his cap and pheran. She watched him say his prayers. She had never seen him do that before. She sat up in bed. It did not distract him. When he was done he came to her and sat on the edge of the bed.

"Does it worry you?"

"Should it?"

"It's a big change . . ."

"Yes. No. Just makes me . . . think."

"We can't win this with just our bodies. We have to recruit our souls too."

She lit two more cigarettes.

"You know what the hardest thing for us is? The hardest thing to fight? Pity. It's so easy for us to pity ourselves . . . such terrible things have happened to our people . . . in every single household something terrible has happened . . . but self-pity is so . . . so debilitating. So humiliating. More than Azadi, now it's a fight for dignity. And the only way we can hold on to our dignity is to fight back. Even if we lose. Even if we die. But for that we as a people—as an ordinary people—have to become a fighting force . . . an army. To do that we have to simplify ourselves, standardize ourselves, reduce ourselves . . . everyone has to think the same way, want the same thing . . . we have to do away with our complexities, our differences, our absurdities, our nuances . . . we have to make ourselves as single-minded . . . as monolithic . . . as stupid . . . as the army we face. But they're professionals, and we are just people. This is the worst part of the Occupation . . . what it makes us do to ourselves. This reduction, this standardization, this *stupidification* . . . Is that a word?"

"It just became one."

"This stupidification . . . this idiotification . . . if and when we achieve it . . . will be our salvation. It will make us impossible to defeat. First it will be our salvation and then . . . after we win . . . it will be our nemesis. First Azadi. Then annihilation. That's the pattern."

Tilo said nothing.

"Are you listening?"

"Of course."

"I'm being so profound and you're not saying anything."

She looked up at him and pressed her thumb into the tiny inverted "v" between his chipped front teeth. He held her hand and kissed her silver ring.

"It makes me happy that you still wear it."

"It's stuck. I can't take it off even if I want to."

Musa smiled. They smoked in silence and when they were done she took the ashtray to the window, dropped the stubs into the water to join the other floating stubs and looked up at the sky before she returned to bed.

"That was a filthy thing I just did. Sorry."

Musa kissed her forehead and stood up.

"You're leaving?"

"Yes. A boat's coming for me. With a cargo of spinach and melons and carrots and lotus stems. I'll be a Haenz . . . selling my produce in the floating market. I'll undercut the competition, bargain ruthlessly with housewives. And through the chaos I'll make my exit."

"When will I see you?"

"Someone will come for you—a woman called Khadija. Trust her. Go with her. You'll be traveling. I want you to see everything, know everything. You'll be safe."

"When will I see you?"

"Sooner than you think. I'll find you. Khuda Hafiz, Babajaana." And he was gone.

In the morning Gulrez gave her a Kashmiri breakfast. Chewy *lavasa* rotis with butter and honey. *Kahwa* with no sugar, but with shredded almonds that she had to scoop up from the bottom of her cup. Agha and Khanum displayed deplorable manners, skittering up and down the dining table, knocking around the cutlery, spilling the salt. At ten sharp, Khadija arrived with her two young sons. They crossed the lake in a shikara and drove downtown in a red Maruti 800.

For the next ten days Tilo traveled through the Kashmir Valley, each day accompanied by a different set of companions, sometimes men, sometimes women, sometimes families with children. It was the first of many trips she made over several years. She traveled by bus, in shared taxis, and sometimes by car. She visited the tourist spots made famous by Hindi cinema—Gulmarg, Sonmarg, Pahalgam and the Betaab Valley, which was actually named after the film that was shot there. The hotels where film stars used to stay were empty, the honeymoon cottages (where, her traveling companions joked, their oppressors had been conceived) were abandoned. She trekked through the meadow from where, a year ago, six tourists, American, British, German and Norwegian, had been kidnapped by Al-Faran, a newly formed militant outfit that not many people knew about. Five of the six were murdered, one escaped. The young Norwegian, a poet and dancer, had been beheaded, his body left in the Pahalgam meadow. Before he died, as his kidnappers moved him from place to place, he left a trail of poetry on scraps of paper that he secretly managed to give to people he encountered on the way.

She traveled to the Lolab Valley, considered the most beautiful and dangerous place in all of Kashmir, its forest teeming with militants, soldiers and rogue Ikhwanis. She walked on little-known forest paths near Rafiabad that ran close to the Line of Control, along the grassy banks of mountain streams from which she would drop down on all fours and drink the clear water like a thirsty animal, her lips turning blue with cold. She visited villages ringed by orchards and graveyards; she stayed in villagers' homes. Musa would appear and leave without notice. They sat around a fire in an empty stone hut high up in the mountains that was used by Gujjar shepherds in the summer when they brought their sheep up from the plains. Musa pointed out a route that was often used by militants to cross the Line of Control:

"Berlin had a wall. We have the highest mountain range in the world. It won't fall, but it will be scaled."

In a home in Kupwara, Tilo met the older sister of Mumtaz Afzal Malik, the young man who happened to be driving the taxi that took Amrik Singh's accomplice Salim Gojri to the camp the day they were murdered. She described how, when her brother's body was found in a field and brought home, his fists, clenched in rigor mortis, were full of earth and yellow mustard flowers grew from between his fingers.

Tilo returned to HB *Shaheen* from her excursions in the Valley, alone. She and Musa had said their goodbyes, casually, just in case. Tilo learned quickly that, in these matters, casualness and jokes were strictly serious, and seriousness was usually communicated as a joke. They spoke in code even when they didn't need to. That was how Amrik Singh "Spotter" got his code name: Otter. (There hadn't been a formal convocation, but the degree they had jested about had been conferred and accepted. Even though Tilo was nothing less than irreverent about the slogan *Azadi ka matlab kya? La ilaha illallah*, she could now certainly, and correctly, be described as an Enemy of the State.) The day after she returned, when she saw Gulrez laying the table for two, she knew Musa would come.

He came late in the night, looking preoccupied. He said there had been serious trouble in the city. They switched on the radio:

A group of Ikhwanis had killed a boy and "disappeared" his body. In the protests that followed fourteen people had been shot dead. Three militants had been killed in an encounter. Three police stations burned. The toll for the day was eighteen.

Musa ate quickly and stood up to leave. He murmured a gruff goodbye to Gulrez. He kissed Tilo on her forehead.

"Khuda Hafiz, Babajaana. Travel safe."

He asked her to stay inside, not to come out to see him off. She didn't listen. She walked out with him to the rickety, makeshift dock where a small wooden rowboat was waiting. Musa climbed in and lay flat on the floor of the boat. The boatman covered him with a woven grass mat and artfully arranged empty baskets and a few sacks of vegetables over him. Tilo watched the boat row away with its beloved cargo. Not across the lake to the boulevard, but along the endless line of houseboats, into the distance.

The thought of Musa lying at the bottom of a boat, covered with empty baskets, did something to her. Her heart felt like a gray pebble in a mountain stream—something icy rushed over it.

She went to bed, setting her alarm to be up in time to catch her bus to Jammu. Fortunately she followed Kashmiri protocol, not because she meant to, but because she was too tired to undress. She could hear Gul-kak pottering around, humming.

·   ·   ·

She woke less than an hour later—not suddenly, but gradually, swimming through layers of sleep—first to sound and then to the absence of it. First to the hum of engines that seemed to come from every direction. Then, when they were switched off, to the sudden silence.

Motor boats. Many of them.

The HB *Shaheen* pitched and rolled. Not much, just a little.

She was already on her feet, braced for trouble, when the door of her carved, embroidered, filigreed bedroom was kicked down and the room was full of soldiers with guns.

What happened over the next few hours happened either very quickly or very slowly. She couldn't tell which. The picture was clear and the sound precise, but somehow distant. Feelings lagged far behind. She was gagged, her hands were tied, and the room was searched. They hustled her down the corridor into the dining room where she passed Gul-kak on the floor, being kicked and beaten by at least ten men.

Where is he?

I don't know.

Who are you?

Gulrez. Gulrez. Gulrez Abroo. Gulrez Abroo.

Each time he told the truth they hit him harder.

His wails speared clean through her body like javelins and drifted across the lake. When her eyes got used to the darkness outside, she saw a flotilla of boats full of soldiers bobbing on the black water, the aquatic equivalent of a cordon-and-search. There were two concentric arcs, the outer arc was the area domination team, the inner one, the support team. The soldiers that made up the support team were standing in their boats, probing and stabbing at the water with knives tied to the end of long poles—improvised harpoons—to make sure the man they had come for did not make an underwater getaway. (They were mortified by the recent, but already legendary, escape of Haroon Gaade—Haroon the Fish—who got away even after the raiding party thought it had cornered him in his hideout on the banks of the Wular Lake. The only possible exit route he had was the lake itself, where a team of marine commandos lay in wait for him. But Haroon Gaade got away by hiding underwater in a clump of weeds, using a reed of bamboo as a snorkel. He was able to remain concealed for hours—until his flummoxed pursuers gave up and went away.)

The boat that had carried the assault team was docked, waiting for its passengers to return with their trophy. The man in charge of the operation was a tall Sikh wearing a dark green turban. Tilo assumed, correctly, that he was Amrik Singh. She was shoved on to the boat and made to sit down. Nobody spoke to her. Nobody in the neighboring houseboats came out to find out what was happening. Each of them had already been searched by small teams of soldiers.

In a while Gulrez was brought out. He couldn't walk, so he was dragged. His big head, covered by a hood now, lolled forward. He was seated opposite Tilo. All she could see of him was the hood, his pheran and his boots. The hood wasn't even a hood. It was a bag that advertised Surya Brand Basmati Rice. Gul-kak was quiet and appeared to be badly hurt. He could not sit up unsupported. Two soldiers held him up. Tilo hoped he had lost consciousness.

The convoy set off in the same direction that Musa's boat had taken. Past the endless row of dark, empty houseboats and then right, into what looked like a swamp.

Nobody spoke, and for a while there was silence except for the drone of boat engines and the plaintive mewling of a kitten that filled the night and made the soldiers uneasy. The mewling seemed to be traveling with them, but there was no sign of a kitten on board. Finally she was located—Khanum the harlequin—in Gulrez's pocket. A soldier pulled her out and flung her into the lake as though she was a piece of garbage. She flew through the air, yowling, with her fangs bared and her little claws extended, ready to take on the entire Indian Army all by herself. She sank without a sound. That was the end of yet another *bewakoof* who did not know how to live in a *mintree* occupation. (Her sibling Agha survived—whether as collaborator, common citizen or mujahid was never ascertained.)

The moon was high, and through the forest of reeds Tilo could make out the silhouettes of houseboats, much smaller than the ones meant for tourists. A ramshackle wooden construction fronted by a rickety wooden boardwalk—a backwater shopping arcade that hadn't seen customers in years—sat just above the waterline on rotting stilts. The shops, a chemist, an A-1 Ladies' store and several "emporiums" for local handicrafts, were all boarded up. Small rowboats were docked on the shores of what looked like boggy islands dotted with old wooden houses fallen to ruin. The only sign that the eerie silence which lay upon the swamp was not entirely unpeopled was the crackle of radios and the occasional snatches of songs that drifted out of the barred, shuttered shadows. The boat sat low in the water. That part of the lake was choked with weed so it felt surreal, as though they were cleaving through a dark, liquid lawn. Debris from the morning's floating vegetable market bobbed around.

All Tilo could think of was Musa's little boat that had taken the same path less than an hour ago. His had no motor.

Please God, whoever you are, wherever you are, slow us down. Give him time to get away. *Slowdownslowdownslowdownslowdown-slowdownslowdownslowdown*

Someone heard her prayer and answered it. It was unlikely to have been God.

Amrik Singh, who was in the same boat as Tilo and Gulrez, stood up and waved to the escort boats, indicating that they should go ahead. Once they were gone, he directed the driver of the boat they were in to turn left into a waterway so narrow they had to slow down and literally push their way through the reeds. After ten minutes of suffocation they emerged in open water again. They made another left turn. The driver cut the motor and they docked. What followed appeared to be a familiar drill. Nobody seemed to need instructions. Gulrez was lifted up and dragged ashore through a couple of feet of water. One soldier remained on the boat with Tilo. The rest, including Amrik Singh, waded ashore. Tilo could see the outline of a large, dilapidated house. Its roof had fallen in and the moon shone through its skeleton of rafters that loomed against the night—a luminous heart in an angular ribcage.

A gunshot followed by a short explosion alarmed the ground-nesting birds. For a moment the sky was full of herons, cormorants, plovers, lapwings, calling as though day had broken. They were only playacting and settled down soon enough. The odd hours and unusual soundtrack of the Occupation were now a matter of routine for them. When the soldiers returned there was no Gulrez. But they carried a heavy, shapeless sack that needed more than one man to lift.

In this way the prisoner who left the boat as Gul-kak Abroo returned as the mortal remains of the dreaded militant Commander Gulrez, whose capture and killing would earn his killers three hundred thousand rupees.

The toll for the day was now eighteen plus one.

Amrik Singh settled back into the boat, this time seating himself directly opposite Tilo: "Whoever you are, you are charged with being the accomplice of a terrorist. But you will not be harmed if you tell us everything." He spoke pleasantly, in Hindi. "Take your time. But we want all the details. How you know him. Where you went. Who you met. Everything. Take your time. And you should know that we already know those details. You won't be helping us. We will be testing you."

The same depthless, blank, black eyes that had pretended to laugh about pretending to forget his pistol in Musa's home now stared at Tilo in the moonlit bog. That gaze called forth something in her blood—a mute rage, a stubborn, suicidal impulse. A stupid resolve that she would say nothing, no matter what.

Fortunately, it was never tested; it never came to that.

The boat ride lasted another twenty minutes. An armored Gypsy and an open military truck were parked under a tree, waiting to drive them to the Shiraz. Before they got in, Amrik Singh removed Tilo's gag but left her hands tied.

In the cinema lobby, busy as a bus terminal, even at that hour, Tilo was handed over to ACP Pinky, who had been summoned from her sleep to deal with this unusual prisoner. The arrest was not registered. They had not even asked the prisoner her name. ACP Pinky led her past the reception counter where nine months ago Musa had left Amrik Singh's bottle of Red Stag whiskey, past the advertisements for Cadbury's chocolate and Kwality ice cream and the faded posters of *Chandni*, *Maine Pyar Kiya*, *Parinda* and *Lion of the Desert*. They threaded their way through the lines of the latest batch of bound, beaten men and the cement kangaroo garbage bins, entered the theater, crossed the improvised badminton court, exited from the door closest to the screen and then took another door that opened on to a backyard. There were more than a few amused glances and mumbled lewd remarks as the women made their way to the Shiraz's main interrogation center.

It was an independent structure—an unremarkable, long, rectangular room whose primary feature was its stench. The smell of urine and sweat was overlaid by the sicksweet smell of old blood.

Though the sign on the door said *Interrogation Center*, it was in truth a torture center. In Kashmir, "interrogation" was not a real category. There was "questioning," which meant a few slaps and kicks, and "interrogation," which meant torture.

The room had only one door and no windows. ACP Pinky walked over to a desk in the corner, pulled out a few blank sheets of paper and a pen from a drawer and slapped them on the table.

"Let's not waste each other's time. Write. I'll be back in ten minutes."

She untied Tilo's hands and left, shutting the door behind her.

Tilo waited for the numbness to go away and the blood to return to her fingers before she picked up the pen. Her first three attempts at writing failed. Her hands were shaking so much she could not read her own writing. She closed her eyes and remembered her breathing lessons. They worked. In clear letters she wrote:

Please call Mr. Biplab Dasgupta, Deputy Station Head India Bravo Give him this message: G-A-R-S-O-N H-O-B-A-R-T

While she waited for ACP Pinky to return she inspected the room. At first glance it looked like a rudimentary tool shed, kitted out with a couple of carpenters' worktables, hammers, screwdrivers, pliers, ropes, what seemed to be scaled-down stone or concrete pillars, pipes, a tub of filthy water, jerry cans of petrol, metal funnels, wires, electric extension boards, coils of wire, rods of all sizes, a couple of spades, crowbars.

On a shelf there was a jar of red chili powder. The floor was littered with cigarette stubs. Tilo had learned enough over the last ten days to know that those ordinary things could be put to extraordinary use.

She knew that the pillars were the instruments of the most

favored form of torture in Kashmir. They were used as "rollers" on prisoners who were tied down while two men rolled the pillars over them, literally crushing their muscles. More often than not, "roller treatment" resulted in acute renal failure. The tub was for waterboarding, the pliers for extracting fingernails, the wires for applying electric shocks to men's genitals, the chili powder was usually applied on rods that were inserted into prisoners' anuses or mixed into water and poured down their throats. (Years later, another woman, Loveleen, Amrik Singh's wife, would display an intimate knowledge of these methods in her application for asylum in the US. It was this very tool shed that was the site of her field research, except that she had visited it not as a victim, but as the spouse of the torturer-in-chief, who was being given a tour of her husband's office.)

ACP Pinky returned with Major Amrik Singh. Tilo saw at once, from their body language and the intimate way in which they spoke to each other, that they were more than just colleagues. ACP Pinky picked up the sheet of paper Tilo had written on and read it aloud, slowly and with some difficulty. Clearly, reading was not her forte. Amrik Singh took the paper from her. Tilo saw his expression change.

"Who is he to you, this Dasgupta?"

"A friend."

"A *friend*? How many men do you fuck at the same time?" This was ACP Pinky.

Tilo said nothing.

"I asked you a question. How many men do you fuck at the same time?"

Tilo's silence elicited a slew of insults along predictable lines (in which Tilo recognized the words "black," "whore" and "jihadi") and then the question was asked again. Tilo's continued silence had nothing to do with courage or resilience. It had to do with a lack of choice. Her blood had shut down.

ACP Pinky noticed the smirk on Amrik Singh's face—clearly in some way he admired the defiance that was on display. She read volumes into that expression and it incensed her. Amrik Singh left with the sheet of paper. At the door he turned and said:

"Find out what you can. No injury marks. This is a senior officer, this person whose name she's written. Let me check it out. May be nonsense. But no marks until then."

"No marks" was a problem for the ACP. She had no experience in that field, because she was not a trained torturer, she had learned her craft on the run, in the battlefield, and "no marks" was not a courtesy that was extended to Kashmiris. She did not believe that Amrik Singh's instructions had anything to do with a senior officer. She recognized the look in his eye, and she knew what attracted him in women. Having to constrain herself offended her dignity and that didn't help her temper. Her slaps and kicks (which came under the category of "questioning") drew nothing from her detainee but expressionless, dead silence.

It took Amrik Singh more than an hour to locate Biplab Dasgupta and speak to him on the hotline to the Forest Guest House in Dachigam. The fact that he was part of the Governor's weekend entourage was cause for serious alarm. There was no question that the woman knew him. And well. The Deputy Director India Bravo seemed to know exactly what G-A-R-S-O-N H-O-B-A-R-T meant. But the predator in Amrik Singh smelled hesitation, diffidence even. He knew he could be in more trouble, big trouble, but it wasn't too late for it to be undone if he released the woman unhurt. There was space to maneuver. He hurried back to the interrogation center to stall any further damage. He was a little late, but not too late.

ACP Pinky had found a cheap, clichéd way around her problem. She called down the primordial punishment for the Woman-Who-Must-Be-Taught-a-Lesson. Her vindictiveness had very little to do with counter-terrorism or with Kashmir—except perhaps for the fact that the place was an incubator for every kind of insanity.

Mohammed Subhan Hajam, the camp barber, was just leaving as Amrik Singh rushed into the room.

Tilo was sitting on a wooden chair with her arms strapped down. Her long hair was on the floor, the scattered curls, no longer hers, mingled with the filth and cigarette butts. While he tonsured her, Subhan Hajam had managed to whisper, "Sorry, madam, very sorry."

Amrik Singh and ACP Pinky had a lovers' tiff that almost came to blows. Pinky was sulky but defiant.

"Show me the law against haircuts."

Amrik Singh untied Tilo and helped her to her feet. He made a show of dusting the hair off her shoulders. He put a huge hand protectively on her scalp—a butcher's blessing. It would take Tilo years to get over the obscenity of that touch. He sent for a balaclava for her to cover her head. While they waited for it, he said, "Sorry about this. It shouldn't have happened. We have decided to release you. What's done is done. You don't talk. I don't talk. If you talk, I talk. And if I talk, you and your officer friend will be in a lot of trouble. Collaborating with terrorists is not a small thing."

The balaclava arrived along with a small pink tin of Pond's Dreamflower talc. Amrik Singh powdered Tilo's shaved scalp. The balaclava stank worse than a dead fish. But she allowed him to put it on her head. They walked out of the interrogation center, across the yard and up a fire escape to a small office. It was empty. Amrik Singh said it was the office of Ashfaq Mir of the Special Operations Group, Deputy Commandant of the camp. He was out on an operation, but would return shortly to hand her over to the person whom Biplab Dasgupta Sir was sending.

Tilo politely refused Amrik Singh's offers of tea and even water.

He left her in the room, clearly keen for this particular chapter to end. It was the last she saw of him, until she opened the morning papers more than sixteen years later, to the news that he had shot himself and his wife and three young sons in their home in a small town in the US. She found it hard to connect the newspaper photograph of the puffy, fat-faced, clean-shaven man with frightened eyes to the same one who had murdered Gul-kak and then solicitously, almost tenderly, powdered her scalp.

She waited in the empty office, staring at the whiteboard with a list of names against which it said (killed), (killed), (killed) and a poster on the wall which said:

We follow our own rules
Ferocious we are
Lethal in any form
Tamer of tides
We play with storms
U guessed it right
We are
Men in Uniform

It was two hours before Naga walked through the door, followed by the cheerful Ashfaq Mir who was accompanied by the scent of his cologne. It took another hour for Ashfaq Mir to complete his histrionics with the wounded Lashkar militant as his prop, for the omelettes and kebabs to be served and for the "handover" to be completed. All through the meeting and the dawn ride to Ahdoos through the empty streets while Naga held her hand, all she could think of was Gul-kak's head lolling forward in a Surya Brand Basmati Rice bag (for some reason the handles, particularly the handles, of the bag seemed demonically disrespectful) and Musa lying at the bottom of a small boat covered by empty baskets, being rowed to eternity.

Naga had very considerately booked her a room next to his in Ahdoos. He asked her whether she wanted him to stay with her ("On a purely secular basis," as he put it). When she said no, he hugged her and gave her two sleeping pills. ("Or would you prefer a joint? I have one rolled and ready.") He called and asked housekeeping to bring her two buckets of hot water. Tilo was touched by this caring, kind-hearted side of him. She had never encountered it before. He left her an ironed shirt and a pair of his trousers in case she wanted to change. He suggested they take the afternoon flight to Delhi. She said she'd let him know. She knew she couldn't leave without hearing from Musa. She just couldn't. And she knew that a message would come. Somehow it would come. She lay on her bed unable to close her eyes, almost too scared to even blink, for fear of what apparition might appear before her. A part of herself that she didn't recognize wanted to go back to the Shiraz and have a fair fight with ACP Pinky. It was like thinking of something clever to say long after the moment has passed. She realized that it was also cheap and mean. ACP Pinky was just a violent, unhappy woman. She wasn't Otter, the killing machine. So why the misguided revenge fantasy?

She missed her hair. She would never grow it long again. In memory of Gul-kak.

At about ten o'clock that morning there was a quiet, barely audible knock on her door. She thought it would be Naga, but it was Khadija. They hardly knew each other, but there was nobody in the world (other than Musa) that Tilo would have been happier to see. Khadija explained quickly how she had found Tilo: "We have our people too." In this case they included the pilot of one of the boats on the cordon-and-search team and people on neighboring houseboats and all along the way, who had relayed information, almost in real time. In the Shiraz Cinema, there was Mohammed Subhan Hajam the barber. And in Ahdoos there was a bellboy.

Khadija had news. The army had announced the capture and killing of the dreaded militant Commander Gulrez. Musa was still in Srinagar. He would be at the funeral. Militants from several groups would attend to give Commander Gulrez a farewell gun salute. It was safe for them to move around because there would be tens of thousands of people out on the streets. The army would have to pull back to avoid an all-out massacre. Tilo was to go with her to a safe house in Khanqah-e-Moula where Musa would meet her after the funeral. He said it was important. Khadija had brought Tilo a set of fresh clothes—a salwar kameez, a pheran and a lime-green hijab. Her matter-of-factness jolted Tilo out of the little swamp of self-pity she had allowed herself to sink into. It reminded her that she was among a people for whom her ordeal of the previous night was known as normal life.

The hot water came. Tilo bathed and put on her new clothes. Khadija showed her how to pin the hijab around her face. It made her look regal, like an Ethiopian queen. She liked it, although she much preferred the look of her own hair. Ex-hair. Tilo slipped a note under Naga's door saying she would be back by evening. The two women stepped out of the hotel and into the streets of the city that came alive only when it had to bury its dead.

The City of Funerals was suddenly awake, animated, kinetic. All around was motion. The streets were tributaries; small rivers of people, all flowing towards the estuary—the Mazar-e-Shohadda. Little contingents, large contingents, people from the old city, the new city, from villages and from other cities were converging quickly. Even in the narrowest by-lanes, groups of women and men and even the smallest children chanted *Azadi! Azadi!* Along the way young men had set up water points and community kitchens to feed those who had come from far away. As they distributed water, as they filled the plates, as people ate and drank, as they breathed and walked, to a drumbeat that only they could hear, they shouted: *Azadi! Azadi!*

Khadija seemed to have a detailed map of the back streets of her city in her head. This impressed Tilo enormously (because she herself had no such skills). They took a long, circuitous route. The chants of *Azadi!* became a reverberating boom that sounded like the coming of a storm. (Garson Hobart, holed up in Dachigam with the Governor's entourage, unable to return to the city until the streets had been secured, heard it on the phone held out to the street by his secretary.) Nine months after Miss Jebeen's funeral, here was another one. This time there were nineteen coffins. One of them empty, for the boy whose body the Ikhwanis had stolen. Another one full of the shredded remains of a little man with emerald eyes who was on his way to join Sultan, his beloved *bewakoof*, in heaven.

"I would like to attend the funeral," Tilo said to Khadija.

"We could. But it will be a risk. We may get late. And we won't get anywhere close. Women are not allowed near the grave. We can visit it afterwards, once everyone has left."

Women are not allowed. Women are not allowed. Women are not allowed.

Was it to protect the grave from the women or the women from the grave?

Tilo didn't ask.

After forty-five minutes of driving around, Khadija parked her car and they walked quickly through a maze of narrow, winding streets in a part of town that seemed to be interconnected in several ways—underground and overground, vertically and diagonally, via streets and rooftops and secret passages—like a single organism. A giant coral, or an anthill.

"This part of town is still ours," Khadija said. "The army can't come in here."

They stepped through a small wooden doorway into a bare, green-carpeted room. An unsmiling young man greeted them and ushered them in. He walked them quickly through two rooms and as they entered the third, he opened what looked like a large cupboard. There was a trapdoor through which steep, narrow steps led into a secret basement. Tilo followed Khadija down the steps. The room had no furniture, but there were a couple of mattresses on the floor and some cushions. There was a calendar on the wall, but it was two years old. Her backpack was propped up in a corner. Someone had risked salvaging it from the HB *Shaheen*. A young girl came down the steps and rolled out a plastic lace *dastarkhan*. An older woman followed with a tray of tea and teacups, a plate of rusks and a plate of sliced sponge cake. She took Tilo's face in her hands and kissed her forehead. Not much was said, but both mother and daughter stayed in the room.

When Tilo finished her tea, Khadija patted the mattress they were sitting on.

"Sleep. He will take at least two or three hours to get here."

Tilo lay down and Khadija covered her with a quilt. She reached out and held Khadija's hand under the quilt. In the years that followed, they would become fast friends. Tilo's eyes closed. The murmur of women's voices saying things she couldn't understand was like balm on raw skin.

She was still asleep when Musa came. He sat cross-legged next to her, looking down at her sleeping face for a long time, wishing he could wake her up to another, better world. He knew it would be a long time before he saw her again. And then only if they were lucky.

There wasn't much time. He had to leave while the tide was high and the streets still belonged to the people. He woke her as gently as he could.

"Babajaana. Wake up."

She opened her eyes and pulled him down next to her. For a long time there was nothing to say. Absolutely nothing.

"I've just come from my own funeral. I gave myself a twenty-one-gun salute," Musa said.

And then in a voice that would not rise above a whisper because each time it did it broke under the weight of what it was trying to say, Tilo told him what had happened. She forgot nothing. Not a single thing. Not a sound. Not a feeling. Not a word that had or had not been said.

Musa kissed her head.

"They don't know what they've done. They really have no idea."

And then it was time for him to leave.

"Babajaana, listen carefully. When you go back to Delhi you must not on any account stay alone. It's too dangerous. Stay with friends . . . maybe Naga. You'll hate me for saying this—but either get married or go to your mother. You need cover. For a while at least. Until we deal with Otter. We'll win this war, and then we'll be together, you and I. I'll wear a hijab—although you look lovely in this one—and you can take up arms. OK?"

"OK."

Of course it didn't work out that way.

Before Musa left he gave Tilo a sealed envelope.

"Don't open it now. Khuda Hafiz."

It would be two years before she saw him again.

The sun had not yet set when Khadija and Tilo went to the Mazar-e-Shohadda. Commander Gulrez's grave stood out from the others. A small bamboo framework had been erected over it. It was decorated with strings of silver and gold tinsel and a green flag. A temporary shrine to a beloved freedom fighter who had given his todays for his people's tomorrows. A man with tears streaming down his face looked at it from a distance.

"He's an ex-militant," Khadija said, under her breath. "He was in jail for years. Poor man, he's crying for the wrong person."

"Maybe not," Tilo said. "The whole world should weep for Gul-kak."

They scattered rose petals on Gul-kak's grave and lit a candle. Khadija found the graves of Arifa and Miss Jebeen the First, and did the same for them. She read the inscription on Miss Jebeen's tombstone out to Tilo:

MISS JEBEEN
2 January 1992–22 December 1995
Beloved d/o Arifa and Musa Yeswi

And the almost-hidden one below it:

Akh daleela wann
Yeth manz ne kahn balai aasi
Na aes soh kunni junglas manz roazaan

Khadija translated it for Tilo, but neither of them understood what it really meant.

The last lines of the Mandelstam poem she had read with Musa (and wished she hadn't) floated back unbidden into Tilo's brain.

Death cleaner, misfortune saltier,
And the earth more truthful, more awful.

They returned to Ahdoos. Khadija would not leave until she saw Tilo back to her room. When Khadija had gone, Tilo called Naga to say she was back and that she was going to bed. For no reason she knew, she said a small prayer (to no god she knew) before opening the envelope Musa had given her.

It contained a doctor's prescription for eardrops and a photograph of Gul-kak. He was in a khaki shirt, combat fatigues and

Musa's *Asal boot*, smiling into the camera. He had a handsome
leather ammunition belt slung across both his shoulders, and
a pistol holster at his hip. He was armed to the teeth. In each
leather bullet loop there was a green chili. Sheathed in his pistol
holster was a juicy, fresh-leaved, white radish.

On the back of the photograph Musa had written: *Our darling
Commander Gulrez.*

In the middle of the night Tilo knocked on Naga's door. He
opened it and put his arm around her. They spent the night
together on a purely secular basis.

TILO HAD BEEN CARELESS.

She returned from the Valley of death carrying a little life.

She and Naga had been married for two months when she
discovered that she was pregnant. Their marriage had not been
what was called "consummated" yet. So there was no doubt in
her mind about who the father of the child was. She considered
going through with it. Why not? Gulrez if it was a boy. Jebeen if
it was a girl. She couldn't see herself as a mother any more than
she could see herself as a bride—although she *had* been a bride.
She had done that and survived. So why not this?

The decision she eventually took had nothing to do with her
feelings for Naga or her love for Musa. It came from a more pri-
mal place. She worried that the little human she produced would
have to negotiate the same ocean full of strange and dangerous
fish that she had had to in her relationship with her mother. She
did not trust that she would be a better parent than Maryam Ipe.
Her clear-eyed assessment of herself was that she'd be a far worse
one. She did not wish to inflict herself on a child. And she did not
wish to inflict a replication of herself on the world.

Money was a problem. She had a little, but not much. She
had been fired from her job for poor attendance, and hadn't got

another one. She didn't want to ask Naga for any. So she went to a government hospital.

The waiting room was full of distraught women who had been thrown out of their homes by their husbands for not being able to conceive. They were there to have fertility tests. When the women found out that Tilo was there for what was called MTP—Medical Termination of Pregnancy—they could not hide their hostility and disgust. The doctors too were disapproving. She listened to their lectures impassively. When she made it clear that she would not change her mind, they said they could not give her general anesthetic unless there was somebody with her to sign the consent form, preferably the father of the child. She told them to do it without anesthetic. She passed out with the pain and woke in the general ward. Someone else was with her in the bed. A child, with a kidney disorder, screaming in pain. There was more than one patient in every bed. There were patients on the floor, most of the visitors and family members who were crowded around them looked just as ill. Harried doctors and nurses picked their way through the chaos. It was like a wartime ward. Except that in Delhi there was no war other than the usual one—the war of the rich against the poor.

Tilo got up and stumbled out of the ward. She lost her way in the filthy hospital corridors that were packed with sick and dying people. On the ground floor she asked a small man with biceps that seemed to belong to someone else whether he could show her the way out. The exit he pointed to led her to the back of the hospital. To the mortuary, and beyond it, to a derelict Muslim graveyard that seemed to have fallen into disuse.

Flying foxes hung from the branches of huge, old trees, like limp black flags from an old protest. There was nobody around. Tilo sat on a broken grave, trying to orient herself.

A thin, bald man in a scarlet waiter's coat clanked in on an old bicycle. He had a small bunch of marigolds clamped to the back seat of his cycle. He made his way to one of the graves with the flowers and a duster. After dusting it, he placed the flowers on it, stood in silence for a moment and then hurried away.

Tilo walked over to the grave. It was the only one, as far as she could tell, whose tombstone was inscribed in English. It was the grave of Begum Renata Mumtaz Madam, the belly dancer from Romania who had died of a broken heart.

The man was Roshan Lal on his day off from Rosebud Rest-O-Bar. Tilo would meet him seventeen years later, when she returned to the graveyard with Miss Jebeen the Second. Of course she wouldn't recognize him. Nor would she recognize the graveyard, because by then, it was no longer a derelict place for the forgotten dead.

Once Roshan Lal left, Tilo lay down on Begum Renata Mumtaz Madam's grave. She cried a little and then fell asleep. When she woke she felt better prepared to go home and face the rest of her life.

That included dinner downstairs, at least once a week, with Ambassador Shivashankar and his wife, whose views on almost everything, including Kashmir, made Tilo's hands shake and the cutlery rattle on her plate.

The stupidification of the mainland was picking up speed at an unprecedented rate, and it didn't even need a military occupation.

Then there was the changing of the seasons. "This is also a journey," M said, "and they can't take it away from us."

—NADEZHDA MANDELSTAM

Word spread quickly in the poorer quarters that a clever woman had moved into the graveyard. Parents in the neighborhood flocked to enroll their children in the classes Tilo held at Jannat Guest House. Her pupils called her Tilo Madam and sometimes Ustaniji (Teacher, in Urdu). Although she missed the morning singing by the children from the school opposite her apartment, she didn't teach her own pupils to sing "We Shall Overcome" in any language, because she wasn't sure that Overcoming was anywhere on anyone's horizon. But she taught them arithmetic, drawing, computer graphics (on three second-hand desktop computers she had bought with the minimal fees she charged), a bit of basic science, English and eccentricity. From them she learned Urdu and something of the art of happiness. She worked a long day and, for the first time in her life, slept a full night. (Miss Jebeen the Second slept with Anjum.) With each passing day Tilo's mind felt less like one of Musa's "recoveries." Despite making plans every other day to do so, she had not visited her apartment since she left. Not even after receiving the message Garson Hobart had sent through Anjum and

Saddam when they went (out of curiosity to see where and how the strange woman who had parachuted into their lives lived) to pick up some of her things. She continued to pay her rent into his account, which she thought was only fair until she moved her things out. When a few months had gone by with no news from Musa, she left a message with the fruit-seller who brought her his "recoveries." But she still hadn't heard from him. And yet, the burden of perpetual apprehension that she had carried around for years—of suddenly receiving news of Musa's death—had lightened somewhat. Not because she loved him any less, but because the battered angels in the graveyard that kept watch over their battered charges held open the doors between worlds (illegally, just a crack), so that the souls of the present and the departed could mingle, like guests at the same party. It made life less determinate and death less conclusive. Somehow everything became a little easier to bear.

Encouraged by the success and popularity of Tilo's tuition classes, Ustad Hameed had begun, once again, to give music lessons to students he considered promising. Anjum attended these classes as though they were a call to prayer. She still wouldn't sing, but hummed the way she used to when she was trying to get Zainab the Bandicoot to learn to sing. On the pretext of helping Anjum and Tilo look after Miss Jebeen the Second (who was growing up fast, getting naughty and being spoiled rotten), Zainab began to spend her afternoons, evenings and sometimes even nights at the graveyard. The real reason—not lost on anyone—was her heady love affair with Saddam Hussain. She had completed her course at the polytechnic and become a pudgy little fashionista who stitched ladies' clothes to order. She inherited all Nimmo Gorakhpuri's old fashion magazines as well as the hair curlers and cosmetics that had been put in Tilo's room to welcome her when she first came. Saddam's first, unspoken declaration of love had been to allow Zainab to flirtatiously paint his fingernails and toenails scarlet, both of them giggling all the while. He did not remove the nail polish until it chipped off by itself.

Between Zainab and Saddam, they had turned the graveyard into a zoo—a Noah's Ark of injured animals. There was a young peacock who could not fly, and a peahen, perhaps his mother, who would not leave him. There were three old cows that slept all day. Zainab arrived one day in an autorickshaw with several cages stuffed with three dozen budgerigars that had been absurdly colored in luminous dyes. She had bought them in a fit of anger from a bird-seller who had the cages stacked on the back of his bicycle and was peddling the birds in the old city. Colored like that, they couldn't be set free, Saddam said, because they'd attract predators in seconds. So he built them a high, airy cage that spanned the breadth of two graves. The budgerigars flitted about in it, glowing at night like fat fireflies. A small tortoise—an abandoned pet—that Saddam had found in a park, with a sprig of clover in one nostril, now wallowed on the terrace in a mud-pit of his own. Payal-the-mare had a lame donkey for a companion. He was called Mahesh for no reason that anyone knew. Biroo was getting old, but his and Comrade Laali's progeny had multiplied, and they tumbled around the place. Several cats came and went. As did the human guests in Jannat Guest House.

The vegetable garden behind the guest house was doing well too, the soil of the graveyard being as it was a compost pit of ancient provenance. Although nobody was particularly keen on eating vegetables (least of all Zainab), they grew brinjals, beans, chilies, tomatoes and several kinds of gourds, all of which, despite the smoke and fumes from the heavy traffic on the roads that abutted the graveyard, attracted several varieties of butterflies. Some of the more able-bodied addicts were recruited to help with the garden and the animals. It seemed to bring them some temporary solace.

Anjum mooted the idea that Jannat Guest House should have a swimming pool. "Why not?" she said. "Why should only rich people have swimming pools? Why not us?" When Saddam pointed out that water was a key element in swimming pools and the lack of it might prove to be a problem, she said poor people would appreciate a swimming pool even without water. She had one dug, a few feet deep, the size of a large water tank, and had it lined with blue bathroom tiles. She was right. People did appreciate it. They came to visit it and prayed for the day (*Insha'Allah, Insha'Allah*) when it would be full of clean blue water.

So all in all, with a People's Pool, a People's Zoo and a People's School, things were going well in the old graveyard. The same, however, could not be said of the Duniya.

Anjum's old friend D. D. Gupta had returned from Baghdad, or what was left of it, with horror stories of wars and massacres, bombings and butchery—of a whole region that had been deliberately and systematically turned into hell on earth. He was grateful to be alive and to have a home to return to. He no longer had the stomach for blast walls, or for that matter for any kind of business enterprise, and was delighted to see how the desolate, ravaged specter that he had left behind when he went to Iraq had blossomed and prospered. He and Anjum spent hours together, shooting the breeze, watching old Hindi films on TV, and overseeing new plans for expansion and construction (it was he who supervised the construction of the swimming pool). Mrs. Gupta, for her part, had also retreated from worldly love and spent all her time with Lord Krishna in her puja room.

Hell was closing in on the home front too. Gujarat ka Lalla had swept the polls and was the new Prime Minister. People idolized him, and temples in which he was the presiding deity began to appear in small towns. A devotee gifted him a pinstriped suit with *LallaLallaLalla* woven into the fabric. He wore it to greet visiting Heads of State. Every week he addressed the people of

the country directly in an emotional radio broadcast. He disseminated his message of Cleanliness, Purity and Sacrifice for the
Nation, either with a fable, a folk tale, or an edict of some sort.
He popularized the practice of mass yoga in community parks. At
least once a month he visited a poor colony and swept the streets
himself. As his popularity peaked, he became paranoid and secre-
tive. He trusted nobody and sought no advice. He lived alone, ate
alone, and never socialized. For his personal protection, he hired
food-tasters and security guards from other countries. He made
dramatic announcements and took drastic decisions that had far-
reaching effects.

The Organization that had brought him to power took a dim
view of personality cults, and a long view of history. It continued
to support him, but quietly began to groom a successor.

The saffron parakeets that had been biding their time were set
loose. They swooped into university campuses and courtrooms,
disrupted concerts, vandalized cinema halls and burned books.
A parakeet committee of pedagogy was set up to formalize the
process of turning history into mythology and mythology into
history. The Sound and Light show at the Red Fort was taken
into the workshop for revision. Soon the centuries of Muslim
rule would be stripped of poetry, music and architecture and collapsed into the sound of the clash of swords and a bloodcurdling
war cry that lasted only a little longer than the husky giggle that
Ustad Kulsoom Bi had hung her hopes on. The remaining time
would be taken up by the story of Hindu glory. As always, history
would be a revelation of the future as much as it was a study of
the past.

Small gangs of thugs, who called themselves "defenders of the
Hindu Faith," worked the villages, gaining what advantage they
could. Aspiring politicians jump-started their careers by filming
themselves making hateful speeches or beating up Muslims and
uploading the videos on to YouTube. Every Hindu pilgrimage

and religious festival turned into a provocative victory parade. Armed escort teams rode beside pilgrims and revelers on trucks and motorcycles, looking to pick fights in peaceful neighborhoods. Instead of saffron flags they now proudly waved the national flag—a trick they had learned from Mr. Aggarwal and his tubby Gandhian mascot in Jantar Mantar.

The Holy Cow became the national emblem. The government backed campaigns to promote cow urine (as a drink as well as a detergent). News filtered in from Lalla strongholds about people accused of eating beef or killing cows being publicly flogged and often lynched.

Given his recent experiences in Iraq, the worldly Mr. D. D. Gupta's considered assessment of all this activity was that in the long run it would only end up creating a market for blast walls.

Nimmo Gorakhpuri came over one weekend with a (literally) blow-by-blow fourth-person account of how the relative of a neighbor's friend had been beaten to death in front of his family by a mob that accused him of killing a cow and eating beef.

"You had better chase out these old cows that you have here," she said. "If they die here—not if, *when* they die—they'll say you killed them and that will be the end of all of you. They must have their eyes on this property now. That's how they do it these days. They accuse you of eating beef and then take over your house and your land and send you to a refugee camp. It's all about property, not cows. You have to be very careful."

"Careful in what way?" Saddam shouted. "The only way you can be careful with these bastards is by ceasing to exist! If they want to kill you they will kill you whether you are careful or not, whether you've killed a cow or not, whether you have even set eyes on a cow or not." It was the first time anybody had ever heard him lose his temper. Everybody was taken aback. None of them knew his story. Anjum had told nobody. As a keeper of secrets, she was nothing short of Olympic class.

On Independence Day, in what had grown to be a ritual, Saddam sat next to Anjum on the red car sofa with his sunglasses on. He switched channels between Gujarat ka Lalla's bellicose speech at the Red Fort and a massive, public protest in Gujarat. Thousands of people, mainly Dalit, had gathered in a district called Una to protest the public flogging of five Dalits who had been stopped on the road because they had the carcass of a cow in their pickup truck. They hadn't killed the cow. They had only picked up the carcass like Saddam's father had, all those years ago. Unable to bear the humiliation of what was done to them, all five men had tried to commit suicide. One had succeeded.

"First they tried to finish off the Muslims and Christians. Now they're going for the Chamars," Anjum said.

"It's the other way around," Saddam said. He did not explain what he meant, but looked thrilled as speaker after speaker at the protest swore on oath that they would never again pick up cow carcasses for upper-caste Hindus.

What didn't make it to TV were the gangs of thugs that had positioned themselves on the highways leading away from the venue of the gathering, waiting to pick off the protesters as they dispersed.

Anjum and Saddam's Independence Day TV-watching ritual was interrupted by wild shrieks from Zainab, who was outside, hanging up some washing. Saddam raced out, followed by a slower, worried Anjum. It took them a while to believe that what they saw was real and not a specter. Zainab, her gaze directed skyward, was transfixed, terrified.

A crow hung frozen in mid-air, one of its wings spread out like a fan. A feathered Christ, hanging askew, on an invisible cross. The sky swarmed with thousands of agitated, low-flying fellow crows, their distraught cawing drowning out every other city sound. Above them in an upper tier, silent kites circled, curious perhaps, but inscrutable. The crucified crow was absolutely still. Very quickly a small crowd of people gathered to watch the proceedings, to frighten themselves to death, to advise each other about the occult significance of frozen crows, and to discuss the exact nature of the horrors that this ill-omen, this macabre curse, would visit upon them.

What had happened was not a mystery. The crow's wing feathers had snagged mid-flight on an invisible kite string that was laced across the branches of the old Banyan trees in the graveyard. The felon—a purple paper-kite—peeped guiltily through the foliage of one of them. The string, a new Chinese brand that had suddenly flooded the market, was made of tough, transparent plastic, coated with ground glass. Independence Day kite-warriors used it to "cut" each other's strings, and bring each other's kites down. It had already caused some tragic accidents in the city.

The crow had struggled at first, but seemed to have realized that each time it moved, the string sliced deeper into its wing. So it stayed still, looking down with a bewildered, bright eye in its tilted head at the people gathered below. With every passing moment the sky grew denser with more and more distressed, hysterical crows.

Saddam, who had hurried away after assessing the situation, returned with a long rope made of several odd pieces of parcel string and clothes line knotted together. He tied a stone to one end and, squinting into the sun through his sunglasses, lobbed the stone into the sky, using instinct to gauge the trajectory of the invisible kite-string, hoping to loop the rope over it and bring it down with the weight of the stone. It took several attempts and several changes of stone (it had to be light enough to spin high into the sky, and heavy enough to arc over the string and pull it through the foliage it was snagged on) before he succeeded. When he finally did, the kite-string fell to the ground. The crow first dipped down with it, and then, magically, flew away. The sky lightened, the cawing receded.

Normalcy was declared.

To those onlookers in the graveyard who were of an irrational and unscientific temper (which means all of them, including Ustaniji), it was clear that an apocalypse had been averted and a benediction earned in its place.

The Man of the Moment was feted, hugged and kissed.

Not one to allow such an opportunity to pass, Saddam decided that his Time was Now.

Late that night he went to Anjum's room. She was lying on her side, propped up on an elbow, looking tenderly down at Miss Jebeen the Second, who was fast asleep. (The unsuitable-bedtime-stories stage was still to come.)

"Imagine," she said, "but for the grace of God, this little creature would have been in some government orphanage right now."

Saddam allowed for a well-judged moment of respectful silence and then formally asked her for Zainab's hand in marriage. Anjum responded a little bitterly, without looking up, suddenly revisited by an old ache.

"Why ask me? Ask Saeeda. She's her mother."

"I know the story. That's why I'm asking you."

Anjum was pleased, but did not show it. Instead she looked Saddam up and down as though he was a stranger.

"Give me one reason why Zainab should marry a man who is waiting to commit a crime and then be hanged like Saddam Hussein of Iraq?"

"*Arre yaar*, that's all over now. It's gone. My people have risen up." Saddam took out his mobile phone and pulled up the Saddam Hussein execution video. "Here, see. I'm deleting it now, right in front of you. See, it's gone. I don't need it any more. I have a new one now. Look."

As she cranked herself up on her bed and creaked into a sitting position, Anjum grumbled good-naturedly under her breath, "*Ya Allah!* What sin have I committed that I have to put up with this lunatic?" She put on her reading glasses.

The new video Saddam showed her began with a shot of several rusty pickup trucks parked in the compound of a genteel old colonial bungalow—the office of a local District Collector in Gujarat. The trucks were piled high with old carcasses and skeletons of cows. Furious young Dalit men unloaded the carcasses and began flinging them into the deep, colonnaded verandah of the bungalow. They left a macabre trail of cow skeletons in the driveway, placed a huge, horned skull on the Collector's office table and draped serpentine cow vertebrae like antimacassars over the backs of his pretty armchairs.

Anjum watched the video looking shocked, the light from the mobile phone screen bouncing off her perfect white tooth. It was clear the men were shouting, but the volume on the phone was turned down so as not to wake Miss Jebeen.

"What are they shouting? It's in Gujarati?" she asked Saddam.

"Your Mother! You look after her!" Saddam whispered.

"*Ai hai!* What will they do to these boys now?"

"What can they do, the poor fuckers? They can't clean their own shit. They can't bury their own mothers. I don't know what they'll do. But it's their problem, not ours."

"So now?" Anjum said. "You've deleted the video . . . that means that you've given up the idea of killing that bastard cop?" She sounded disappointed. Disapproving, almost.

"Now I don't need to kill him. You saw the video—my people have risen up! They are fighting! What is one Sehrawat for us now? Nothing!"

"Do you make all your life's big decisions based on mobile phone videos?"

"That's how it is these days, *yaar*. The world is only videos now. But see what they've done! It's real. It's not a movie. They're not actors. Do you want to see it again?"

"*Arre*, it's not that easy, babu. They'll beat up these boys, buy them off . . . that's how they do it these days . . . and if they leave this work of theirs, how will they earn? What will they eat? *Chalo*, we'll think about that later. Do you have a nice photograph of your father? We can hang it up in the TV room."

Anjum was suggesting that a portrait of Saddam's father be hung next to the portrait of Zakir Mian garlanded with crisp cash-birds that graced the TV room. It was her way of accepting Saddam as her son-in-law.

Saeeda was delighted, Zainab ecstatic. Preparations for the wedding began. Everybody, including Tilo Madam, was measured up for new clothes that Zainab would design. A month before the wedding Saddam announced that he was taking the family out for a special treat. A surprise. Imam Ziauddin was too frail to go and it was Ustad Hameed's grandson's birthday. Dr. Azad Bhartiya said the treat-destination Saddam had chosen was against his principles and in any case he couldn't eat. So the party consisted of Anjum, Saeeda, Nimmo Gorakhpuri, Zainab, Tilo, Miss Jebeen the Second and Saddam himself. None of them could in their wildest dreams have predicted what he had in store for them.

Naresh Kumar, a friend of Saddam's, was one of five chauffeurs employed by a billionaire industrialist who maintained a palatial home and a fleet of expensive cars even though he spent only three or four days a month in Delhi. Naresh Kumar arrived at the graveyard to pick up the pre-wedding party in his master's leather-seated silver Mercedes-Benz. Zainab sat in front on Saddam's lap and everybody else squashed in behind. Tilo could never have imagined enjoying a ride through the streets of Delhi in a Mercedes. But that, she discovered very quickly, was only due to her severely limited imagination. The passengers shrieked as the car picked up speed. Saddam would not tell them where he was taking them. As they drove through the vicinity of the old city, they looked out of the windows eagerly, hoping to be seen by friends and acquaintances. As they moved into South Delhi, the mismatch between the passengers and the vehicle they were in drew plenty of curious and sometimes angry looks. A little intimidated, they rolled the window-glasses up. They stopped at a traffic intersection at the end of a long, tree-lined avenue where a group of Hijras dressed up to the nines were begging—they were technically begging, but actually hammering on car windows demanding money. All the cars that had stopped at the lights had their windows rolled up. The people in them were doing all they could to avoid eye contact with the Hijras. When they caught sight of the silver Mercedes, all four Hijras converged on it, smelling wealth and, they hoped, a naive foreigner. They were surprised when the windows rolled down before they had even launched their strike, and Anjum, Saeeda and Nimmo Gorakhpuri smiled back at them, returning their wide-fingered Hijra clap. The encounter quickly turned into an exchange of gossip. Which Gharana did the four belong to? Who was their Ustad? And their Ustad's Ustad? The four leaned through the Merc's windows, their elbows resting on the ledges, their bottoms protruding provocatively into the traffic. When the light changed, the cars behind them hooted impatiently. They responded with a string of inventive obscenities. Saddam gave them one hundred rupees and his visiting card. He invited them to the wedding.

"You must come!"

They smiled and waved goodbye, sashaying their leisurely way through the annoyed traffic. As their car sped away, Saeeda said that because sexual-reassignment surgery was becoming cheaper, better, and more accessible to people, Hijras would soon disappear. "Nobody will need to go through what we've been through any more."

"You mean no more Indo-Pak?" Nimmo Gorakhpuri said.

"It wasn't all bad," Anjum said. "I think it would be a shame if we became extinct."

"It *was* all bad," Nimmo Gorakhpuri said. "You've forgotten that quack Dr. Mukhtar? How much money did he make off you?"

The car floated like a steel bubble through streets wide and narrow, smooth and potholed, for more than two hours. They glided through dense forests of apartment buildings, past gigantic concrete amusement parks, bizarrely designed wedding halls and towering cement statues as high as skyscrapers, of Shiva in a cement leopard-skin loincloth with a cement cobra around his neck and a colossal Hanuman looming over a metro track. They drove over an impossible-to-pee-on flyover as wide as a wheat field, with twenty lanes of cars whizzing over it and towers of steel and glass growing on either side of it. But when they took an exit road off it, they saw that the world underneath the flyover was an entirely different one—an unpaved, unlaned, unlit, unregulated, wild and dangerous one, in which buses, trucks, bullocks, rickshaws, cycles, handcarts and pedestrians jostled for survival. One kind of world flew over another kind of world without troubling to stop and ask the time of day.

The steel bubble floated on, past shanty towns and industrial swamps where the air was a pale mauve haze, past railway tracks packed thick with trash and lined with slums. Finally they arrived at their destination. The Edge. Where the countryside was trying, quickly, clumsily and tragically, to turn itself into the city.

A mall.

The passengers in the Merc fell dead silent as it turned into the underground parking lot, lifted its bonnet and its boot like a girl lifting her skirts, for a quick bomb-check and then drifted down into a basement full of cars.

When they entered the bright shopping arcade, Saddam and Zainab looked happy and excited, completely at ease in the new surroundings. The others, including Ustaniji, looked as though they had stepped through a portal into another cosmos. The visit began with a hitch—a little trouble on the escalator. Anjum refused to get on. It took a good fifteen minutes of coaxing and encouragement. Finally, while Tilo carried Miss Jebeen the Second, Saddam stood next to Anjum on the step with his arm around her shoulders, and Zainab stood on the step above her, facing her, holding both her hands. Thus reinforced, Anjum went up wobbling and roaring *Ai Hai!* as though she was risking her life in a dangerous adventure sport. As they wandered around awestruck, trying to tell the difference between the shoppers and the mannequins in shop windows, Nimmo Gorakhpuri was the first to regain her composure. She looked approvingly at the young women in shorts and miniskirts, with huge shopping bags and sunglasses pushed up into their lush, blow-dried hair.

"See, this is what I wanted to look like when I was young. I had a real fashion sense. But nobody understood. I was too far ahead of our times."

After an hour's window-shopping and absolutely no buying, they ate lunch in an outlet called Nando's. Mainly, huge helpings of deep-fried chicken. Zainab was assigned to supervise Nimmo Gorakhpuri, and Saddam took care of Anjum, because neither of them had been to a restaurant before. Anjum stared in frank amazement at the family of four at the next table—an older couple and a younger one. The women, clearly mother and daughter, were both dressed alike in sleeveless printed tops and trousers, their faces caked with make-up. The young man, presumably the girl's fiancé, had his elbows on the table and frequently gazed down admiringly at his own (huge) biceps that bulged out of his blue, short-sleeved T-shirt. Only the older man did not appear to be enjoying himself. He peered furtively out from around the imaginary pillar he was hiding behind. Every few minutes the family suspended all conversation, immobilized their smiles and took selfies—with the menu, with the waiter, with the food and with each other. After each selfie they passed their phones around for the others to see. They did not pay any attention to anyone else in the restaurant.

Anjum was far more interested in them than in the food on her plate, which she had not been in the least impressed by. After he paid the bill, Saddam looked around the table with a sense of ceremony:

"You all must be wondering why I brought you all the way here."

"To show us the Duniya?" Anjum said, as though it were a quiz question on a TV show.

"No. To introduce all of you to my father. This is where he died. Right here. Where this building now stands. Before it came up there were villages here, surrounded by wheat fields. There was a police station . . . a road . . ."

Saddam then told them the story of what happened to his father. He told them about his vow to kill Sehrawat, the Station House Officer of the Dulina police station, and why he had given up the idea. They all took turns to pass his mobile phone around the table and watch the video of the dead cows being flung into the District Collector's bungalow.

"My father's spirit must be wandering here, trapped inside this place."

Everybody tried to imagine him—a village skinner, lost in the bright lights, trying to find his way out of the mall.

"This is his mazar," Anjum said.

"Hindus aren't buried. They don't have mazars, badi Mummy," Zainab said.

Maybe it's the whole world's mazar, Tilo thought, but didn't say. *Maybe the mannequin-shoppers are ghosts trying to buy what no longer exists.*

"It isn't right," Anjum said. "The matter can't be left like this. Your father should have a proper funeral."

"He *did* have a proper funeral," Saddam said. "He was cremated in our village. I lit his funeral pyre."

Anjum was not convinced. She wanted to do something more for Saddam's father, to lay his spirit to rest. After a great deal of discussion, they decided they would buy a shirt in his name from one of the shops (like people bought chadars in dargahs) and bury it in the old graveyard so that Saddam and Zainab's children would feel the presence of their grandfather around them as they grew up.

"I know a Hindu prayer!" Zainab said suddenly. "Shall I recite it here in memory of Abbajaan?"

Everybody leaned in to listen. And then, sitting at a table in a fast-food restaurant, as a missive of love to her late as well as future father-in-law, Zainab recited the Gayatri Mantra that Anjum had taught her when she was a little girl (because she believed it would help her in a mob-situation).

Om bhur bhuvah svaha
Tat savitur varenyam
Bhargo devasya dhimahi
*Dhiyo yo nah pracodayat**

---

* O God, thou art the giver of life / Remover of pain and sorrow / Bestower of happiness / O Creator of the Universe / May we receive thy supreme sin-destroying light / May thou guide our intellect in the right direction

❧

ON THE MORNING of Saddam Hussain's father's second funeral, Tilo put something else on the table. Literally. She brought out the little pot that contained her mother's ashes and said she would like her mother to be buried in the old graveyard too. It was decided that there would be a double funeral that day. If the cremation in the electric crematorium in Cochin counted, it would be Maryam Ipe's second funeral too. Saddam Hussain dug the graves. A stylish, Madras-checked shirt was interred in one. A pot of ashes in the other. Imam Ziauddin demurred a little at the unorthodoxy of the proceedings, but eventually agreed to say the prayers. Anjum asked Tilo if she wanted to say a Christian prayer for her mother. Tilo explained that the church had refused to bury her mother, so any prayers would do. As she stood beside her mother's grave, a line that Maryam Ipe had repeated more than once during her hallucinations in the ICU came back to her.

I feel I am surrounded by eunuchs. Am I?

At the time it had seemed like nothing more than a part of her regular barrage of ICU insults. But now it gave Tilo a shiver. *How did she know?* Once the pot of ashes had been buried and the grave filled with earth, Tilo closed her eyes and recited her mother's favorite passage from Shakespeare to herself. And at that moment the world, already a strange place, became an even stranger one:

And Crispin Crispian shall ne'er go by,
From this day to the ending of the world,
But we in it shall be remember'd—
We few, we happy few, we band of brothers;
For he to-day that sheds his blood with me
Shall be my brother; be he ne'er so vile,
This day shall gentle his condition;

And gentlemen in England now a-bed
Shall think themselves accurs'd they were not here,
And hold their manhoods cheap whiles any speaks
That fought with us upon Saint Crispin's day.

She had never understood why her mother had so particularly loved this manly, soldierly, warlike passage. But she had. When Tilo opened her eyes, she was shocked to realize that she was weeping.

Zainab and Saddam were married a month later. There was an eclectic gathering of guests—Hijras from all over Delhi (including the new friends they had made at the traffic lights), Zainab's friends, most of them students of fashion design, some of Ustan-iji's students and their parents, Zakir Mian's family, and several of Saddam Hussain's old comrades from his varied career—sweepers, mortuary workers, municipal truck drivers, security guards. Dr. Azad Bhartiya, D. D. Gupta and Roshan Lal were there of course. Anwar Bhai and his women and his son who had outgrown his mauve Crocs came from GB Road, and Ishrat-the-Beautiful—who had played a stellar role in the rescue of Miss Jebeen the Second—came from Indore. Tilo's and Dr. Azad Bhartiya's little cobbler friend, who had outlined his father's lung tumor in the dirt, dropped in briefly. Old Dr. Bhagat came too—still dressed in white, still wearing his watch on a sweatband. Dr. Mukhtar the quack was not invited. Miss Jebeen the Second was dressed as a little queen. She wore a tiara and a frothy dress and shoes that squeaked. Of all the presents the young couple were showered with, their favorite was the goat that Nimmo Gorakh-puri gave them. She had had it specially imported from Iran.

Ustad Hameed and his students sang.

Everybody danced.

Afterwards Anjum took Saddam and Zainab to Hazrat Sarmad. Tilo, Saeeda and Miss Jebeen the Second went too. They made their way past the sellers of ittars and amulets, the custodians of pilgrims' shoes, the cripples, the beggars, and the goats being fattened for Eid.

Sixty years had gone by since Jahanara Begum had taken her son Aftab to Hazrat Sarmad and asked him to teach her how to love him. Fifteen years had passed since Anjum took the Bandicoot to him to exorcize her *sifli jaadu*. It was more than a year since Miss Jebeen the Second's first visit.

Jahanara Begum's son had become her daughter, and the Bandicoot was now a bride. But other than that, nothing much had changed. The floor was red, the walls were red and the ceiling was red. Hazrat Sarmad's blood had not been washed away.

A wispy man with a prayer cap striped like a bee's bottom held out his prayer beads to Sarmad beseechingly. A thin woman in a printed sari tied a red bangle to the grille and then pressed her baby's forehead to the floor. Tilo did the same with Miss Jebeen the Second, who thought it was a good game and did it many more times than was really necessary. Zainab and Saddam tied bangles to the grille and laid a new velvet chadar trimmed with tinsel on the Hazrat's grave.

Anjum said a prayer and asked him to bless the young couple.

And Sarmad—Hazrat of Utmost Happiness, Saint of the Unconsoled and Solace of the Indeterminate, Blasphemer among Believers and Believer among Blasphemers—did.

Three weeks later there was a third funeral in the old graveyard.

ONE MORNING Dr. Azad Bhartiya arrived at Jannat Guest House with a letter that was addressed to him. It had been hand-delivered by a woman who would not identify herself, but said the letter was from the Bastar forest. Anjum didn't know what or where that was. Dr. Azad explained briefly about Bastar, the Adivasi tribes that lived there, the mining companies that wanted their land and the Maoist guerrillas who were waging a war against security forces that were trying to clear the land for the companies. The letter was written in English, in tiny, cramped handwriting. There was no date on it. Dr. Azad Bhartiya said it was from Miss Jebeen the Second's real mother.

"Tear it up!" Anjum roared. "She throws away her baby and then comes back here saying she is the real mother!" Saddam stopped her from lunging for the letter.

"Don't worry," Dr. Azad Bhartiya said, "she is not coming back."

It was a long letter, written on both sides of the pages with whole passages scored out, sentences running into each other as though paper was in limited supply. Between the pages there were a few pressed flowers that had crumbled when the papers had been folded into the pellet that was delivered. Dr. Azad Bhartiya read it out, roughly translating it as best he could as he went along. His audience was Anjum, Tilo and Saddam Hussain. And Miss Jebeen the Second, who did all she could to disrupt the proceedings.

Dear Comrade Azad Bharathiya Garu,
I am writing this to you because in my three days time in Jantar Mantar I observed you carefully. If anybody knows where is my child now, I think it might be you only. I am a Telugu woman and sorry I don't know Hindi. My English is not good also. Sorry for that. I am Revathy, working as a full-timer with Communist Party of India (Maoist). When you will receive this letter I will be already killed.

At this point, Anjum, who had been leaning forward, listening with rapt attention, rocked back, looking visibly relieved. She seemed to have lost interest. But gradually, as Dr. Azad Bhartiya read on, she grew riveted again and listened without interrupting.

My comrade Suguna knows to send this letter to you when she hears that I am no more. As you know we are banned, underground people, and this letter from me you can call as underground of underground, so it will take minimum five or six weeks to come to you through a safe channels. After I left my child there in Delhi, my conscience is very much bad. I cannot sleep or take rest. I don't want her. But I don't want her to suffer also. So in case if you know where she is, I want to tell you her frank story a little. Rest is for your decision. Her name that I have gave her was Udaya. In Telugu it means sunrise. I gave her this name because she was born in Dandakaranya forest during sunrise. When she was born I frankly felt hatred for her and I thought to kill her. I felt really she was not mine. Really she is not mine. Really if you see her story that I have written here, I am not her mother. River is her mother and Forest is her father. This is the story of Udaya and Revathy. I, Revathy, hail from East Godavari district of Andhra Pradesh. My caste is Settibalija which comes under BC (Backward Caste). My mother's name is Indumati. She is a SSLC school pass. She is married with my father when she is 18 years. Father worked in army. He was older to her by many years. He saw her when he was home for vacation and fell in love because Mother is very fair and pretty. After engagement but before marriage Father was

court-marshaled from army for smoking near the
armory. He came to live in his village which was
on opposite side of Godavari river from Mother's
village. His family is same caste, but was rich than
hers. During marriage ceremony itself they made
my Mother to got up from the pandal and demanded
for more dowry. My grandfather had to run for loan.
Only then they agreed and marriage continued.
Immediately after marriage Father developed some
perversions and sadism. He wanted Mother to wear
short dresses and do ballroom dancing. When she
refused he cut her with blades and complained she
was not satisfying him. After some months he sent
her home to my grandfather. When she was five
months pregnant with me my Mother's younger
brother took her back to Father's village in a boat.
She was dressed in a very good sari and jewelry and
took two silver pots of sweets and twenty-five new
saris for her mother-in-law. Father was not there
in the house. In-laws refused to open the door and
came out and kicked the pot of sweets. Mother felt
very much ashamed. On the way back, in middle of
the river she taked off her jewelry and jumped from
the boat. I was in her stomach five months then.
Boatman saved her and took her home. I was born in
my maternal grandfather's house. During pregnancy
time Mother's stomach was huge. She was expecting
twins. White color, like her and her husband. But I
came out. I was black and weighty. Seeing my color
Mother was unconscious for two days. But after
that she never left me. The whole village talked. My
father's family came to know how black I was. They
had that caste and color feeling. They said I was not

theirs but a Mala or Madiga girl, not a BC but a SC Schedule Caste girl. I grew up in my grandfather's house. He worked in Animal Husbandry. He was a communist. His house had a thatch roof but many books. When he became old my grandfather became blind also. I was in school then I would read to him. I would read *Illustrated Weekly, Competition Success Review* and *Soviet Bhumi.* I also read the story of the Little Black Fish. We had many books from People's Publishing House. Father would come to my grandfather's house at night to trouble Mother. I would hate him. He moved around the house at night like a snake. She would follow him, he would torture and cut her and send her back. Again he would call her and again she would go. For some time afterwards he took her and kept her with him again in his village. Again she became pregnant. In my grandfather's village the women prayed for her second baby to be also black so Mother could be proved a faithful wife. They sacrificed thirty black hens in the temple for this. Thanks god my brother is born also black. But then again Father sent Mother home and married another woman. I wanted to be a lawyer and put my father behind bars forever. But soon I became influenced by Communism and revolutionary thinking. I read communist literature. My grandfather taught me revolutionary songs and we would sing together. My mother and grandmother stole coconuts and sold them for paying my school fees. They bought me small things and kept me very fashionable and many boys liked me. After passing Intermediate I sat for Medical entrance and got selected but we had no money for fees. So

I joined government degree college in Warangal.
There Movement was very strong. Inside forest, but
outside also. In my first year itself I was recruited
by Comrade Nirmalakka and Comrade Laxmi
who would visit women's hostel and talk to us girls
about exploitation by the Class Enemy and terrible
condition of poverty in our country. From college
itself I worked as a part-timer and courier for the
Party. Afterwards I worked in the Mahila Sangham—
women's organization, creating class awareness in
slums and villages. We became a channel for Party's
communication all over Telangana. We would travel
by bus to meetings carrying booklets and pamphlets.
We would sing and dance at protest meetings. I read
Marx and Lenin and Mao and became convinced of
Maoism.

At the time situation was very dangerous. All
police, Cobras, Greyhounds, Andhra Police would
be everywhere. Hundreds of Party workers were
killed like anything. Maximum hatred police had
for women workers. Comrade Nirmalakka when
she was killed they ripped her stomach and took out
everything. Comrade Laxmi also they not simply
killed, but cut, and removed eyes. For her there
was big protest. One another Comrade Padmakka
they captured and broken both her knees so she
could not walk and beat her so she has kidney
damage, liver damage, so much damage. She came
out from jail now she works in Amarula Bandhu
Mithrula Sangham. Wherever Party people are
killed and family is poor and cannot afford to travel
to get their person's body back, she goes. In tractor,
Tempo, anything, and brings the body to family for

funeral and all those things. In 2008 the situation
much worst inside the forest. Operation Green
Hunt is announced by Government. War against
People. Thousands of police and paramilitary are
in the forest. Killing adivasis, burning villages. No
adivasi can stay in her house or their village. They
sleep in the forest outside at night because at night
police come, hundred, two hundred, sometimes
five hundred police. They take everything, burn
everything, steal everything. Chickens, goats, money.
They want adivasi people to vacate forest so they
can make a steel township and mining. Thousands
are in jail. All this politics you can read outside.
Or in our magazine *People's March*. So I will only
tell you about Udaya. At the time of Green Hunt,
Party gave a call for recruitment to PLGA—People's
Liberation Guerrilla Army. At the time I and two
others went into Bastar forest for arms training.
I worked there for more than six years. Inside
sometimes I am called Comrade Maase. It means
Black Girl. I like this name. But we keep different
names also, each other's names. Although I am
in PLGA, since I am an educated woman, Party
also keeps me for outside work. Sometimes I have
to go to Warangal, Bhadrachalam or Khammam.
Sometimes Narayanpur. This is most dangerous,
because now in villages and in towns there are many
informers working against us. That is how, one time
when I was returning from outside, I was captured
in Kudur village. At the time I was dressed in a sari
and bangles and handbag and two string pearls. I
could not fight. My arrest was not shown. I was tied
up and given chloroform and taken to some place I

don't know. When I waked up it was dark. I was in
a room with two doors and two windows. It was a
classroom. There was a blackboard but no furniture.
It was a government school. All schools inside the
forests are police camps. No teachers and no students
come. I was naked. There was six police around me.
One was cutting my skin with a knife-blade. "So
you think you are a great heroine?" he asked me. If
I closed my eyes they slap me. Two are holding my
hands and two are holding legs. "We want to give
you a gift for your Party." They are smoking and
putting their cigarettes on me. "You people shout
a lot! Shout now and see what happens!" I thought
they would kill me like Padmakka and Laxmi but
they said "Don't worry Blackie we will let you go.
You must go and tell them what we did to you. You
are a great heroine. You supply them with bullets,
malaria medicines, food, toothbrushes. All that we
know. How many innocent girls have you sent to join
your Party? You are spoiling everyone. Now you go
and marry someone. Settle down quietly. But first we
will give you some marriage experience." They kept
on burning me and cutting me. But I am not crying
at all. "Why don't you scream? Your great leaders
will come and save you. You people don't scream?"
Then one man forced open my mouth and one man
put his penis in my mouth. I could not breathe. I
thought I would die. They kept putting water on my
face. Then all raped me many times. One is Udaya's
father. Which, how can I say? I was unconscious.
When I waked again I was bleeding everywhere.
The door was open. They were outside smoking. I
could see my sari. I slowly took it. The back door

was open slightly and outside was a paddy field. They saw me running, first they ran after me and I fell but then they said, "Leave it, let her go." This is the experience of so many women in the forest. From that I took courage. I ran through the fields. It was only moonlight. I reached a tar road. I came onto it. I had only sari. No blouse, no petticoat. I wrapped it somehow. A bus came. I got in. I was barefeet. Bleeding. My face is like a pumpkin. Mouth is huge because they bit it many times. The bus was empty. Conductor did not say anything. He did not ask me for a ticket. I sat near the window and slept because of the chloroform. In Khammam he woke me and said, "This is the last stop." I got down from the bus. When I came to know it was Khammam I was happy because I know very well one Dr. Gowrinath who has a clinic. I went there. I was walking like a drunk man. I knocked on the door and his wife opened it and screamed. I sat on her bed. I was looking like a mad person. All the cigarette burns were bubbles, on my face, breast, nipples, stomach. Her whole bed was blood. Dr. Gowrinath came and gave me some first aid. I am sleeping always because of chloroform. When I am awake I am only weeping. I only want to go to my comrades inside the forest, Renu, Damayanti, Narmada akka. Dr. Gowrinath kept me for ten days. After that we got a contact from inside and I went back to the forest. I walked for twelve kilometers then a PLGA squad came and we walked five hours more to a camp where District Committee members were. The main leader, Comrade P.K., asked me what happened. He is no more now. He also killed in encounter. At the time I told them, but

I was crying and he could not understand anything.
First he thought I am complaining about a Party
comrade. Comrade P.K. said, "I don't understand
this feelings nonsense. We are soldiers. Tell me like a
report without emotions." So I told him the report.
But without my knowledge my eyes are weeping.
I showed my injuries for inspection to female
comrades. After that they sat for two days to think
what to do. Then the committee called me again and
said I must go outside and form a "Revathy Atyachara
Vyathireka Committee"—Committee Against
Revathy's Rape. In addition I was given responsibility
for another program to take over a slum colony
with 2000 people and only two handpumps. I am so
sick and I have to organize people's rally for more
handpumps. I could not believe it. But they said I
must help myself. But I could not go outside because
by then I could not walk. Bleeding was not stopped.
I was having fits. My wounds were got septic. I could
not go out. I could not march with the squads. Again
I was left in a forest village. After three months I
could walk. By then I was pregnant. But I did not
bother. I rejoined PLGA. But when Party came
to know they again told me to go outside because
PLGA women are banned to have children. I stayed
in a forest village till Udaya was born. When I saw
her first I felt very much hatred. I felt that six police
fellows cutting me with blades and burning me with
cigarettes. I thought to kill her. I put my gun on her
head but could not fire because she was a small and
cute baby. That time there was a big campaign going
on outside the forest against War on People. Big
Delhi groups organized a public tribunal. Adivasi

people who had become victims were called to
Delhi to speak to National Media. Party told me to
accompany them along with other local lawyers and
activists. As I had a small child it was a good cover. I
was a very good speaker in Telugu and knew all the
facts. They had good translators in Delhi. After the
Tribunal I sat with tribal victims for three days public
protest in Jantar Mantar. I saw many good people
there. But I cannot live outside like them.

My Party is my Mother and Father. Many times
it does many wrong things. Kills wrong people.
Women join because they are revolutionaries but
also because they cannot bear their sufferings at
home. Party says men and women are equal, but still
they never understand. I know Comrade Stalin and
Chairman Mao have done many good things and
many bad things also. But still I cannot leave my
Party. I cannot live outside. I saw many good people
in Jantar Mantar so I had the idea to leave Udaya
there. I cannot be like you and them. I cannot go on
hunger-strike and make requests. In the forest every
day police is burning killing raping poor people.
Outside there is you people to fight and take up
issues. But inside there is us only. So I am returned to
Dandakaranya to live and die by my gun.

Thankyou Comrade for reading this.

Red Salute! Lal Salaam!
Revathy

"LAL SALAAM ALEIKUM," was Anjum's inadvertent, instinctive
response to the end of the letter. That could have been the begin-

ning of a whole political movement, but she had only meant it in the way of an "Ameen" after listening to a moving sermon.

Each of the listeners recognized, in their own separate ways, something of themselves and their own stories, their own Indo-Pak, in the story of this unknown, faraway woman who was no longer alive. It made them close ranks around Miss Jebeen the Second like a formation of trees, or adult elephants—an impenetrable fortress in which she, unlike her biological mother, would grow up protected and loved.

What came up for immediate discussion in the graveyard Politburo, however, was whether or not Miss Jebeen the Second should ever know about the letter. Anjum, the General Secretary, was absolutely unambiguous about that. While Miss Jebeen the Second stood on her lap and almost twisted the nose off her face, Anjum said, "She should know about her mother of course. Never about her father."

It was decided that Revathy should be buried with full honors in the graveyard. In the absence of her body, her letter would be interred in the grave. (Tilo would keep a photocopy for the record.) Anjum wanted to know what the correct rituals were for the funeral of a communist. (She used the phrase *Lal Salaami*.) When Dr. Azad Bhartiya said that as far as he knew there were none as such, she was a little disparaging. "What kind of thing is it, then? What kind of people leave their dead without prayers?"

The next day Dr. Azad Bhartiya procured a red flag. Revathy's letter was put into an airtight container and then it was wrapped in the flag. While it was buried he sang the Hindi version of "The Internationale" and gave her a clenched-fist Red Salute. Thus ended the second funeral of Miss Jebeen the Second's first, second or third mother, depending on your perspective.

The Politburo decided that Miss Jebeen the Second's full name would, from that day onwards, be Miss Udaya Jebeen. The epitaph on her mother's tombstone simply read:

COMRADE MAASE REVATHY
Beloved mother of Miss Udaya Jebeen
Lal Salaam

Dr. Azad Bhartiya tried to teach Miss Udaya Jebeen—she of the six fathers and three mothers (who were stitched together by threads of light)—to clench her fist and say a final "Lal Salaam" to her mother.

". . . 'al Salaam," she gurgled.

II

THE LANDLORD

I'm still here. As you must, no doubt, have guessed. I never did check in to that rehabilitation center. It lasted on and off for almost six months, the binge that started when I first arrived. However, I'm sober now—sober *for* now, is probably how I'm meant to put it. It's been well over a year since I touched a drink. But it's too late. I've lost my job. Chitra has left me and Rabia and Ania won't speak to me. Oddly, none of it has made me as unhappy as I imagined it would. I have come to enjoy my solitude.

Over the last few months, I've lived the life of a recluse. Instead of binge drinking, I've been binge reading. I have made it my business to pry into every last piece of paper—every document, every report, every letter, every video, every yellow Post-it and every photograph in every file in this apartment. I suppose you could say that I brought the attributes of an addictive personality to this project too—by which I mean single-mindedness coupled with acute guilt and useless remorse. Once I had been through the whole, weird archive, I tried to make amends for my prurience by putting some logic and order into its chaos. Then again, maybe that just counts as further transgression. Either way, I've refiled the papers and photographs and packed them into sealed cartons so that, if and when she comes, she can take them away easily. I've taken down the noticeboards and made sure the photographs and Post-its are packed in a way that she can put them up again in the same order with little difficulty. All this to say that I have moved in. I live here now, in this apartment. I have nowhere else to go. The rent from the flat downstairs constitutes the better part of my income. Tilo does continue to pay rent into my account, but I plan to return it to her whenever, if ever, I see her again.

The upshot of my prying, I should admit, is that I have changed my mind about Kashmir. It might sound a little cheap and convenient for me to be saying this now, I know—I must sound like those army generals who wage war all their lives and then suddenly become pious, anti-nuke peaceniks when they retire. The only difference between them and me is that I'm going to keep my newly formed opinion to myself. It's not easy though. If I wanted to, and if I played my cards right, I could probably parlay it into some serious capital. I could create a political storm if I "came out," so to speak, because I see from the news that Kashmir, after a few years of deceptive calm, has exploded once again.

From what I can tell, it's no longer the case that security forces are attacking people. It seems to be the other way around now. People—ordinary people, not militants—are attacking the forces. Kids on the streets with stones in their hands are facing down soldiers with guns; villagers armed with sticks and shovels are sweeping down mountainsides and overwhelming army camps. If the soldiers fire at them and kill a few, the protests just swell some more. The paramilitary are using pellet guns that end up blinding people—which is better than killing them, I suppose. Although in PR terms it's worse. The world is inured to the sight of piled-up corpses. But not to the sight of hundreds of living people who have been blinded. Pardon my crudeness, but you can imagine the visual appeal of that. But even that doesn't seem to be working. Boys who've lost one eye are back on the street, prepared to risk the other. What do you do with that kind of fury?

I have no doubt that we can—and will—beat them down once more. But where will it all end? War. Or Nuclear War. Those seem to be the most realistic answers to that question. Every evening as I watch the news I marvel at the ignorance and idiocy on display. And to think that all my life I have been a part of it. It's all I can do to stop myself writing something for the papers. I won't, because I'd lay myself open to ridicule—the sacked, drunk, conscientious objector. That sort of thing.

Of course I know about Musa now—in the sense that I know he didn't die when we thought he did. He's been around all these years, and of course, needless to say, my tenant has known that all along. All it took was an extended power cut for me to find the things she had stored in the freezer.

So imagine my pleasure one night, when the key turned in my door and Musa walked in and was more shocked to see me than I was to see him. The first few minutes of the encounter were fraught. He made to leave, but I managed to persuade him to stay and at least have a cup of coffee. It was good to see him. We had last met as very young men. Boys, really. Now I had almost no hair and his was silver. When I told him that I was no longer with the Bureau he relaxed. We ended up spending that night and most of the next day together. We talked a lot—when I look back on that meeting, I'm a little unnerved by the skill with which he drew me out. It was a combination of quiet solicitousness and the sort of curiosity that is flattering rather than inquisitive. Perhaps because of my eagerness to reassure him that I was no longer the "enemy," I ended up doing most of the talking. I was astonished at how intimately he seemed to know the workings of the Bureau. He talked of some officers as though they were personal friends. It was almost like exchanging notes with a colleague. But it was done so coolly, almost nonchalantly, most of it just casual chatter that bordered on gossip, that I only realized what had happened after he was gone. We didn't really talk politics. And we didn't talk about Tilo. He offered to cook me lunch with whatever ingredients I had in the kitchen. Of course I knew that what he really wanted was to take a look at my freezer. All there was in there now was a kilo of good mutton. I told him that the stuff in the apartment, including his many passports and other personal belongings, was packed and ready to be removed whenever Tilo wanted to take it.

We circled around the subject of Kashmir, but only in abstract ways.

"You may be right after all," I said to him in the kitchen. "You may be right, but you'll never win."

"I think the opposite," he smiled, stirring the pot from which a wonderful aroma of rogan josh arose. "We may turn out to be wrong, but we have already won."

I left it at that. I don't think he was aware of the extent to which the Government of India would go to hold on to that little patch of land. It could turn into a bloodbath that would make the 1990s look like a school play. On the other hand, maybe I had no idea how suicidal Kashmiris were prepared to be—to become. Either way, the stakes were higher than they had ever been. Or maybe we had different notions about what "winning" means.

The meal was delectable. Musa was a relaxed, accomplished cook. He asked about Naga. "I haven't seen him on TV of late. Is he OK?"

Oddly, the only person I have been seeing occasionally in my new life as a recluse is Naga. He has resigned from his paper and seems happier than I remember him ever being. Maybe, ironically, we're both liberated by Tilo's conclusive and categorical disappearance from our lives and the world we know. I told Musa that Naga and I were planning—it was still nothing more than a plan—to start a sort of yesteryear music channel, on the radio or maybe a podcast. Naga would do the Western music, rock 'n' roll, blues, jazz, and I'd do world music. I have an interesting, and I believe excellent, collection of Afghan, Iranian and Syrian folk music. After I said it, I felt shallow and superficial. But Musa seemed genuinely interested and we had a nice little chat about music.

The next morning he organized a small Tempo from the market and two men loaded it up with the cartons and the rest of Tilo's things. He seemed to know where she was, but didn't say, so I didn't ask. There was one question, though, that I did need to ask him before he left, something I desperately needed to know before another thirty years went by. It would have troubled me for the rest of my life if I didn't. I had to ask. There was no subtle way of doing it. It wasn't easy, but finally I came out with it.

"Did you kill Amrik Singh?"

"No." He looked at me with his green-tea-colored eyes. "I didn't."

He said nothing for a moment, but I could tell from his gaze that he was assessing me, wondering if he should say more or not. I told him I'd seen the asylum applications and the boarding passes of flights to the US with a name that matched one of his fake passports. I had come across a receipt from a car-hire company in Clovis. The dates matched too, so I knew that he had something to do with that whole episode, but I didn't know what.

"I'm just curious," I said. "It doesn't matter if you did. He deserved to die."

"I didn't kill him. He killed himself. But we made him kill himself."

I had no idea what the hell that was supposed to mean.

"I didn't go to the US looking for him. I was already there

on some other work when I saw the news in the papers that he had been arrested for assaulting his wife. His residential address became public. I had been looking for him for years. I had some unfinished business with him. Many of us did. So I went to Clovis, made some inquiries and finally found him at a truck-washing garage and workshop where he would go to have his truck serviced. He was a completely different person from the murderer we knew, the killer of Jalib Qadri and many others. He did not have that infrastructure of impunity within which he operated in Kashmir. He was scared and broke. I almost felt sorry for him. I assured him that I was not going to harm him, and that I was only there to tell him that we would not allow him to forget the things that he had done."

Musa and I were having this conversation out on the street. I had come down to see him off.

"Other Kashmiris had also read the news. So they began to arrive in Clovis to see how the Butcher of Kashmir lived now. Some were journalists, some were writers, photographers, lawyers . . . some were just ordinary people. They turned up at his workplace, at his home, at the supermarket, across the street, at his children's school. Every day. He was forced to look at us. Forced to remember. It must have driven him crazy. Eventually it made him self-destruct. So . . . to answer your question . . . no, I did not kill him."

What Musa said next, standing against the backdrop of the school gates with the painting of the ogre nurse giving a baby a polio vaccine, was like . . . like an ice-injection. More so because it was said in that casual, genial way he had, with a friendly, almost-happy smile, as though he was only joking.

"One day Kashmir will make India self-destruct in the same way. You may have blinded all of us, every one of us, with your pellet guns by then. But you will still have eyes to see what you have done to us. You're not destroying us. You are constructing us. It's yourselves that you are destroying. Khuda Hafiz, Garson bhai."

With that he left. I never saw him again.

What if he's right? We've seen great countries fall into ruin virtually overnight. What if we're next in line? That thought fills me with a kind of epochal sadness.

If this little back street is anything to go by, perhaps the unraveling has already begun. Everything has suddenly fallen quiet. All the construction has stopped. The laborers have disappeared. Where are the whores and the homosexuals and the dogs with fancy coats? I miss them. How could it all disappear so quickly?

I mustn't keep standing here, like some nostalgic old fool.

Things will get better. They must.

On my way back in I managed to avoid my voluptuous and voluble tenant Ankita on the stairs as I returned to my empty apartment that will forever be haunted by the ghosts of the cardboard cartons that have gone, and all the stories they contained.

And the absence of the woman who, in my own weak, wavering way, I will never stop loving.

What will become of me? I'm a little like Amrik Singh myself—old, bloated, scared, and deprived of what Musa so eloquently called "the infrastructure of impunity" that I have operated within all my life. What if I self-destruct too?

I could—unless music rescues me.

I should get in touch with Naga. I should work on that podcast idea.

But first I need a drink.

12

GUIH KYOM

It was Musa's third night in Jannat Guest House. He had
arrived a few days ago like a deliveryman, with a Tempo full
of cardboard cartons. Everybody was delighted to see the anima-
tion on Ustaniji's face when she set eyes on him. The cartons
were stacked against the wall in Tilo's room, crowding up the
space she shared with Ahlam Baji. Tilo had told Musa as much
as she knew about everyone in Jannat Guest House. On that last
night she lay next to him on her bed, showing off her prowess in
Urdu. She had written out a poem she'd learned from Dr. Azad
Bhartiya in one of her notebooks:

Mar gayee bulbul qafas mein
Keh gayee sayyaad se
Apni sunehri gaand mein
*Tu thoons le fasl-e-bahaar**

___

* She died in her cage, the little bird, / These words she left for her captor— /
Please take the spring harvest / And shove it up your gilded arse

"That sounds like the anthem of a suicide bomber," Musa said.

Tilo told him about Dr. Azad Bhartiya and how the poem had been his response to police questioning in Jantar Mantar (on the morning after the *said* night, the concerned night, the aforementioned night, the night hereinafter referred to as "the night").

"When I die," Tilo said, laughing, "I want this to be my epitaph."

Ahlam Baji muttered a few insults and turned over in her grave.

Musa glanced at the page in the notebook that faced the one in which Tilo had written the poem.

It said:

> *How*
> > *to*
> > *tell*
> > > *a*
> *shattered*
> > *story?*

> > > > *By*
> > > *slowly*
> > > *becoming*

> *everybody.*

> > > *No.*
> > > *By slowly becoming everything.*

That was something to think about, he thought.

It made him turn to his love of many years, the woman whose strangeness had become so dear to him, and hold her close.

Something about Tilo's new home reminded Musa of the

story of Mumtaz Afzal Malik, the young taxi driver whom Amrik Singh had killed, whose body had been recovered from a field and delivered to his family with earth in his clenched fists and mustard flowers growing through his fingers. That story had always stayed with Musa—perhaps because of the way hope and grief were woven together in it, so tightly, so inextricably.

He would leave for Kashmir the next morning, to return to a new phase in an old war from which, this time, he would not return. He would die the way he wanted to, with his *Asal boot* on. He would be buried the way he wanted to be—a faceless man in a nameless grave. The younger men who would take his place would be harder, narrower and less forgiving. They would be more likely to win any war they fought, because they belonged to a generation that had known nothing but war.

Tilo would receive a message from Khadija—a photograph of a young, smiling Musa and Gul-kak. On the back, Khadija would write *Commanders Gulrez and Gulrez are together now*. Tilo would grieve deeply at Musa's passing, but would not be undone by her grief because she was able to write to him regularly and visit him often enough through the crack in the door that the battered angels in the graveyard held open (illegally) for her.

Their wings did not smell like the bottom of a chicken coop.

On their last night together, Tilo and Musa slept with their arms wrapped around each other, as though they had only just met.

Anjum was restless that night and unable to sleep. She pottered around the graveyard inspecting her property. She stopped for a moment at Bombay Silk's grave and said a prayer and told Miss Udaya Jebeen, who was perched on her hip, the story of how she had first set eyes on Bombay Silk while she was buying bangles from the bangle-seller at Chitli Qabar and had followed her all the way down the street to Gali Dakotan. She bent down and picked up one of Roshan Lal's flowers from Begum Renata Mumtaz Madam's grave and put it on Comrade Maase's grave. That little act of redistribution made her feel much better. She looked back at Jannat Guest House with a sense of contentment and accomplishment. On impulse, she decided to take Miss Udaya Jebeen out on a brief midnight ramble to familiarize her with her surroundings and see the city lights.

She walked past the mortuary, through the hospital car park on to the main road. There wasn't much traffic at that hour. Still, to be safe, they stayed on the pavement, threading their way through parked cycle rickshaws and sleeping people. They passed a slim, naked man with a sprig of barbed wire in his beard. He raised a hand in greeting, and hurried off as though he was late for the office. When Miss Udaya Jebeen said, "Mummy, soosoo!" Anjum sat her down under a street light. With her eyes fixed on her mother she peed, and then lifted her bottom to marvel at the night sky and the stars and the one-thousand-year-old city reflected in the puddle she had made. Anjum gathered her up and kissed her and took her home.

By the time they got back, the lights were all out and everybody was asleep. Everybody, that is, except for Guih Kyom the dung beetle. He was wide awake and on duty, lying on his back with his legs in the air to save the world in case the heavens fell. But even he knew that things would turn out all right in the end. They would, because they had to.

Because Miss Jebeen, Miss Udaya Jebeen, was come.

ACKNOWLEDGMENTS

I wove the love and friendship that I received from those whose names I mention below into a carpet on which I thought, slept, dreamed, fled, and flew around during the many years it took me to write this book. My thanks to:

John Berger, who helped me start and waited for me to finish.

Mayank Austen Soofi and Aijaz Hussain. They know why. I don't need to tell.

Parvaiz Bukhari. Same as above.

Shohini Ghosh, beloved madcap, who queered my pitch.

Jawed Naqvi for music, wicked poetry and a house full of lilies.

Ustad Hameed, who showed me that you can skydive, snorkel and hang-glide between any two notes of music.

Dayanita Singh, with whom I once went wandering, and an idea was ignited.

Munni and Shigori in Meena Bazaar for long hours spent shooting the breeze.

The Jhinjhanvis: Sabiha and Naseer-ul-Hassan, Shaheena and Muneer-ul-Hassan, for a home in Shahjahanabad.

Tarun Bhartiya, Prashant Bhushan, Mohammed Junaid, Arif Ayaz Parray, Khurram Parvez, Parvez Imroze, P. G. Rasool, Arjun Raina, Jitendra Yadav, Ashwin Desai, G. N. Saibaba, Rona Wilson, Nandini Oza, Shripad Dharmadhikary, Himanshu Thakker, Nikhil De, Anand, Dionne Bunsa, Chittaroopa Palit, Saba Naqvi and Reverend Sunil Sardar, whose insights are somewhere in the foundations of The Ministry.

Savitri and Ravikumar for our travels together and for so much else.

J. J. (Heck.) But she's in here somewhere.

Rebecca John, Chander Uday Singh, Jawahar Raja, Rishabh Sancheti, Harsh Bora, Mr. Deshpande and Akshaya Sudame, who have kept me out of prison. (So far.)

Susanna Lea and Lisette Verhagen, World Ambassadors of Utmost Happiness. Heather Godwin and Philippa Sitters, who woman the base camp.

David Eldridge, jacket-designer extraordinaire. Two books, twenty years apart.

Iris Weinstein for perfect pages.

Ellie Smith, Sarah Coward, Arpita Basu, George Wen, Benjamin Hamilton, Maria Massey and Jennifer Kurdyla. Close readers, serious-shit copy-editors and brilliant protagonists in the transatlantic comma wars.

Pankaj Mishra, First Reader, still.

Robin Desser and Simon Prosser. Dream editors.

My wonderful publishers, Sonny Mehta, Meru Gokhale (for publishing plus comfort food), Hans Jürgen Balmes, Antoine Gallimard, Luigi Brioschi, Jorge Herralde, Dorotea Bromberg and all the others whom I have not personally met.

Suman Parihar, Mohammed Sumon, Krishna Bhoat and Ashok Kumar, who kept me afloat when it wasn't easy.

Suzie Q, mobile shrink, dear friend and best cabbie in London.

Krishnan Tewari, Sharmila Mitra and Deepa Verma for my daily dose of sweat, sanity and laughter.

John Cusack, supersweetheart, co-drafter of the Fleedom Charter.

Eve Ensler and Bindia Thapar. Beloveds.

My mother like no other, Mary Roy, most unique human.

My brother, LKC, keeper of my sanity, and sister-in-law, Mary, both of whom, like me, survived.

Golak. Go. Oldest friend.

Mithva and Pia. Littles. Still mine.

David Godwin. Flying Agent. Top Man. Without whom.

Anthony Arnove, comrade, agent, publisher, rock.

Pradip Krishen, love of many years, honorary tree.
Sanjay Kak. Cave. Since forever.
And
Begum Filthy Jaan and Maati K. Lal. Creatures.

Special acknowledgments:
The passage which the weevil professor reads aloud to his weevil class is adapted from *Straw Dogs* by John Gray.
The lyrics of "Dark to Light and Light to Dark" are from "Gone" by Ioanna Gika.
The poem "Duniya ki mehfilon se ukta gaya hoon ya Rab" is by Allama Iqbal.
The couplet on Arifa Yeswi's gravestone is by Ahmed Faraz.